FIRE RISING

BLUE PROMETHEUS SERIES #3

NED MARCUS

ORANGE LOG PUBLISHING

Copyright © 2019 by Ned Marcus

First Edition (paperback).

ISBN 978-986-95833-6-7

All rights reserved.

No part of this book may be reproduced in any form or by any electronic or mechanical means, including information storage and retrieval systems, without written permission from the author, except for the use of brief quotations in a book review.

This book is a work of fiction. The characters, places and events are products of the author's imagination or have been used fictitiously and are not to be construed as real. Any resemblance to persons, living or dead, is entirely coincidental.

Published by Orange Log Publishing

Cover Design by Damonza

CONTENTS

Prologue	1
Chapter 1	5
Chapter 2	13
Chapter 3	23
Chapter 4	33
Chapter 5	40
Chapter 6	47
Chapter 7	55
Chapter 8	63
Chapter 9	73
Chapter 10	79
Chapter 11	87
Chapter 12	98
Chapter 13	109
Chapter 14	114
Chapter 15	124
Chapter 16	133
Chapter 17	141
Chapter 18	150
Chapter 19	159
Chapter 20	166
Chapter 21	177
Chapter 22	189
Chapter 23	198
Chapter 24	206
Chapter 25	211
Chapter 26	220
Chapter 27	228
Chapter 28	235
Chapter 29	245
Chapter 30	252
Chapter 31	261

Chapter 32	266
Chapter 33	274
Chapter 34	286
Chapter 35	294
Chapter 36	300
Chapter 37	311
Chapter 38	321
Chapter 39	329
Chapter 40	344
Chapter 41	352
Chapter 42	359
Chapter 43	364
Chapter 44	370
Chapter 45	383
Epilogue	394
Free Stories	397
Please Leave A Review	399
Books By Ned Marcus	401
About the Author	403
Acknowledgments	405

PROLOGUE

Far away, in the distant peaks of the Eastern Rim, a golden dragon was born. She shone in the early morning sun, her scales glittering brightly as she crawled from her cracked egg towards the frothing pool.

But her difference unnerved some—she was smaller and brighter than a normal dragon. Older dragons watched from the shore of the mountain lake, while the rest of the newly born Tangle croaked at their tiny sister as she struggled towards them.

A fighting red dragon, one of the Thunder, spread his wings in the cold wind. *"The worm'll die!"* He spoke in the True Language—the telepathic language of dragons. Others agreed: only the strongest survived.

She slipped on the rocks, but struggled up again, and crawled on towards the water and the other wingless dragons of her Tangle. She felt the pain of her past lives as they flickered through her mind. She knew she was born to struggle, but slowly her memories faded, and the tiny golden dragon slipped into the lake.

Many of the dragons gathered around the shores of the mountain lake bellowed, waiting for the first struggle of life to begin. Only the great black dragon, the First of the Wisdom, watched silently as the Tangle swirled in the water.

The bright golden dragon joined the group of immature dragons, each two or three times her size, as they rushed beneath the frigid surface of the lake. Steam rose from the cold water as the young dragons adjusted their inner fire. When an immature maroon dragon blasted his feet with fire, a larger dragon hopped back from the water's edge to bellows of laughter. The maroon dragon, one of the largest of the Tangle, dived back beneath the surface, rejoining the swirling mass of his brothers and sisters.

When some of their brothers attacked a sister, the golden dragon swam at them, knocking them away with her snout. When her larger brothers turned on her, she backed off, readying herself to fight.

"She's finished," one of the Flight whispered. But the maroon dragon swam close to her, sending away their more aggressive siblings. They continued to chase and fight in the swirling waters. Many tried to bite the golden one, but she was faster. It was almost as if she knew where they would be before they did as she twisted and turned in the water.

Then the atmosphere changed. The golden dragon seemed to be calming them. The Tangle had gathered around her. She appeared to be speaking to them.

"What're they doing?" one of the Flight asked.

"They're showing weakness," a white dragon said.

A few of the older dragons hissed in frustration; this was not the first struggle of life they'd expected to witness. The red sent a forceful stream of fire into the frigid water.

The tiny golden dragon leapt from the water, stumbling

over the rocks. From there, she issued an immature bellow in challenge to the red. She'd exposed herself to attack from behind, but from the lake there was silence—the young dragons watched their sister.

"At least she has spirit," the fighting red said.

1

"Dreams don't raise the dead." Lucy was sweating heavily; she wiped dirt from her face.

Thomas felt a heaviness in his body—a disappointment. He'd thought she would've understood. They stood in a dark tunnel on the outer edges of Min Flo, deep beneath the prison. He swatted one of the black flies that followed them, causing the finger stub on his left hand to throb again; he didn't need this discussion. He glanced at the silhouette of the ice demon—apart from her long tail gently tapping the tunnel wall, Chloris was silent as usual.

He remembered what Aina had said to him in the centre of the planet. *Raise the fire, and I'll return.* "I promised Aina I'd raise the Fire."

"Look what's the Fire's doing to us," Lucy said, pulling back the sleeve of her jacket. Burns had begun to mark her, just as they did him. "We've been travelling from the deepest parts of the planet for months, and it hasn't got any better."

The new magic hurt, but it had benefits. "Perhaps we just have to get used to it. It's a small price to pay . . ." He almost said to save Aina but stopped himself. He knew Lucy's opinion.

"We still don't know what the Fire is," Lucy said. "Aina would never trick us, but dragons might. Perhaps we were wrong about the nature of the Fire. Perhaps it does more than give us magic. We're both changing—no one told us about that. Not Aina, and not the black dragon. Perhaps raising the Fire is not what we thought."

"What do you mean?"

"We're raising it now," Lucy said. "But is that what Aina meant?"

"That was all she said. I'd assumed that raising it to the surface of Prometheus was enough."

"What if it isn't? What if there's another purpose?"

"For example?" Thomas asked.

"I don't know, but I know it isn't what I thought it would be." The ice demon hissed her agreement. "You saw Aina in the centre of the planet, but it was her spirit. How much would she know of the dragons' intentions?"

Emotion and magic mingled within him, and again he felt the pain inside. "I saw her," he gasped, leaning against the tunnel wall.

"I believe you," Lucy said. "But can't you see that something's wrong? I can hardly use this dragon magic for the pain."

The tall ice demon hissed again, her neck frills fluttered open and closed. "Don't trust them; the desires of dragons are not human ones."

"I don't trust them," Thomas said. "If there are dragons —I've only ever seen one." But Thomas didn't want to talk about dragons. "She told me she'd return."

"The Aina you saw was spirit."

"But . . ."

"She's dead, Thomas. If she was reborn, she'd be a baby. How would you find her amongst the millions of babies born every day? And then she wouldn't know you. Thomas, stop this. You're worrying me."

He had to believe she lived. Without that hope . . . He shook his head to stop that line of thought.

Oliver, one of the Copper Fighters—fellow gladiators he'd freed, and who had followed him from the city of Copper in the hope of finding a better life—approached. "We have a problem: a mercenary's killed the miner."

Thomas's heart sank. The mercenaries had been a problem since he'd recruited them in Tartaros, deeper inside the planet. At the time he'd believed that he'd need greater numbers, and that he could persuade some of them to join the Silvan Resistance with him. That was seeming less and less likely, but they could still prove useful in the escape.

Thomas thought of the dead miner. He'd been speaking about life in Nassopolis to the man less than an hour ago. When he'd first seen them, Thomas had been reluctant to let him join, but he'd grown on him. "What happened?"

"Something about a hat."

It felt so pointless. "I'll be with you soon." Oliver left them.

"I'm sorry," Lucy said.

He nodded. "The mercenaries are becoming a problem; I need to sort this out." But his thoughts returned to Aina. "I promised her I'd raise the Fire. At least, I'll take it to the surface."

"What difference do you think that will make?" Lucy asked.

Thomas sighed. He knew he'd been avoiding thinking about this. "Maybe if I do, I'll find her in Silva."

"What if she's not there?"

"Then I'll look somewhere else, but it was her home. I think it's a good place to start."

She turned to Chloris. "Do you know why the dragons would want us to raise the Fire?"

"We suspect they sleep," she hissed. "If so, it may wake them, but if they wake, it won't be good. They dislike my race, but they hate humans."

"Do you care what they think of humans?" Thomas asked.

"I care for Lucy." Chloris's tail hit the tunnel wall. Lucy laid her hand on the ice demon's arm.

"Will you be able to pay the mercenaries?" Lucy asked, changing the subject.

"Getting them into Nassopolis is the payment. And any who come to Silva will get more money. They've heard stories about the governor's store of tags and blockers, too—they're better than gold in this economy."

"Who told them he has tags?"

Thomas shrugged. "I might have spread a rumour."

She raised an eyebrow.

"It's probably true. And it motivates them."

"For now."

Big Tom appeared at the end of the passage. "We need you."

Tom was one of his Copper Fighters. They were tough, but there were only six of them, while the mercenaries numbered twenty-five. He followed the man down the roughly cut passage. Despite being forced to stoop, they moved fast until the tunnel joined a small cavern. It was lit by torches and lamps stolen from the prison.

The mercenaries that he'd gathered from the underworld stood on the far side of the body. Jack of Clubs, a

Copper Fighter named for his gambling habits as much as the club he carried, held a man by his arm. The other Copper Fighters stood by Jack. One of his men was worth three of the hired men, but he hoped to avoid bloodshed—beyond what was necessary.

"What happened?" Thomas asked.

"He killed the miner," Jack said, twisting his arm.

"Let him go, Jack." The sullen-looking man wearing the miner's hat stared at him.

"Your name?" Thomas asked. He walked closer to the man.

"Sammy."

"Did you kill him?"

"I was just playing." Some of the mercenaries smirked.

"You killed him for a hat?" Thomas asked.

Sammy scowled. "He should've just given it to me."

Thomas glanced at Jack, who shook his head slightly. "We're here to escape. Not kill miners."

Glancing at his friends, who grinned back at him, Sammy said, "It's nothing."

"It's called murder."

The man shrugged.

In one smooth motion, Thomas drew his sword and decapitated him. The mercenaries stared at the grinning head on the ground, open-mouthed. Before any of the men could react, Thomas continued. "He murdered a man, disobeyed orders, and endangered us. Our lives depend on us staying focussed."

Thomas called over his Fighters and spoke to them as if nothing was out of the ordinary. The mercenaries stared, but he ignored them. Eventually they formed smaller groups—still hostile. It was hard, but he'd done the right thing. This wasn't a game; those they opposed were deadly and would soon kill them if he couldn't maintain discipline. His Copper Fighters waited impassively. For them, death was a normal part of life.

"Any others I should watch for?" Thomas asked.

"About half of them," Jack said. "That was nicely done, though. I don't think there'll be any more problems today."

That was as good as Thomas could hope for. "We'll be leaving the mines soon. Once they get some action, they'll be too occupied to think too much."

Chloris walked into the cave, and the mercenaries backed away. No one spoke when she hooked the mercenary's corpse with her claws and took a deep bite.

"Leave the other," Thomas said in the True Language. She hissed her assent, sending the men further back.

Thomas was used to her, and watched calmly when she spat a finger at a scowling mercenary. He didn't move, but when she hissed, with her neck frills expanding, he disappeared deeper into the tunnel.

Thomas resisted a smile. "What?"

"Lucy needs to speak to you."

"Can't it wait?"

"No." The ice demon disappeared back down the dark passage, taking the remains of the corpse with her.

"At least we don't have to get rid of the body," Jack of Clubs said.

"True," Thomas said with a slight grin. "Put the miner in the small cave along the tunnel. He can rest there. I'll be back." He followed Chloris down the passage.

Lucy was waiting for him close to the point where the tunnel descended back towards the underworld. He sensed she was going to say something he wouldn't like.

"What is it?"

"I'm leaving with Chloris."

His stomach tightened at her words. "We need you."

"I can't stay."

They'd argued about taking the secret passages to the surface before. He'd thought he'd convinced her. "We're in this together."

"I'm not going to Silva. We have to go separate ways for now. I have to reach the rocs."

"But..."

"We've discussed this already. The rocs were important in defeating the Empire in the first war. It wasn't just the dragons."

"I know, and I agree that they're important, but we could go there later."

"The rocs might also be able to shed some light on the nature of the Fire, and what raising it actually means."

He rubbed the tunnel wall with his fingers while he thought. "I'm not sure they would know. Also, it's a dangerous path. Those dark passages could lead anywhere."

"Chloris knows the way to the ancient forest."

"What about me?"

"Thomas, I have to do this. We'll meet later. On the surface."

"I thought I'd convinced you the best way to fight the Empire is to break through the prison and find our way to Silva to join the Resistance. We'd be between the imperial colony and the ancient forest."

She shook her head. "We need allies against the Empire, and the rocs are a formidable force. They also have ways to tap into the imperial intelligence systems."

"An alliance with the rocs is a good idea, but it's the timing. And working with the Resistance could help us attack the Empire from the inside." Chloris hissed at the mention of the avian species. Thomas knew that no ice demon would be comfortable in their presence.

"You asked the oracle cards, didn't you?" She relied too much on the strange animal oracle.

"I did. Thomas, the oracle has never let me down."

He knew it was true, but he didn't feel comfortable with it. "It's risky," he said. He had friends in the prison who he wanted to free, and he wanted to work with the Resistance, but he knew that he mostly objected because of his need to find Aina.

"Everything we do is risky. Using the magic is risky."

"Lucy..."

She raised her hand, and he saw the scarring the Fire's magic had caused on her palms. "I have to try. I'm not sure the magic will solve our problems. It may have another purpose. I want to ask the rocs. They may know something about it."

"What do you think it is?" Thomas asked. He could feel the Fire burning in his belly as he spoke. And, like Lucy, he didn't trust it.

"Something for the dragons. They may be very selfish creatures. Thomas—"

He interrupted her. "I want you to stay."

"I know."

With a sinking feeling, he realized that she'd already made up her mind. And, once decided, she was as stubborn as he was. He sighed.

She squeezed his arm. "I'm sorry." She glanced into the darkness. Chloris had already disappeared down the tunnel. "I'll find a way to reach you." And then she was gone.

Thomas stared into the darkness, feeling more alone than he'd ever remembered. It was several minutes before he moved.

2

"Tom."

"How did you know it was me?" the man asked after he walked around the bend in the tunnel.

"Your footsteps are distinctive." All footsteps vibrated in a unique way, and Thomas recognized each of his Fighters.

"I thought I moved quietly."

"You do. What is it?" Thomas asked.

"The men are waiting."

Thomas followed him back. They were all there.

"It begins. Tonight I'll test the escape route; tomorrow we go. I know the prison and can move quickly and unseen. Micky, wait for me near the miners' cave and bring the men after I deal with the gangers—or, if there's a problem, before. Tomorrow evening we'll join the prisoners as they return to their cells, but unlike them, we won't stop until we reach Nassopolis."

Thomas turned to the sergeant of the mercenaries. "I need you to continue scouting the area. Pay attention to the movements of guards, bots, and gangers. They have no reason to come this way, but keep alert."

The sergeant nodded. "And you?" he asked. "You're just going to walk into the prison?"

"I know it well; I spent almost a year there." The men looked at him sceptically despite his reputation for being able to steal into places no one else could. They knew nothing of magic. They thought him lucky. "I'll return tomorrow morning."

The meeting ended, and Thomas moved quickly through the dark tunnels, seeing with his rock sense. Half an hour later, he reached a small cave and stopped. Prisoners were working a rock face separated from the cave by a short tunnel. A pair of gangers, supervisors of the other prisoners, sat in the cave. One was overweight, a rare sight in a prison so short of food. He coughed repeatedly. The wiry one was Decker—a man Thomas'd had problems with when he'd been a prisoner. It sounded as if he'd recently been assigned to this gang. Thomas waited.

When the distant bell rang, eight prisoners crawled from a narrow tunnel, all covered in sweat and dust. Decker shouted, and they followed him up a tunnel that led to the shafts. The other ganger followed at the rear. Thomas waited several seconds, then followed, blending into the darkness with a soft magic suggesting shadows in the minds of the men ahead. When they reached the shaft, other prisoners joined them, and he relaxed the invisibility spell enough that he was seen but not noticed. Looking at the haggard faces, he wished he could take them with him. If what he hoped happened, he'd close this prison down.

He climbed the shaft quickly and was soon in an upper tunnel that led to the hall with the lifts. Unless the schedules had completely changed, his old team would pass this way. He'd already recognized a few men, although they'd not noticed him. He suspected that no one would notice him, even if he removed the spell, but he didn't want to risk it yet. Then he saw Jackson. The man was limping. Thomas stepped close to him.

"Jackson," he whispered.

The man started. Then he strained to see.

"I'm here."

"Thomas?" Jackson rubbed his eyes. He blinked rapidly. "I can hardly see you. Your face looks like it's been half-erased."

Thomas allowed himself to appear more visible. "Jackson, some people know magic."

"I remember the strange things that happened around you when you escaped. You were always different. And now you're back?"

"Just visiting," Thomas said. "We can talk more tonight. Who are you sharing with?"

"No one. Everyone's dead; I'm the only one left. A rockfall took most of them, and an argument with gangers..."

Thomas noticed the man was breathing more heavily than he had before. "I'll stay with you tonight."

Some of the men were looking at them, and they walked the rest of the way in silence, joining the queue of prisoners waiting to enter the giant lifts.

"The lift?" Jackson whispered.

"Won't notice." Thomas was confident he could access its mind, although he'd have to draw on the Fire. He felt it burning inside him now, like the pilot light of a gas burner permanently alight. He'd never possessed such suggestive power before, but the Fire could force certain things to happen, even things he'd not had the knack for before. Although, there was a physical cost.

The men shuffled into the lift, and he suggested to the

artificially intelligent machine that he was not really there. It accepted the suggestion completely.

The gangers entered last, as usual. Thomas made sure he was right at the back, and he looked down, not wanting any of them to recognize him. There were none of the old gangers there, which was a relief, but someone might notice he shouldn't be there. He counted thirty-eight men in the lift, which was the limit—and the lift counted. His escape plan involved taking over a single lift.

There were six levels: the lowest was for the mines, the highest was for prisoners with family able to bribe the governor. Jackson's level was the second, and when the lift stopped, they walked into the communal area, which led to the washrooms and eating place. As much as Thomas wished to eat, he forced himself to wash first. Twenty minutes later, they sat at a table.

"When did you last eat?" Jackson asked, watching him hold the bowl to his mouth.

Thomas started eating more slowly. He didn't want to do anything that would draw attention to himself. "More than a day."

"It's a hard life in the spaces beneath the prison?"

"The better places are deeper down, but none are comfortable."

"I can imagine."

They stopped speaking when strangers sat next to them, instead focussing on finishing the dinner. Then they returned to the cells. They looked smaller than when he'd last been there. He noticed the new metal bars on his old cell.

"They've replaced everything," Jackson said.

Thomas followed Jackson into his cell, which was opposite his old cell. He remembered Victor sitting on that bed.

"Old memories?" Jackson said.

He nodded and sat on the bed opposite Jackson's. "Of Victor."

"I take it he didn't make it."

Thomas shook his head, surprised by the sudden intensity of emotions he was feeling for the old man. The other cells were still empty; the men were enjoying their half hour of freedom before they had to return.

"What are you doing here, Thomas?" Jackson asked. Thomas told him the highlights of his story. When he was finished, Jackson's eyes widened. "This is big stuff."

"It'll probably cost us our lives."

Jackson gave a cold laugh. "Doing nothing has cost lives."

"I'm escaping to Nassopolis tomorrow. I want you to join me."

Jackson gave Thomas a long look. When he finally spoke, he said, "I'll come. I'm the last one, and I don't think I'll last much longer here. It's getting harder."

His old friend looked older: more worn and fragile. Thomas tried to imagine how he'd feel if he'd remained in the prison. Many men gave up. "My visit is also reconnaissance for my escape. I wanted to remind myself of the route and to see if anything had changed."

"New metal bars."

Thomas stood and looked up at them, and then he noticed a dark patch on the passage roof. He immediately reached out mentally, testing the nature of the substance. He hoped it was what he suspected.

"What?" Jackson asked.

Thomas grinned. "Do you remember the crystal garden I grew?"

"I'll never forget it. Why?"

"There's a bit left."

Jackson laughed nervously. "I hope you're not going to grow a crystal garden again."

Thomas shook his head. "I don't need to, but they may come in useful." He spoke to the dark crystals, and they responded with a feeling that he could only describe as love. But he'd need magic to free them from the ceiling.

He stretched his hand out and the Fire roared inside. His stomach and gut burned. Seconds later, the clump of crystals dropped into his palm, and he sat on the bed again.

"Midnight blue," Thomas said.

Jackson gave a slight shake of his head. "What?"

"Their name."

"These are strange things," Jackson said. "Stuff like this, and humming songs that vibrate rocks."

Thomas grinned. "That's a good trick." He studied the crystals. They were midnight blue and beautiful. Their life pulsed in his hand, and he stroked them with soft rock magic, polishing them. "They want to grow."

"Can you really speak to rocks?"

He glanced at the worn man opposite. "These are crystals and are more alive than other rocks, but yes."

"Well, they certainly grew the last time you were here."

Thomas placed the crystals into his pocket.

When two prisoners entered Thomas's old cell, they glanced at him but didn't speak. It wasn't unusual for prisoners to appear or disappear. Before sleeping, they planned the next morning; Thomas had to join the work unit he'd watched earlier. Luckily, Jackson's team was working nearby tunnels. He'd join them later in the day.

The next morning he woke, unrefreshed, minutes before the bell. When the doors opened, he joined the shuffling line of men on their way to the eating place. Upon entering, he memorized the positions of the artificially intelligent guns. There were three of them. Some of the lifts were already descending from the upper floors. They took their food. Thomas ate everything, including the grub cooked in his gruel.

"We need to go higher than the sixth level."

"Must be another lift up there."

Thomas remembered it vaguely from the day he'd arrived.

However hungry he felt, he knew his men were hungrier. They'd not eaten in almost two days, and a problem he foresaw was stopping them from gorging themselves when they reached the upper eating place. He'd have to deal with that then.

"How will you deal with the gangers?"

Thomas looked at Jackson but was silent. Jackson nodded. "And the other men in the team?"

Thomas was quiet for a few seconds. "We won't have the space. The lift takes thirty-eight, and it counts. There are thirty-three of us, but I want a team that works together."

"So four more could fit in," Jackson said. Thomas nodded. "Unless we take two lifts."

"We take one," Thomas said. Controlling the artificially intelligent minds of two was too much. "I'm not returning for a second batch."

"It's time," Jackson said. "We'll be in the same lift, but my group will leave you at the fork in the tunnel." He glanced at Thomas. "What just happened to your face?"

"A partial invisibility spell. I want to be seen but not noticed."

"My brain goes cloudy when I look at you."

"It's for the best. From now on, we don't speak. Not until tonight. I'll wait for you by the shaft."

They joined the line of men, and minutes later pressed into the lift. A guard watched, but as normal, the management of the prisoners was left to the gangers. There were only eighteen men in the lift, including the four gangers. One of them stared at Thomas, looking like he wanted to speak, and he opened his mouth a few times, but no sound came out. Thomas was still learning the finer details of invisibility—or mental suggestion, as it really was. From the first level, they walked to the shaft and climbed back down to the tunnels.

Jackson's team of eight men and two gangers took one fork in the tunnel. Thomas pretended to be with them, following the rear ganger, then stopping to allow the other team of eight to descend deeper into the tunnel. Then he turned back and followed the other team. Decker led them; the fat man was at the rear. He still coughed—the death cough of Min Flo. Thomas moved silently ten yards behind him. It would be easiest to kill the man before they reached the larger space ahead.

The ganger didn't notice him sneak up behind and was coughing blood as he cut his throat. Thomas pulled the body back to a narrow adjoining tunnel, finding space in a crevice. He quickly returned to the rest of the group. They'd reached the small cave, but no one commented on the ganger's disappearance. Decker gave orders—and was free with his club. Thomas remembered that club too well. After the obligatory shouts and threats, four of the prisoners crawled to the rock face. The others waited to carry the rocks back towards the shaft, where another team would haul them up.

Thomas waited in the tunnel for Decker to investigate the disappearance of his colleague, but an hour later, the man was still berating the prisoners. Thomas had learnt patience, and he continued to wait, but it became obvious that the ganger had no concern for his colleague.

A prisoner crouched by the low tunnel to the rock face. "The men need a break." A normal ganger might or might not grant a break, but Decker had never been normal. He was bored, and he liked inflicting pain. Perhaps this gang hadn't learnt his ways yet. He struck the stooping prisoner in his stomach with the end of his club. The man doubled over, holding his stomach. "Why?" he gasped.

There is no why, Thomas thought. Decker hit him again. The other gangers had crawled back to the cave at the sound of the club. There were eight of them, but they were intimidated by the man. And to raise a fist to a supervisor meant death.

"You just can't help yourself, can you?" Thomas said, still standing in the shadows—still only partially visible.

Decker turned to Thomas and squinted. "Who are you?"

"Don't you remember me?" Thomas remembered the beatings this man had given him and his crew over a period of five weeks, until he'd been moved to another crew.

The ganger walked closer, and Thomas stepped from the shadows, slowly releasing his spell of invisibility. The man bared his teeth and made a guttural growling sound. "You!"

Thomas grinned.

Decker swung his baton, but for Thomas, such a simple attack seemed like slow motion. This man wouldn't last more than a few seconds against any of his fighters—he relied on status and intimidation. Thomas stepped inside the blow, knocking the club away. He felt no need to draw his short sword. But this just enraged the ganger, who charged him head down. Thomas caught his head in a hold and, after a few attempts, broke his neck. He dropped the body to the ground.

Footsteps came from the deep passage, and Micky Two Tooth, another of his Copper Fighters, stepped out. "I thought I'd keep you company."

"What's happening?" a miner asked.

"We're just a group of people passing through," Thomas said. "But we need to wait here until the bell rings."

As he spoke, his men emerged from the tunnel. Soon over thirty mercenaries and Fighters squeezed into the cave and nearby tunnels. The prisoners sat quietly in one corner, trying not to stare at the armed men.

Thomas sat against the wall, Adela the psychic beside him. She'd attached herself to Oliver, one of the Copper Fighters, and followed him from the underworld. Her psychic skills were real, he now believed that, but compared to Lucy, she seemed like a beginner. She'd tried to disguise herself as a man, and it had partly worked. It was possible no one would look too closely.

"I had a dream."

He didn't want to listen, but she wasn't going away. Without looking at her, he said, "What?"

"You were by a black tower. A woman was with you."

Thomas sat up straight and turned to face her. "A woman?"

"A woman you love."

"What else?"

She shook her head. "It was cold."

Thomas laughed. "When isn't it?"

"I just wanted to tell you what I saw." She rejoined Oliver.

He wanted to deny it. Why would Aina come to him on the top of the mountain? Why not Silva—her home?

3

The bell rang.

They walked ahead of the prisoners through the maze of mine tunnels to the shaft. Their weapons, mostly knives, short swords, and clubs, were concealed inside their clothes, or wrapped in cloth. It would have to be enough.

Thomas knew the way through the tunnels well, and with each turn, he led them upwards. Half an hour later, they reached the vertical shaft that led up to the eating place and hall. "Start climbing." He looked around for Jackson. He could wait ten minutes, but no longer. Another group of prisoners pushed past him, and one of the gangers stared at him but said nothing.

As soon as he saw Jackson, he nodded and began to climb the shaft. Jackson caught up with him. "I hope you have a way to control the lifts."

"I told you last night."

"Today it seems more real."

Thomas knew that too well. "I have a way." He only hoped it would work; it wasn't always certain.

The mercenary above him paused. "We're almost there."

"Keep going," Thomas said.

He climbed out of the shaft and into the lift hall. His men were standing to one side, trying to look inconspicuous. The clothes they wore were worn and dirty, making them almost indistinguishable from the prisoners. Queues were forming in front of the lifts. The thirty-three of them formed a large group, but there were larger groups in the hall, and Thomas knew that no one counted the men here; they'd wait until they returned to their levels and cells.

Thomas led them to the lift with the fewest prisoners waiting. They joined the queue. There were so many prisoners here that it was impossible to know each one, but that would change once they stepped out of the lift.

The queues moved more slowly than Thomas would have liked, and he hadn't managed to access the machine mind of the level. Touching metal would help—if the machines had been made from rock, then he'd be able to enter their minds from where he was. Artificial eyes watched, but nothing appeared out of the ordinary. As he'd ordered, all his men stared at the ground—he didn't want any type of facial recognition program attempting identification.

"We can fit three more in," the ganger said.

Thomas shook his head. "My gang's new, and I want to keep them together."

The man just nodded, and the doors closed. Ten slow minutes later the lift returned. "Inside," he said, standing back to allow his men in. He wanted to enter last.

His men pushed into the lift. The Copper Fighters played the part of gangers well. They could do attitude when they wanted, and nobody entered with them. The doors shut, and the machine waited.

"Identify," the lift said.

Thomas rested his hand on the metal wall and imagined himself inside the machine; his vision blurred, and his head hurt.

"Identify," the dead voice of the lift asked in his mind.

Thomas had expected this—the lift would now be scanning and trying to identify his men. "New gang," he said aloud, sensing confusion in the cold circuits of the lift's mind.

"Not recognized," it said.

"We had an accident in the mines," Smiler, one of his Copper Fighters, said as Thomas searched for a way in. "It's changed our look."

The lift was quiet for several seconds while Thomas went deeper into its cold mind. In a way, this coldness compensated for the Fire burning inside his belly. It was a simpler machine than a bot. He spoke in the True Language: *"All is fine. Sixth floor."* It accepted.

The lift ascended, but he needed to do more, or else face walking out into the barrels of automatic weapons. The circuits of its computer brain felt similar to some minerals, and he pretended to himself that that was what they were. His aim was to make it forget the past couple of minutes had existed, and then to access Imperial Security. Thomas found its most recent memory. He ordered it to erase all memories from that point. Then, he told it to switch off its gun. It complied without comment. Thomas opened his eyes and breathed deeply, relaxing for a few seconds. He looked up. They'd just passed the fourth level.

"Thirty seconds," Oliver said.

"I've switched off the lift gun; now the sixth-floor guns."

"Use them against the gangers," Micky said.

Thomas shook his head. "Too dangerous; they may turn

on us after." He leant heavily against the lift wall, and despite a throbbing headache, he pushed into the artificial mind again, but this time he sought access to the greater mind of Imperial Security.

"Ten seconds," Oliver said.

Thomas was breathing heavily and sweating when he found a way in. *"Lock down all weapons on the sixth level."* The order was countermanded. He repeated the order. *"Technical problem. Lock down weapons."*

"We're there," Oliver said.

Opening his eyes, he saw lights. Jackson supported him, and he called the Fire, which flowed through his body, flushing away feelings of faintness.

"Did you shut them down?" Jackson asked.

"I don't know." He breathed heavily and cursed the pain that coursed through him. The lift was slowing down.

"What's happened to her?" Danny, one of his Copper Fighters, said, looking at Adela.

As the lift stopped, Thomas glanced at her. Her eyes were wide, and he knew she was having one of her visions. She turned to Thomas and gripped his arm.

"Kill the guard in blue!"

"We've got him," Big Tom said. Danny and Jack of Clubs nodded.

The doors opened and they ran out, pushing prisoners to the floor. Thomas staggered through, waiting for the rattle of machine guns that didn't come. To his left, two guards were chatting; one was wearing blue. To his right was a table of ten gangers. Half the mercenaries charged at them.

The guards looked at them in surprise. Thomas walked unsteadily forward, still supported by Jackson.

The guard in grey drew a pistol and shot Big Tom. Then

he killed Danny before Jack clubbed his arm. The pistol clattered to the ground. For a second, Thomas wondered why the man in blue hadn't drawn his gun, but when he felt the sudden rising of magic, he knew the man was more than just a guard—his Fire rose in response.

The man in blue clapped his hands, and Jack and several of the nearest mercenaries fell to the floor. Jackson also fell to his knees. The guard in blue's eyes widened slightly at seeing Thomas still staggering towards him. The man chanted magic, making Thomas feel nauseous, but his Fire was burning through the toxic energy.

Thomas reached the man, barely managing not to faint. He wasn't even sure what he could do. When the man clapped his hands again, Thomas suddenly felt hot, and he vomited on him. Then the world turned black, and he silently cursed his body for failing him.

"Wake up!" Jackson shouted. Someone threw water on his face.

Thomas opened his eyes. "How long?"

"Seconds," Jackson said.

Thomas sat slowly with the man's help. The guard in grey lay in a pool of blood; one of the men had slit his throat. The man in blue was obviously dead, but his stomach had been burnt away, and there was a look of terror etched on his dead face.

"What happened?"

"You tell me," Jack of Clubs said. "One minute you threw up on him, and the next minute he was on fire."

"You vomited fire," Adela said in his ear.

He looked at her for a second, not quite understanding what she said, before he turned back to Jack. "How many did we lose?"

"Big Tom and Danny," Jack said. "The mercenary sergeant, too."

Still feeling sick, Thomas studied the man's body. He had no idea how he'd done this, but he'd burnt a hole through the man's abdomen, and the smell coming from his guts was nauseating. But his limbs were intact, and on one of his fingers was a large ring. Thomas removed it.

"I think this is a key." He hoped it was. Thomas saw that the men were devouring the prisoners' food, while the scared convicts clustered against the far walls.

"You need to eat," Jackson said.

"Yes." He turned his attention to the other lift. "But I need this lift working more." He walked to the lift, feeling better the further he got from the dead man. His energy began to return. He put the ring on and placed it against the pad by the lift. He heard the lift descend.

Jackson passed him food, but he couldn't eat; he took the water offered. "Take the food, too."

Thomas put a piece of hard cheese in his mouth, and Jackson stuffed some bread in his pocket. The food was better on this level. He looked around the room. The men were feasting, but looking at the bodies of Big Tom and Danny lying near the minor lord, Thomas lost his hunger.

He felt the lift descending. "Come here," he tried to shout, but his voice croaked instead. "Jackson."

"Here!" Jackson shouted. Some of the mercenaries glanced at him, but most were absorbed by the food.

Thomas regained his voice. "The lift's here. We're leaving now!"

The Copper Fighters joined him, but the mercenaries moved too slowly. A door opened on the far side of the room, and a bot, followed by armed guards, rushed into the hall.

The lift doors opened as the first men fell. "To me!" Somehow, the mercenaries managed to partially disable the bot, which started bobbing along the floor and shooting at random. They'd also killed two of the guards, but he counted ten of his men dead, and three were bleeding badly. "Leave them!" Some of the men were reluctant to leave their injured friends. "Run!"

He stepped into the lift with Adela, Jackson, and his Fighters. When another bot flew through the far door, the mercenaries ran into the lift. Thomas shut the doors and pressed the ring against the inner pad, ordering the lift to ascend.

"There were five men still out there!" an angry mercenary corporal shouted.

"Nothing I could do." Thomas didn't bother mentioning that he'd called the men away from their food several times before the attack.

"We'd all be dead if we'd waited," Jack said, almost snarling at the mercenary.

"What now?" Oliver asked. "They'll know we're coming." He glanced up at the small gun.

"You've got us all killed!" the mercenary yelled, and Thomas punched him. He fell to the ground, losing consciousness for several seconds before being shaken awake by his friends.

There were nine mercenaries and four Fighters left. It had gone much worse than he'd imagined; he'd underestimated their attachment to the food and his own magical abilities. "We're not dead yet." Turning to Jack and Micky, he motioned at the mercenaries. "Keep them off me. I need to access its mind."

Thomas placed his palms against the lift wall, and despite his headache, he called the Fire and let it mingle with his primary magic of rocks, minerals, and metal. He listened to the machine, and as he did, his mind flowed beyond the metal lift, reaching towards the artificial mind located at some other location in the prison complex. The lights, impulses, and vibrations of the artificial mind spoke a unique language.

"What?" the controlling artificial mind asked telepathically.

"Lock all weapons."

"Authority?"

"Imperial Security." Thomas waited. He was unsure how aware this artificial mind was. Some were highly aware and would fight intruders. The trick was to appear as part of the mind or the Empire.

"Denied. Identify yourself."

Thomas had no codes or numbers to enter, instead remembering something he'd once learnt from Aina. He imagined he was one of the most powerful imperial lords, the man he and Lucy had raced against to the centre of Prometheus for the Fire. *"I am Lord Frore."* Thomas almost felt the sorcerer's signature energy, and for that moment, he *was* the lord.

"Apologies, my lord." The weapons locked, and he heard exclamations from the men around him.

Thomas accessed the prison plans, memorizing alternative ways out. One route was better than the others; he'd try for that. Feeling as if a pin had been pushed into his head, he realized that someone was trying to reactivate the weapons.

"Denied." He sent his message to whoever was attempting to override his control. *"Show me images from outside the lift doors at each level."*

The artificial mind showed him pictures of guards gathering outside the doors at each floor. There were about twenty men waiting for them at the upper level, which was their destination. He wished he could reactivate the weapons to kill the men, but that would mean they'd be shot dead inside the lift before it arrived.

He turned off the lift lights, leaving only the red floor indicator turned on, and without opening his eyes or leaving the machine mind, he shouted, "Silence!" Jack and Micky maintained order while he found the light control for the upper level, and he turned it on full, watching the men look up at the lights. "Get ready. There are armed men waiting for us. Kill them and take their weapons. Then follow me down the third passage to the left. It's the smallest and leads through the prison stockrooms to a delivery area. Once we get through the large delivery doors, we're in Nassopolis."

"Is that all?"

With his eyes still closed and his mind half inside the machine mind, Thomas heard one of his men slap the man. "The guards are waiting in a small hall, and I've turned the hall lights on full. It's bright there. When our doors open, I'll switch them to the lowest level. They'll be blinded for a few seconds—use those seconds to kill them!"

"Did the ring connect you to the system?" one of the mercenaries asked.

Thomas chose not to answer. He knew that most of the men would assume that what he did was via tags and devices like the ring. As the lift slowed down, Thomas dimmed the lights outside to the lowest levels he could without turning them off. He watched the guards glance up at the lights, and as the doors began to open, he opened his eyes and disconnected from the artificial mind. Anger at the pain wracking his body made his magic explode, and with a blast, he sent the nearest half dozen men to their knees. His men attacked with blades and stolen guns.

Then the guards opened fire.

4

Lucy couldn't forget seeing Thomas standing alone in the dark tunnel after she'd left him. He hadn't known she'd turned to look, but she had, several times. And each time he was still there, unmoving. Thinking about it gave her a lump in her throat. She'd abandoned him, and she'd spoken more harshly than she'd intended about Aina. She wondered whether she should have used kindness instead of truth, but his irrational pursuit of a dead woman troubled her. Aina could not re-enter the world as she had been, whatever dreams, ghosts, or dragons said. In part, she wished she'd given him the hope he desired, but it was too late. He'd chosen a hard path. It was demanding enough to lead a gang of killers against a dangerous enemy, but that seemed easy compared to his search for a dead woman.

Lucy now moved through the darkness silently; the magic within her was helping her sense her surroundings in a way she never had before, and she moved through the dark tunnels without a sound. She'd gained new senses since finding the Fire, too, but it'd burnt her. It wasn't as she'd expected, and she still had to learn how to use it fully, but the thought of what it might do scared her. Lucy could now sense vibrations in the air, and heat sources at a distance, but she still felt she needed a teacher.

Chloris moved silently ahead. Lucy was learning a lot from her, and although Chloris knew no magic, unless you counted her telepathic skills, she had given Lucy ideas on applying her magic to martial situations. But, apart from teaching some basic skills, the ice demon had rejected the role of teacher, telling her she should trust and be herself. She was trying.

Climbing had become easier, too. She doubted she'd ever equal Thomas's skill with rock magic, but he'd given her hints and pushed her to do basic exercises as they'd travelled from the centre of the planet. Since then, she'd developed a certain stickiness to rocks, which was helping her climb faster now. She followed Chloris up a vertical shaft that would have been impossible for her before.

Then she stopped.

"What?" Chloris asked from above.

Lucy was impressed by the ice demon's ability to listen to all of her environment. "I felt something."

"Heard?"

"No, I just felt something wrong."

Chloris rushed down to her. The ice demon had incredible ability in running up and down vertical rock faces. Even upside down. "Where?"

"Down." It was all she knew. "I think we're being followed."

"I'll look," Chloris hissed. And she vanished down the shaft.

Lucy extended her senses down like a cone, searching for life beneath her, but apart from Chloris and a few small animals, she sensed nothing. But she had had an ominous feeling.

Chloris returned quickly up the side of the shaft. "There's nothing."

"I—" Lucy began.

Chloris silenced her with her claw. "What you hear is the magic of the planet, and the disturbances in its field. If we're followed, they're not yet close."

Lucy had never thought of it like that, but it made sense. "How do you know this?"

"I was a fighter of the Dark Moon." Lucy knew Chloris had served in an elite unit. "We were personal guards to the Imperial Order, and we heard."

"They discussed this in front of you?" Lucy was a little surprised.

"They made us, but they didn't understand us. They wanted intelligent animals, but animals are more aware than they think."

Lucy knew from experience how true this was. "So they know as little about you as the subjects of the Empire know about their rulers."

"Ignorance is bliss," Chloris said with a widening of her jaw, indicating an ice demon smile. Her friend was right. The subjects of the Empire chose to live in ignorant bliss: tagged and plugged in to the imperial network. They didn't experience the world she did, but an infantile one without care. They continued their climb, undisturbed, for several hours.

Lucy could sense water and simple plants, but most were inedible. With dread, she began to realize that there might be nothing edible growing here at all, and she hated the idea of eating any of the small animals—dreading that they may speak to her. She knew that Chloris had already eaten a family of rats, but even if desperate, she wasn't sure she could eat a raw rat or insect.

Finally, they left the series of shafts and began scrambling up a steep tunnel. Chloris went on ahead, and Lucy sensed her moving in the distance. Lucy knew she was hunting for more mice. Turning her attention back to the tunnel, she remembered that she'd once been afraid of the dark, but now, with her sharpened senses, the dark no longer seemed so dark. Until she had the feeling of something being wrong again. She stopped and listened. There was no sound, but something felt wrong. She waited on the upper part of a boulder. If there was anything there, surely she'd be able to sense it. Then she knew. She'd heard the tiny sounds of insects moving in the rocks for most of the journey, but now there was silence.

"Chloris. Something's wrong."

"I'm coming."

A hand grabbed her right wrist, and she screamed as its fingers tightened, its nails cutting into her skin. She slipped and slid along the top of the boulder as the hand tugged her. In her rising panic, she forgot her magic, instead hitting as hard as she could with her free hand. The grip tightened. Then she saw shadows moving around her. The scent of ice demons was strong.

A man crawled towards her. He was hurting her; his nails had punctured her skin. "Who are you?" Shaking with fear, she tried to pull back, but he wouldn't let go. Bending his head down to her wrist, he sniffed.

It was Scanlon—the imperial assassin who had once caught and imprisoned her in a room in Nassopolis. She pulled away in disgust. From the roof of the tunnel, an ice demon stared at her. Another clung to the side of the tunnel.

"You can't escape."

"What do you want?" She didn't know whether he recognized her or not with the dirt covering her. He pulled her closer and stared, and as he did, she subtly influenced his mind, masking her scent by suggesting the scent of a plant she'd passed in the passages.

"Who are you?" he asked.

"I escaped from the prison." She felt him push at her mind, but he lacked her skill. She allowed him to think he was entering.

"How did you know where I was?" Lucy asked, watching the demons sniffing their way along the walls.

"Why am I mopping up for the Hag?"

Startled, Lucy listened. He hadn't meant to communicate anything, but he'd left his thoughts unguarded. Lucy had no idea what it meant. "Are you hunting prisoners?"

"They'll be caught." He sneered and pressed harder into her mind, as he once had before. She'd been weaker then, but still able to divert him. This time she was in control, but she wasn't sure she wanted him to know who she was. Whilst she showed the assassin fake memories of her prison life, which he lapped up, she reached for her knife with her free hand. He smiled, and her heart sank until she realized he was smiling at a false image of her cringing in fear.

With her knife in her hand, she twisted and slashed his wrist. He let her go with a curse—a blade appearing in his hand. She slashed, but he was faster, and he slapped her hand away. Her knife clattered onto the ground. She saw the ice demons watching her, ready to help the assassin, but she continued to attack, this time with both hands.

Scanlon let go and looked at the blood on his hands. Frowning in confusion, he stared at her. "What did you do?"

She wasn't sure. Looking down, she saw a faint golden

light coming from her hands. Blood dripped from her fingers, and for a second, she imagined her hands were blades.

A loud crash startled both her and Scanlon, and one of the ice demons tumbled to the ground with its throat cut open. The other demon screamed as Chloris attacked; seconds later it was dead on the ground. When Lucy turned back, Scanlon was gone.

"You should've killed him," Chloris said. "Now he'll follow us."

Killing a human, even one like him, was hard. She'd killed in self-defence, but this time he'd already let go. There had been no immediate threat, although she knew Thomas would have killed him—Aina, too. It just wasn't something she could do in the same way Chloris could. "I didn't understand what was happening."

"Your magic awoke, but your fear blocked it for too long," she hissed. "That will kill."

She was right, but it was too late now. Lucy could no longer sense the assassin. He had his own small magic. Enough to hide himself away in dark places. And she didn't want Chloris risking herself finding him. He was dangerous. "We should keep moving," Lucy said.

This time, Chloris made her climb ahead of her, which was slower, as Chloris was natural at finding the best ways up through the steep incline of the tunnel. Lucy felt herself plodding along compared to her companion, but Chloris never complained.

"Do you know him?" Chloris asked.

She thought about the assassin and shivered. "He tried to kill me once. He's an imperial assassin and has a special sense of smell."

"And small magic," Chloris said.

"You noticed."

"I can sense such things, but compared to you, he's weak. How did he nearly overpower you?"

It was a good question. "I was scared. Chloris?"

"Yesss?" she hissed.

"I saw something in the assassin's mind; something I didn't understand. When I asked him how he'd found us, he had a thought. It seemed strange."

"And?"

"Who is the Hag?" Chloris let out such a long rattling sound that Lucy felt alarmed. "Chloris? You're making me nervous."

"As you do me."

"Explain if you know what he meant."

"The Night Hag's an associate of Lord Frore."

Lucy's heart sank. "A sorcerer?"

"One of their worst."

This was the last thing she needed. "Do you think she's coming?" Lucy asked.

"I don't know, but I do know the brothers I killed were from the tower."

Lucy remembered the black tower on the peak of Nassopolis, the headquarters of Imperial Intelligence and the Imperial Order on the planet. "Were they part of your unit?"

"No. A lesser unit, but still dangerous."

Forgetting about her hunger, Lucy began climbing much faster than before—fast enough for the fire lichen to spark as she moved over it.

5
―――

As she climbed, Lucy practiced using the magic she'd acquired in the core, particularly the martial magic. She didn't want to, but Chloris had mithered her until she'd agreed.

With no cup to focus the energy through, using the Fire felt strange, and it left a hangover worse than wine, but she was learning to better control the blade hand magic, and now she could send energy into her hands at will, even focussing it in her fingertips. When she practiced cutting the fire lichen, it fell from the wall in clumps.

Chloris watched her, making Lucy feel like a student. All ice demons were trained in martial arts from birth, and Chloris had belonged to an elite unit.

"Which weapon do you find most natural?"

Lucy pulled out her knife. "This." She'd never liked firearms, but had become comfortable with the blade.

"Then, after you master the knife hand, you should practice with the knife. Try sending your magic into the blade."

She did and was surprised at how easily she'd done it.

Her blade glowed slightly in the dark. "Thomas talked about infusing magic into his sword," she said, looking closely at her knife.

"If you can do this with a knife, you can do it with a sword," Chloris said. "Now cut the lichen."

Lucy did, and a large clump fell away. It hit the ground hard, and she picked it up. "I've cut off part of the rock, too."

"Good," Chloris said.

Lucy remembered the magic-infused knife Lazolteotl had given Chloris when they'd visited her realm. "Whatever happened to your silver knife?"

"I wondered if you'd notice," Chloris said. "I gave it as a gift—a sign of trust."

Lucy wanted to know more, but the ice demon climbed quickly, and was soon hard to see in the darkness. She knew Chloris well enough to know that she didn't want to say any more. They continued climbing through the twisting tunnels for the next hour, and when they took another break, Lucy sat on the ground by the wall. "I need food and a bath." The streams of water they'd passed had been too small to wash in.

"We're above the prison level," Chloris said. "You can enter the lowest levels of Nassopolis, if you want."

"Have you been there before?" Lucy asked.

"Yes. I passed through on the way down."

"I'd like to go," Lucy said, suddenly feeling excited at the thought of taking a bath.

"There are many criminals."

Remembering the stories she'd heard about the New Cities of Nassopolis, she looked down at her hands and made them glow again.

"Yess, you'll need that."

"These are the poorest levels then."

"Not just that, but those who want to avoid the Empire live here. Many are untagged."

That suited Lucy fine. "I'll need money."

"The criminals will donate."

Lucy smiled until she realized the ice demon's meaning. "I'm not sure I want to steal."

"Is stealing from thieves theft?" Chloris asked.

Perhaps that would be okay, Lucy thought. Then she felt movement in her pocket. "The oracle cards." The frills around Chloris's neck fluttered questioningly. "They're restless." She took them out and they jumped in her hand.

"What does this mean?" Chloris asked.

"It means they want to tell me something." Chloris immediately became more alert, listening for movement down the tunnel. Lucy shuffled the cards, and on the second shuffle, a card jumped out, landing upright on her leg. "This one." Putting the others away, she studied the card in front of her.

Chloris came closer. "It's all black."

"Wait," Lucy said. She studied the dark scene, letting her intuition guide her. Then she saw a pair of eyes moving to the right. When she looked more closely, she saw a black and yellow chameleon waiting by a dark waterfall. A dark moon hung in the sky—one she could only sense. "A chameleon is by a waterfall." Chloris looked silently. "And a dark moon in the sky. It's hidden, but I can feel it." Chloris became agitated. "What?" Lucy asked.

"Continue," Chloris said.

"I can see something sniffing along the ground, and . . . This is really strange."

"What?" Chloris asked.

"Four lizards. The first acts as if he's the king, the second is sniffing, just like a dog, the third has skin hanging from his body . . ."

Chloris looked up at Lucy. "And the fourth is beautiful."

"How do you know?" Lucy was sure that her friend couldn't see the images on the card as she could.

"The Dark Moon is coming. And your assassin may be with them." Lucy was beginning to feel uncomfortable. "We were the best."

"I sensed a dark moon, but..." Lucy started to deny it, but she knew she was deceiving herself. She worried that Chloris was right.

"The four lizards were in my team: Duke, Sniffer, Skinner, and Beauty. All are deadly." Chloris's tail was beating involuntarily against the wall of the tunnel. "What was the other animal?"

"A chameleon. They're lizards, too. They can change colour with their surroundings, and they have a prehensile tail—"

"It's a warning! We must go now!"

"But—"

Chloris interrupted. "We must choose our own ground; we must choose where we fight them. We need every advantage." The ice demon was nervous, and that was making Lucy nervous, too. They continued their ascent through the tunnels, but this time, Chloris was gently pushing Lucy on with her long head. Lucy climbed and walked up through the tunnels and shafts faster than she ever had before; thoughts of a bath were now gone.

"I can't just keep doing this," Lucy said.

"Not much further," Chloris whispered. "Then you can rest before they come. Water's there, and maybe mushrooms, too."

Lucy's stomach rumbled at the thought of even a few

raw mushrooms, and she pushed herself on. Her legs now felt as if they were made of lead, but she continued to place one in front of the other.

After what felt like hours, Chloris told her to stop. They were in a chamber, and the ground was covered in water. A curtain of water fell from the ceiling, and Lucy cupped her hands beneath it, catching water to drink.

"Here," Chloris said.

Lucy joined her and saw the patch of mushrooms. They were an edible kind, and they accepted her eating them, asking only for her to spare the tiniest ones. They were so small that she couldn't eat them anyway. The dozen or so mushrooms were not enough, but it put something in her stomach. Her cards jumped again in her pocket. This time she sensed the approach of Scanlon. "They're coming."

With her knife in hand, she hid behind a boulder, much as the chameleon in the card had done, and like the chameleon, she blended into the background, but in her case through a simple invisibility spell. Chloris had attached herself to the inside of the curtain falls. They waited.

The cave was silent apart from the water falling. It was only Lucy's psychic sense that alerted her. *"Chloris,"* she whispered in the True Language, so softly that she was sure only her friend could hear.

"Yes?"

"They're here. But only one demon—Skinner."

"Are you sure the others aren't in the passages below?"

"They're not here."

Lucy heard Chloris's silent laughter. *"Then they've made a mistake, but not one they'll repeat, not when they know who we are."*

Lucy felt a strange relief that Chloris just believed her intuition. Some people would have questioned the truth of her vision, but not Chloris. Thinking about what had changed the minds of the other three demons did worry her a little, though.

"Focus," Chloris whispered.

And she did. The ice demon was good. It moved without any sound, and was close to the curtain fall. Lucy only felt it because of a sense of displacement—the place it stood felt different. *"Chloris."* Her telepathic whisper was soft, and she knew Chloris listened. *"It's almost beneath the falls."* She showed her friend its position. And that was enough for Chloris. She dropped silently with the water, and her razor claws cut Skinner's throat open; his neck frills fell from his neck.

When Scanlon turned to the ice demons, Lucy stabbed him through his heart with her magic infused knife. He died with a confused expression on his face. She felt only a twinge of pain as the magic subsided.

Chloris's wet nose touched her. "Are you alright?"

"Fine." She didn't feel fine at all, but she was alive. "I didn't think it could be so easy to kill him."

"Sometimes death comes quickly, and he was distracted. But you did well."

"You, too."

"Your night sight helped me. How did you see them?" Chloris asked.

"I didn't. I felt a difference in the spaces they stood." Chloris hissed her approval. "I'm worried about what I saw in the card. I saw more of them."

"They work as a team. They'll be here."

"And the Hag?" Lucy asked.

"Imperial lords used to lead teams of us on special missions. If the Dark Moon is here, the Hag could be nearby, too."

"I'm still scared," Lucy said. "I think we should keep moving." The fight had made her too alert to rest.

"Agreed," Chloris said. "And feeling nervous is good; it keeps you alive. But first, you need food." Lucy's stomach rumbled at the thought of food, and for a short while, she forgot about what hunted them and followed Chloris along the tunnels that led to the deepest of the New Cities.

6

The entrance to 27th, the lowest level of the New Cities, was a rusted door that hung from its lower hinge. Lucy stepped into the dark, rubbish-strewn alley. Chloris remained inside the maintenance passage that ran around the underground city.

"Chloris?"

"I'd attract too much attention." The ice demon pushed her large head into the alley and sniffed the stale air. "I'll wait for you here. Call me if you need me."

Stepping carefully over piles of trash, Lucy left the alley. The street it led to was not much cleaner, but at least there were some streetlights. The city appeared as poor as she'd heard—27th was a place where no one wanted to live. A common opinion amongst richer Nassopolitans was that anyone living beneath 14th by the time they were forty had failed in life.

Lucy turned a corner and walked into a desolate market. An old woman sold two varieties of limp looking vegetables from a piece of cardboard on the ground, and a man sat with a chained rabbit. Blood covered the sheet of dirty plastic in front of him. Her heart went out to the poor animal, but there was little she could do. If she helped it escape, it'd be caught again.

Feeling dejected, she moved past the line of poor vendors. Further into the market, she found an eating place. She had no money. Chloris had told her to use her magic to create the illusion of wealth to the seller. She guessed that she might be able to do that, but it made her feel dirty. She sat on one of the three upside down metal casks serving as seats.

The man glared at her, and she pointed at whatever was in his pot. Giving her a curt nod, he scooped two ladles of soup into a bowl. There was no spoon, and she wiped the side of the bowl, then lifted it to drink. She tried not to think where this food had come from; she'd heard that in the poorest parts of Nassopolis, there were people who made a living from collecting waste food, washing it, and recooking it with spices. This soup was spiced.

She stood and sent the man a sensation of success and happiness. He nodded as she left, and she saw a smile on his face. She'd paid him, in a sense.

Wherever the food had come from, she felt better. Looking back, she could still see the entrance to the alley. Once she entered the next street, it would be out of sight. She didn't want to wander too far, but she hoped to find more and better food, and she'd heard Thomas once say that you could always find hotels and eating places around train stations. She asked for directions from the next person she saw.

The train station was a large wall on one side of a shabby square. It was one of the horizontal stations linking parts of this city, but not ascending to the higher levels. Still, she wondered at the possibility of making her life easier and taking a train to a main station, and then going up to the surface the easy way. But there was no way Chloris could travel in the open.

As some shady-looking characters in front of the train station took notice of her, she realized she'd been lost in her thoughts for too long. The atmosphere had turned predatory, and she considered turning back. She knew that she was dangerous, too, but she didn't want to be forced to use magic if there was a chance that the Night Hag was nearby. Looking around for somewhere she'd be safe, she saw the liveliest restaurant and walked quickly to it.

As she entered, a buzzer sounded, and the diners all turned to look at her. A robot server raised its hand. "We don't serve your sort."

"What?" Lucy asked, feeling her face grow hot as everyone stared.

"Untagged." Now more people were staring at her. "Leave immediately or I'll be forced to call the police."

"Is it a crime?" She felt angry with the stupid robot, but remembered that only those with tags were within the economy.

"Leave the restaurant." Some of the diners were shaking their heads.

She walked out of the restaurant feeling a shame she knew she shouldn't feel. Perhaps she could influence the robot, but possibly not before it called the police. When she left, a young man in stained pants approached her.

"You're not from around here," he said.

"No." There was no point in denying the obvious; she would never have walked into that restaurant if she'd known its policy towards untagged. And they'd been right: she had no credits.

"I can show you a nice restaurant."

This seemed like a bad idea, but she was still hungry, and she couldn't sense any obvious hostile intentions, although she was sure he wanted to scam her in some way. No chance of taking what she didn't have—apart from her hidden oracle and magic-infused knife. She doubted even two or three men like this could take them.

"Where is it?"

"Not far."

Not the best answer. "How far?"

"I'll show you."

Her oracle cards seemed to have the habit of warning her of danger, but they remained still in her pocket. The man grinned and walked towards an alley next to the one she'd entered the square from. There was a look in his eyes that gave her a bad feeling.

"I live down there." She pointed the way she'd come. She had no wish to get further from Chloris; she already wandered far enough.

He gave a crisp nod that made her feel she'd just made a worse choice. But there was always Chloris. "Not much this way." That much was true, at least. "I do know a small place, but it's further." Other men lounging around the square watched him lead her back the way she'd come; one of the men said something to the man, but he ignored him and started walking faster. "It's better not to hang around here. It's a dangerous neighbourhood; you can't trust anyone."

Including you, Lucy thought. But perhaps he'd lead her to food before he tried whatever scam he practiced. As they walked, he spoke on his earphone. They passed the market she'd eaten at earlier and walked past the alley where Chloris waited. Then he turned to the right. The street looked desolate. "There's nothing here." She was guessing.

"A small place. Very good." The energy coming from the man was becoming more erratic and disturbed.

"I don't think this is a good idea," she said. The oracle cards fluttered in her pocket.

"Not far. I promise!" He smiled. "Down here."

She looked into the dark alley, and she couldn't sense anyone there, but she was starting to feel uncomfortable. "Okay, I'll just take a look." Keeping her eyes on the man, who was still smiling, she rested her hand on her knife.

Five men stepped out of the shadows, and her guide disappeared. "You're coming with us," one said. He was better dressed than the rest, and she sensed a hint of magic. Lucy backed up, but she was surrounded.

"Chloris?"

"What?"

"I may need help; I'm not sure."

"I'm coming."

"What do you want?" she asked the men.

"A lady wants to speak to you." She could think of no lady, in this city or any other, who would want to speak to her. "Come with me. You won't be hurt."

She didn't believe him and cursed herself for not having listened to her intuition, or to the cards—they had since stilled in her pocket.

She pulled out her knife. The men laughed, and the leader nodded at a large man, who grabbed her wrist roughly. She sent a magic shock down her arm, and the man quickly let go.

"She's strange." He slashed her quickly, but she responded by cutting his hand, the magic guiding her. His knife clattered to the ground.

"I'll deal with her," the leader said.

She felt his magic building up, which meant he was

Imperial Intelligence. His magic was a clasping sort, and she felt it squeezing and restraining her. Cutting the unseen bonds with knife hands, she took a thread and threw it back at the man. Then she whipped a second around his neck. He fell back into the men, choking and holding his throat.

"What did you do?"

"I'm leaving," Lucy said. The magic of the Fire burnt steadily within her, having the potential to turn into a firestorm if she was threatened. The men laughed, and too late, she noticed them glance behind her.

A sharp blow to her head sent her to the ground. Ignoring the grazes on her body, she turned round, her magic alight. An older woman grinned at her as a magical blast knocked her onto her back.

Lucy lay on the ground, stunned and unable to see clearly. The oracle cards were frantically tearing their way out of her inner pocket. Shadows loomed before her; she knew she had to force herself to move. She stood but stumbled into the wall as her legs weakened. A hand took her knife, and then another slapped her.

Her vision was blurry. *"Chloris,"* she called weakly.

Lucy looked at the woman. Her magic was strong, and it was overpowering her. Two ice demons appeared from deeper within the alley. They stood to her left, and the sorcerer and men to the right.

"Night Hag," Lucy gasped.

"Charming," the woman said. "My name is Lady Hay, and I work for Imperial Intelligence. You'll be coming with me. I have some questions for you."

Lucy called her magic, but she felt a sickening burning pain inside.

"What magic you had has gone. I've locked it."

Was that even possible? Lucy tried again, but she felt

nothing.

"You have no choice but to cooperate, so be reasonable."

She didn't feel reasonable, and the desperate movement from her pocket was telling her to move, but her body felt numb. Still, she knew she must escape, and she searched for a way. The Night Hag glistened with sickly magic, and as she stepped closer, Lucy saw movement behind the magician.

Chloris struck the sorcerer hard enough to kill, but it only stunned the woman. *"Get out of here! Escape the city!"* Her tail struck the man holding her knife, sending it to the ground.

"No!" Lucy said. She picked up her knife, and then turned to help the ice demon, but Chloris forcefully pushed her through the group of men, biting a chunk out of one man's head and slicing another in half with her tail as she propelled Lucy out of the alley. "Whatever happens, don't return!"

Lucy staggered into the street, shocked by the force Chloris had used on her. But then the two other ice demons took hold of her friend, and the Night Hag struck her with dark magic.

Chloris fell to the ground and didn't move. She was about to run back to Chloris when the oracle cards moved violently in her pocket. She stared back into the alley. Chloris appeared to be dead, and the two ice demons had also been stunned by the magical shock. The Hag looked drained of energy, too. "Get her!" the Night Hag said.

The three remaining men ran at her, and she slashed with her knife. It was still infused with magic, but the flow had stopped. She felt a burning sensation in her chest, but no magic.

The men circled around her, and she hesitated. Chloris lay still on the ground, and a dark shadow moved close to her. It sniffed the air and hissed. Lucy remembered the sniffing demon she'd seen in the cards.

"Chloris!"

Sniffer hissed. "My sister's dead." The other demon was moving towards her.

Lucy felt a sharp pain in her leg, and a shadow moved by her side. She cursed, ready to fight, but then she saw the shadow wolf from the oracle. *"Follow me!"* The wolf slipped through the line of three men, unseen by them, and waited for her at the mouth of the alley.

She held her knife tightly and ran, trying to remember Thomas's training. He'd made her practice breaking through a line of men, and she wished she'd paid more attention, but she did remember him telling her that attitude was the most important thing. Shouting wildly, she slashed her way through the line, and then stabbed the first man to turn.

Although she couldn't call her magic, the knife still cut into them like butter. They yelped and fell back. She didn't wait, but ran back out of the alley, then sprinted after the shadowy wolf as it crossed the road and turned into the first alley.

Shouts came from behind her, but Lucy kept running. She jumped through the broken door and ran deeper into the underground tunnels. She heard the pursuit but didn't stop until she could no longer move her legs.

Sounds behind her told her that the howler monkey from her oracle was helping distract, which was strange, because only one card could ever appear at once. But then looking around, she realized that she was running alone through the darkness.

"Never alone," the shadow wolf's familiar voice whispered in her mind.

7

Their eyes had adjusted to the dark, and when they stepped out of the lift and into the dimly lit passage, they could see, unlike the waiting guards attempting to adjust to the sudden darkness. But fighting guns with knives and magic had limits.

Thomas cut through the cluster of guards with his magic-infused knife, and when a guard aimed his gun at Jack, Thomas cut the man's throat, and then cut his way through the guards, leaving a path behind him. The lights brightened and the killing continued. Guards, mercenaries, and Fighters died.

A minute later it was finished. Thomas looked at the dead and dying, and then, moving quickly, he finished off the injured guards.

"We got them all," Jack said.

The cost had been high, but there had been no choice. Adela was weeping over the body of her lover, Oliver. Smiler lay dead in a corner, and Jackson's body had been riddled with bullets. This death, he regretted most of all. There were limits to his magic, and the results lay in front of him. Four mercenaries had also died. In all, there were nine of them left alive.

"We can do nothing for them," Thomas said. "Follow me!" Adela glared at him, and he took her by her arm, forcing her along the passage. "He's dead."

She shook herself free. "What sort of plan was that?"

"A desperate one." He didn't tell her that the losses had been light considering what they were doing. "Are you coming?" He didn't wait for an answer, but led the men along the passages he'd memorized from the machine mind.

A guard came out of a door, and Thomas threw his knife into the man's throat. They didn't meet anyone else on the way to the storage depot. As he'd expected, the doors were locked.

"Can you access the system again?" Micky asked.

Thomas nodded, but when he tried to access the artificial mind again, he found nothing. He tried again, and then stepped back in confusion. "I can't feel anything. It's as if the mind of the computer's disappeared."

"They may have switched it off," Jack said. "Since you keep breaking in."

"So we're trapped," a mercenary said. He kicked the thick metal doors. They didn't move an inch. "This could be a massacre."

"Only if we stay here," Thomas said. He felt the doors and allowed his mind to explore them for weaknesses. He couldn't find any; these doors were as tough as those on warships. Perhaps he could use his magic, but it would take too long.

"When the women escaped from prison, your friend created a strange fungus that ripped everything apart," Adela said. "Do you know how to do that?"

His frustration disappeared at her words. "Thank you,

Adela." He reached in his pocket and took out the midnight blue crystal. *"Break for me."* The crystal split into two pieces, and he placed the one against the metal doors. Sending a spurt of magic into the crystals, he spoke to them. *"Grow!"*

"What are you doing?" Micky asked.

Thomas fed the crystals with his Fire and watched them spread over the surface of the door, working their way into small gaps and holes. Only he could see the dark crystals as they grew.

"You'd better do something," a mercenary said. "They're coming."

"They're not here yet," Thomas said. He'd already felt their vibrations. "Two minutes before they reach us, and by then we'll be gone."

"Are you a seer?" the man asked sarcastically.

Adela watched him as he continued to feed magic through the metal door into the crystals. He sensed them enter the gaps in and between the doors. Then he laid both hands against them and sent a blast of his Fire into the doors. The doors moaned as they twisted, then one snapped and cracked. "Stand back." Thomas kicked a door, sending more magic into the metal. There was a loud snap.

"What's happening?" the mercenary asked nervously.

"Kick the doors!" Thomas said. He stood back, hot and exhausted. Some of the men kicked, and cracks appeared. "Again!" And then part of the door exploded outwards, leaving a hole in the middle.

A shot rang out, and a mercenary collapsed against the door. Guards were moving towards them. Thomas fired at them while the men jumped through the hole, then he followed.

He looked onto a grey concrete and plastic square. It was

the ugliest he'd seen, but it was beautiful at that moment. And it was almost deserted. "That way."

"You promised money," the corporal said as they ran.

"I agreed to help you reach Nassopolis, and here we are. There might be money in the top level of the prison. You can go back if you want." The man looked unhappy but said nothing. "You can do as you wish, but I've seen maps of 27th. There's a market where we can eat and drink."

That changed their minds. "Then we're together a little longer," the corporal said.

They ran behind Thomas, bloody swords and guns in their hands. Without warning, Thomas turned down a narrow path, which was more a gutter running between buildings. He hardly noticed his wet feet and the smell of sewage, but kept moving deeper into the maze of alleys.

Thomas wasn't so concerned about being seen with blood and knives. In the upper levels of Nassopolis, all well-to-do subjects were tagged, but in the lower levels like this, the people were poor and often untagged, meaning less eyes for the Empire. From the Imperial Security computer systems, he'd pieced together a mental map of the city. It helped, also, that he was able to see through rocks, ores, and metals as most people saw through water. Sometimes it was cloudy or dark, but often he could make out patterns and shapes, and then he could often sense the shapes themselves. His world was more than the narrow alley through which they ran; he saw the maze of alleys and was aware of the people watching them from cracks in doors and windows.

Micky, Jack, Adela, and four mercenaries ran with him.

"Do you know where you're going?" the corporal snapped.

"Murine Market." Thomas knew the men were angry,

tired, and hungry, but at the moment, none of that mattered—only living was important.

"What's that?"

"Where rat-catchers sell meat."

The man laughed. "I've been eating rats for years." At the mention of food, the mood of the men improved. None of them were fussy eaters.

When they began walking through piles of rotten mushrooms and other decaying food, Thomas knew they were getting closer. He found some dirty rags and wrapped it around the gun he'd taken. "Hide your weapons." The men did the same, then they walked out of the pathway into the market.

"We have no money," Micky said.

"I think I can influence the vendor."

The men grinned, misunderstanding his meaning. But if his method of mentally influencing the seller didn't work, then he'd have to resort to the more basic method. The market had dozens of small eating places. Thomas picked one with a picture of a rat eating a chilli. The menu was clear, and Thomas doubted any of these stalls were different. They sat, and a stone-faced vendor looked at them.

"What do you want?"

There were only two vats of food: a spicy one, and a bland, watery one. Thomas pointed at the spicy one. "And ale."

The vendor hesitated, and Thomas attempted to influence the man's mind, suggesting good business. The man frowned but served them. The dirty cup of mild smelt and tasted sour, but it was better than what they had been drinking. And rat or not, the spicy meat tasted good. Food had been scarce in the climb up to the prison.

"More," Thomas said.

"Money."

Thomas suggested mental satisfaction to the man, but only received an angry glare. "What's this? Pay or I'll call the market police!"

Micky grabbed the man, but the vendor started shouting. Other vendors approached. Some of them held sticks and knives.

"Let's leave and find more food somewhere else," Thomas said. He was sure they could fight their way out, even without magic, but he didn't want the vendors' blood on his hands. He didn't blame them; he just had no choice. They stood.

"You're not going anywhere," the rat vendor said.

"We've got no money," Thomas said. It was the simple truth.

"Then the market police will deal with you."

"We've not eaten for days," Adela said.

"Not my problem."

Thomas wasn't sure what market police were, but although they sounded better than imperial police, he wasn't going to wait for them. He considered offering to pay in the future, but he knew it was a lie. He'd never return to this city.

"It's too late," Adela said.

Several men dressed in dark green moved towards them, holding truncheons in their hands. Thomas pushed past the vendor and walked in the opposite direction, followed by Adela and the men. Shouts came from behind. "Time to run," Thomas said. They ran down the street. The market police and several vendors gave chase, slowing down when five imperial police officers turned the corner. One of them wore the cloak of a junior member of the Imperial Order.

"Lord Ford," the vendor called out. "They've refused to pay."

"Who are you?" the lord asked Thomas. For a second, the lord's eyes were unfocussed. A sign of a mental download in process. Then he looked at Thomas anew. "You can't escape—"

Thomas punched the first man, stopping him midstream, and he shot the second. His men pulled the rags from their guns and fired. The lord and another man lay unconscious, and the other three were dead. A shot from behind killed a mercenary. The market police charged towards them, but his men fired, sending the police and vendors diving for cover. Thomas quickly led the men back into the maze of alleys.

Despite possessing a mental map of the alleys and a rock sense that helped Thomas sense the vibrations of their pursuers, it still took more than twenty minutes to lose the market police. They now walked through a quiet neighbourhood consisting mostly of warehouses. He felt the doors as they passed.

"What?" Jack asked.

"We need a place to rest while they search." He also hoped that there would at least be fresh water inside.

"Your plans killed most of my men," the corporal said.

"I took you from a difficult situation in Tartaros and led you into Nassopolis. You knew the risks," Thomas said. Stopping by a pair of large metal doors, he laid his hands on them. The room wasn't empty like most of the others. "Let's see what's inside." A short shock of magic unlocked the door, and they slipped inside. Once inside, he locked it again.

They found the light switches. The warehouse had a large pile of crates in the centre, and then smaller piles of boxes around the edges. Nobody was there, but he saw an office and walked towards it. There was a washroom with running water. They drank in silence.

"A fridge," Micky said. He held up a lump of some sort of cheese.

It took less than ten minutes to empty the fridge. It was enough to remove their immediate hunger, but they needed more food. He divided them into groups and had them start searching the crates and boxes for anything useful.

A shout came from Jack. Thomas drew both his knives and ran across the warehouse, stopping when he saw Jack grinning with a pair of opened ale bottles in his hands. "Cheers!"

He put away his knives and caught a bottle Jack tossed to him. It was better than what they'd drank in the market. He had mixed feelings about them drinking, but for now, they deserved the chance to relax.

Thomas sat apart from the others, thinking about the lives he'd changed and ended, many of whom he'd loved. The Fire possessed great power, but not the power to save the lives of those around him. He thought about Jackson, and about Oliver, and his eyes drifted to Adela, who was sitting alone clutching her unopened bottle.

8

Thomas could hear the drinkers from the far side of the warehouse, which meant someone outside might, too. It was time they left. He moved from the dirty window and walked slowly back across the warehouse floor to rejoin the men, pleased to have discovered that they were close to a horizontal line train station.

Adela's scream roused him from his thoughts. A man lay dead on the floor, and Jack of Clubs stood over him with a bloody dagger. Micky stood by him, and the one-eyed corporal and another mercenary faced them. Adela was behind Jack with a dagger in her hand.

"What happened?" Thomas asked.

"He touched me!" Adela pointed at the dead man.

"Jack?" Thomas asked.

"He said the girl was his now that Oliver was dead. I stopped him." Jack's stare was fixed on the dead man.

"He was just playing," the corporal said, glaring at Jack.

"He touched you?" Thomas asked. He liked the Fighters, but they were a rough lot and were quick to take offence.

"He touched me where he shouldn't." She briefly touched her breasts.

"So you killed him?" he asked Jack.

"I didn't mean to," Jack said. "I told him to stop first, but he got mouthy, so I poked him with my blade."

Thomas got the picture. But there was nothing he could do.

"What are you going to do?" the corporal asked.

Thomas sighed. "What can I do?"

"What you did in the mines when one of ours killed a prisoner."

"It was different." The man scowled. "He did a small wrong and paid a high price; the man in the mines murdered an unarmed man and threatened our escape."

"The difference is that he's your friend." The corporal pointed at Jack.

That was part of the truth, but not the whole truth. One look at the two men told him that no explanation would be adequate. Instead, he just shook his head. "We're leaving. I've found a way."

One of the mercenaries rushed at him with a knife in his hand, but he knocked it to the floor with a short burst of magic. Stepping in closer, Thomas pushed the man away, leaving the smell of burning flesh.

The man stepped away and touched his face. "What did you do?"

"A touch of magic." The man's chin was burnt.

"Let's go!" he said to Adela and his remaining Fighters.

The corporal and burnt man shouted threats as they left the warehouse through the door nearest the station. Thomas locked the door behind him. If anybody thought it unusual that three men and a woman walked out of a warehouse, they didn't show it.

"We need tags and blockers," Thomas said.

"Then we must find a place where thieves hang out," Micky said.

Thomas nodded. "How can we pay them?"

Micky grinned. "We don't."

"We'd be making enemies."

Micky shrugged. "We have lots, what's a few more?"

"Any ideas where to find them?"

"On the edges of society," Jack said.

Thomas remembered Chloris's stories about the passages around, under, and over each of the New Cities. They'd been used when the cities had originally been cut from the rock, and they consisted of both natural spaces and manmade passages. He had no idea whether criminals had found these spaces on the edges of the city, but if they had, then he was sure they'd use them. Chloris had also told him that it was possible, with patience, to use them to climb to the Inner Cities of Nassopolis, which lay within the mountain but above the surface.

"Then let's find these edges." Thomas stopped in front of the artistically designed map decorating the outer wall of the tram station. "We're here, and we need to go there." He pointed to where the city ended.

"But we don't have any credits," Adela said.

If the picture map was to scale, then it wasn't far to the end of the city. "We can walk." He laughed at Adela's face, but Jack nodded, and Micky seemed indifferent. He led them back past the warehouse and continued on along a road of commercial properties. Few people walked on 27th, so they had the road to themselves.

A tram passed them. "Can't we just jump on?" Adela asked.

Thomas shook his head. "We don't want to draw attention to ourselves. Nobody will notice poor people walking along a road."

Two hours later, they reached the edge of the city. It was darker than the central parts—perhaps no one here could afford the electricity used to light the streets—and people paid more attention as they passed. The air was stale, too. Several men were drinking spirits on a broken sofa; they laughed as the four walked past.

"It's very local," Micky commented.

The street had become a passage—or more like a hallway in someone's house, just a little wider. Some of the doorways had doors, but through the ones that didn't, Thomas caught glimpses of life at the bottom in Nassopolis: a family sitting on a broken bed, and an old man sleeping on a dirty floor. Further along the passage were businesses, of a sort. The doors had names painted on, and there was a bar with smoked glass windows. The Uranium was written on the window.

He'd drunk in every kind of bar, and he had a good idea what type this was just from its look. "A beer?" Neither Jack nor Micky took much persuading.

The barman looked them up and down. "What?"

None of them had changed their clothes in weeks, and they smelt, but this wasn't a high-class establishment. "Four ales." Thomas pushed between the two men leaning against the bar. They looked like brawlers.

"You stink!" the nearest one said.

Thomas gave a cold grin and repeated his request.

"We don't serve your sort here," the barman said. "Do you even have money?"

"No."

"Then get out!"

Thomas leant into the man next to him, picked up his

beer, and drank it. The man reached for a weapon, but Thomas gripped his wrist. "We need tags and blockers." He pushed the man away.

"They cost money," a man said as he walked into the bar from the back room. Thomas guessed he was the landlord.

"But you have them?"

"That's not your business."

Thomas listened to the man's feelings and felt a slight emotional rush. He was sure the man had them; now he had to find where they were. "Where are they?"

"You're incredible," the landlord said. "You know you're going to pay for that beer and more." Thomas finished the bottle and dropped it to the floor.

"Show me the tags!" He asked in the True Language, too, and the man unconsciously responded by thinking of their location. Thomas saw an image; he glanced at the rusty wall.

"Get out!" The landlord called for help from a back room.

"We can leave now," Thomas said. They left the bar, and Thomas gestured to the rusty outer wall of the city. "Somewhere behind there."

The landlord rushed out of the bar, followed by the bartender and the two men from the bar. "You're going to hurt, and then you're going to pay."

Ignoring them, Thomas began rubbing his hands along the rusty wall. It was more like tissue, and even without magic, he could punch a hole through it. On the other side was a passage, and from the passage, he felt the footsteps of men moving past.

"Thomas?" Micky said.

Three men were walking towards them. "Show them your weapons."

Micky drew a pistol, Adela a knife, and Jack took out his club. The men reached for guns, and Micky shot one.

Thomas punched a hole through the rusty wall and pulled out a man from the other side, thrusting him into the bartender, followed by a second. Thomas climbed through the wall.

"Follow me."

They squashed inside a stifling metal passage, and Thomas moved quickly towards the hollow area he'd sensed. A single electric bulb lit the small room, bare but for boxes piled against the walls. There were two doors.

"They're coming," Jack said.

Thomas slammed the door to the room shut, slamming back a bolt.

"That won't help much." Micky said.

The other door opened, and Thomas threw his dagger into the throat of a man.

"How did you know?" Jack asked.

"I told you," Adela hissed.

"The magic stuff?"

Thomas held out his hand, and the knife flew back into his palm. He moved back to the first door, which was already buckling from kicks on the other side. "Open them," he said, pointing at the boxes. He placed his hands on the edges of the door. A man screamed on the other side.

"What was that?" Jack said.

Thomas just grinned. He continued to generate rock magic, and soon his hands were glowing orange. He welded the door to the doorframe.

"I never really believed you," Jack said as he watched.

"Find the tags and blockers," Thomas said. "They're here somewhere."

He heard them throwing boxes to the floor as he

crouched lower to finish sealing the door. Then he touched the metal wall, creating a series of shocks that resulted in several loud bangs. The men on the other side shouted and struggled to get away from the door.

"That's given us a few minutes," Thomas said.

He pulled more of the boxes to the ground and opened them, kicking away the ones with junk. Then, one of the boxes broke open. Inside were packets of disposable tags and a tag meter. He tossed two packs to each of them.

"Check them." Then he found a small box of blockers and passed a handful to each of his companions.

Micky whistled. "We're rich." He glanced at the dead man lying in the second doorway. "If we get out of here alive." Men were moving cautiously along the passageway to the second doorway.

Thomas called more Fire; it was a warmth suffusing his body, relieving the pain of the magical hangover. As it flowed, so did his vision, and the metal around him became part of his body. He tapped a wall. "The bar's through this wall. Do you want a drink?" Thomas asked. "They can't accuse us of having no money."

"There's only two problems with that," Micky said. "The wall and the landlord."

"The first is easy. Let's worry about the second later." Thomas took Adela's hand. "Come closer."

"What are you going to do?" she asked, frowning.

"Whatever happens, don't let go. Do you understand?" She nodded. Pulling her closer, he stepped through the wall. It was the first time he'd done this in months, and it felt strange, but there was none of the pain that sometimes came with rock walking. It helped that the metal wall was less than an inch thick.

Adela stared at him with eyes wide open, as did a solitary drinker in the corner. Before she could speak, he let go of her and stepped back through to take hold of Jack. "Relax." They walked through together. Seconds later, he returned for Micky.

Listening through the wall, Thomas heard the men enter the storeroom.

"We have another problem," Jack said.

"What?"

"The imperial police are outside."

"Then I really need a drink," Thomas said. He walked to the door to the taproom and helped himself to a jug of mild. Micky took the glasses.

Thomas rejoined his friends at the table by another frosted window. He leant back against the wall and let his senses extend into the metal. It was thinner than the wall they'd just passed through. His magic was humming.

"We can't sit here drinking ale," Adela said.

"We can't go back through there," Thomas said, glancing at the wall, "and leaving is unadvisable at the moment." Voices came from the taproom.

"What's the plan?" Jack asked.

"Hope the imperial police go away and then deal with the criminals."

"What if they don't go away?" Micky asked.

"Sit closer," Thomas said.

Imperial police walked into the room. "There they are," the landlord said.

Lord Ford ordered his men to approach. Five imperial police officers stood around them with weapons drawn. "You're under arrest."

"Stay close to me," Thomas whispered, "and when I say now, hold me tightly and get ready to fall through the wall." He looked up at the lord. "We're just finishing our drinks."

"I don't think so," Lord Ford said. "Take them!" he ordered his men.

Thomas's magic swelled, and Lord Ford laughed. "That won't help you." The lord's magic expanded, too, but Thomas had a few seconds head start, and his bubble of magic pulsed through the room, knocking the men to their feet.

"Now!"

Together, the four drinkers fell back through the wall, rolling onto the metal street. Thomas stood and sent a smaller shockwave of magic into the pair of police standing by the entrance. Some of the criminals watched them from the side of the street, but none approached.

"Run!" Thomas said as the door of The Uranium opened and Lord Ford staggered out, gasping for air.

"That wasn't too bad," Micky said as they ran down the street. He laughed, then there was silence. Thomas turned to see Micky's confused expression. His mouth opened, and he tried to speak, but he was silenced when a second bullet passed through his head. Thomas knelt next to him, but he was dead before he reached the ground. He rested his hand on Micky's arm.

"I've been with him half my life," Jack of Clubs said, wiping away a tear.

Thomas literally felt the heaviness in Jack's heart. His ability to listen to the feelings of others was now almost overpowering.

"Take the sword and gun," Jack said. "He'd want you to have them."

Thomas took them in silence.

"The death mark of the Uranium Union is on you!" the landlord shouted.

Thomas felt cold rage. "I'm going back."

"But not now." Jack gripped his shoulder.

Another shot fired as they turned a corner. They ran for twenty minutes through the alleys, eventually stopping to catch their breath.

Adela was shaking. "They'll kill us. They'll never give up."

She seemed more disturbed by the criminal gang than she was by the imperial police. Thomas didn't know what this gang had done to her inside the prison, but he knew they were one of the most violent gangs in Min Flo. It couldn't have been anything good.

Jack held Adela's hand and looked to Thomas. "We can't stay with you any longer. I'm sorry. After losing Micky..."

Thomas nodded. He didn't blame them. "Go to Silva. Life's freer there."

Adela gripped Thomas's wrist. "I dreamt the same dream last night. She's waiting for you."

And then Jack of Clubs and Adela were gone.

9

Thomas put the short sword and black knife in his belt, and his second knife in his boot; all three were infused with magic. The pistol had a single bullet.

He was calmer now, but determined to kill the landlord and his thugs. The death mark, which at one time would have frightened him, only angered him more. He'd kill them for Micky's death, but he had practical reasons, too. In the tight passage behind the outer wall of the city, he'd noticed shafts leading up to the next level. Now he was alone, he'd climb the dark passages on the edges of Nassopolis.

He walked quickly, keeping to the shadows. This, and the invisibility spell, meant that he walked unnoticed through the streets. When a police patrol approached, he sat on a pile of rubbish, sending the suggestion he was a tramp. They laughed when they passed but didn't stop.

Soon, he reached the line of shops. He passed the same four beggars, sitting in a row, but this time they didn't notice him. In front of him was the line of decrepit businesses. Next to The Uranium was a hardware shop. He walked inside, and an old man looked up. It was the back room that Thomas wanted.

"You can't go in there," the man said, following Thomas into a cluttered back room.

Thomas drew the short sword and as the old man backed off, Thomas walked through the wall into the kitchen behind the bar. A man sat at a table sorting out packets of drugs. As he looked up, Thomas stabbed him in his neck. He slumped onto the table.

Hearing voices in the taproom, Thomas followed the wall away from the door to the bar. He wanted to deal with any gangsters in the public lounge first. When he was a few feet from the corner, he sensed the bigger space of the lounge on the other side, and felt the vibrations of five people sitting at a table on the other side of the wall. Someone moved on the far side of the room; possibly the same solitary drinker he'd seen earlier.

Thomas listened to the conversations while trying to ignore the pain his use of magic had set off. He was still uncertain why he'd been able to rock walk without pain before. His best guess was that the spirit keys had helped control the energy. Now his body absorbed the magic directly. He'd drifted away from the conversation. They were discussing a brutal punishment for a boy who'd not paid them.

Thomas studied the men's energy. He'd learnt how to distinguish emotions through their vibrations. These men vibrated at a low level; one in particular was toxic. He'd heard enough. He pushed his hands through the metal wall, almost as if it wasn't there, and around the necks of the nearest two men. Then he stepped back, pulling the surprised men's heads through the wall. They stared at him with wide eyes. Then he let go, and their heads fell to the kitchen floor. He placed them on the table.

The screams in the lounge had sent the landlord, barkeeper, and two others running into the room. And again Thomas watched with his rock sense. They were examining the headless bodies. A man claimed he'd seen hands come through the wall. The landlord dismissed his claims as nonsense with a slap.

The man with toxic energy touched the metal wall, only inches from Thomas. Thomas touched the same place, and his Fire burnt the man, then he pulled with magic, and the man screamed as his hand stuck to the wall. Thomas pulled harder, but his companions pulled from the other side. He wasn't inside far enough for Thomas to drag him through.

The landlord took out a pistol and shot at the wall, and Thomas leapt to the side to avoid the bullet that passed through. The man with bad energy fell back with a scream. Thomas tossed his finger onto the table with the heads.

Next, he walked to the doorway to the bar—it was empty. There were four taps for beer—he flipped each one on. Returning to the kitchen, he slammed the door shut and bolted it. Hearing the noise, the landlord and most of the men rushed back through the bar and began banging on the door to the kitchen.

Thomas stepped through the wall into the lounge. Three men were in the room, but only the solitary drinker by the window had noticed him. The man with toxic energy had changed seats, where he was tending his wound. Another man talked to him. Thomas threw his black knife into the second man's neck, and as he collapsed onto a chair, Thomas projected his magical reach, directing the knife to cut the toxic man's throat. The dagger flew back into his hand. The solitary drinker sat silently at his table.

"Who're you?" Thomas asked.

"Bobby," the man said. "I just drink here."

"You might want to leave," Thomas said.

The man looked at his half-full glass of ale reluctantly, and Thomas touched the table, causing it to vibrate. The man grabbed his glass, but Thomas pointed at the glass, imagining heat, and the ale steamed. The man dropped the glass and rushed from the room.

When he was gone, Thomas walked into the empty taproom and locked the front door. An argument was taking place inside the kitchen. Leaning over the bar, he poured himself a glass of ale and looked back into the lounge with his rock sense. He saw where the energy condensed and where it left hollow spaces in the rocks. A narrow vertical shaft was located behind the wall at the far end of the lounge. He'd begin his long climb from there.

The discussion abruptly stopped, and Thomas moved to the corner of the taproom. He imagined invisibility, and as the first man walked into the room, he threw the short sword, stabbing him through his chest.

A second man rushed forward, then stopped, confused. He couldn't see anyone. The landlord, barkeeper, and another man joined him. They looked around the room, not seeing the motionless man in the corner. The barkeeper pulled the short sword from the dead man, and Thomas mentally pulled. The sword swung round and cut the second man's throat. Now there was only the landlord, barkeeper, and one more.

Eyes wide, the barkeeper looked at the dead man at his feet. "I didn't do anything, really." The barkeeper was scared.

"What have you been doing, Joe?" the landlord asked, glaring at the man.

"Nothing!" The man looked down at the sword in his hand.

Thomas caused the sword to point towards the landlord. The barkeeper dropped the blade in shock. "Something's wrong with it."

"Something's wrong with you," the landlord said. He shot the man dead. Now there were two men left. Thomas waited patiently.

"Did he kill everyone?" the man asked.

"Who else?" the landlord asked.

The landlord noticed the half-empty glass at the table, and then his eyes widened. "You!"

Thomas put the empty pistol on the table.

"Who are you?" the landlord asked. The other man stood beside him.

"Thomas Brand."

The landlord wiped sweat from his forehead, and slowly his hand moved for his pistol.

"It's time to pay." Thomas held both knives in his hands. When the landlord and his companion drew their pistols, he threw them. The first penetrated the landlord's skull, and the second the other man's heart. Thomas called both knives back. He then found a suitable pistol and put it in his pocket.

The bar was quiet, and he needed somewhere to rest, but the bodies were bleeding and unappealing to see. His anger had subsided, and he felt slightly sick. He dragged the corpses into the kitchen.

Opening the fridge, he found some cooked meat. Then he took a bottle of spiced rum into the lounge and poured a glass. On the other side of the wall was the passage he intended taking. He listened in the True Language. It was empty.

He'd already tried to contact Lucy but failed. He tried again, but again there was no answer. Distance shouldn't really matter, but there were several reasons why it didn't always work. Her mind might be elsewhere, or perhaps he was blocking himself in some way. The death around him didn't exactly lift his spirits. He poured a second glass.

His thoughts returned to Aina. And to what Lucy had said. If that were true, then Aina would be a baby. Surely that was not what she'd meant when she'd told him she was returning to this world. How could she have meant that? What use would it be to be born a baby again? It must be wrong—it just didn't make any sense.

But he couldn't get Lucy's words out of his mind—she was so perceptive in some ways. And he was very aware that he didn't want to believe her. He wanted a lover, not a daughter, or worse, a stranger he'd never meet.

He sipped the spiced rum.

The thought of Aina being reborn on this world worried him, too. She'd be completely defenceless.

He'd lost his hunger, but his mouth was dry.

He poured another glass of rum.

10

The golden dragon noticed the light in the sky as she slowly rose to the surface of the lake. She adjusted her inner fire to remain warm. The pale blue shape of her sister swam closer. Na enjoyed feeling Kaylie's warmth next to her. She was bigger than Na, but was timid and frequently followed her. Yet, her blue sister was lovely in many ways, and Na knew that all dragons changed when they grew their wings. Few other species saw them at such an early stage.

"It's flying towards us," Kaylie said.

"It's not," Na said. *"It's going to land in the second lake."*

Her brothers joined them.

"We should see what it is," Seth said. She silently agreed with her silver brother.

"Seth's right," Warth said. *"We should see it."*

Her maroon brother swam close to her; she felt protected by his presence, and by the fact that he was already several times her size. Only Kaylie protested. The second lake was closed to the Tangle. Then Na saw the sleek black shape of her other sister swimming towards her. Allie pressed against her, trying to get a better view of the object as it disappeared from sight.

"I want to get closer," Na said.

"We'd be exposed if we crossed the rocks," Kaylie said.

No young dragon liked being vulnerable, but Na was curious. She wished she could fly—it was every immature dragon's dream. But she had to wait. Her wings were still growing, and for the moment, she had no choice but to swim with the Tangle.

"It's a short distance," Warth said. *"We can follow a gully."* Na swam to the best place for crossing. *"How did you know we'd cross here?"*

"I followed you the night you crawled to the second lake." She felt his amusement.

Warth climbed over the boulders and crawled through a shallow stream. Perhaps it was because he was growing so fast, but he wasn't yet able to walk on two legs as she could. She followed her brother, carefully avoiding his tail, which was longer than she was. Allie was right behind her; Seth came last. Her pale blue sister waited in the water.

Warth stopped behind a large boulder.

She pushed close up to him. *"What?"*

"Wait while I look."

She didn't want to wait and ran through the boulders and splashed into the second lake. The others followed her. Her irritated big brother came last.

"I said look first," he said.

"Look now," Na said.

A spherical object flew over the surface of the lake. It seemed familiar, and it stirred a memory that she couldn't recall. She sensed danger.

Allie splashed her tail in the water. Seth turned his long head towards her and hissed. *"Quiet!"* Allie was embarrassed; Na felt her emotion as heat. None of the others seemed to notice.

"What is it? It's giving me a bad feeling," Na said.

"A human machine," Seth said. Warth rumbled his hostility.

"Don't you remember the first war?" Allie asked.

Na was embarrassed that her memories hadn't appeared. She remembered nothing of her previous lives—this was almost shameful for a dragon.

"You really have a bad memory." Allie looked back to the flying black machine. *"This is one of their war machines."*

"She may not have lived during the first war," Seth said. *"She may have lived much longer ago."*

"True," Allie said.

Na wondered if that were true. Perhaps that was why she couldn't remember the object, but it did seem familiar. *"Can they speak?"* Na asked.

"They use sounds to speak to humans," Warth said.

"Why?" Na asked, confused. *"Why would they do that?"*

"Humans can't speak the True Language," Warth said.

She heard his contempt when he said humans, but she hooted anyway, assuming it was a joke. *"How do they speak?"*

"Through sounds."

Na could hardly believe it. All life spoke the True Language. At least, she'd assumed it did.

"Let's burn it," Allie said. Warth agreed.

"I sense danger," Na said.

"You sound like Kaylie," Warth said.

"Something's wrong."

But they were too excited, and she followed her siblings as they swam under the water and then circled up towards the surface. Pushing her head out of the water, she watched the machine. Overwhelmed again by ominous sensations,

Na sank inches beneath the surface and continued to watch. She didn't understand where her feelings were coming from. Normally, she'd be excited to attack, but not today. *"We should tell the Thunder,"* Na said. The others looked at her. *"What?"*

"How?" Warth asked.

Surprised by the question, Na paused. She wasn't sure why she'd said it; it just seemed obvious. Eventually, feeling a little confused, she spoke. *"In the True Language."*

"None of the Tangle can speak at that distance," Seth said.

She was surprised. She'd never considered this before. As her siblings argued about the best way to attack, she thought of the older dragons. The ones in the Flight still seemed immature to her; they just seemed like a flying Tangle. She was sure they'd be flapping into the air to attack the machine. She wanted to speak to a more mature dragon. She thought of the Thunder, but realized that the great dragons intimidated her.

But pushing aside her fears, she visualized one of them. *"Help us!"* There was silence, and Na wondered whether her siblings had been right. Perhaps there was a physical distance beyond which young dragons of the Tangle could not use the True Language. Or perhaps she needed to focus on a particular dragon. She called again, and instantly the head of a black dragon appeared in her mind. She swallowed water in shock.

"What is it, Na?"

She was taken aback. The First of the Wisdom spoke directly to her, and she almost lost her voice. *"We've seen a human machine flying over the second lake."* She felt the burning intensity of the black dragon's mind as she shared her vision with him.

"Is it aware of you?"

"Not yet, we've remained hidden. But the others are planning to attack."

"Do not attack!" His voice vibrated through her body. *"Stay submerged and wait for me."*

She opened her eyes and saw her siblings rising to the surface. She swam into them, trying to push them back. But all her siblings were far bigger than her.

"What are you doing, sister?" Warth said.

"I've spoken to Night Sun. He told us not to attack. He's coming."

"Your imagination is too active," Seth said.

"If you spoke to him, why couldn't we hear?" Allie asked.

"I don't know." Na really had no idea. *"I just thought of him, and he came to me."* She was still learning about the True Language. *"Perhaps there are hidden levels of True Language."*

Her brothers laughed, but she knew that she'd annoyed them. She knew that Warth was still going to attack the machine, and she swam hard into his belly. He turned to bite her, but she was faster, sensing his movements before he made them. Seth stopped her maroon brother, and she was grateful. A single bite could cripple her.

"What's wrong?" Warth asked her. *"The humans are invading our world. We must fight."*

"We mustn't attack."

Warth tried to nip her again.

Night Sun's voice rocked the Tangle. *"Retreat to the shores of the lake."* Two dragons of the Thunder flew with him.

There was no option. The First of the Wisdom had spoken. They swam towards the shore, and as they swam, Na noticed her siblings looking at her in surprise. She felt the distant vibrations as the large dragons dived into the lake. Seth's eyes widened. She knew he'd felt it, too. But not the others. She realized that not all dragons experienced the world in the same way.

The three great dragons swam silently through the lake: Night Sun, Spere, and Willa. They watched the robot with their inner eye, and she joined them, watching quietly.

Spere turned his head to Night Sun. *"I'll call from the falls."*

"I want to know what it knows," Night Sun said, swimming with the other two.

Na listened, and she was sure she'd missed some parts of the conversation. Adults were good at hiding their words from the Tangle.

"Dangerous," Willa said.

"Can we read its mind from here?" Na asked.

There was silence, then Willa spoke. *"Are you eavesdropping?"*

"No." She'd not considered it eavesdropping. *"You didn't conceal your thoughts."*

Fire belched from Night Sun's mouth into the cold water, but a slight widening of his mouth showed approval. She wasn't sure if it was because of her idea, or that it was her right to listen if she could. He watched the machine, and she felt his mind enter. It rocked slightly in the air before continuing its flight. The black dragon's eyes glazed over slightly, then came back into focus. *"It's ignorant. Collecting information for the human invasion."*

Spere flew into the waterfall. Na imagined him clinging to the rocks beneath the sheets of water pouring into the lake. He whistled. The machine stopped in midair over the lake. Na waited near the shore, but she projected her mind freely and could sense movement near the falls. Willa had joined them, and had made her siblings swim deeper, but had not objected when Na had floated closer to the surface.

She watched the machine with her physical eyes, and it seemed to stir a memory. With relief, she realized that she was beginning to remember her dragon past. She recognized what Night Sun had just done—she knew that she could also enter machine minds. It flew low over the lake, stopping in front of the waterfall.

Its eyes were pointed at the falling water, and it never noticed the vast dragon rising from the lake, nor the jaws that crushed and then spat out its broken body. Night Sun washed his mouth out, then breathed fire to remove the bad taste. Na learnt more about her telepathic ability—she actually tasted the unpleasant metallic taste of the machine in her mouth, too, and sent out her own short blast of fire.

Misunderstanding, and thinking she was mimicking the First of the Wisdom, her siblings laughed at her.

"Go back to the first lake. I'll speak to you later," Night Sun said. Na turned to go. *"Not you."* Her brothers and sister swam back to the gully linking the two lakes, leaving her alone with Night Sun. The other adult dragons had gone. Na was nervous, unsure what the great dragon was going to say or do.

"None of the Tangle, nor many of the Flight, could call me from such a distance. How long have you been able to do this?"

This was not the question she'd expected. *"This was the first time. I just tried."*

"Do you sometimes know things?"

She laughed, for a moment forgetting who she was speaking to. *"I know many things."*

"I mean things that you shouldn't be able to know."

"I'm not sure what I shouldn't be able to know."

"Do you know that things are about to happen and then they do?"

"Sometimes."

"Can you feel the emotions of others?"

"Of course, all dragons can."

"All of the Wisdom can, but not all dragons."

"I didn't know." She felt the great black dragon studying her, and she wondered how much he could see.

"Psychism grows slowly in dragons, and magic even more slowly. Few outsiders meet our species until we're developed, and it was good you stopped the machine from doing so."

"I know," she said. Actually, she realized she knew little.

"I plan to punish your siblings, but you acted well, and your actions have protected dragons. Swim back to our lake. Someone is waiting for you by the shore. The second lake is closed to the Tangle." Night Sun spread his wings, and he silently rose into the sky.

Na swam back to the gully, wondering who was waiting for her. She hoped it wasn't Warth, not after he'd tried to bite her so many times.

"Na."

She was startled. *"Kaylie?"* Her pale blue sister swam to her. *"You came."*

"I waited for you. The others didn't see me."

Na felt sudden affection for her sister. Perhaps she wasn't as timid as she'd thought.

11

Na walked through the shallow water by the shore. Several months had passed since the incident in the second lake, and as all dragons did, she'd matured over those months. Night Sun had insisted she be tested for psychic abilities. The First of the Thunder was also interested in her abilities, but her only concern was to leave the Tangle. Night Sun had named her Daughter of Fire, an honorific she felt she didn't deserve, but he believed it would make it easier for her to deal with older dragons later. She wasn't sure of his meaning. She felt the vibrations of a dragon walking towards her.

"You're not a real dragon," Geris said.

Na was infuriated by his infantile behaviour, but she knew that some of the Thunder watched. Anyway, the grey was too big for her to fight.

Warth, Seth, and Allie were the first of the Tangle to fly, and she was proud of them. They were now members of the Flight, and they encouraged her. She flapped her wings. They were growing stronger, but she'd not yet managed to lift more than a few inches off the ground. Geris mocked her again. She chose to keep practicing and not waste energy reminding him that he couldn't fly either.

She flapped her wings harder, sending a spray of water in his face. Feeling his emotions change, she continued to beat her wings. She sensed that he was going to do something stupid and that he didn't yet know it. Feeling the weight taken from her feet, she continued to beat her wings.

He rushed at her, but instead of swimming away, she beat her wings harder. Hearing encouragement from her sister in the sky, she lifted into the air as a jet of fire hit the water, sending steam into the air.

"Grow your wings!" Na hovered twenty feet in the air, and she breathed fire down, singeing his head.

Geris leapt in the air in an attempt to bite her tail that was hanging low but was knocked into the lake. He turned angrily, stopping when he saw the great red.

"Apologies, First of the Thunder."

Even a fool like Geris wouldn't argue with the great red.

"Respect your seniors!"

Na felt her golden skin flushing at the reprimand, until she realized that it was for the dragon splashing in the water. *"She's a member of the Flight."* Turning to her, Spere spoke. *"Why do you play with the Tangle? Take to the skies. Your first task as a member of the Flight is to survey the forests around our mountain."*

She needed no further prompting. She rose higher into the air, too scared to stop beating her wings. Hearing Allie's laughter, she turned but continued to rise. Her sister whispered words of advice. Then, relaxing, she soared through the sky with her black sister.

"We can fly to the forests together," Allie said.

Laughing in delight, Na flew fast, enjoying the feeling of cold air rushing around her body. She didn't care if the task set by Spere was only for her to test her wings. Excitedly, she flew low over the misty forest, projecting her psychic sense of seeing before her like a beam of sunlight, listening to the life of the forest with the True Language.

Later, she listened to a lecture with her Flight. *"The mountains of Prometheus are our home."* Na knew the words were true, but she sensed a change coming, and she felt they would need to adapt to it. *"The humans will be killed or driven from Prometheus,"* Roth continued.

For most dragons, the anticipated war with humanity was an adventure—one they expected to win within months—but Na thought the dragons too complacent. Bombast excited some, but not her, nor did the hatred of her brother. Warth was now hostile to all mention of humanity.

Some of her Flight trumpeted at the talk. All dragons felt the energy of their bodies change after growing wings. They wished to test themselves. *"The moons of Prometheus must be retaken first."* The moons interested her. She looked up at the three visible moons. Mature dragons could recycle oxygen and maintain enough air to breathe for flights to the moons. She'd heard that dragons in ancient times could even fly between planets, but that had required a magic that was now lost.

Several dragons blew steam at the rocks in anticipation of the morning flights around the mountain ridges and peaks. She hoped to find a basoo, one of the four-legged animals inhabiting the lower parts of the mountains, for breakfast. She drank from the pool, and steamed the nearest boulder, too, as she listened to Roth clarify the returning memories of her kin. She'd kept quiet about her lack of memories, although the closest of her siblings knew. She couldn't understand why this was happening to her. In other ways, and despite her size, she competed well with her peers

—and her psychic abilities were already beyond many of the Thunder, although she kept quiet about that, too.

Roth spoke of the three great races of Prometheus. Na already knew of the division of the world: the dragons ruled the mountains and moons, the rocs ruled the forests, and the leviathans the oceans.

A red flash was followed by the clap of thunder. She looked up to see the great red landing. Many in the Flight were nervous of Spere. None would say, but she could sense it. Roth, despite being a member of the Thunder, was also deferential. Their teacher left them and joined Spere by the river. It was respectful to give senior dragons space, even though their words were hidden from the Flight. However, Na could hear deeper levels of the True Language than most in the Thunder. She didn't attempt to eavesdrop this time, though. Spere was too good at detecting her.

"Something's happening," Allie said.

Na waited, hopeful for a special mission. She was sometimes chosen to scout the more distant mountain peaks, and she'd once seen a bright red and blue roc flying over a distant valley. She'd longed to speak to it, but it had been too far away. She wished to gain skill as a flyer. Despite his great size, Spere flew adeptly. Na still struggled to control her much smaller body and occasionally flew into the branches she was attempting to land on. Her siblings were now too big to even attempt this, except on the biggest branches. The two dragons of the Thunder finished their conversation and approached them.

Her brothers and sisters whispered as Spere's long head moved close to her. She was excited and nervous all at once. *"I have a mission for you."*

Na's senses were heightened. He was speaking to her in the True Language, and nobody else could hear. She knew she was transmitting her excitement and desire without speaking.

But Spere ignored her whirling emotions. *"You'll scout the ancient forest for signs of human incursion."*

After the moons of Prometheus, the ancient forest was where she most wanted to go, but she thought about Roth's recent words. *"Isn't that roc territory?"*

"We have permission."

Her heart jumped again. *"What should I do if I find any humans?"*

"Report what you see directly to me or Night Sun. You have the ability." Her telepathy was good, but she was unsure how good it would be at such a distance. As if guessing her thoughts, he continued. *"For dragons, distance is less important than for many species. It's the connection that's important."*

"What if the humans attack?"

"Kill them!"

She was pleased with the answer. *"Should I communicate with them directly?"* She wondered if speaking to a human was even possible. She'd heard they were dumb, but she could speak with many animals; perhaps they wouldn't be so different. She'd experimented, and she knew she could even bring peace to a basoo before she ate it. But humans were a novelty. Unlike her brothers or sisters, she was curious about these tiny two-footed creatures that ran about on the surface.

"You're a dragon. Decide your own course. But know that humans cannot speak the True Language."

"None?" Although Warth had told her this, she hadn't believed him. She'd assumed it was his hatred of humanity that had coloured his feelings. She waited, half-expecting Spere to say he was joking. Then she realized that the Thunder didn't joke—not as the Tangle did.

"We appreciate humour. But this is serious." She was embarrassed, and a little annoyed, that he'd read her thoughts so clearly. *"Most humans don't believe telepathy is possible, but it's true that a handful do have limited ability."*

"But how do they communicate?" Her eyes widened as she watched the great dragon.

"Through sounds."

She still didn't understand. *"But even animals and plants use the True Language, even if it's in a simpler way than us."*

"True, but humanity has turned its back on much of what is natural. They seek other ways."

The fire in her belly momentarily chilled as her respect for humans diminished.

Spere must have sensed her change of emotion. *"Many animals use sounds and also empathically understand the emotions and intentions of other creatures. The rocs use both; they're skilled in the True Language, but they also use sounds."*

Na had long wished to hear their songlike language, but humanity was annoying her. *"They don't even have an empathic sense?"*

"Some do. But most humans look down on other species because they assume they have no language. But it's the humans who are deaf."

"So that's why they're so removed from nature. They can't hear it speak." She was beginning to understand, but she was still surprised. She thought about the poetry and song of dragonkind. It was hard for her to imagine any species lacking this source of inner beauty. She shook her head to rid herself of such strange ideas.

"They think we're dumb animals because we don't have a language based on sound," Spere said.

"But it's because we don't use sounds that our knowledge of the True Language is the deepest." She knew that even the rocs,

skilled as they were, could not match the richness or subtlety of a dragon using the True Language.

Spere rumbled his amusement.

"*What?*" She tried to see what she'd said that was funny, but couldn't.

"*Dragons are proud, but we also need intelligence and appreciation of truth.*"

"*What truth?*"

"*The rocs are so close to us in their use of the True Language that it makes little difference. The leviathans may surpass us. But for now, focus on humanity. Learn what you can.*" Spere shared a mental map of the part of the ancient forest she was to investigate.

"*Will I fly alone?*"

"*Yes. We lack the human numbers. And they're spreading fast.*" She already knew of the environmental damage they'd caused in other parts of Prometheus. She could hardly believe that any species would act in such a way. "*Their actions are unacceptable. We fear this will be worse than the first war.*"

Na was now very alert. He'd spoken of her fears. "*I feel we face a great danger,*" she said, immediately wishing she'd remained silent. Great dragons didn't always like direct comments, but Spere listened.

"*Night Sun thinks the same. Take care. Hiding is not our nature, but you must conceal yourself. Your size is ideal for this.*" Those words, although not malicious, punctured her pride, and she felt deflated. But at least it meant she would be doing something worthwhile. "*Learn what you can. We must purge our planet of this infestation.*"

∾

NA LIFTED into the air and rose on a current of warmer air, and then she dropped over the mountain edge. It was a clear sunny morning, and she could see the ancient forest far beneath her. As she swooped towards it, she wondered at why so many dragons had awoken after such a long sleep, and why so many young dragons had hatched. There were four hundred and fifty dragons in her family, and up to ten thousand throughout Prometheus. Roth's explanation that they'd awoken because of the danger the dragons faced, although accepted by the Tangle and Flight, didn't feel completely true. Something seemed to be missing. Although she lacked full dragon memories, she did possess some. Usually, the awakening dragons waited decades before hatching a new generation. It only made the encroaching human presence feel more ominous. Night Sun had spoken of the need for dragons to replenish their strength before a new hatching occurred, but the latest Tangle had already been born. Pushing her questions aside, she spread her wings and flew low over the humming forest.

Some vegetable-like animals puffed their bodies up and rose on warm currents of air. They drifted towards her with their mouths wide open—as if a tiny creature like that could eat her. She gulped a few down, but they didn't taste good, even after burning them in her stomach. At least a dragon didn't have to care too much about what it ate; a dragon's fire could purify most food, even if it didn't add much flavour.

Apart from a few more of the vegetable animals, she didn't see much life. She knew from her experiences in the high mountains that most forms of life feared dragons. They were right to, and it gave her a certain pride. She flew with conviction, but she soon realized that she didn't know where she was going or what she should really be doing. Through boredom, she turned her attention on the green canopy below her.

The forest was noisy, and it seemed to have a sound of its own. She wasn't sure what caused it to hum. When she spoke to it, it seemed to answer, but it spoke in a strange language.

Curious, Na spoke again. *"Are you in pain?"* She immediately felt an emptiness. Had the forest spoken to her? *"Show me."* And an image of a distant part of the forest appeared in her mind. It was burning, and she saw the tiny two-legged humans sending fire into the trees. It was far from her mountain home, but she could fly there within a day. She decided to attempt to end the forest's pain.

Na underestimated the distance. It took her almost three days to reach the smoking trees, and she was shocked by what she saw. A huge swathe of the forest had been destroyed, and machines buzzed in the sky. She felt an enormous sense of loss.

Landing in a high tree, she looked down at the destruction and tried to make sense of it. She now understood Spere's words. She'd not really believed that humans could be so dangerous. Dragons killed to eat, and sometimes burnt trees, too, but always for a purpose. She decided to discover what the human purpose was.

A black metallic thing that sounded like a drone bee flew over the tops of the trees towards her, and she crawled down the trunk, deeper into the foliage. It was similar to the one she'd seen in the second lake and was shaped like one of the spherical fruits of the forest when cut in half. Na didn't think it'd seen her, but she wasn't sure of its sensory capabilities. She probed its mind, as Spere had suggested.

She shivered as she entered. This was not the fiery mind of a dragon, but a cold place of mechanical circuits. She learnt it was called an attack bot. She didn't like being there and flicked the switches in its brain. It went out of control and crashed into the tree next to her, falling onto a large branch. Withdrawing her mind, she blew a short jet of fire in front of her to rid herself of the bad taste. She'd been too hasty; the next time she'd have more patience and search for the information she needed.

As the bot had died, Na had heard it send out a short communication. More would come to investigate, but she knew that it'd died without understanding what had attacked it. She didn't have to wait long for two more to arrive. The first flew to the tree where its companion lay; the second circled the area, watching.

As it entered the dead mind of its companion, Na accompanied it, hoping this would disguise her presence. She wasn't even sure that a bot would notice her presence, but dragons would—unless the spy was skilled. But even then, a perceptive dragon would see the intruder in their mind as a moving shadow. When she was sure the dead bot contained no memories of her, she left its mind and concentrated on the circling bot. It was open to her.

Softly she stepped through its thoughts, climbing higher up the tree as she did so. It wasn't wise, but its mind did contain a richness of images of the surrounding area. The humans wanted the resources from Prometheus; they mined for metal. Na continued to probe, meeting a few basic blocks, which she evaded. It was a security model and carried guns, which could kill a dragon if their bullets hit sensitive parts of the body.

Na studied humanity's fears. Their fear first appeared to be other humans. There was no mention of dragons. Despite her previous conversations with Spere, she was shocked to see that this simple machine, and presumably its human masters, considered rocs to be animals. She rescanned its memories twice to check. What sort of species saw rocs as animals?

She pulled out of the machine mind, feeling slightly dirty, but she resisted her impulse to breathe fire. She thought about what she'd seen. It was true that sometimes dragons fought and killed other dragons, but they'd never threaten dragonkind. Her opinion of humans had sunk to a new low. She'd hoped them to be above the primitive races of the forest. The sooner she learnt what she needed, the sooner Prometheus could be purged.

12

Lucy stopped on the banks of a roaring underground river. Without thinking, she knelt and drank deeply. She must have slept for a few moments, for she came quickly awake when the howler monkey slipped back into her pocket. At least the oracle deck was at rest—a sign that she'd lost the Hag. Then she thought about Chloris's death and her part in it. If she'd listened to her intuition, she wouldn't have followed the man, and if she hadn't followed him, Chloris would be alive. It made her feel sick.

Some time later, the oracle deck shifted in her pocket. It wanted to speak to her, but she still felt sorry for herself and wasn't in the mood to read. She realized how alone she was, despite what the shadow wolf had told her. When they twitched again, she spoke aloud. "What?" But she knew they wanted to be read.

Reluctantly, she took them from her pocket, feeling them calm as she gave them her attention. She composed herself for her reading, grounding herself and breathing as calmly as she could. She had no question for the cards; she'd let them speak to her. As usual, they chose themselves.

The first one jumped out as she shuffled, and it landed on her lap. The card glowed in the dark, and she soon became drawn into the scene taking shape.

A lizard looked at her plaintively. "Chloris?" The lizard in the card didn't hear her. "She's alive?" Lucy was scared to hope. Then she noticed the chains attached to the lizard's ankle. Nearby, there was an empty set of chains. The scene disappeared, and there was light filtering through the trees. It was the surface of Prometheus—she saw a roc flying in the distance. Then the card became dark. She put it away and leant back on the wall of the cavern.

She'd been too fast to assume the worst. She had a choice: return and help her friend and risk being captured herself, or continue on her journey to engage the help of the rocs. She already knew her decision, but she wanted more guidance. No card stirred. The right thing was to rescue her friend, but the empty set of shackles in the card was a warning.

Lucy briefly wondered if the rocs would help her rescue Chloris, but the more she thought about it, the more she realized how unlikely that was. Rocs hated ice demons and would most likely try to charm her into following them deeper into the forest. Even if she did convince them, the avian species were so big that they couldn't fit through many of these tunnels. If she was to rescue Chloris, she'd have to do it herself.

But her magic was gone. She crouched on the floor for a long time, thinking of what she could do, but without the magic, all she had was her knife, her oracle, and herself. She wasn't sure it was enough. As she sat there, she studied the rushing river in front of her. It scared her, but Chloris had spoken of following a river. She was avoiding making a decision, but she had more questions. First, she had no idea how to get her magic back. Lucy took out her oracle cards and shuffled in the dark, focussing on a single question: "*How can I regain my magic?*"

She turned over the card and strained to see in the moonlight. Then she saw a giant spider in the middle of a web at the edge of the forest. It was so still that she wondered whether it was alive. "*What are you telling me?*" she asked, secretly hoping it wouldn't step out of the card. Luckily, it didn't move, although its eyes momentarily glowed in the darkness.

The message of the card was hidden from her; she waited and watched. If the message was stillness, then this spider was the perfect messenger. A fly landed on the web, and the spider rushed to it. Then all was still again. "*Does this mean the magic is still inside me, and all I have to do is wait like the spider?*" The light of the card faded.

"I'm not sure that helps," she said to the darkness. Was the lack of magic a temporary situation? Still not wanting to move, she shuffled the cards again. "*Is the river a good way to escape?*" It was a yes, but she couldn't see how this dangerous river could help. "*Who can help me?*" The wolf looked at her quizzically. "*Alright, don't help.*" She shoved him back in the pack. "*What weapons can I use?*" The spider appeared again. "*You're really not helping.*" She kept getting stranger and stranger answers to her questions, and nothing made any sense. She began to doubt herself—whether she was really as psychic as she liked to believe.

Then the giant spider appeared again. Its cobweb was tattered and it looked different. She realized that it was being attacked by a cloud of tiny biting flies. White fluid leaked from the spider, and it started to lose its grip. Shocked, Lucy looked around the cavern. Her heart beat hard, and she was covered in cold sweat. She knew that something was wrong.

Putting the oracle cards back in her pocket, she worked her way quickly back along the tunnel. She'd already spent hours procrastinating in the cave. Too long. They were coming after her. Instead of returning to the alley, she took the steps that Chloris had said led up to the next level. She ran as fast as she could and didn't care about sweat or tiredness. Scrambling through a small round entrance, she found herself in the maintenance section of the city, a place where pipes and electrical equipment ran along tunnels.

Hearing people speaking, she moved towards them. She felt cold as she realized a possible meaning of the tiny biting flies in the oracle—nanobots were hunting her. Scared, she ran faster along the passage.

13

Lucy burst into a dimly lit utility room. Five men sat talking—one of them was the man who'd tried to sell her to the Hag. When they saw she was alone, they relaxed, exchanging grins.

She walked straight up to the one she recognized and put her knife to his throat. One of the men laughed, and thinking they weren't taking her seriously, she pressed the magic infused blade into his neck, making him cry out.

"She's cut me." That made the men laugh more. She guessed their confidence was backed up by hidden weapons.

Lucy removed her blade, but when he reached for her, she poked the point of her knife in his chest.

"What do you want?" he asked.

"Blockers and tags with credits."

"They're expensive," a dark-eyed man said.

He was more sure of himself than the rest. She wondered if he knew that she didn't really want to kill anybody. "How much are your lives worth?" Lucy asked.

"Ask yourself the same question," he said. "There are

five of us, and we have bigger blades than you. You might kill him, but you wouldn't get anyone else."

"I'm being hunted. My life's worth nothing if I don't get what I need."

"That's just made them more expensive."

"Who's after you?" another man asked.

"Nanobots." She looked at them. "They won't stop with me." She had no idea if it were true, but she knew Imperial Intelligence wouldn't care about a criminal gang.

"We don't carry those sorts of things."

"Find them."

They rushed her with knives in their hands, but she sensed their attack before they'd even moved. She cut deeply into the wrist of the nearest man, as Thomas had taught her, and his knife clattered to the floor. Then she stabbed at another man. She didn't know if it was the magic inside the blade or her desperation, but the men were wary about coming too close. "I mean it. I have nothing to lose by dying here."

The men stepped back and spoke to each other, but she couldn't wait. She needed something to make them decide quickly in her favour. Unseen by the men, she took out her oracle deck and drew a card, knowing it would be the one she needed. She didn't even look at the card but held it low in her hand and pointed it at the men. A black cloud left her hand and spiralled around the small room—then it struck them. She wasn't sure whether the black flies really bit them or whether it was a suggestion, but their yells were real.

She raised her hand and the screams stopped. But the men were still covered in black spots. "Give me blockers and tags with credits!" She dropped her hand, and the screams continued. Again she raised her hand. "Now!" A man took something from his jacket and threw it at her. She grabbed the tag, turned it on, and shook her head at the low number of credits.

"It's all I have!"

But she knew it was enough to get her a train out of this place. *"Return."* She held out the empty card, and the flies flew towards her in a spiralling black cloud, seeming to disappear into her palm. No one noticed when she slipped the card back into her pocket.

The leader frowned, looking at the others as if for an answer to what they'd just seen. "She's a witch," one of the men said.

She smiled, watching them glance uncertainly at each other. "I want someone to accompany me to buy tickets, and then accompany me to the upper levels. They're looking for a single woman." She sat on the only chair in the underground space. "I'll let you decide who it will be."

They moved to the far side of the room and whispered. Lucy listened to their conversation—they were completely unaware of her sharp hearing. The leader spoke. "If she's wanted by the Empire, this could be profitable." They nodded. "Take her to the station. I'll call them when she's on the train. They'll pick her up, and we'll collect our fee." They then argued about who would take her.

Lucy listened calmly. As long as they bought her the ticket, she'd find a way around Imperial Intelligence. "Have you decided?"

The man who'd tried to sell her stepped forward. "I'll take you." They left immediately. She followed him along a dirty passage that led to a door into the city. He walked fast, moving ahead without looking back. That was fine; she didn't want to speak to him. They took one of the sleek blue trams to the V-station, with vertical as well as horizontal trains.

On entering the station, they walked towards the giant tubes, the ones enclosing the spherical trains that regularly ran from the lowest to the highest levels of Nassopolis. She bought a snack from a passing robot vendor; its taste was chemical. She was untagged, and therefore unable to download a flavour into her mind. For the tagged, there were thousands of flavours to choose from. Any could be downloaded into the consumer's mind. She just suffered the cardboard texture and chemical taste, knowing that at least it contained the calories she needed. Despite the bad taste in her mouth, she was excited to be moving forward again.

Feeling her cards vibrate, she glanced at her guide and had the gut feeling he was thinking of running. Moving very close to him, she slipped a card into her hand without looking and half-opened her palm. The sounds of the clicks of cicadas were swallowed up in the huge station, but the man heard clearly. He changed his mind.

"Buy a ticket for five levels." The man swiped a tag; the ticket was stored inside. He gave it to her, but she needed to switch tags. It was certain that the tag he'd used would be tracked, and the person with the ticket arrested.

She probed his mind, searching for fears, and was pleased when she found an easy one: he was terrified of spiders. She showed him the black widow of her oracle. His eyes widened, and she took the tag from his pocket, replacing it with hers. He stepped away from her in horror.

He still saw a giant spider. *"I can help you escape it,"* she whispered in the True Language. The man unconsciously heard and allowed her to lead him through the turnstiles to the open doors of the train. All he could see was the scene from the jungle. His tag clicked as he entered, and he sat down—still unaware of his surroundings.

Lucy waited for the train to ascend. Then she moved to

the opposite platform, where she bought a ticket down a level. Hopefully this tag had no name attached to it. It was a guess that Chloris would still be on 27th, and a hope that she was in the jail. It was possible they'd moved her somewhere else—or killed her.

On entering the train, Lucy sat alone. She glanced around her compartment and saw that everyone was absorbed in mental movies, other inner entertainment, or asleep. It was peaceful, but she couldn't relax. Instead, she visualized escaping from the police or criminals who may be waiting for her even now.

14

Lucy walked out into 27th. The smoke from the fires of homeless people cooking scavenged food mixed with the stale air. They lived in the streets behind the station, but their smoke drifted into the areas beyond—the city's air-conditioning units only absorbed so much. Nobody noticed her walking along the street; with her stained clothes, she blended into the neighbourhood.

Touching the tag she'd clipped to her earlobe, she accessed an audio map of the level. More expensive external tags connected to contact lenses that showed images, but the audio guide was enough. She'd asked for eating places near the jail, despite having lost her hunger. She was cautious not to draw attention to herself by searching for the jail itself. She was unsure what was considered suspicious search behaviour.

Half an hour later, she'd reached the square with the largest police station and jail on 27th. She sat on a bench and watched the people move around a small outdoor market that was between her and the jail. The only good thing about losing her magic was that the pain in her joints had subsided. She studied the palms of her hands and her fingertips; they were scarred, but only slightly sore.

Two boys sat on the other end of the bench, oblivious to her presence, being far more interested in their small white dog. They jumped up and ran in circles while the dog chased them. She smiled as she watched them play and laughed as the dog nipped one boy on his backside. Watching their antics took her mind away from her problems, and for a few moments she felt as if her worries had been washed away. The dog seemed to notice her watching, and it walked over to her. It stared up at her. The boys looked at her, and she shifted nervously; she didn't want to attract any attention at all.

"Food?" the dog asked in the True Language.

Lucy was taken aback. It was rare for an animal to initiate a telepathic conversation with a human. *"No, I'm sorry."* Unsure what else to say, she waited.

"Why do you have a black cloud over you?"

Lucy looked up and saw nothing. Then she shivered in realization of what the dog was seeing. This time, with her psychic sense, she noticed a darkness.

"When you laughed, it changed colour," the dog said.

"What colour did it change to?"

"Grey." The boys called the dog, and he ran back to them, and Lucy returned to her fears. Although she wasn't familiar with this kind of black magic, she'd heard about it. It was something the Hag had attached to her, and it was probably what was locking her magic.

She wasn't sure how she could get rid of it. *"Can I just laugh it away?"*

The dog didn't answer, but followed the boys across the square; they were walking in the direction of the jail and its adjoining police station. On impulse, she followed them as they joined a noisy crowd developing close to the jail.

About forty men, and a few women, crowded round a fight. Many were betting, including a man wearing a dark grey cloak—a junior lord of the Imperial Order. The boys and their dog pushed to the front. Not wanting anyone to notice her, she stayed at the back. The fighters were stripped to the waist and circling each other, throwing occasional jabs. One wore the boots and grey pants of the company police; the other, more muscular man, wore only shorts.

The company man charged, but the stockier man swept his legs from under him, and the police officer fell to the hard ground. The bigger man was immediately on top, raining punches in his face. Then, picking up the dazed man, the stocky man smashed the back of his head against a rock. He went limp while the stocky man continued to punch him. The lord smiled and walked away.

Lucy was shocked at the callousness. The man was unconscious, but no one cared. The winner collected his prize money, then pushed through the crowd. No one paid any attention to the man on the ground. She considered helping him, but that would attract attention. Looking at the figure on the ground, she realized that the Night Hag would never expect her to return. If imperial lords cared so little about their own men, how much would they expect her to care about an animal—which was all Chloris was to them?

She hesitated too long as the crowd dispersed. The lord stopped and turned round. He must have sensed her attention focussed on him. She felt magic—the smallest amount. He was staring directly at her. Pretending not to notice, she turned and followed the boys and their dog. They'd just jumped over an open sewer that flowed along one side of the square.

Out of the corner of her eye, she saw that he was following her, and she quickened her pace. She still doubted that he recognized her, but she was worried that he saw the dark cloud above her.

"Stop!" the lord called.

She didn't, still pretending not to notice, but now people were staring at her. The stream of sewage was about a yard across, and she jumped over, feeling sudden relief as she did. Gasping, she leant on the side of the building as her magic filled her, and the familiar pain returned. "The water," she said aloud.

The lord stood on the other side of the stream. He laughed, but his eyes were cold. "That's what you people think of as water." But it wasn't that. She remembered that crossing running water could remove the power of a spell. She turned, but the man tutted. "I've called nanobots." Lucy looked up at the dark swarm that had just flown past the children and was flying towards her.

"What do you want?" she asked in Dnassian.

"Come with me to the police station. There's something about you..."

She knew better than to argue with an imperial lord, especially when he wanted to take her where she wanted to go. She nodded and widened her eyes, hoping to look nervous. It wasn't difficult with a cloud of nanobots hovering over her.

Gently, she felt her magic. She sensed it had returned, but she couldn't test it, not with this man in front of her. Glancing up, she noticed the black cloud had gone, and she noticed that she was better able to listen in the True Language. The man showed signs of a nascent magic, but he seemed to lack focus and control. This was normal for a junior member of the Imperial Order.

Of all the skills she'd learnt, listening in the True Language was the one she was most confident with. She knew she could listen to life around her, as well as a roc. This wasn't her ego—it was simply true. The man was attempting to push into her mind, but she brushed him away without him even being aware of what she was doing. She noticed his expression of surprise change to annoyance, but she kept her expression neutral, apart from a look of wide-eyed nervousness, which she hoped she wasn't overplaying. "This way." He attempted to push her into the jail building, but she hopped forward with a cry; he seemed more satisfied now.

"Chloris." She sensed the ice demon immediately on entering the building.

"Lucy?"

"I've been arrested."

"That's not good," Chloris hissed in her mind.

"It's fine. I have my magic back." Chloris was two floors beneath her, at the lowest level of the jail.

"Lord Plane," a desk sergeant dressed in dark blue said. So this was a regular, not company, jail. The man jumped up. "Do you require the interrogation room?" She noticed his attempts to smooth his perfect uniform; she didn't have to even listen with the True Language to sense the man's anxiety.

"No, I'll take her straight to B2." Lord Plane pointed Lucy to a lift. She walked inside, noticing a set of stairs behind a door to her left. The desk sergeant was nervously glancing at the cloud of nanobots circling by the ceiling as the doors closed.

She sensed and smelt the ice demon immediately. "What's that smell?" she asked. She heard the lord chuckle. The first two cells, on either side, were of the larger communal type. The one to her right had several ragged people inside—all were either watching her, or staring at Chloris in the cell opposite. Further down the metallic grey corridor was a series of solid metal doors, presumably leading to individual cells.

She stopped by Chloris's cell. The ice demon was chained to the back. *"This is becoming a habit,"* she said.

"Yess," the ice demon hissed. Immediately, all eyes turned to her, including the lord's.

"Did it speak?" the lord said, apparently to himself.

"Ice demons can speak, you know," Lucy said. She held the bars of Chloris's cage. "Am I going in here?"

"I can arrange that."

"Yes, please." Lucy grinned at the lord and was amused to see his mouth hang open in surprise.

"You don't want to go in there, lady," an old man said from the other communal cell. She looked at him, feeling his kindness as clearly as she sensed the lord's hostility.

"Thank you, Joe," she said. She was almost as surprised as the old man that she'd known his name. I must be getting better at this, she thought. Turning back to Chloris's cell, she tapped the door. "Open it please."

Lord Plane was now staring at her with an intensity that would have once unnerved her, but now she shrugged it off. He was nothing compared to Frore or the goblin sorcerer she'd once known.

"Can you open it?" Chloris asked.

Lucy began to enter the small machine mind controlling the mechanism of doors when she realized that she no longer needed to. With the magic of the Fire she could blast it, but as she called on the Fire, she remembered the pain that came after using this magic. Breathing deeply, she let it recede, but when the lord took hold of her, she pressed her palm against his chest and gave him a shock.

He fell back, gasping. "Who are you?"

She nearly told him, but it was better if she didn't. As soon as the Night Hag knew she was there, she'd have a problem again. Quickly, she entered the machine mind of the door and, overriding its security settings, ordered it to open. The pain coming from this type of augmented natural magic was less than blasting things. The door to Chloris's cell slid open, and Lucy walked inside to gasps from the communal cell behind her.

The lord was attempting to close the door, but she'd mentally jammed it; he entered behind her, giving her an idea. She smiled into his cold eyes. "I want to talk to her."

The man glanced up at the reptile. "It'll kill you."

She touched Chloris's chains—the blasting type of magic would be fastest, and she braced herself. *"Take care, Bright One,"* the ice demon said softly. The chains snapped with Fire coming from her hands. She looked down at the darkening to the centre of her palms. They stung.

"How did you do that?"

"A trick," she said. Focussing her full attention on the man for the first time, she rushed into his mind. His legs wobbled like jelly, and he fell neatly to the floor. He was a new lord, concerned about advancing in his order, but she found nothing else of interest. It was easy to do to him what the Night Hag had done to her. "I've locked your magic." He looked at her with wide eyes.

"Chloris, we should go." As they left the cell, she ordered the door shut.

"The stairs?" Chloris said. She nodded, stopping outside the communal cell. *"What?"*

"A distraction might help. And at least one of these men

doesn't belong here." Turning back to the cell, she spoke aloud. "Open!" The mechanism of the door hummed as it slid open.

"Did you do that?" Joe asked.

She grinned at him. "If you want to escape, you should come with me and my friend now." She enjoyed watching them stare at Chloris. "Before it's too late."

She followed Chloris up the stairs and heard some of the men following behind her, then she remembered the cloud of nanobots. "I should go first." Squeezing past Chloris, she pushed the door to the ground level open. The desk sergeant began to speak but stopped, open-mouthed, when he saw Lucy, an ice demon, and a group of ragged prisoners peering around the reptile.

"What's happening here?"

"Jailbreak." Lucy glanced up at the nanobots—they were already moving towards her. She sent a magical shockwave towards them. Then, with a snap, they dropped to the floor en masse, crackling and smouldering. They gave off a smell of burning electrics. Brushing them aside with her feet, Lucy touched the sergeant's face. "I'm sorry." She sent a small shock, and he fell back into his seat.

"Did you kill him?" one of the men asked.

"Of course not. He's just stunned. He'll wake up in a few hours." She led the ragtag group out of the jailhouse. It was evening, and the lights had already been dimmed. She and Chloris ran into the darkness as the other prisoners disappeared in their chosen directions.

There was no need for words. They ran back to the dead-end alley, and the door to the world between cities. They met a few people on the streets, but no one tried to stop a wild-looking woman and an ice demon. They soon reached the alley, walking past the place where the Night Hag and her ice demons had attacked them.

"We were too confident," Chloris said.

Lucy nodded. It wasn't the first time she'd made that mistake, but she didn't intend to make it again. It was the intoxicating power of magic that had that effect. They stepped through the broken metal door into the tunnels beyond.

"Where now?" Chloris asked.

She knew that one option was to climb up to the surface city by city, but it was slow and risky. "The river?"

"It's dangerous," Chloris said.

"The Night Hag won't expect it."

"No one will expect it because it will probably kill us."

But Lucy's intuition was that it was the best way. "It'll take us away from the imperial colony and into the forest valley. From there, we can find our way to the ancient forest and the rocs."

Chloris turned to face her. "Bright One, we cannot be sure that there will be any oxygen to breathe on the way, nor that the river will ever go to the surface. We are already deep underground."

"I think there'll be air. And I know we're underground, but we're underground in a mountain range. Normal ground level is lower than this, and we want to reach the forest valley, which is lower still. I've flown over the valley; it's deep enough to hide a mountain in."

"But we can't be sure of air. I can swim underwater for thirty minutes without breathing, but I do need to breathe. And if you remember our river escape, even with magic, you can only last about ten."

Lucy did remember escaping under the filthiest water

she could imagine. "But I'm stronger now. And my feeling is that this is the best way."

Chloris flicked her tail uneasily, but she said, "If you go, I'll follow."

Lucy's stomach felt dread as she ran through the dark passages, knowing clearly that her decision could kill them both. Despite running for over half an hour through tunnels, it felt as if only seconds had passed, and she wished the river had been further away. When they finally reached it, she stood there with her eyes closed, the feeling of lead in her stomach.

"We don't have to go this way," Chloris said quietly.

She opened her eyes, and despite the darkness, she saw, perhaps with inner sight, the foaming black river that roared past—rushing from a dark tunnel to the right into another equally dark tunnel to the left. The times she hadn't trusted her intuition had led to problems, but sometimes she misinterpreted it, too. She was scared of what she was about to do. "Chloris." She held out her hand, which Chloris took, and they stepped into the icy water. The current dragged them down, and they disappeared into a frigid darkness. The power of the river overwhelmed her, upturning her world.

Now she was terrified of the foolish thing she'd done, her body was pulled by a power beyond her control down a pitch-black tunnel. She felt Chloris's arms tighten around her, and then Lucy silently screamed as she span around a whirlpool before being sucked deeper underground.

15

Thomas woke up to banging on the door. His head was sore, and an empty bottle of spiced rum sat on the table. The banging on the door was getting louder and not helping his head. Looking around, he realized he was still sitting in The Uranium.

Luckily, someone had invested in a strong door. It would take more than a few kicks to break it down. The walls were thick enough to stop regular bullets, too. He'd noticed that earlier. He felt no urgency; whoever it was could wait. Instead, he rubbed his throbbing finger stub. The nausea of his hangover lessened when he let the magic flow, and slowly his headache receded, but the banging didn't stop. Again, he tried to contact Lucy, but there was nothing.

After several minutes, the magic had resolved the problem of the hangover, but not the men outside. Remembering the night before, he was annoyed with himself for indulging in self-pity.

"Thomas Brand!"

His eyes widened. Although he knew he'd be recognized at some time, this was earlier than he'd expected.

"The corporal has told us a lot about you. We know you're in there. We can see you."

Turning, Thomas placed his hands on the metal wall behind him. With his rock magic flowing, he could look outside, but he still wasn't too concerned. This place was built like a fortress. His eyes opened wide; he swore and the men laughed. An imperial bot was inches from his head on the other side of the metal wall. It had heat scanning and an audio sensor, too. It could definitely see him, and it could definitely shoot through the wall. Thomas was seldom shocked, but he was now, and, without thinking, he sent a magical shock of his own into the bot, melting parts of its mechanical mind. The bot fell to the ground.

He stood and walked to another part of the room. Again he placed his hands on the wall and watched the activity outside. At least he'd wiped the smiles from their faces, and he was pleased to see that he'd destroyed the only bot.

"We come in friendship, yet you damage our property. Expensive property, too." The speaker had a narrow red stripe on his cloak—a knight of the Order of the Empire. Next to him was Lord Ford. Both had magic.

"Who are you?" Thomas asked, vibrating his voice through the walls of the passage outside. The police and their officers looked at the walls.

"I'm Sir Ordin, and this is Lord Ford."

There was also a third person—a boy wearing a dark green page's uniform. Thomas studied the boy more carefully; there was something about him. Not his appearance, which was nothing out of the ordinary—something in his attitude. He stood silently while the lord and knight spoke. Then Thomas knew what he was seeing. The boy was listening telepathically, or attempting to.

Thomas laughed, purposely making his laughter sound

strange as it vibrated through the metal. "Since when did the Imperial Order do friendship?"

"I don't know what you mean," the knight said. "We're an order devoted to the well-being of all imperial subjects."

Thomas was mildly surprised. Sir Ordin seemed to believe what he was saying. Shifting his perspective, Thomas extended his magic sense, and he was fairly sure that none of the three magic users felt him probing them.

The knight's magic was in harmony with the lord's; Thomas guessed that they'd practiced their magic together, making them more difficult opponents in a fight. The page was an unknown. Either he was a fledgling sorcerer without skill, or something more, but with an ability to mask his magic. Thomas thought it was safe to assume the former.

The aristocrats stood in the centre; police were spread out around the building. He was surprised, and relieved, they hadn't discovered the passages in the walls yet. The criminal gang's efforts to conceal the passages by piling rubbish against the wall seemed to be working.

While the knight was talking, Thomas collected weapons inside. He found a third knife, another pistol, and an automatic rifle. It was cumbersome, but might be useful. Magic worked, but not in all situations. He was now alight with it, and as pain moderation, it was working well enough; although, if the results of using magic continued as they had, he'd soon need a walking stick for when he wasn't using it.

"We know you're a magic user," Sir Ordin continued. Thomas stopped to listen. He'd used magic against them, but he was interested in how much they really knew. If they'd passed on information to their seniors, then someone would know quite a lot about him, including how he'd killed the prison governor.

But the more the knight spoke, the more Thomas realized that they were not privy to very much information about him. Realizing that this talking could simply be a delaying tactic while they waited for more bots, which would be able to cut or blast their way through the walls, or for a more experienced practitioner of magic who may prove much more challenging for Thomas, he filled a flask of water and prepared to leave.

He'd been about to step through the wall and climb up the narrow shaft to the next level of city when Sir Ordin said, "We have good news! We've found the woman you're looking for."

Thomas chilled inside.

"We have Aina Kay."

Thomas felt sick. "Prove it!" He couldn't believe they had her. It made no sense. He knew they liked to play mind games.

Lord Ford nodded to someone behind him, and a man brought a woman forward.

Thomas gasped. Feeling disoriented, he leant heavily against the wall. It was Aina. Her skin was a little lighter than he remembered, but otherwise, it looked like her. She stumbled as she was led; her wrists were chained together. Feeling confused, Thomas wasn't sure what to say. When the man pushed her forward, he found his voice.

"Free her!"

Lord Ford smiled. "Of course not, but if you surrender, you can speak to her. I guarantee that."

"And then?"

"You'll be put on trial for your crimes." He turned to the woman. "She'll be tried, too. But after we've tagged you both, then we'll allow you a life. The Empire is big."

Thomas wasn't sure whether he was referring to its size

or its heart, but either way, it was a lie. "Let me speak to her."

Sir Ordin started speaking, and Thomas stopped listening. Instead he spoke to Aina directly, in the True Language. *"Aina?"* She looked in his direction but didn't speak. *"Can you hear me?"*

She stared ahead but didn't appear to hear. She'd been fluent in the True Language. Was it possible that she'd lost the ability? Thomas noticed the page was listening more intently, and he stilled his magic, instead focussing it inwards. It was time to use the Fire he distrusted. He wasn't sure whether this really was Aina or not, but he was determined to find out.

The page's eyes widened as Thomas's magic flared, and if any had been able to see him, they would have seen a flaming orange man sinking into the ground.

Aware of all his surroundings, Thomas attempted what he normally would have been reluctant to do. He dropped through the ground—a mixture of metal and rock, but also plastics that he had to burn as he descended. Some things he couldn't simply pass through. The floor of the world was thick, with narrow gaps, wires, startled rats, and dirt. He didn't care. He descended for several minutes.

First he felt his feet come free, then his legs, and finally his whole body dropped a dozen feet into the administrative section of the 28th level—the prison. A man and a woman stared at him, and he was very aware that his body was on fire with the magic. He'd memorized exactly where Aina had been standing, and he walked fifteen paces ahead, straight through a wall into a dark room.

He leapt into the air, and as his fingers touched the ceiling, he stuck. Using his magic, he drew himself upwards into the layer of materials between the two worlds. He almost screamed as he passed through some asbestos-like material, burning it with magic that changed its form. The magic pulled him up until he was just beneath the surface, only feet from Aina.

His Fire burnt, and he rose from the street as a burning orange man, and the police fell over themselves to get away from him. The knight shuffled back a step, and the young lord yelped. But seconds later, they'd recovered enough to draw weapons, and the knight rushed forward.

For Thomas, physical attacks usually seemed as if in slow motion. He'd trained magically and martially too long to retain normal perception. The knight drew a knife and rushed forward, belatedly rousing his magic in an attempt at shielding. Thomas touched Aina's chains and they fell away, and then he issued a short blast that shocked the men around them; many dropped their weapons. The knight slowed his attack, and Aina took his knife and stabbed him in his stomach. He fell to the ground with a look of surprise; he was bleeding badly and wouldn't survive if left without prompt medical aid.

"Thomas, take me with you," Aina said. He adjusted his magic, allowing her to come closer without burning. If she wanted to attack him, it would be the perfect time, but she didn't.

"We're going," he whispered.

But then, the hairs on his body stood up. The page was doing something. Without looking behind, Thomas pointed his hand towards the dying knight and called the knife. It shot into his hand, and he turned, throwing it at the page and breaking his concentration. The page screamed as the grey cloud surrounding him contracted, pushing against his body, running back into his nostrils and through his lips. He dropped to his knees, choking on the sticky substance. Then he fell headlong onto the ground.

The men around him stared with wide eyes at the dead page.

"You've killed Lord Frore's son!" Lord Ford gasped.

Thomas almost laughed. That explained a lot, and it explained the fear on the young noble's face. To Thomas, the knife in the boy's side seemed superfluous. "His black magic killed him, and good luck explaining that to Frore."

As some of the men were picking up their weapons, Thomas took hold of Aina and allowed the Fire of Prometheus to blaze. They dropped back down into the dark room a dozen or more feet beneath the road.

"Where—"

Thomas silenced her. "Not yet. We can speak later." He took hold of her, and calling more magic, they walked through the wall, back into the prison office. Several men were there, speaking to the distraught pair of office workers. A security guard struggled to draw a pistol, but Thomas just pointed at it, and it glowed as orange as he was. The man screamed and desperately undid his belt, throwing it to the floor, and then he poured a glass of water over his smouldering trousers.

"Who are you?" a man asked.

Thomas grinned and reached up to the cracked part of the ceiling. Aina yelped as his magic pulled them up, and again, he stuck to the ceiling, allowing his magic to pull them through. This time, he took special care to burn all materials that his rock magic didn't work with—with the Fire, his rock magic was specially supplemented. He worried that the workers below might try to shoot their legs, but perhaps they'd been too shocked to do more than look.

Minutes later, they climbed out of the floor of the bar. The banging on the door continued.

"Where are we?" Aina asked.

"In The Uranium." Seeing her confused look, he continued, "The bar in front of you on the street."

"Couldn't you have taken us a bit further away?"

"Not easily. It takes a lot of energy to work against gravity, especially though mixed materials." It was almost impossible to go far this way—he was already exhausted and covered in sweat. He wanted to ask her questions, but it was not the time or place.

Touching the wall again, he saw the confusion outside. The prone knight was being attended to, and the lord was kneeling by the body of Lord Frore's son, but unless he could bring people back from the dead, there was little he could do. The door was beginning to break. "This way," he said to Aina, taking her hand and moving to the far wall of the lounge.

Despite tiredness, his rock sense was alert, and he studied their escape route—a narrow shaft on the other side of the metal wall. The front door fell from its hinges, and he took her hand. "Whatever you do, don't let go, and don't speak."

They passed through the thin metal wall in seconds. On the other side, they were squashed against each other, and the last thing he wanted to do was climb up the shaft, but there was no choice.

"Can you climb?"

"Yes."

He pushed her up to the metal rungs of the ladder attached to the side of the shaft. "Start now!"

It was a tight climb and having Aina above him was distracting. She could move more freely, but he had to keep his elbows tucked close to his side. He moved quickly, though, burning magic instead of calories as he rose.

"I have lots of questions," she said.

Thomas thought of all the questions he had, and some of them were hard ones. He wanted this to be Aina, but he kept thinking of Lucy's words about her having to be reborn as a baby. The Aina above her seemed a little younger and her skin was a little lighter than the Aina he'd known, but not by much.

"You're quiet," she said.

"I'm tired."

He was, but it wasn't that. He was well aware that many nobles were hardly human. Not just their attitudes, but also the extent to which they'd made themselves machine—or synthetic, as they preferred to say. He listened to her body with his magic senses, feeling gently inside. He knew Aina's body better than just a lover, which he had been in another life, but he'd also healed her injuries and had sent his mind and magic into her body several times. Tentatively, he reached inside again.

He had to know if she was human.

16

"Thomas? Was that you? I felt as if you were touching me."

"I was..." Thomas had a heavy feeling in his stomach.

"Why?" She sounded upset. He hesitated; he needed to gather his thoughts.

The rungs ended. They'd reached another stale passage. It appeared to be a maintenance passage on the outside of 26th.

"Not here," Thomas said. "We need to find somewhere we can speak."

She wasn't happy, but accepted that they needed to keep moving. "Do you think they'll follow us?"

"I tried to disguise the direction we took, and it might work for a while. But Lord Ford could probably find our trail."

Thomas stopped in the dirt-covered passage. Touching the walls, he saw patchy images of the city on the other side. It was the 26th, and it looked just like the 27th. A man slept in a pile of trash; a rat was eating something by his head.

"What can you see?" Aina asked.

"Nothing interesting. I think we should find the way up to the next city." It had taken over forty minutes to climb up one level, and there were still twenty-five left. He'd have days of climbing, assuming everything went smoothly, which it never did. The passage was partially blocked where part of the roof had collapsed. They climbed over the pile of metal and concrete. "Down here."

"How do you know?"

"I have special senses: I can feel vibrations coming through the walls. There's an empty space ahead."

"Where can we talk?" she asked.

"On 25th."

To Thomas's relief, the shaft to the next level was wider and straighter than the last, and they were able to climb quickly. Half an hour later, they were standing in the passages beyond the edge of the 25th New City. Sensing an open space ahead, Thomas kept walking.

It was a dirty space that housed dozens of water pipes for the city. A hole at the bottom of the wall let light into the room, as did the cracks and smaller holes above it.

"It looks like a giant mouse hole," she said.

Thomas imagined a homeless person crawling through it. The smell of dried urine was strong, and old food rotted on the floor.

"It looks like we've walked into someone's home," Thomas said.

"Not much of a home."

"No." The place depressed him, but not as much as what he'd seen inside her. However, before he acted, he wanted to be sure. There would be no going back.

Aina was investigating an adjoining room. He joined her. There were some upturned plastic barrels on the far side of the room next to a wooden table. "It's smells better in here.

We can sit on the barrels. It's not too bad; the floor's almost clean."

He joined her, sitting on the other barrel, studying her profile in the dim light as she talked. In appearance, she was almost identical to the woman he'd lost, but on the inside she was not the woman he'd known.

"Now speak to me!" She looked him straight in the eyes. "Something's wrong."

That was an understatement. "What are you?"

She stiffened. "What do you mean?"

"I saw inside of you, and you're not human."

She winced and tears formed. "Not human?"

He had to force himself to continue. "Your body is mostly synthetic: your heart and organs, and much of your skin."

"All of it?"

"About two-thirds."

"There's more, isn't there?" she asked, looking at him intently.

"Aina, I saw you die. How are you here?"

"You left me."

His stomach sank, but when he quickly searched his memories, he could only see her lying dead. "You were dead. We took you back to the mountain, and when the black dragon came, we burnt the pyre. Your body was on top."

"That's impossible! I woke up in hospital alone. I was desperate to see you, but no one knew who or where you were."

"Aina, I spoke to your spirit in the centre of the planet."

She smiled as if he were a little simple. "I woke up alone in hospital. I was seriously hurt. I've been in hospital for over a year, and through rehabilitation for almost as long."

He shook his head. "How is this possible?"

"I don't know. I was unconscious after the stabbing."

"What were your last words to me?" His eyes narrowed as he waited for her answer.

"I don't remember. Thomas, it's hard to remember. I was in a lot of pain. Perhaps the dragon you saw took me to Nassopolis. I remember something about dragons. Perhaps it wanted something."

Again doubts clouded his mind. He felt a burning sensation inside: the magical hangover was beginning.

"What's wrong?" Aina asked.

"Nothing." He looked away.

"It's not nothing."

What if she were right? What if the black dragon had actually taken her body? They were capable of subtle magic; perhaps it'd disguised its actions. But he'd carried her dead body.

"Thomas, I was unconscious—I never died!"

Had the dragon used Aina as bait to entice him to recover this dangerous Fire that wracked his body with pain? And if so, why? Lucy and Chloris both suspected the dragons of duplicity.

"I spoke to you in the inner sun."

"I don't know what happened there. How do you know what you saw?"

He was very aware that the inner sun was a place of illusion and deception. He'd not been so uncertain of anything for a long time.

"I was in the hospital for a long time. The doctors told me I nearly died. They said they had to replace some parts, but I didn't think it was that much." She paused, blinking away a tear. "They said my injuries became worse because they'd been untended for so long. I had gangrene; some parts of me had to be amputated." She squeezed his arms. "Thomas! I'm Aina!"

He wanted to believe, plus the thought of killing her now sickened him. But what if she was an imperial spy? He closed his eyes and listened carefully in the True Language for deceit, but sensed none. She believed what she was saying. He opened his eyes and saw her shoulders quivering.

"Many imperial subjects are half synthetic. You know that," she said.

It was true, and what if he was wrong? What if she had really been alive, in a coma? And what if to save her, surgeons really had replaced most of her body with artificial parts? He wasn't sure what to think.

"Thomas, I hate the Empire. I'll sacrifice my life to fight it!"

She held his hands, and when he held them and listened to her, she still felt like Aina. "I thought you were dead."

She gave a sad smile. "You know how advanced their biotechnology is." She looked at him intently. "Do you think I'm a robot?"

As she spoke, he felt each vibration her heart sent out. When he touched her mind, she moved closer.

"You're untagged."

"You can see that?"

He nodded, searching for ideas as doubts almost overwhelmed him. Not for the first time, he wished Lucy was with him. She would know the truth in this kind of situation, but when he called her, he heard nothing.

He realized that he was no longer sure. He wanted to believe her, but Aina's spirit had seemed so real. He felt the most confused he'd ever felt in his life, but when she wrapped her arms around him, she began to feel more real than the spirit in an illusory world. When she pushed him onto the table, and her clothes fell away, he forgot his concerns.

THEY LAY TOGETHER for what felt like a long time, but Thomas guessed was no more than half an hour. The sex had been almost the same, except that she was more passive than before. She'd told him she'd been recovering. Perhaps that was it. "We should go."

"Yes, it's not too comfortable." She stood and got dressed. "You've still not told me where we're going."

"I planned to go to Silva to find you." He stood and put his clothes on.

"And now you've found me?"

"Silva's still the best choice. The Resistance is there, and we must rejoin the fight. And it's your home." He'd been thinking about finding Aina for so long that now he'd found her, it felt like an anticlimax. Perhaps it was because he had hoped their strength together could damage the Empire, but this Aina lacked the magic of the old Aina, and she lacked some of her spirit. Or perhaps he was losing trust in the dragons and the Fire, despite its power. "I still need to discover the true purpose of this Fire."

"Fire?" she asked.

"The magic." Thomas chilled inside. She should have known, and he couldn't understand why she didn't, unless she had amnesia because of her injuries. He knew she'd been injured badly to need so many replacement parts. Perhaps he just needed to give her more time to recover.

"Wouldn't it be better to fight the Empire in the Crown —the centre of power on Prometheus?"

"Adela saw us near the black tower." He told her about the vision of the psychic, Adela.

"The tower is in the Crown. Have her prophecies come true before?" He nodded. "Then you should pay attention."

"Do you still want to end the Empire on Prometheus?" he asked.

"Yes. I think we should take the fight to them. The Emperor's here celebrating the completion of his Empire."

This was more like the Aina he knew, but the plan lacked sense. It was simply too dangerous to challenge the Imperial Order directly. "I have power, but I'm not all powerful. I can kill a man with a thought, but I can't defeat the Emperor and his inner circle by myself."

"We can find allies."

"Perhaps." He thought about the rocs and dragons. But despite synthetic parts that should, in theory, make her stronger in some ways, he had doubts that Aina could fight. "Going to the Crown unprepared is dangerous."

"I've lived with danger before. Thomas, it feels right."

He shook his head. "We must reach Silva first. When I've spoken to the Resistance, then I might consider attacking the Crown, but not until then."

"Then we have a long journey," Aina said. "And a chance to get back my athletic body." She rested her hand on his chest. "Maybe one as rock hard as yours."

He gave a brief grin. "It's the only way if we want to remain concealed."

"So we climb up to the Inner Cities?"

He nodded. "And then we take a train to Naskopole Junction. From there, we travel to the Hanging Cities, and then fly to Silva."

She nodded, then they heard something in the other room. Quickly entering, they looked towards the man-sized mouse hole in the wall. Somebody was squeezing through.

Thomas pointed to a narrow passage, and they quietly left. He led the way along the passage. At one point, they had to crawl under a series of water pipes. The pipes eventually turned and rose vertically.

"There's a space beside the pipes," Thomas said. Aina looked at him dubiously. He was holding the pipes, and he could feel the spaces all the way up to 24th. "There are rungs in the wall, too."

She shrugged. "Okay, lift me."

As Aina climbed quickly above him, Thomas stared after her for a moment. Losing her had hurt so much, and he wanted to believe so much that she had returned.

17

Na turned her long head towards the circling bot and blasted it with fire. The other bot reacted like a wasp, but for a dragon with a developed psychic sense, entering a simple mind like this was as straightforward as breathing fire. She entered its mind, ensuring there were no more communications with the humans. Then, she simply told it to die, and the bot tumbled to the forest floor.

Thinking about the wasted resources within the bots, she dropped to the ground next to its body. If she'd killed an animal, she could feed now; nothing would be wasted. She was beginning to dislike humanity even more. They took from her world to create things for a single use instead of training themselves to live as dragons and rocs did. However, despondency wasn't a part of her nature, and curiosity soon uplifted her mood as she noticed the forest around her.

She ran on two legs through the forest, fascinated by the colours of the bright flowers. Her forelegs, like those of all dragons, could be used for crawling on all fours when necessary, but dragons moved fastest on their hind legs. All around her the ancient forest shone, and, for a moment, she forgot her mission and became absorbed in the simple pleasures of the life in the forest.

Dragons were not vegetarians, but she accepted the offer of fruit that one of the trees made. The shining fruit was sweet and juicy, but not as satisfying as a basoo. A warning call from a bird about thirty yards ahead alerted her to a possible danger. She told the flowers to turn off their lights, and one by one they did, leaving the forest in darkness.

Whatever moved towards her was not of the forest. She was sure. No forest creature would make such a noise. Instructing an extensive patch of hanging vines to let her pass, she was surprised at their hostility. Then she rumbled her amusement. *"You're like little dragons."* She breathed fire towards them, and they opened. *"I am a dragon,"* she said as an explanation, wondering if they were intelligent enough to learn. They simply echoed, *"Dragon."* That was enough. Life in the ancient forest was not used to dragons—she couldn't expect the same respect given to her in the mountains, not immediately. She climbed up to one of the lower branches and waited.

NA LISTENED to the strange sound coming from the forest floor—some sort of jabbering. Listening carefully, she tried to determine what sort of animal would make that sound. And then she saw her first humans.

Human language was not as she'd expected. It was not as harsh as the language of the haloons, the mammalian, two-footed creatures living in the foothills of her mountains, and not as beautiful as birdsong. She couldn't understand the words, but she could listen in the True Language for ideas, intentions, and emotions. With practice, she was sure she could understand their thoughts on a finer level; they seemed to do little to hide them.

Five humans approached, three males and two females. All wore grey uniforms, apart from one of the females, who was wearing blue. All were unhappy. She noted the chaotic emotional disturbances within them. "What're we doing here?" a tall male said. "We should wait for more bots to arrive."

"I've told you we can't." Na recognized his authority within the group. "Something's killing them, and we have to find out what." Surely they weren't talking about her. Curious, Na listened more carefully to their thoughts. "We've lost seven in less than a week." Na grinned a wide dragon grin to herself. She understood. The ancient forest hated them, too. Impulsively, she suggested that the snapping vines attack the humans. They liked the suggestion, and immediately whipped them, causing the group to fire into the forest. But bullets did little to the vines, and they were forced to go around the large patch. Na followed from tree to tree.

Many of the human thoughts were petty, and they bored her, but she listened for information. After an hour, she decided to be more aggressive. She probed the mind of the weakest member, causing him to stagger into a snapping vine.

"What's wrong with you?" the short female said.

The male whose mind she entered shook his head. "I'm not sure. I feel a little strange." She searched its thoughts but found little of practical use, but she learnt that he desired drug downloads. She searched more to try to understand. She understood that he wanted escape, but that he had to wait to download feelings of intoxication from his tag.

Na stopped on her branch. Again she was surprised. These humans had made themselves part machine; their mind was part mechanical, tying them more to the material world. But worse, they tied themselves to a larger machine mind controlled by their leaders. She shuffled through its most recent uploads and downloads. He didn't appear to notice her presence at all, making her even bolder. Humanity was doing something strange: it was moving in the opposite direction to dragonkind, chaining itself to smart but simple machines. Dragons sought to free their minds, to become more aware. She realized she still had a lot to learn.

The forest was becoming thicker; she was entering an older part. She felt its whispers, and listening to this ancient consciousness was far more interesting than listening to humans. She sent it warm feelings and it returned them. It seemed to recognize her, but she didn't know how. She'd never entered before, and she doubted that she'd visited in past lives. Dragons seldom spent time in the forest.

The trees and plants allowed her to pass unhindered, but not so the humans. They struggled with each pace. Na had heard Night Sun say that it was sometimes that way for dragons, too, especially in the oldest parts.

The male whose mind she'd read cried in pain as a predatory whelk on the trunk of a tree bit its arm. She thrummed with amusement, recognizing the scene from somewhere. She knew that the whelks grew from those trees. It was something to do with shell-shaped fruit, but she didn't know where the memory came from. Her thrumming sound became a louder humming, and the humans shone lights towards her. "There's something there," the biggest male said. "What the—" They gasped as they stared at her.

She was annoyed. It was her fault they'd seen her. Now she had to decide what to do. She was already monitoring their tags for outward messages, and she believed she could block any attempts they made to communicate.

"It's pure gold," the big male said. "We're rich if we can catch it."

"An animal like that would be worth a fortune on the inner planets," the tall male said.

Na was heating with anger.

"I saw it first," the big male said.

"It's too big," the leader said. "We'd never smuggle a thing like that off-planet." The man glanced at the woman in blue. "This must be our secret."

The woman stood straighter. "The flora and fauna of this planet are protected." The female was better, but she still considered her an animal. "I must contact headquarters."

Na understood that they were blocking their thoughts while they planned how to dispose of her. The fire rumbled in her belly.

"What was that?" the short female in grey asked.

"We'd be better killing it and selling the parts. Its head would make a fantastic trophy."

The energy within the woman wearing blue changed—she'd switched her tag on. It was time for Na to act. She sent a psychic shock through the group, and they screamed, holding their heads. Directing her flames at the leader, she sent a short blast through his heart. The man died instantly.

She watched the others crawling around on the ground in pain, but she had no sympathy for any of them, even the one in blue, who, she had to admit, was slightly less offensive. The tall male was the first to reach for his weapon, and the next to die. The big male and short female followed. Na was surprised at how slowly humans moved. The bleeding male and the female in blue stared at her; she smelt their fear.

These creatures were only a little above animals, but animals attempting to kill her had to be dealt with. She probed the female's mind and found something different from the other. This one believed she had an interest in the planet, although it was a human interest, not the interest of the inhabitants of Blue Prometheus.

"I don't know if it did anything to us, but something has fused my tag."

"My tag's finished, too," the male whimpered. Na had a strong impulse to kill him, but she waited. Night Sun had often told the Tangle to develop patience.

"Well? Are you going to kill us?" the female yelled.

"Not yet," Na said in the True Language. She wasn't sure how these creatures would respond. Even plants understood the language of all life, but her thoughts in their minds seemed to startle them.

"What was that?" the male asked.

Na breathed fire, and the man almost fell back against the shell tree, pulling his hand away just in time.

"It's a dragon," the woman said. "There were encounters when we first came to Imperial Uranus, but I never really believed they existed."

"I know what it is. I mean what happened? I heard a sound in my head."

"I think it spoke to us."

"You've invaded our planet. You must leave."

"We can't do that," the female said.

"Have you gone mad?" the man asked.

"It's speaking telepathically—it's strange."

"Why not?" Na asked.

"This is our planet. The Emperor has arrived to celebrate our victory and conquest. Imperial Uranus belongs to us."

Na knew the woman expected to die and was therefore speaking honestly, but it didn't excuse it. *"The true name of this planet is Blue Prometheus, and it belongs to . . ."* She hesitated. She'd never thought of the ownership of the planet before.

The female continued. "I'm sure that the Emperor will permit some species to remain, but if you kill me, he'll send an army to hunt you."

"Prometheus is not yours to take."

"The Emperor brings order to chaos."

Na guessed that the woman only partially understood the thoughts she directed at her, and she sensed the final sentence was an implant in the human's mind. *"The three great races govern Prometheus."* Uncurling her long golden tail, Na stepped closer. The male raised a weapon, and she sliced off his arm with one of her talons.

The female screamed, and the sound was unpleasant, but her panic opened her mind wider than before, and Na's curiosity took over. She plunged inside, learning more about this species. She saw clearly how they'd moved from planet to planet, destroying each one. Words would not stop humanity, only strength. Through the memories of the woman, she saw the imperial fleets patrolling the dark space around Blue Prometheus.

The woman was staring up at her. "The Empire is progress, and you can't stop progress." Another implanted sentence, Na thought. She burnt the recent memories, and some more, from the woman, but left her with most of her mind. The woman looked at the golden dragon a final time and disappeared into the forest.

Opening her wings, Na rose between the giant trees before flying through a hole in the forest's canopy. Her heart was heavy as she flew low over the dark forest. It seemed to speak to her, but she could only think of the danger facing the dragons. Contact with humanity had sickened her; nothing had prepared her for that. They were not like most animals, which, however fierce, had something attractive about them. This species repulsed her.

As she flew, she reached out in the True Language. *"Night Sun."* Almost immediately, an image of the black dragon appeared in her mind. It was as if he'd been waiting for her.

"Daughter of Fire."

"I'm coming back!" She felt a little embarrassed at the emotions she felt.

But the black dragon breathed fire in relief. *"We worried for you, Daughter."*

Na felt warmth towards him, particularly after her encounter with the humans. *"I'm worried, too."*

"I've seen some of what you've seen," he said. Na was upset her thoughts had escaped her. *"You still need to practice shielding your thoughts; we now think that some humans might be able to read them."*

"The female showed some ability, but it was primitive. They're animals, after all, and all animals possess some ability with the True Language."

"They appear as animals, but some can be wise. However, I wasn't referring to the woman you just questioned, but to ones with training."

She didn't believe humans could be wise, and she listened, waiting for Night Sun to qualify his words, but he didn't. *"I've met them, read their thoughts, and seen their actions. They're animals."*

"But sometimes they can be more than that," Night Sun said. *"You'll understand in time."* He stopped her from speaking, and she quietened. *"Fly fast, Daughter of Fire. When you return, eat, drink, but don't sleep."*

Na felt unhappy with the instructions—all dragons loved to sleep after a long flight. *"Why not sleep?"*

"You'll address the Thunder and Wisdom."

She was surprised. *"All of them?"*

But Night Sun was gone, and she flew faster into the cold Promethean wind.

18

The dragons waited in the drizzle of Blue Fell for her to speak. Only about half of the four hundred and fifty dragons from her group were there—some were too young—but there were also almost a thousand dragons from other parts of Prometheus. Many of those were led by Twrch, a great brown dragon.

Na felt small. She was a dragon of the Flight, speaking to the combined Thunders and Wisdoms of dragonkind. Physically she was less than a third the size of most of these dragons, and her group was a minority. But she knew she was strong, too, and she adjusted her inner fire, making her eyes glow red.

"Daughter of Fire," Night Sun said, indicating that she should begin.

With a breath of fire, she began. *"I studied the memories and thoughts of a group of humans in the ancient forest . . ."* She told them what she'd learnt.

"How can you know this?" a green dragon from a distant Thunder asked.

"I read their memories."

"Immature dragons can't read memories," he said.

Night Sun spoke. *"She's the first golden dragon born in two hundred years—the Daughter of Fire has unusual psychic skills."*

"All dragons have psychic skills," Twrch said.

"Not like her," Night Sun replied.

"She must be tested," the green dragon said.

"She's not ready for that," Night Sun said.

"Then how can we trust her?" Na was sure this rudeness was a breach of protocol. The green turned his head to a long yellow dragon. Na felt something pass between them. Then they turned to Na.

"No!" Night Sun said.

Because of Night Sun's warning, the psychic attack only shocked Na, and she moved within her mind, deflecting the double attack, pulling the attacks into each other, and then mentally tripping them. She felt the pain of the two dragons, but then they attacked again.

She felt dizzy, as if she were being sucked down into a whirlpool. She allowed herself to be pulled into the swirling pool of energy, searching for the leak in their power—there always was one. She found it in the centre of the swirling, and imagining herself flying into the centre of the vortex, she took the dragons with her. At first, they pushed her on, but when they tried to pull away, she held them tightly.

Screeches and hisses from the assembled dragons made her open her eyes, and she blinked in surprise at the pair of prone dragons before her.

"What did you do?" a dragon asked.

"I defended myself," she said to the assembled Thunders and Wisdom.

The dragons spoke to each other, and she listened to their conversations, some supporting and some opposing her.

"It's rude to listen to the thoughts of the Thunder," Spere said.

"Then they shouldn't think so loud!" she said before realizing who she was speaking to.

She felt Night Sun's amusement; Spere merely nodded his large head. Fire dripped from Twrch's mouth, but he remained silent.

"The Daughter of Fire has passed your test," Night Sun said.

None of the assembled dragons disagreed, and they looked away as the defeated dragons crawled back to their groups. *"If we've finished with tests, perhaps we can speak of action,"* Night Sun said.

Na listened to news that shocked her again. There had been an unprovoked assault on the rocs' forest home, and dozens had been killed. Even the most insular and isolationist dragons were angered. And then she heard of the attacks on dragons; a Flight from the other group had been killed while flying over the mountains by a spaceship orbiting Prometheus, and another Flight had been attacked over Twrch's territory.

The dragons roared. The war council began, and Na lifted into the air to leave. Only the Thunder and Wisdom were permitted places in such meetings.

"Wait!" Night Sun said. She gently landed by the great black dragon.

"I grant her special permission," Night Sun said. Ignoring the rumbles of a few dragons, he continued. *"She's the most gifted dragon of her generation, perhaps in several generations. And we need her skills to counter the human machines. I propose that she accompanies the group attacking the Moon of Oberon."*

A series of attacks was proposed. Her group was to attack Oberon. Even if her role was only support, Na could barely contain her excitement to have been chosen for an attack on a human moon base. The attack on Oberon would take place before dawn, and it would be led by Night Sun.

One hundred dragons from her group gathered hours before dawn, and she joined them. Sixty were from the Flights, forty from the Thunders. They rose silently into the dark sky together. The Thunder was named for the combined sounds of the dragons' wings, but the sounds were for show; when they wanted, dragons could fly in silence.

As she flew, Na thought about the humans and their complacency; they thought themselves the only intelligence in the solar system. It was their weakness, and the dragons' advantage. No human could imagine animals rising from the surface of the planet to attack their moon base.

They flew hard through the upper atmosphere, gaining speed in preparation for entry into space. She'd never flown into space before, but she'd swum without oxygen, and the principle was the same. Dragons recycled oxygen within their bodies, allowing them to swim deep underwater or fly in space for several hours at a time. She'd had plenty of practice in the mountain lakes when she'd been a part of the Tangle. Her role in the attack focussed her mind. Unless she broke into the human base, where she and the others could replenish their oxygen, many of the younger dragons, including herself, would never return.

Once in space, the dragons folded their wings and glided silently, relying mostly on their initial speed to propel them, but they could also use small magic to manoeuvre. Although many dragons termed it magic, Na really just saw it as a manipulation of energy not yet known to other species except, perhaps, the leviathans. Na watched Night Sun closely. He was the only dragon with knowledge of the more powerful, older magic. She suspected he used that, too.

Hours later they reached the moon, and the hundred dragons silently beat their wings in the thin lunar atmosphere. They gathered in the crater. Although distance usually didn't matter with the True Language, it was sometimes better to be physically present. She left the rest of the dragons and flew low over the rocky surface towards the moon base.

The human base was a flat dome structure, it looked like a rodent mound on Prometheus. Like the rodents, they'd burrowed underground. She sensed the life crawling under her feet, but her destination was the largest of the three mounds—the place they stored their transports, and the only one with an entrance large enough for full-sized dragons.

When she was about a hundred yards from the base, she projected her consciousness towards it, feeling the life there. The machine mind was guarded, but not against a dragon. She surveyed the whole system and then dropped inside. It accepted her as if she were a download from the imperial headquarters in the inner planets. Finding the controls to the hangar doors, she opened her eyes and spoke to the Thunder.

"I'm inside its mind."

She landed in front of the hangar door, misleading the four glass eyes that stared outwards. She could trick the eyes, but could see no way to open the doors without alerting the humans inside. She counted eight of them.

There was no choice. She ordered the doors open, and as they opened, she heard the humans inside shouting. Crawling up the outer wall of the mound until she was above the opening doors, she waited. *"They're open."* The dragons in the crater had heard.

Waiting above the door, she decided to pounce on the humans, but no one came out. Listening carefully, she realized they'd gone deeper into their tunnels. She dropped to the ground and entered, blowing flames at each of the mechanical eyes—far easier than maintaining mental control. Relaxing a little as she breathed in oxygen from a vent on the ceiling, she probed deeper into the machine mind. The humans were aware something was wrong but weren't reacting as she'd expected. She'd once poked her head into a hive of Promethean hornets and had quickly learnt her lesson, but these humans were still scurrying about deep under the surface.

Turning her head, she saw a dark cloud in the distance. The dragons would arrive within minutes, and she looked for something to do. Five fat transports lay to one side; on the other was a row of sleek spacecraft. Night Sun had told her to leave the fighters. The Thunder would deal with them as one, but she could start with the unarmed transports. They were open, and she ran inside the most distant one first. The inside was puzzling, and she didn't understand the human instruments, but she knew that the delicate electrical equipment was important for the transport, so she blasted it with fire. Once the fire had taken hold, she moved to the next, and gradually worked her way along the row. By the time the fourth transport was smoking, the dragons had arrived.

"You've done well. Return to the crater and wait," Night Sun said.

Na ran outside, glancing at the dragons as they tore machinery from the walls. She knew they'd finish by burning the fighters, which would cause an explosion, damaging many of the tunnels beneath. She flew low over the lunar surface, keeping to the shadows where possible. Twenty minutes later she was in the crater, and she turned to watch.

Flames came from the human dome, and the Thunder rushed from the structure. The mound exploded, more flames shooting up twenty or thirty yards into the sky. They'd destroyed a large part of the human base, but some parts of it would remain intact. However, without their spacecraft or landing area, it would be harder for them to launch more attacks on Prometheus.

She was pleased but knew that the damage inflicted was only one small battle. Then she saw something that made her go cold. Running to the top of the ridge, she strained to see. In the blackness of space, near the planet, there seemed to be a deeper darkness. She projected her mind towards it.

"A trap!" she shouted in the True Language. *"Get away!"* She sent a mental image of the dark shapes to Night Sun.

"I see something. What do you see?" Night Sun asked.

She struggled for the words or concepts to describe human machines. She'd been studying human technology with one of the older dragons, then she remembered. *"Fighters!"* She sent an image of the space where they were, and she felt the shock of the great black dragon.

"Stay hidden." And then he was gone from her mind.

The Thunder of dragons flew towards the attacking squadron of fighters. Na counted seventeen spacecraft, and she relaxed. What could so few do against so many dragons? She waited for her family to destroy the humans, and only Night Sun's direct order kept her hidden in the dark crater. She shifted on the small ridge around the crater, blowing a short blast of fire at some rocks in frustration and watching the small rockslide she caused.

The human fighters were clearer now—sleek, long craft with long projections from the front. Each fighter was slightly smaller than a dragon. Then the fighters breathed fire on the dragons, and two exploded before her eyes. Na cried out in shock and concern. Another dragon caught fire, and she felt his pain.

The dragons fought back, destroying one of the fighters, but the human machines were fast and manoeuvrable, and they quickly turned back for another attack. Three more dragons died. Na felt cold inside. The humans were killing her family, and she couldn't understand it. She uttered a soft cry—unable to control it.

Dragon fire destroyed another fighter, but they were so fast, and more dragons caught fire. She saw Night Sun clinging to one of the fighters, and that gave her an idea. He was struggling to break his way in, but she knew a way. No longer caring about his instructions, she lifted off from the ridge and flew towards the fight. As she flew, she became invisible, passing the bodies of her family; she was already entering their machine mind systems. But dragons were still dying, and she hadn't discovered a way to stop it yet. She flew fast, but it took fifteen more minutes before she reached the battle. Of the hundred dragons, only sixty-three were left. The remaining ones had become better at fighting the human machines, but they were still struggling against the final two fighters.

Na hit the fighter hard—right next to Night Sun, making him start. *"Daughter of Fire?"*

"It's me." She realized he couldn't see her properly because of the spell of invisibility. *"I'm using magic."* Then she felt embarrassed at stating the obvious.

"Can you help?"

"I must!" She entered its mind, distressed out at how

such a stupid machine could kill so many. She turned off its weapon systems, and then communicated the same to the other fighter.

"Destroy it! I'll take this one."

Dragons attacked the other fighter. Turning her attention to the fighter beneath her, she looked inside via the ship's computers and saw the humans desperately trying to regain control of their weapons, but before they could do anything, she told the outer doors to open, sucking the air and life from inside. Minutes later, the other fighter had exploded, while this one was a listless metal hulk, devoid of life, drifting silently in space.

19

Lucy's magic flared—she no longer cared whether the Hag heard. She was drowning, and Chloris was semi-conscious. Despite the pain and pressure, she pushed the bubble of air around them outwards, forcing the water back. Chloris opened her eyes. "Thank you, Bright One," she gasped.

"I'll keep this sphere of air around us as long as I can." She was surprised at how much energy something so simple took.

"Can you add heat?"

"I'll try," Lucy said. This was the first time she'd ever heard Chloris complain about the cold, but she was right, the river was frigid. She'd forgotten because the Fire burnt inside her. The river was fast, and she needed to protect against rocks, too. A journey of hours felt like days, but Lucy knew it was less than two hours since she'd been foolish enough to step into the river.

Doubts about her intuition beset her as the dark current swirled and dragged them down, deeper into the planet. She was not surprised that she'd found no life here bigger than the mould clinging to stones. She desperately needed a rest from pushing them away from sharp rocks and maintaining the bubble of air around them. She had no energy to speak.

Suddenly, they hit rocks, despite her best attempts to keep them away. *"I don't understand,"* Lucy whispered. With her eyes tightly closed, she reached out with her mind. *"The pressure has gone."*

"Here," Chloris said. The ice demon lifted her out of the water.

"Are we there?" she asked, feeling like a five-year-old asking a parent on a long journey. She noticed that the water had stopped splashing onto her face.

Chloris sputtered water out, perhaps in an attempted laugh. "Open your eyes and look."

Lucy didn't really want to, but she knew she was no longer in the river, despite its loud roar around her. She opened her eyes to a depressing darkness, but then, through her inner sight, she saw her surroundings.

They sat on a narrow shore deep underground—the river rushed past her feet. "I feel like sleeping for a week."

"Not here," Chloris said.

"I'm joking," she said aloud, but she knew she wasn't. She didn't even mention the food they didn't have. "At least we have lots of water to drink."

"They may follow us," Chloris said.

Lucy shivered, not only from the cold. "The Hag won't swim this river, and her nanobots couldn't take it either."

"The Dark Moon could," Chloris said. "Especially if they've had time to prepare a device to hold onto."

"We might have a day's start on them."

"Perhaps."

Lucy bent over and screamed as the pain from having used the magic worsened. She vomited on the shore.

"Use magic," Chloris said.

"Magic to stop the pain of magic. That'll make it worse later." She retched again, but there was little left in her stomach. Despite what she said, she allowed a low level of magic to vibrate through her body, reducing the immediate pain a little.

"The curse of dragons," Chloris said. "They tricked you into taking the Fire."

Lucy had no answer. She had no idea of the true role of dragons. She'd only encountered one.

"They're using you to raise the magic."

She wondered how the magic of the Fire could help the dragons. She'd always imagined them as powerful creatures ruling the mountains and skies as the rocs ruled the forests. But despite her time outside the human colony, she still only knew a small part of the giant forest planet.

"I'm ready." She stood, cringing in pain. Chloris looked at her. "I'm fine." Her friend lifted her and, holding her firmly, leapt back into the river. The pain lessened when she used her magic to create another bubble of air around them, but this time the journey was smoother. They'd stopped descending and had no more of those terrible whirlpools sucking them down endless tight tunnels. In some places there were two or three feet of air above the river, and they floated more peacefully.

"You know the Night Hag will've heard my magic," Lucy said.

"It's done. We have to move on," Chloris said.

"Do you think the Dark Moon's hunting us?"

"Perhaps. They may swim the river, but they may travel with her, too."

The journey continued for hours; at least Lucy had the opportunity to feel bored, and even her magical hangover was tolerable. She started drowsing, pleased that the tunnel ceiling was now about four feet above her head.

"Lucy?"

"What?"

"Use your magic; we need protection."

"What do you mean?" Lucy asked.

"We're about to leave the mountain."

"That's good."

Lucy screamed as she flew out of the mouth of the tunnel. Hundreds of feet below was a river flowing through deep forest. Cold wind rushed around her, and she called her magic, creating a magical sphere that pulled them closer together.

"You took your time," Chloris hissed.

"Sorry." By the time they were halfway down, she was completely awake. She studied the wide valley. "The ancient forest is beyond the ridge." She pointed to a distant range of mountains.

"How do you know?" Chloris asked. "There's forest everywhere."

"It feels different." She now understood what Aina had said about the difference between the ancient forest and rest of the forest. "When we get close enough, you'll see that it looks different, too."

"How?"

"The shapes of the trees are unique."

As they rushed towards the river, she noticed pink shapes by the shore. Then they hit the river, and the weight of water falling on them pushed down, but her sphere of magic rolled away from it, rising quickly to the surface.

"There," Chloris said.

"We can run," Lucy said, almost immediately regretting it when the ice demon sprinted within the spinning sphere, sending her sprawling to the bottom. As they reached the shore, she let go of the magic, and it evaporated, along with most of her energy. Chloris helped her wade ashore.

The beach was narrow, and at the top was thick forest. Pink shapes watched them from the trees, but Lucy only wanted to rest, and lying on the damp grey sand of the beach, she closed her eyes. Chloris hissed, which she knew meant that something was approaching. Pushing away thoughts of sleep, she rolled over and saw scores of deep pink birds moving towards them. She sat up quickly. Chloris was ready to fight.

"No," Lucy said to Chloris.

The birds were about four feet tall. Some of them stretched their necks a further two feet into the air to see her better; others kept their necks curled up, making their large heads look as if they grew directly out of their feathered bodies.

"They're too close," Chloris hissed.

Lucy ignored her friend's bad mood. *"Hello."* She staggered to her feet, grasping hold of Chloris, partly for balance, and partly to stop her from doing anything stupid.

A chorus of hellos greeted her, and she knew the creatures meant no harm. But Chloris jumped towards them, and several rose into the air, looking like flames. One of them sent a blast of fire onto Chloris's head. The ice demon snapped quickly, but the bird was faster.

"Stop!" she shouted aloud and in the True Language. The birds slowly sank to the ground. Many whistled at Chloris. Lucy pushed past her and walked towards the nearest birds. *"She was just trying to protect me. She didn't mean any harm."*

"Cook it," one said.

"That won't be necessary," Lucy quickly replied. *"I like her exactly as she is."*

"*Strange taste,*" a bird said. Some of the pink birds spoke or sang in a tinkling song.

"Can you give me directions to the ancient forest?" Lucy asked.

The bird shared a mental image of the mountains opposite. "*I know, but I need a fast way to get there. Something is following me.*"

"*Can you fly?*"

"*Only off mountains.*"

She heard musical laughter. "*We saw you fly down, but if you can't fly up, then you must travel through the forest. It's dangerous. And you are only two.*"

Lucy reluctantly admitted the truth of that. "*What are you?*"

"*Rising flames.*"

"*A beautiful name.*" She mollified the pink birds slightly, and again they pushed towards her; she quickly sent a secret message, deep in the True Language, telling Chloris to take a bath.

The most aggressive of the birds laughed. "*How did you learn to speak the True Language like that? Even some rising flames wouldn't hear you.*"

"*I once spent time with the rocs; they were good teachers.*"

Now she had the attention of the whole flock, and again she asked about ways to the ancient forest.

"*There's danger.*"

"*I can speak to all the species of the forest, including the trees and plants. I'll just have to avoid the basilisks,*" Lucy said. Some of the rising flames clicked in disgust at the name of the serpent people.

"*You misunderstand,*" the bird said.

"*What then?*"

"Humans have invaded our world; otherwise, we wouldn't come so close to these mountains."

Lucy's heart sank. *"How many?"*

"Ten thousand or more. And they bring machines."

"Where are they?"

She saw the river. The soldiers had advanced into the forest for about two miles on either side, creating a barrier that prevented her from reaching the mountains on the far side of the valley.

She turned to Chloris. "I have an idea. I'll explain as we run."

20

"Your plan's like sticking a branch into a hornets' nest," Chloris said.

"I knew you'd approve." Lucy grinned at the impassive demon, then she returned her gaze to the forest. When the distant mynah birds imitated the sounds of engines, she glanced at Chloris.

"Taking the cutters will be easy," Chloris said. "Crossing the river unnoticed and then losing any pursuers will be harder."

"I wish I knew this forest better," Lucy said. "It could make it easier to lose them."

Chloris turned her large head towards Lucy. "It seems to speak to you. Why don't you ask it?" She spat acid on a snapping vine that snapped too close. "A few diversions would help."

"The plants here respond to me, but in the ancient forest, the forest itself speaks to me. I'm a part of it. This is newer forest; it's not developed the same awareness." Resting her hands on the trunk of the nearest tree, she asked her question, but the answer was a blur of images.

"Is the ancient forest really so different?" Chloris asked.

Lucy looked around the exotic forest of glowing fruits and flowers, but she knew that although they looked similar, the feeling was different. "The ancient forest is awake." She wasn't sure that even Chloris could understand this. "It's aware of what happens inside it, and it sometimes intervenes in events taking place within it."

"It's intelligent?"

"It's sentient." She wasn't really sure how intelligent it was. It was so different from other forms of intelligence she'd encountered. It seemed like a communal intelligence of trees, plants, and possibly other life forms. Now she understood how Aina had seen the wild forest as a refuge and protection against the hostile Empire.

She looked up at the sound of the approaching machines. A pair of cutters—flying imperial motorbikes—raced through the forest a hundred yards ahead of them.

"Bring them closer," Chloris said.

Lucy disliked using her power this way, but there was need. Focussing her thoughts on the lead rider, she silently called him. Unless he was unusual, he would consciously hear nothing, but his unconscious mind would be drawn to the trees beneath Chloris, who had just crawled along a branch.

The greens and greys of Chloris's uniform camouflaged her well. Lucy hid behind a tree as a rider turned towards them. There was little more she could do without using the painful Fire. She heard Chloris drop onto the cutter and saw a flash of grey as the flying bike flew past her and into the trees. When it re-emerged, the imperial rider was gone, and Chloris rode with a sub-machine gun in one hand.

"We must get the other," Chloris said.

The other rider would be attempting to contact his

colleague via his tag, and all responses, or lack of, would be recorded by Imperial Security. "I'll call him." Killing like this felt dirty—and she knew that both Chloris and Thomas would agree that it was. The cutter approached more slowly, and Chloris accelerated towards it, shooting the rider before he saw her. She span her cutter round and caught the other machine, forcing it to the ground. Minutes later, Lucy was riding through the forest behind Chloris. She'd already accessed the cutter's computer, which was now blocking all communications with the soldiers' base.

Chloris had insisted she carry one of the sub-machine guns, despite the cutter having inbuilt guns. They reached the river too soon for her liking and were soon flying low over the grey water towards the distant forest on the other side. Even at the speed they were flying, Chloris estimated that it might take twenty minutes to reach the far shore. Her estimate was good, and Lucy was relieved not to see an imperial welcoming party.

"We might not have been noticed," Lucy said.

"They're waiting for us," Chloris said. Lucy's stomach sank as she saw the cutters rising from the trees. They surrounded them, and one of the riders pointed to a clearing. Chloris followed, and Lucy, unable to think of doing anything else, followed her.

"Who are you?" a corporal asked.

"Imperial scouts," Lucy said.

The man examined her clothes. "You don't look like an imperial scout." He shouted at a soldier, who approached carrying a small device—one with which Lucy was familiar. He scanned her.

"Untagged."

"Impossible."

"Imperial Intelligence," Lucy said. She knew Chloris was

choosing her moment to kill the men, but there were ten of them, and all were armed.

"Stun them with magic. I'll finish them," Chloris said.

Lucy had used vibrations within people's minds and bodies before, and now she had greater power. *"I'll stun them, and then we'll escape. No more."*

Chloris hissed a reluctant agreement.

But Lucy was sure that these men should be allowed to live. They were merely servants of the Empire and had no need to die today.

"We have no record of any imperial spy with permission to cross the river at this point. Wait here." The corporal clapped his hands, and a swarm of nanobots rushed from the trees. Lucy sent out a short shock wave of magic, and with a sharp crack, the entire swarm fell to the forest floor.

"Good," Chloris said. *"And the men."*

She tried to remember how exactly she'd done this before. A different frequency, she thought.

"What happened?" The corporal studied the tiny, immobile nanobots. "That was a new batch. They'd just reproduced."

Lucy experimented with different frequencies of magic, feeling the beginning of magical nausea. Chloris glanced at her.

The corporal left the nanobots where they lay and walked towards her.

The man stiffened, as if listening—she knew he was. Lucy inwardly groaned as the men pointed their weapons at them again. This had happened to her before—information was downloading into their tags.

"You're under arrest," the corporal said.

Finding the frequency to shock men, she vibrated her breath and felt a bubble of magical energy expand within her. The man's eyes widened, but it was too late. She blew the bubble outwards. At first it crackled while the men held their ears. When the corporal pointed his gun at her, she quickly expanded the bubble until it silently exploded, sending a shock wave through the camp. All the men fell to the ground, and Lucy collapsed with them, feeling completely drained of energy.

Chloris helped her to her feet, and she staggered back to the cutters. "That was well done," Chloris said. "Are you all right?"

"Yes," she lied. She was shaking. Chloris passed her water, and drinking it made her feel a little better.

"The curse of the dragons." Chloris repeated her regular condemnation of the creatures.

Lucy sat astride the cutter, feeling better when the engine roared to life. They left the unconscious soldiers on the forest floor and rode fast through the trees, and as the air rushed against her face, her feelings of nausea lessened.

Seeming to sense when she was ready to talk, Chloris spoke. "The Night Hag will already know where we are. She'll be flying here now with the Dark Moon." They raced up the steep mountain forest towards the ridge. "They may already be waiting on the ridge. I must search for sentries first." The ice demon decelerated, flying more slowly through the trees. Then she stopped.

Chloris dismounted and ran up towards the ridge. She returned forty minutes later. "There are no more sentries."

"Let's hope half the imperial army isn't there," Lucy said.

Chloris cackled, spraying acidic spit on the forest floor. Lucy watched the leaves of a plant sizzle and disappear. "Don't exaggerate. There are no more than ninety soldiers, I think."

Lucy sighed. That felt like half the army to her.

"We have some advantages," Chloris said.

"For example?"

"Your magic."

Lucy inwardly groaned at the thought of the nausea and pain. "She has magic, too."

"Not like yours. And if she is there, we have a surprise: she thinks your magic is locked."

"Not if she saw what happened by the river with the nanobots."

"The Empire can see through a tagged mind, if it knows the one to look through. But there are many subjects, and memories can become distorted," Chloris said. Lucy was wondering how she knew this. They moved up closer to the ridge. The vegetation here was shorter. Once they moved over the ridge, they would be visible to anyone looking. "What can you sense?"

Lucy listened to the plants, and then to all life. She noticed several bright mynah birds watching her. She asked them about ice demons, and they showed her an image. "Your unit is further back, closer to the ancient forest."

"My ex-unit," Chloris stressed. "And the Hag?"

Lucy dreaded this. To probe for a sorcerer created a serious risk of exposing yourself. It took a lot of skill to hide from someone of the Night Hag's power. "I'm worried she'll see me."

Chloris left her cutter and crawled the remaining distance to the ridge. Lucy was concerned she'd make herself visible, but she merely placed her large nose on the rocks and sniffed. Minutes later she edged back down, being careful not to make a sound. "She's there. I'd never forget that smell."

Lucy had almost forgotten an ice demon's specially designed sense of smell. "Won't they smell us?"

Chloris's mouth widened into a grin. "The wind blows towards us."

Lucy pushed aside her annoyance at her lack of observation, and instead focussed on the kind of observation she was best at: she listened to the web of life stretching out around her. Feeling the oracle cards move in her pocket, she took them out. They itched in her hands, and she shuffled. The feeling to stop was sudden and strong. She turned over the card, and her heart sank.

"What?" Chloris asked, leaning closer.

They looked at the picture of the ancient forest as the trees swayed slowly in the wind; a swarm of insects flew from the forest, then rushed back inside.

"What does this mean?" Chloris asked.

Lucy quietened her and pointed at the two silver birds that flew towards the forest. "That's us."

Chloris hissed quietly, and Lucy sensed her displeasure. "Direct but difficult."

"Two more things." Lucy pointed at the swarm of insects that had re-emerged from the trees. "The first distraction."

"They may be distracted for a few seconds, if the insects are loud enough." Chloris's tail twitched. "It would help us get closer, but they'd shoot us in our backs as soon as we passed. And then there's the Hag."

"The second distraction." Lucy pointed to the right of the picture. Chloris stared without seeing, and Lucy flicked the card. A black bird turned its bright yellow eyes towards them. "A mynah bird."

"And?" Chloris hissed quietly, staring at the bird.

Lucy continued a little impatiently. "They can speak."

"All life speaks."

"No, I mean they can speak like humans. They can imitate sounds."

Chloris's neck frill flicked back for a second. "And there are mynah birds in the forest?"

"I've already spoken to them. They hate what's happening here and I think they'll help. Once the Hag and your old unit go to investigate, then we can follow the path of the silver birds." She motioned the direct path from the ridge to the ancient forest with her hand. "The place where your old unit waits has no soldiers. I think they'd be too frightened to get too close."

Chloris hissed her approval. "The Dark Moon would kill them, and the Hag would just laugh. But what if they don't go to investigate the noise? What if they send soldiers instead?"

"We can wait here. If they don't move, then we'll have to think of something else."

"It's good," Chloris said.

Lucy spoke to the ancient forest in the True Language, surprised by its fast response. She felt a pent-up hatred of the invaders pushing into its territory. In her mind's eye, she saw a swarm of tens of thousands of insects rush from the forest, buzzing and clicking loudly.

She felt Chloris touch her arm and gesture to the cutters. Still in the mind of the forest, she moved to her cutter and edged it towards the ridge. They stopped at the top, and Chloris waited for her signal. The soldiers' attention had turned to the forest. Lucy knew it made them nervous, but the ice demons were watching all directions. She couldn't see the Hag.

The forest moaned as the insects returned. Lucy then spoke to a pair of mynah birds. Their fierce yellow eyes watched her, and she wasn't sure they'd agree. But they appeared amused by the idea. She gave them words to say, warning them of the danger they faced, particularly from the Hag. They were much larger than the mynah birds she'd seen before, and highly opinionated. Like the forest, they hated the humans, and fiercely squawking, they argued about how to apply her idea.

"Fly fast if the witch approaches," Lucy said.

She heard a whisper of *"not scared"* in her mind. The birds of the ancient forest were tough, she thought. And proud. She opened her eyes and looked at Chloris. "Get ready."

Foul language came from the trees at the top of the ridge, about thirty yards to their right. Chloris sniggered at the obscene insults directed at the Hag and Empire.

"I didn't teach them those words," Lucy said, feeling a little embarrassed. "They must have found them in a memory I shared."

"Those mynah birds speak the truth," Chloris said.

The three ice demons of the Dark Moon, all that was left of Chloris's old elite unit, were already moving towards the trees. The insults continued. Lucy hadn't realized her vocabulary was that colourful.

"What about the Hag?"

Lucy wasn't sure. The woman was hard to sense, and she still didn't want to search too hard. "I think she's with them."

"Good. Then we go."

Lucy nodded, and they edged closer still to the ridge. "Now!" she said, and their two grey cutters flew over the ridge and raced down the steep descent towards the line of soldiers and the ancient forest, which was about ninety yards beyond them. They raced over low shrubs and boulders. Some of the soldiers pointed at them. She now wished she used a spell of invisibility. It wouldn't make them invisible, not with the noise the cutters were making, but it would make their outlines harder to see and shoot.

"*Change direction,*" Chloris said in the True Language. It was too noisy to speak aloud.

"*Why?*" And then she saw the Night Hag standing alone, blocking the space before them. The woman sneered and pointed at Lucy. "*I can't run from this,*" she said, already feeling the pain that would come from her use of magic.

They accelerated, still moving towards the witch. "*You can't run from me,*" the Night Hag said, echoing Lucy's own thoughts. "*I control you, but the tricks with the bugs and birds were good. I should have locked your animal speech, too.*"

Lucy called her magic, feeling it rush from the Fire within the planet and through her body, making her cringe as the burning sensation filled her. The Hag's eyes widened, and Lucy imagined whips of energy striking the sorcerer, and each of these whips bound her, wrapping around her arms and legs. The Night Hag cried out and fell to the ground.

"*Kill her!*" Chloris shouted.

"*She's bound. If we attack, her magic will break free.*"

"*Then faster!*"

Lucy accelerated, hitting the Hag as she attempted to stand, sending her spinning to the ground a second time. Lucy and Chloris now flew fast towards the ancient forest. She cast a spell of invisibility around the pair of them, and when the soldiers fired, their shots went wide.

Behind them, screeches came from the returning ice demons. "*Come to me!*" Lucy called the forest, and it responded with a swarm of black flies, the biting type she most hated. But this time they flew past her and Chloris and dived onto the ice demons.

"*The effect will be limited,*" Chloris said. "*Our skin is too thick to feel, but our eyes are vulnerable. It'll slow them.*"

Lucy blinked. When the pain began, she almost hit a boulder.

"Slower," Chloris said. *"We've lost them."*

Lucy's body burnt, and she wanted to vomit. She'd seen the ice demon unit with her inner eye, their bodies covered in thousands of the fist-sized flies. But even such a sight didn't lessen her pain.

21

They stepped over the bodies of the sleeping people in the passage—so many in such a small place. Thomas knew he smelt, but the stench here made him feel ill. His Fire burnt low to cleanse himself.

"What is this place?" Aina asked.

He wasn't sure; they'd seen nothing like this before. At most, a few homeless people occupied some corners of the corridors on the edge of the cities. He'd asked some people, but they'd been incoherent, abusive, or silent.

"They're poor," Thomas said. That was clear, but not much else was. One man watched them, and Thomas tried again. "Why are you here?"

"For the Second Empire."

Thomas didn't understand. He'd heard the name before, but couldn't remember its significance. He got no more out of the man, and they continued, but now their progress was slow, and sometimes difficult. Some people didn't like them being there, and some people liked a girl being there too much, but the automatic rifle slung over Thomas's shoulder was a deterrent. However, eventually, they were forced to stop.

A makeshift barrier blocked the passage that led up to 19th. A rusty metal sign proclaimed the Second Empire. He clutched onto a piece of metal for support, now remembering the meaning.

Aina glanced at him. "Are you all right?"

Drawing more magic than he wanted, he nodded. It was like a drug, and he was addicted, despite what it did to him. He pulled at a long piece of plastic; it didn't move. Metals and other materials intertwined to make the barrier solid—rock walking into this was extremely dangerous. Some parts were electrified, too. It was their first obstacle since leaving 27th.

The homeless treated it as a part of their home. A woman was hanging clothes on it.

"You can walk through it, right?" Aina asked.

Thomas looked at the mixed materials: metals, plastics, wood, and broken glass. He could walk slowly, very slowly, burning impurities away as they moved. But they'd be vulnerable when they passed through it. "I'd rather not. My energy is not exactly high. It might be better to do this by hand." He'd allow himself a little magical help to loosen the pieces, that was all.

"What's the Second Empire?" Aina asked.

"One of the smaller criminal gangs, but in their territory, they're kings."

"And this is their territory."

"It looks like it," he said. "And it looks like they don't want poor people wandering into their space."

"If they're thieves, wouldn't they steal from these people?"

"And take what?"

She was quiet. "Can you dismantle it?"

He removed a linen bag that hung from the barrier and pulled on a piece of plastic piping. A woman yelled at him. He kept pulling, and she jumped up and hit him, then she screamed and stared at her hand. Thomas had hardly felt her touch him. She wasn't strong, but he should have felt something.

Aina challenged her, but Thomas rested his hand on her shoulder. "There's movement on the other side." They stepped back into the shadows while the woman reattached her bag to the plastic pipe.

"Before I try to dismantle anything, I'd like to know a little more." He glanced back at Aina. "Perhaps this is a good time to rest. This may take some time." She sat against the wall and glared at the woman opposite.

Placing his palms on the rock wall by the barrier, he listened to the vibrations of the rocks. The old passages connected to a system of underground caves, and all of them were occupied. Someone was getting closer. A man walked along the passage carrying a torch. He shone it into the barrier, and Thomas realized it didn't matter if he saw him, not with all the homeless there. The man sat on a box and began to mutter through his earphone. He listened to the man's complaints. It was clear that the Second Empire wouldn't be welcoming.

"Can we just walk through? I mean, once you open a way," Aina asked.

Thomas smiled as he imagined it. "They'll try to stop us. They're in charge of eight levels, and people who build walls to keep people out like having control."

"If we walk fast, they may not notice us."

He gave a short laugh, but the pain stopped him. "We can try. I doubt if the imperial police know about this place, or if they do, they look away. That gives us one advantage."

Aina looked at him. "Which is?"

"We can make a lot of noise, and nobody will come."

She grinned, but then looked serious. "That means they can, too. How many are there?"

He shrugged his shoulders. "One on this level, but I expect the other levels will have a lot more people."

She strained to see through the barrier. "You know there's only one man there, just by listening?"

"To the vibrations; I can feel life vibrating. With the upper levels, it's just a guess." He glanced at her, slightly surprised that she looked sceptical. The old Aina would have understood instinctively.

She looked at him accusingly. "Don't compare me to what I was. I've suffered and changed."

Whatever she was, she was perceptive. "But why don't you remember natural magic?" He couldn't see how she would forget something that had been so fundamental to her.

She shook her head. "I don't know. I've tried, but I can't feel it."

Controlling his irritation, which he knew concealed a deeper unease, he told her about his magic, hoping that by explaining he could reawaken something inside her. If it was inside her.

"There are two things. First, I can hear vibrations on the rocks when people move; that's the most basic level. Second, everything vibrates at its own rate. With natural magic, I can listen to those vibrations."

"I thought you had rock magic?"

"Rock magic is a specialism of earth magic, which is one type of natural magic. Lucy has another kind, and you used to blend several sorts." Aina was quiet, and Thomas guessed she was searching her memories. He prayed she'd remember something soon. The old Aina would be helping him; this Aina helped, in her own way, but not actively.

"I know, but I don't like it." The man on the other side was speaking on his earphone. He looked tough, but Thomas sensed his anxiety. When the man touched the barricade, Thomas touched his mind. The man's name was Jonny. It only took a few seconds to see what distressed him. He'd murdered his lover. Thomas just felt sad as he looked into her eyes the moment before she died. The man felt remorse, but mostly from fear. He'd dreamt of the sound of her feet coming for him every night since he'd murdered her.

"Thomas?" Aina asked.

"He's done bad things."

He touched the metal part of the barrier, ignoring the woman and her bags, and projected his mind again. He illuminated parts of the metal barricade, running harmless magic through it, and then he shaped the light into the form of a woman. The man gripped the other side of the barrier in fear as the apparition of his dead lover walked towards him. Then, Thomas caused materials in the barrier to expand and contract, creating sounds similar to footsteps.

"He's gone," Aina said. "What did you do to him?"

"I reminded him of something."

Thomas quickly pulled out pieces of the barricade, sending many of them flying into the passage behind him to the dismay of those whose home it was. He dismantled it faster than he'd anticipated. Twenty minutes later, they stepped through a crooked path into the Second Empire.

THE GREY PASSAGE of the Second Empire was dull compared to the homeless spaces, but it was just as dirty.

Aina wrinkled her nose at the remains of old food on the floor. "What's the plan?"

Thomas gave a short laugh. "We walk through their territory until we're stopped."

"What then?"

"I'll decide then."

She sighed. "I'd assumed you'd have a plan."

Thomas felt the jarring difference between the old Aina and one he'd have to get used to. The new Aina was passive; she depended on him in ways she never had before. "I'll use an invisibility spell. That means we must remain still if we meet anyone."

"Isn't there a moving invisibility spell?"

"It can work, sometimes. I may be able to disguise us as someone else. Let's see the sort of people we meet."

They walked to the end of the corridor, coming to a vertical shaft. "I'll go first," Thomas said. He climbed quickly, listening in the True Language as he ascended to the eighteenth level. Boxes were piled against the walls and shelves had been fitted above them. It was a storage area.

"What do you think's inside those boxes?" Aina asked when she'd climbed out of the shaft.

He pushed one; it was light. "Drugs, I'd guess. We know criminal gangs make money from them."

"But downloads can safely simulate the feelings of drugs."

"The downloaded feelings are regulated and safe; the drugs give excitement and danger." She raised an eyebrow. "The illegal stuff gives a bigger buzz."

The locations of shafts in the passages outside the cities were at irregular distances apart, and some weren't functional. The first vertical shaft they encountered was blocked. This level connected to natural caves, too. The first three they'd passed were full of boxes. At the fourth, a man walked out.

"Who are you?"

"I'm looking for Jonny," Thomas said, placing a small suggestion in his mind that they were new members.

"He's where he always is," the man said. Thomas nodded, and they walked quickly past him.

"That was easy," Aina said. "Where do you think Jonny always is?"

Thomas thought about the short time he'd spent inside the man's mind. "It probably has something to do with food." They walked quickly along the passage and met two more men—each time, Thomas mentioned Jonny. He also placed the same suggestion in the men's mind. He was surprised how easy it was.

Their luck ran out on 17th. Three men surrounded them in a cave where workers were packaging drugs. "You're not one of us," a man said, despite Thomas's attempts to influence his mind. The man was stubborn. Their weapons were taken, apart from the black knife that had the habit of remaining unseen.

"We're looking for Jonny," Thomas repeated. The three men exchanged glances, and Thomas guessed their thoughts. "He's seen a ghost."

The man turned round. "Jonny!"

"What?"

"Come here."

Jonny appeared, looking confused. "What?"

"Do you know this pair?"

Suggestion was easier in the man's disturbed mind, but unpredictable, too. "I saw her," Thomas said. Again he imagined the image of the murdered lover and shared it with the man.

Jonny moaned. "I told you it was real," he said to the three men. "She's come for me."

"Come with me," the man said. "You, too, Jonny." He nodded to the other two who pointed guns at Thomas and Aina. "You can see the twins."

Unsure of his meaning, Thomas followed Jonny and the first man. Aina was right behind him. The two armed men were at the rear. They moved quickly through the rest of 17th, and then up to 16th, which was more workshops, except here they seemed to be making the drugs.

From glimpses of the men's thoughts, Thomas learnt that the twins ruled the Second Empire. The first man knocked on a metal door. A large man opened it. "What?"

"I've found intruders, and they're saying strange things. I think the twins need to hear."

The man looked at Thomas and Aina and then slammed the door shut. It seemed to be normal behaviour. Several seconds later, the door reopened. "In."

They walked into a well-lit cave. A tapestry hung from one of the walls, and old carpet covered most of the floor. Five men sat on old leather armchairs. Thomas felt a heaviness as he looked at them. He instinctively knew the bosses.

"The twins?" he asked.

One had dyed orange hair and a tattoo of a black spider in its web on his neck. The other man had softer, more rounded features; he almost looked jovial, except for his eyes.

"What have we here?" the jovial-looking one asked.

"We found them in the tunnels. They claim to have seen the ghost of Jonny's lover," the first man said.

The jovial twin laughed. "I doubt if her ghost has come for you yet, Jonny."

"I saw her on 19th."

"What did you see?" He turned to another man. "Check the barrier."

"Yes, Squire." The man left the room.

Thomas noticed the man's stick; it would make a good walking stick. With the increasing pain the Fire was bringing, he was beginning to need one. "Are you a squire in the Empire?"

"I'm called Squire. How did you get in?"

"We walked through the barrier," Thomas said.

"How could you do that?" the spider-tattooed twin asked.

"Pulled it apart and walked through."

"Pulled it apart and walked through," the man repeated. "Why enter the Second Empire?"

"We're just passing through."

"We decide who passes through."

"Why are you here?" Squire asked.

"We're tourists," Thomas said. A sudden jolt of pain almost made him double over, but he refused to show it. He felt as if something had changed inside him, and looking at his hands, he saw the hardening of his skin had spread to his wrists.

The jovial man laughed. "We can make you subjects of the Second Empire. How would you like that?"

"Not much," Thomas replied. He looked at Squire's stick. He could sense the metal blade inside.

The man turned to Aina. "And you? What do you say?"

"The same," Aina replied. "We're passing through."

The man shook his head. "We all know that can't be. And it would be such a waste. I think you should stay."

"For how long?" Aina asked.

"For as long as it pleases me. You might become my personal assistant for a few years; after that we have a workshop training scheme."

Thomas had heard enough. He'd noticed containers of gas in the corner; his Fire was rising in preparation, and with it came relief. The Fire eased the pain, but like a drug, it took larger doses each day.

"I don't like the look of him," Spider said.

Squire walked closer. "He's awfully scarred—not a pretty boy." The man laughed. "Perhaps too old to be useful." Thomas had already noticed the aging effects of the Fire. He called more, and soon felt its heat warming him.

The door opened, and one of the men returned. "The barrier's been breached. It's being fixed now. We've just thrown out some beggars."

"How could you pull apart our barrier?" Squire asked. "It would take more than the two of you, and she doesn't look like she'd be much use at the job." His smiles had gone. "Take them!"

Hands grabbed Thomas, and he released his Fire, burning the men who touched him. A single strike sent the man who held Aina somersaulting backwards. "We're leaving," Thomas said, taking the stick from the no longer jovial man.

The twins took out their gun, and with his mind Thomas reached for the gas containers, hoping to create a distraction. But Squire shot him. The bullet grazed his side, and the man aimed again. But the spike in pain caused a surge in his magic, and the gas container in the corner exploded. A small explosion, but enough to shock the men.

Thomas took Squire's gun and scooped another that had fallen to the ground. "Let's go," Thomas said to Aina.

"How did you do that?" Squire asked. The men still didn't want to let them go.

Thomas touched an armchair, and it caught fire. The thick black smoke coming from it seemed to change their minds.

Spreading his arms wide like a gracious host, Squire said, "We're happy to escort you out of the Second Empire. We didn't realize you were a man of importance." His eyes moved to the stick Thomas held. "But I request you return my stick."

"Then escort, but I need the stick to walk." It wasn't completely true, but it helped.

Squire nodded to two of the men who'd been in the room when they'd arrived, and then to Jonny. "Take them to 12th." Then he turned and began instructing the men to put out the fire. The three men walked ahead, leading them to what looked like a newer shaft. It was a long climb, but the ladder took them up two levels.

"Do you trust them?" Aina whispered.

He shook his head, then put his finger to his lips. He was listening in the True Language. The message coming through the men's earphones was clear: *"Take them to 12th and kill them. And get my stick back."*

"I understand," one of the men said aloud.

They followed the men up the final set of steps. Thomas wasn't surprised to see more men waiting for them. The twins were not taking any chances. Only half feigning pain, Thomas leant against a wall, his senses reaching into it. As he suspected, it led to the city.

"Get ready to rock walk," he whispered to Aina.

"A change of plan," the man said. The men drew their guns.

"You can have mine," Thomas said, carefully taking out

his guns and putting them on the floor. He needed a little time. "We can talk." As he spoke, he backed against the wall that separated the Second Empire to the first. Aina was by his side. He wanted to step through but didn't want the men to know where they'd gone.

"We have them," the man said on his earphone.

"Kill the man and bring the girl back," the voice said.

Thomas burst into flames, and the men moved back in shock. They lowered their weapons as they looked at each other. From within the Fire, Thomas felt comfortable. He vibrated the wall behind him, sending energy into the metal floor and then through the wall behind them. When it banged, the men jumped, quickly turning around.

Thomas took Aina's hand, and they stepped, unobserved, through the metal wall into 12th.

22

The owner of the restaurant started when he turned to see two people sitting at one of the two tables inside the tent he'd erected against the city wall.

"Sweet white wine." Thomas glanced at Aina. "Food?"

She nodded and looked at the menu written on the wall. "Artificial white meat—spiced."

"Me, too," Thomas said. The owner was about to speak, but then changed his mind. He soon returned with the wine.

Aina drank hers in one go. "I needed that." The man looked a little surprised, but quickly refilled her glass.

Thomas tensed, sensing wisps of magic nearby. It was nothing strong, but just as each food had a flavour, so did magic—and this one left a bad taste. Imperial agents, but they seemed to be moving away.

"I'm hungry," Aina said. "Did you know this was here?"

"Not before I touched the wall."

She touched the city wall. "To think that inches from our heads is a gang of vicious criminals."

Thomas listened. "They're arguing about what happened."

A little later, the man placed their dishes on the table. Food was fast in Nassopolis. When he left, she spoke. "We can take a train to Dnaskat, another to one of the Hanging Cities, and then fly to the Crown."

"Aina, we've discussed this already. We need to go to Silva and join the Resistance. I can help them."

"You told me the psychic woman said you should go to the tower."

"Adela? She said I met you at the black tower, but—"

She interrupted. "We have to go there."

He frowned. "Why?" He couldn't understand why she wanted this. It made no sense. In everything else she just followed him—sometimes too much.

Her brow furrowed. "If we want to stop the Empire, we must destroy its heart."

She was annoying him. The plan was dangerous and illogical. Aina had always taken chances, but they'd been ones that had a chance of success. "Aina, this doesn't make sense. What can two people do against the Imperial Order?"

"You have magic."

"Yes." He lowered his voice when he noticed the owner watching them. "But they do, too. And if the Emperor's there, then so will some of the Empire's most powerful sorcerers. I might be able to kill one, but not seven or eight of them." Thomas knew that even with the Fire, defeating the Emperor might not be possible.

He used his walking stick to help manoeuvre his legs to one side. The soles of his feet hurt, and his legs ached. He was feeling like an old man. "We can take a train to Naskopole Junction, and then take a series of shorter trips to Blue

Orchid." He didn't add that from there, they'd fly to Silva, not the Crown.

She gave a curt nod. Switching topics, he said, "Do you miss Silva?"

"Yes, but the people I know are dead. I'd be starting again."

"What about your grandfather and younger sister?" He remembered that they lived in the village on stilts—her childhood home.

She was quiet, and then shook her head. "I think my memory loss is worse than I thought."

He wasn't sure what to say to her, and he watched her continue to eat. He couldn't believe she wouldn't remember her own family, but perhaps her mind was still recovering from the trauma she'd gone through. But his mood improved a little when she described the neighbourhood he and Lucy had stayed in when they'd first arrived on Prometheus.

"I think my memory's returning. I remember more details now."

Thomas prayed this was true. By the time they'd finished their meal, the smell of magic had dissipated, and Thomas wanted to move. "Let's go."

Hours later they sat on a train as it ascended. As the train approached the stop beneath Naskopole Junction, Thomas had a feeling of something being wrong. Pushing on his stick, he sat up and looked out of the window. They were pulling into the station and would stop there for fifteen minutes while people boarded and alighted. That was more than enough time for them to be discovered. He looked for police, but even more he listened for magic. He heard something, but it was distant. Then he had a sudden realization. He shook Aina awake. "We're getting off!"

She became alert and looked out of the window. "We're not there yet."

"There's something wrong." She was reluctant to move, but when he stood and took his bag, she got up. "We can still travel to the Hanging Cities."

"But it's not convenient."

"I've had a premonition. Something's wrong."

"What?"

"If I knew, I'd tell you." He left the small cabin, and she followed several paces behind him. As soon as they'd left the train, his anxiety lessened. The station was busy, although not as big as Naskopole Junction, and it linked vertical and horizontal lines. He booked a train to the nearest hanging city, hardly noticing its name. Aina relaxed once he'd bought the tickets, but she still mentioned more than once that there were direct flights to the Crown. Thomas had already checked the flights via the disposable tag. Unlike the implants, this type either projected a screen into his eye or spoke into his ear; he chose the audio option. There were two weekly flights to Silva, which meant waiting for three days. A delay was dangerous, but travelling overland would take longer and had its own risks.

Hours later, their train stopped at the border of Dragon Orchid. This city hung several hundred yards beneath Blue Orchid, and like its spectacular twin, it had a burst of flower-like pods, each one the home to thousands of people. The Hanging Cities were semi-autonomous, at least in name, and there were border checks on entering.

"We're not going to the Crown," Thomas said. He'd had enough of her sulking. "It's death for us."

"Trust in your ability."

"I do," he said. "But there's trust and stupidity. I've overestimated my magic before, and I nearly died because of it. I'll fight the Empire, but I'll choose the time and place." The train was now moving through the tunnel connecting it to Dragon Orchid.

"You must to go to the Crown!" She was sweating, yet it wasn't that warm.

This was the strangest conversation he'd had with her. They'd disagreed before, but not over something like this. He shook his head. "Why must I go?"

"To kill the Emperor."

"I'd like to, but not like this. If I go there, I'd need friends or allies."

"You have me."

Thomas wasn't sure how to answer that. "Aina, I love you, but you're not the same as you used to be." She was glaring at him. "Your magic, for one. In the past, you were a fighter . . ." He stopped before finishing his sentence.

"I can help you fight." She looked at him earnestly, but not with the eyes of a fighter.

He felt sad. "They'd kill you before you could help."

"I'm still alive," she said.

"The people we've faced so far have just been an annoyance; facing master sorcerers is something else. Aina, they'd kill you with a flick of their fingers."

She took her bag and walked out of the cabin. Hoping time away from him would calm her down, he let her go. When the train pulled into the station, she still hadn't returned. He disembarked with the other passengers and looked for her on the platform. Then he saw her moving quickly towards him. She looked distraught.

When she'd caught up to him, she said, "Thomas, I'm being followed."

He saw the two men. They looked like Imperial Intelligence. It was the way they moved, their confidence as they pushed through the crowd. "What happened?"

"I don't know. Suddenly they were following me." The men had stopped and were looking at them.

A train on the opposite platform was about to return to the inner cities. Thomas took her hand and started walking. "Onto that one."

"But they might not have recognized us." She started to look back but Thomas squeezed her hand. They were suspicious; that was enough. He led her onto the train, and this time she didn't argue. "We're safe," she said as the doors closed.

He shook his head. "They've boarded the train."

"You didn't see them."

"I just know." He looked on the platform as the train pulled out of the station, but he couldn't see the men anymore. "Come." They walked quickly through the train, towards the front. That would give them a few minutes to think. The train would enter the mountain in about ten minutes and would arrive in the inner cities about twenty minutes after that. He knew that even if they weren't onboard, a welcoming committee would be waiting for them at the other end. They had to leave the train.

"Can't we hide?" Aina asked when they reached the front of the train.

He shook his head.

"But..."

The men walked into the far end of the carriage. "Into the toilet."

"I'd rather fight," Aina said. He locked the door behind

them. She was squashed up against him. "What are we doing here?" she asked. "It's better outside. How can you use your magic to defend us hiding in a toilet?"

Kicking the toilet lid shut, he stood on it, and calling Fire, he burnt the plastic coating from the ceiling. Aina was coughing, but he continued, throwing the melting plastic against the wall. A minute later, the bare metal roof was exposed.

"Give me your hand."

"Thomas, no. I hate this."

Someone was knocking on the door. "Quickly," he whispered. His left hand rested on the ceiling, which was already melting.

"It's dripping!" she whispered.

"I'll protect you from that. He put his arm around her, drawing her close and extending his protective bubble around her. As long as the imperial agents didn't shoot through the door, they'd be all right.

"Imperial Intelligence. Open the door!"

Thomas had calculated the thickness of the train roof— no more than a quarter of an inch of hard material, but it was metal, and that was his element. They were only minutes from the tunnel into the mountain, and he wanted to be through before then. Pushing his hand through the soft metal, he pulled them both up. His ever-present pain lessened with the magic, and by the time the imperial agents were using a key to open the door, they were already sitting on the roof of the train.

"Your legs."

She pulled them through, and Thomas rubbed his hands on the red-hot metal, using cooling magic to hide their escape. There was nothing he could do about the pieces of plastic that covered the toilet wall and floor. He felt the vibrations as the agents entered.

"Let's move," he said. The train was moving fast towards the tunnel, and only his magical attraction to the metal prevented them from flying to their deaths down the side of the mountain.

"Thomas!"

He didn't blame her for being frightened. Even when he'd known her before, this would have made her nervous. He was on edge, too. The next trick was something new.

"Get ready!"

"For what?" She looked at the mountain rushing towards them. "Thomas, no! Get down!"

He jumped, holding Aina tightly. If this didn't work, their bodies would be tumbling down the mountain in seconds. Reversing the magical attraction to the rocks, they slowed as they flew towards the mountain. The train beneath them rushed into the tunnel. Aina screamed as they flew into the mountain.

The rock softened around them, but Thomas kept moving, knowing the dangers of slowing down too much when inside rocks. He climbed up and out of the rocks, back onto the side of the mountain.

"I can't believe you did that," she gasped. When she saw the drop, she started shaking. Looking around, she said, "There are no places to grip."

"I can find places." He began to climb up the mountain.

"Thomas? Where are you going? The tunnel is down."

"That's where they'll be looking for us when they can't find us inside the train. We're climbing up to the next level."

"Outside?"

"It's faster." He moved steadily up the mountain, despite the constant rain.

When they'd been climbing for over an hour, Aina asked, "How long until we reach the next level?"

"We passed the first level about forty minutes ago, and the second twenty minutes ago."

"Where are we going?"

"Lower Dnaskat." It was the inner city he knew best. "We can go to a hanging city on the other side of the mountain, and fly from there." He felt her tense and expected her to say something, but she remained silent.

A ravine opened up before them, and Thomas followed a narrow path along the side. Moving was much faster here, despite the path only being three or four inches wide. When you stuck to rocks like a magnet, it became safe. The wind was less severe, too. He stopped and looked around. The view would have been incredible if they hadn't been inside the clouds. "We're almost there. We can walk through the cave and then through tunnels into the city.

"I can't see any caves," she said.

"Here."

"Thomas, no!"

Holding Aina firmly, he walked into the mountain, ignoring her stifled scream.

23

"*Humans are our enemy,*" Warth said.

Many whistled agreement. Her brother was now a member of the new Thunder after so many of the old ones had been killed, and although he hadn't taken part in the first battle, many dragons listened to him.

Night Sun turned his fiery eyes on the dragons, and as he spoke, smoke rose from his mouth. "*While dragonkind slept, I alone flew the skies, keeping watch and protecting our world.*" They listened out of respect, although some rumbled their discontent.

"*Dragonkind has slept a disturbed sleep since the last war. We were woken too early that time, and although we pushed the humans back, we paid a high price for it.*" Na listened intently. He spoke of things she didn't know.

"*We should be sleeping the great Promethean winter,*" Night Sun said. Na had wondered why it was so cold, and many of the Flights had spoken of a late spring. "*To awaken from such a deep sleep, we needed someone to take the Fire of Prometheus and raise it. While you slept, four beings descended to the inner sun and attempted to take the Dragon Fire.*"

"Dragons?" Willa asked.

"No."

Na sensed the collective surprise.

"What then?" The powerful young dragon of the Thunder whistled as she spoke.

"Three humans and a goblin," Night Sun said. The dragons bellowed and hissed. Na was also shocked.

"How could humans descend to the centre of the planet?" Spere asked.

"They were special."

More dragons rumbled, and Warth glared at the First of the Wisdom.

"One was a sorcerer of the dark path." Na's heart sank as the story worsened; she shuddered at the thought of such beings possessing the Fire.

"And the others?" Spere asked.

"Two humans from another universe."

"How?" Na asked, stunned into interrupting the older dragons. Some of the Thunder hissed at her interruption, but Night Sun spoke.

"As Daughter of Fire, she may speak at our meetings. And her question is good. They were brought into our world by the last of the ancient Mariners."

Such strange events, and Na struggled to make sense of them. All dragons knew of the Mariners, one of the oldest races in all universes, and ones that had helped dragonkind in the early days. *"So are these two humans good?"* She felt as if she were still in the Tangle when she asked her question and immediately burned with embarrassment.

"They're good. And we must seek their help," Night Sun said.

Na couldn't believe it. *"We're dragons,"* she said. Some hooted agreement. Dragons needed no help, especially not from humans. *"I thought only dragons could raise the Fire."*

"There have been two occasions when other species did so. Once a roc descended into the Fire."

She hadn't known that, but having a roc take the Fire was nowhere near as bad as having humans touch the sacred Fire.

"The situation is serious," Spere said. *"I presume they all succeeded."*

"All four survived the Fire, but only two of them bear the true Fire, yet they still need help in learning how to wield it. And it is on this I wish to speak. I propose that we find and help these humans."

"A goblin and a sorcerer of the dark path?" Spere asked. Na couldn't imagine any dragon doing such a thing.

"Fortunately, the Fire is held by the two humans from the stars."

Na breathed out a jet of fire in relief, almost burning Seth's behind. He turned and gave her one of his intense dark looks. *"Sorry,"* she whispered.

"These humans paid a heavy price." Na was hardly concerned about that, but she listened as Night Sun continued. *"The Fire Bearers are now in the process of raising the Fire, and changes have already taken place. But the process will not be completed until the two human Fire Bearers fully embrace the Fire."*

"What does that really mean?" Na asked.

"To tell you might influence the course of events. But you will play an important role. Na, you are their guide, and you'll help them embrace the Fire."

"Even if I don't know what I'm supposed to do?"

"When the time comes, you'll know."

"Will the old magic return?"

"That's my intention." Night Sun continued. *"I propose we search for and help these two humans."*

"Dragons don't need human help," Warth said. Many others trumpeted their agreement.

"We need all the help we can find," Night Sun said. *"There is one more thing that you need to know. The black tower is also a device designed to pull the souls from living creatures."* Many dragons hissed in disgust.

"I've heard rumours that the Emperor can personally do this," Spere said.

"He can pull a human soul from a man's body, but a dragon is too powerful; therefore, he built his dark tower. It's alive, and its purpose is to control the store of souls."

"What does he want them for?" Na asked.

"They extend his life and that of his followers, and they also power a large part of their black magic."

"Then we must destroy the tower," Spere said.

"Yes," Night Sun said. *"But to do that, we need the help of the Fire Bearers and their Fire."*

Apart from a low rumble from discontented dragons, there was silence. Smoke rose from Warth's mouth, and she noticed him glaring at her. She wondered what she'd done wrong.

"Consider my words," Night Sun said. *"We meet again at the new moon."* The meeting was over.

ATTITUDES HARDENED over the coming days. Only Night Sun wished to search for the two humans, and although he was First of the Wisdom, no dragon could force others to act against their will.

Na worked hard training psychic skills. Although all dragons had natural ability, and all were born fluent in the True Language, they needed help in some areas. It was through her tireless teaching that she found a way into the hearts of many dragons. She didn't know why her psychic skills were greater than others, but there were few other dragons with her talent. Only Night Sun bettered her, but not every time. He also worked tirelessly instructing a small group of dragons in the older magic. She was in that group along with Allie, Kaylie, and Seth.

Slowly, with a few other dragons, she helped develop a deeper ability in many dragons. She successfully taught a few how to enter the mind of the human machines. Night Sun insisted that this was their best chance of defeating the humans.

When she wasn't teaching or sleeping, Na flew alone into the forests, seeking intelligence on the movement of the humans. Often she saw their ships flying overhead as she watched, invisible from their eyes. Each time the dragons attacked human encampments, it only seemed to make it worse. Although they destroyed the camps, more came, like angry ants swarming over the forest. She realized that humans had far greater numbers than the dragons, and that even if they killed millions, millions more would come. The dragons numbered ten thousand and each loss was hard to replace.

The next morning she flew down into the forest. She was becoming more familiar with its smells and sounds, and she knew the creatures that lived there; she could even listen to the dreams of the ancient forest itself—dreams that were primal but full of energy.

Then the atmosphere changed, and she heard a scream. The ancient forest moaned in response. Flying low, she continued listening. A deep sense of unease passed through her. Something very bad had happened.

"Allie!"

Fire Rising

Na flew fast. Her sister was in great pain—burning and falling. Invisible tears formed within the double lenses of her eyes, blurring her vision, but she flew using her inner eye. She knew exactly where her sister was.

A large human spaceship flew in circles over the forest; beneath it lay the bodies of ten dragons. Dropping down, totally invisible to the humans and their machine, she flew to her sister, who lay twenty yards from the others. Na landed gently next to her. She still breathed.

"Allie!"

"Na, I knew you'd come."

Na listened with the True Language to her sister's body. The True Language could do many things, and it could sometimes be used to bring a dragon back to life, but when she saw the extent of the damage, she knew she could do nothing. Allie was dying.

"What happened?"

"We were flying over the forest, and a ship appeared. It attacked us, and we fought. It was only one ship." Allie was breathing heavily. "We fought hard. I did what you taught me, Na." Na heard her sister's pride and love for her and choked back her tears. "I entered the machine mind, but something inside it attacked me."

Na became very alert. "What?" She'd never been attacked inside the machine minds. Blocked, yes, but not attacked. "Do you mean it tried to stop you?"

"No. Na, it was alive." Allie was fading fast, and Na touched her head to her sister's body. "You must stop these invaders. Listen to Night Sun." Na's pain only increased. "Na, listen to me. Find allies. I don't care who. Find them. I was wrong." Na remembered her sister's opposition to finding allies, whether roc or human. "I love you, sister."

And then Allie was dead. Na bellowed the fire of pain

into the forest, unconcerned that the humans might hear. She felt the unfairness of life, but she was a dragon and could control her reaction. She already knew what that would be. Looking up at the dark shape of the spaceship above her, she silently rose. At first, nothing happened, then, as she flew closer, it attacked. But she flew on, dodging its fire, which she sensed before it was sent. Her golden body hit the metallic craft hard, sending vibrations through it. She knew the humans inside could feel her. She plunged into the machine mind, which was too open and easy. It was a trap, but she didn't care, diving deeper into its control systems and burning everything she encountered. The ship shook, and she felt its human captain command it higher; she countered the command, and it rocked in the air.

Then something attacked her, but she was ready, and even the black magic within the machine didn't surprise her. It made her angrier. A psychic hound within the machine's mind bit her, and she blasted it with fire, watching as its head and neck burnt. Barking, it attacked again, and again she burnt it, sending it back. It resisted her fire; however, the circuits of the computer did not, and the melting machine mind blocked the spirit hound's attacks. She changed her tactics, and instead of attacking the chained creature, she again attacked the metal mind itself. The ship was losing altitude, sinking into the ancient forest, but still she clung to the outside, attacking its mind repeatedly.

The ship crashed through the trees—burning fiercely. But still she refused to let go, and still she attacked. Only when it hit the ground was she knocked away. A door opened, and humans rushed out; she burnt them instantly, sending jets of fire into the heart of the ship until she was exhausted.

She crawled away from the burning ship, expecting more humans to come out. She would kill them, too, but none did. Na collapsed unconscious to the forest floor.

24

"Wake up!" It was Night Sun.

Na opened an eye but had no energy to speak. He pushed her with his mouth, but it was no good. She couldn't move—she just stared at the burnt remnants of the human ship.

It was three days before she could move, and young dragons from her Flight brought her food and water, which they blew into her mouth. Night Sun stayed with her for much of the time, and eventually she was strong enough to tell him her story.

"It's worse than I'd thought," he said. *"If the Empire is using its black magic on many of its ships, then we have a serious problem."*

"I destroyed it," she said weakly.

"Yes, you did. One of our most powerful dragons only just survived a fight with one spaceship." She wanted to laugh at being called powerful, but she lacked the energy, and only a puff of smoke emerged from her mouth. *"You're more than you think, young Na."* She liked the sound of his voice but felt too tired to reply. *"The chained spirit killed Allie, and she was*

one of our more promising students." Na felt empty. It was true, and she hadn't even killed the psychic hound, not directly. *"What if more ships have these things inside?"* The thought made her feel unwell; she knew the answer to that. The dragons were dead.

"Tomorrow, you can return to the mountains."

"I will avenge Allie."

Five days later, the dragons met for a war council. Night Sun landed, and the energy radiating from him caused the dragons to back away. He was magnificent, shining with magic. He looked at the Thunder directly; only Spere returned his gaze. *"We've lost too many."* Na had been shocked by the bombing of a mountain lake and the killing of a Tangle—thirty-six young dragons had been killed. All shared the shock. The dragons listened in dismay as he spoke of the black magic being employed by the Empire. *"We have the need to reawaken, not just our psychic skills, but the older magic."* All dragons listened carefully. Na wasn't even sure if this were possible. She'd felt the power in Night Sun, but he'd lived so long; he'd had time to learn. They lacked time.

"Despite your refusal to send dragons to the rocs, and despite your refusal to consider human allies, I still believe this is the best way."

"With respect," Bere said, *"we disagree."* Several dragons trumpeted.

"We're almost ready to attack the human army," Warth said.

The mood chilled when Night Sun interrupted. *"I'll send dragons to find the humans and rocs."*

"Who?" Warth asked.

"I ask Seth to fly into the ancient forest to seek an alliance with the rocs. The Daughter of Fire will find the humans."

Fire dropped from Na's mouth. She was shocked. All

dragons stared at her and Seth, but Warth's look was menacing.

"*Do you agree?*" Night Sun asked.

"*I agree,*" Seth said.

Agreeing to form an alliance with the rocs, whilst disapproved of by traditionalist dragons, was not the same as seeking human help, but Na thought about Allie's final words.

"*Na?*"

"*I agree.*"

Warth rumbled, and fire fell from his mouth, but it was the hatred in his eyes that shocked her. However, thinking of Allie gave her strength.

"*Thank you,*" Night Sun said softly. She was sure no other dragon heard.

The dragons left, ignoring them. Night Sun spoke in deep True Language—Na knew that only the three of them could hear. First he spoke to Seth. "*Our needs are severe. Find the rocs; form an alliance, if possible.*" He looked at Na. "*I want you to find the Fire Bearers. Find and learn about them. Later you'll need to help them.*"

Na felt sad and deflated and couldn't see the point of this, but neither could she refuse—not after what had happened to Allie. She lowered her head but felt like exploding in fire.

"*Any questions?*"

Protestations came quickly, but only one question. "*How will I know them?*"

"*You will know. You must trust your feelings. Now go.*"

Na and Seth rose into the air and flew towards the forest. They flew in silence for several minutes, the silver and golden dragon together. Then she spoke. "*Where will you look for the rocs?*"

"To the west. We once had contact with a large community of rocs almost two day's flight from the human colony."

"They might all be dead."

"The humans are not all powerful, Na. The rocs have had more skirmishes with humans than we have, and they've learnt about them. The rocs are tough birds."

She knew it was true.

"Where will you fly?"

She thought of what Night Sun had said. *"Where my heart takes me."*

And with that, the two dragons parted ways, with Na turning southwest, flying fast through the cloudy Promethean sky.

NA'S HEART took her deeper into the ancient forest. After hours of flying, she heard the sounds of human machines. She glided down to the trees, flying between their vast trunks. In the mid-levels of the forest there was little life compared to the forest floor, or the canopy above, and it was easier to fly here, too.

The sounds of machines were becoming more frequent, but they remained above the canopy of trees, and she knew their sensors would be confused by the energy field the ancient forest emitted. She doubted if the humans were fully aware of the energies it released—after all, they were spirit energies, the kind no machine could measure. As she listened to its energy, she noticed it lessen. Concerned, she spoke to the forest and relaxed at the simple visual answer —she was coming to the end of the ancient forest and the beginning of its child. The younger forest of the planet had not yet awoken, but given thousands of years, it, too, would become ancient forest.

The light changed, and Na slowed her wingbeat, landing on a wide branch at the edge of the forest. She was high in the mountains, and she looked up at the ridge—she knew that the younger forest grew on the far side of the ridge. Between the two, only low bushes and sparse vegetation grew. But there were human smells; the smell of metal machines made her tighten her nostrils, and she only just resisted the impulse to blow out a jet of fire. The imperial army was camped beneath the ridge, and they seemed to be waiting for something.

Feeling curious, Na waited, probing the minds of the humans in the camp. There were lizards, too. She disliked their smell more than that of the humans.

Then something probed her mind. She pulled away, but it tightened, like a hook tugging her towards the human camp. Instinctively, Na blew a jet of fire, not caring about the sound. The humans were too far away to hear anyway.

It vanished, and she breathed more easily. Taking more care than before, she studied the camp. Something in it was strongly psychic, and she remembered Night Sun's warning of black magic. She was annoyed that she hadn't seen the trap. In normal times, she and her siblings would have remained in the Tangle longer while they learnt such things. But these were not normal times.

25

Na was lost in thought when the ancient forest burst into life. Insects buzzed loudly, and she listened, now fully alert, sensing a huge movement of insects rushing to the forest's edge. She hopped to the next branch to see with her physical eyes, too. A swarm of a hundred thousand insects tore from the forest, twisting in the air as they flew, and then they hurtled back inside.

"Why are you doing this?" she asked the ancient forest, for she was sure it was the forest's intention.

She saw a vision of two silver birds flying over the camp and into the forest. They were strange mechanical birds. And the invaders were trying to kill them. Now very alert, Na watched carefully. The pack of lizards rushed through the camp.

Then a pair of silver objects flew from the ridge—they were the silver birds of her vision. She willed them to escape because anything the ancient forest helped with such intensity, and anything the invaders wanted to kill so badly, was something she wanted to live. Her heart dropped when she sensed the same sorcerer who'd touched her mind—the woman's dark magic opposed them, but a flash of bright magic overwhelmed her magic, and the silver birds rushed towards the forest. She'd already decided to follow.

Na had to fly fast as they weaved their way through the trees. They seemed to instinctively know where they were going, and the forest accepted them. Eventually, they stopped. Na recognized the silver birds as human machines—cutters. But she was taken aback to see a human and a reptile speaking to each other. The ancient forest whispered to the woman, and although Na tried, she couldn't hear their conversation, which also surprised her.

Again, they flew, and Na was embarrassed to admit to herself that she was beginning to tire. They moved deeply into the forest, and she was no longer concerned about pursuit from the other humans. The cutters dived into a green hole, and Na followed. She was flying into the deepest part of the ancient forest. The feeling was magical. The flowers were bigger and more vibrant than the ones she'd seen before. Even the black flowers shone brightly.

Scenes from a previous life came to Na; she'd seen places like this before. These were secret parts of the ancient forest. To enter without permission was death—even for dragons. But the forest not only called the woman, it called Na, too. Realizing the connection this human had with the forest, Na felt less embarrassed at her failed attempts to probe her mind. She'd never encountered such strong psychic skills in a human before—not even the sorcerer on the mountain had mastered the intricacies of the True Language as well. Na had never thought it possible. In some ways, this woman reminded her of a dragon.

She wanted to make contact, and perhaps now they seemed to be reaching their destination, she'd have the opportunity. However, she still had to deal with the reptile.

Her preference was to kill it, but it seemed to be the servant of the woman, possibly even a friend, although Na's mind rebelled at such a thought. Either way, killing the reptile would probably upset her. She'd have to find another approach.

The woman had sent the reptile into the forest, and she knelt in the middle of a clearing by a pile of lightstones. She seemed to be making a fire. But it didn't make sense; stones didn't burn. Moments later, the reptile returned with more stones, and soon the pile was several feet high. Golden magic rippled in waves around the woman, and Na watched in amazement. She now had no doubt that she'd found one of the Fire Bearers. The Dragon Fire burnt strongly within her, and the stones burst into bright red, blue, and orange flames.

LUCY FLEW through the dark forest, leading the way, seeing not with her eyes, but as a part of the mind of the forest. She felt its love, and a lessening of her pain. It had accepted her as one of its own, and as such, she felt no separation between herself and the rich web of life around her. The forest's senses became hers, and through her, the forest saw. She flew deeper, towards the forest's secret heart, instinctively knowing where she was going.

She stopped in a deep glade, and its flowers and fruits brightened for her, shining a welcome.

"Thank you."

The glade radiated energy—even the fungi glowed in pale blues and violets.

Turning to Chloris, she spoke. "Now we must find the rocs."

"Rocs have no love for me, and dragons for no one."

"You're my friend. The rocs will accept you for that." Lucy felt a momentary burst of affection from the ice demon.

"Do you know we're being followed?" Chloris asked several minutes later.

"I know," Lucy replied. She'd been listening to its movements in the True Language, trying to decide what it was. She knew it wasn't human, but also that the forest accepted it, for the forest was completely at rest. And it had considerable psychic skill. Lucy knew from experience that very few creatures could so effectively block her psychic probing.

"I can circle back."

"No, leave it." She doubted that Chloris would find it. "I think it's curious, but I sense no harm." She sensed magic, too.

Chloris spat on the ground, showing her unhappiness with the situation. "How can we find the rocs if we stay here?"

"A good question."

Again she connected with the energy of the ancient forest, and asking the same question, she waited, completely confident that she'd receive an answer.

A sound came from behind them, and Lucy smiled. "Chloris, leave it alone."

The ice demon reluctantly returned to her side. "We're taking a chance. Even if it's not an imperial spy, it could be dangerous."

"It's young and curious, and not an animal. It was surprised when I spoke to the forest."

"I didn't hear you."

"I know." She thought about the creature. Its psychic power was much greater than she'd thought, yet it was also young and a little clumsy. It'd concealed itself again. She turned her thoughts back to finding the rocs. And then a vision came to her. A stone fire burnt before her.

"This is a magical place." Chloris sniffed the air. "And dangerous. We should keep moving. We don't know what could be drawn by scent or magic."

"We must wait here. The forest is our ally in the fight." Then she thought of the practical problem of contacting the rocs. "Can you find lightstones?"

"Perhaps. I've seen some. Why?"

"I want to make a fire," Lucy said.

"Stones don't burn."

"Just find them."

She also searched for the stones, and half an hour later, they had a pile of the glowing stones. Lucy knelt by them and called the Fire. Perhaps it was the special nature of the place, but it came quickly, and the stones in front of her flared. Red, blue, and orange flames leapt several feet in the air, crackling with pure magic.

"Every magic user within hundreds of miles will see that," Chloris said.

Lucy shook her head. "It'll only be seen by those who are supposed to see it." She glanced at the forest. "And I think it's time to meet one of them. Keep still when she comes out. She may be nervous with you so close." Chloris's neck frills had expanded at the possible threat.

Lucy sensed its power and strong emotions, but also curiosity and passion. Touching her pocket, she found that the oracle cards were at rest, which was a good sign. Listening intently in the True Language, Lucy projected her mind towards the trees. Despite what she'd said to Chloris, she admitted to herself the possibility of trouble. It was only the second time she'd met a dragon.

"Hello, my name is Lucy." She waited but there was no reply. *"Join us."* There was still no answer, so she continued. *"I didn't know dragons hid in flowers."*

A golden dragon walked from the forest. *"It's called a tree. Flowers don't grow a thousand foot into the air."*

Lucy grinned. *"What's your name?"* Though she was unsure if the dragon would answer; she'd heard that they never revealed their names.

"You're right, we don't reveal our full names."

"You heard that?" Chloris's neck frills extended, and Lucy leant forward and slapped her leg. "Stop it," she whispered. The frills immediately settled.

The golden dragon sat next to her at the fire. Chloris sat opposite the dragon, who appeared not to notice the ice demon, which Lucy knew was a ruse.

"I'm Na," the dragon said. *"You bear the dragons' Fire."*

The dragon's attitude was irritating. *"It belongs to those who take it."*

"Yet it burns you," the dragon said.

Lucy looked at the scarring on her arms and hands. Her feet had the same darkening, but the marks were concealed by her boots. *"It hurts."*

"Because you're not a dragon. Yet you still took it," Na said.

"I had to take it." She felt annoyed with the black dragon, too. *"A black dragon pressured us to take the Fire. If it's the dragon's magic, why would he do that?"*

"Night Sun told me the story. The Fire you raise has awoken the dragons. We grow in strength."

"So the dragons used us?" Lucy said.

Na's eyes glowed red. *"You agreed to take the Fire before you were born. It was a sacrifice you accepted. Night Sun was right to tell you to take it. He was also right not to remind you of the danger. The Dragon Fire has woken us from hibernation. We rise against the invaders."*

Lucy's anger dissipated a little as she considered what the dragon had said. *"Someone else once said that to me,"* she said.

"The Mariner?" Na asked.

"How do you know?" Lucy now wondered how deep this young dragon could enter her mind.

"I'm not reading your mind. Night Sun told your story. But I wasn't sure of it until I met you. He sent me here to speak to you, and help if needed."

Lucy wondered why Night Sun had sent such a young and small dragon. *"Aren't you very young for a mission like this?"*

"I am what I am. I'm the Daughter of Fire. The First of the Wisdom sent me."

"Wisdom?"

"Night Sun."

Lucy sensed strong emotions within the golden dragon: both sadness and anger. *"I'm sorry for your loss."*

"You see a lot."

"I've also lost loved ones to the Empire."

Na nodded her understanding. *"Where's the other Fire Bearer?"*

"Thomas?" She'd searched for her friend but had found nothing. He was either far away, in trouble, or worse. *"He's taken another route. He's taking men to join the Silvan Resistance."*

Na curled her long tail around her body and sat on it. *"How will you use the Fire?"*

"We don't know," Lucy said. *"How should we use it?"*

"Night Sun said that you had to embrace the Fire, and that I was to help you do this, but he refused to say how."

"*Typical,*" Lucy said.

"*He did mention the true purpose of the tower.*"

"*Which is?*" She'd only thought of it as the imperial headquarters.

Na told Lucy about the device to catch souls.

Lucy remembered hearing before that the tower held human souls, and she remembered Mauricio's search for his lover, who he'd insisted was trapped in the stones of the tower. "*We need to destroy it.*"

"*All dragons agree on that. Shouldn't Thomas join us?*"

"*I hope he does. I'm not sure that the real fight is in Silva.*" She thought about Thomas. He'd set himself on a hard path in his search for a dead woman. She worried at what might happen when he finally realized she was dead.

"*What're you thinking?*" Na asked.

Lucy knew the dragon could sense her emotions as well as she could sense hers. "*My friend searches for a dead woman, and I think it can only bring tears.*"

"*Dragons know tears.*"

Lucy was a little surprised. "*Can dragons cry?*"

"*Hidden tears.*" Lucy wasn't sure what she meant. "*Human invaders killed my sister.*"

Lucy sat in silent sympathy until Na touched her hand. "*Show me.*" Lucy showed her scars. "*Beautiful,*" Na said.

That wasn't what Lucy had expected, but when she studied them, she recognized that for a dragon, the dark, hardened skin might look attractive.

"*Your feet are burnt, too.*"

It was more of a statement than a question, but Lucy nodded. "*I fear that Thomas will suffer more than me. He relies on his rock magic; I usually just talk to animals.*"

The dragon's expression changed, and her eyes held a faraway look.

"What?"

"An old memory."

"Do you have a spoken language?" Lucy asked.

"Dragons speak in the True Language."

Na had relaxed. Like ice demons, they seemed to spend much of their time in silence. She glanced at Chloris, who stood by the fire like a statue. For an ice demon, this behaviour was normal. Chloris sometimes stood still for several hours at a time. It unnerved most people, but Lucy was used to it. And she wasn't tricked—she knew that Chloris was aware of her surroundings at all times.

But unlike this young dragon, there were things that ice demons didn't notice, and the call of the ancient world was one. The sentient forest stirred, and Lucy looked up.

"The rocs are coming!"

26

After finding their way to lower Dnaskat and buying new clothes, Thomas found a cheap hotel and rented a room for three hours to get some rest. The noises from next door made clear the purpose of the hotel.

"I wondered why you chose this hotel?" Aina grinned at Thomas.

He shook his head. "I need sleep."

About twenty minutes later, when she walked out of the bathroom naked, he put aside ideas of sleep.

Hours later, Thomas felt a shove on his side. When he opened his eyes, Aina said, "We only have half an hour left." They dressed in their new clothes.

She leant forward and stared into his eyes. "We must challenge the Emperor while he's in the tower."

"Aina, not this again." He knew she was trying to wear him down so he'd just say yes, and it *was* wearing him down. But he had no intention of agreeing with her. "It's because the Emperor's there that it's the most dangerous place in the nine planets."

"Then they won't expect us," she said.

Thomas stepped back, surprised by her intensity. He was starting to question her sanity. "The tower itself is sentient—it will know when we approach." He hoped she didn't remember that he was able to disguise them from the tower.

"I just know we must go there."

"How do you know?"

"My intuition."

She'd shown few signs of her old intuitive abilities so far, and this seemed far from intuitive. More like suicide. "Aina, I'm tired of this. I'm not scared of death, but I see no point in looking for it. I'm going to Silva."

She got up and walked out of the door.

Thomas took his stick and stood to follow, but instead, he bent over double as shooting pain stabbed his body. This was the worst attack he'd had. Again, he felt that something wasn't quite right inside him. For the first time, Thomas suspected he might be dying. Walking to the mirror took almost a minute. Shocked, he stared. His eyes were scarlet, and his skin a reddish brown. He touched his face. His skin was thick, and his sense of feeling had gone.

Almost fainting, he staggered across the room. Then someone started banging on the door. The hotel clerk stared at him. "I'm keeping the room for the rest of the day." He had no idea how long that was, perhaps seven or eight hours.

"Pay."

Thomas slammed the door shut and fell on the bed. He put his hands to his head. They felt strange. Looking at them, his stomach sank even further. The skin had hardened, and his fingers were difficult to move. He could hardly make a fist. He knew the Fire would relieve the pain—even make him feel good. But at what cost?

Slowly, he ran his hands through his hair. He'd always

kept his hair short, but never this short. He rubbed harder, trying to feel his hair, and when he looked at his hands, a handful of hair dropped to the floor.

There was more banging on the door, and Thomas went to open it. The clerk and a man Thomas guessed was a manager stood there. Thomas roared at the two men—they left him alone. Again shutting the door, he thought about Aina's strange reactions. As much as he wished, he couldn't rid himself of doubts about her. He lay on the bed and replayed her death in his mind. He decided that he'd send his mind inside her body again—deeper. He'd been surprised by what he'd found the first time and hadn't looked as closely as he should have. This time, he'd search more carefully.

He woke, covered in sweat, and couldn't understand why he felt so hot. Then he noticed the banging on the door. He couldn't believe the persistence of the hotel staff. Sitting up, he took a long drink of water, and then he took hold of his walking stick. He stumbled to the door as someone started shouting. Leaning heavily on his stick, he opened the door. A police officer staggered into him; he'd been trying to break open the door. Thomas hit him, and the man lost consciousness. Three other police officers and the receptionist stared at him.

For a few seconds, it felt as if time stood still—then it started again. They drew weapons, and this time Thomas roared with magic, his previous resolution forgotten. Fire poured from him, and he slammed into the men. Two went straight down and didn't get up; the third raised his gun, which Thomas sidestepped and took from his hand, snapping several fingers as he did so. A sharp blow to the back of the man's head sent him to the floor. The terrified clerk backed away, but Thomas slapped him with a magical shock. The man fell to the floor unconscious.

Thomas looked at the prone men. None of these men had any reason to die. They'd wake up with sore heads, and he'd be far away. The disturbance apparently hadn't been noticed in any of the rented rooms. He climbed down the stairs with his magic burning inside him.

Kicking open the front doors of the cheap hotel, he stepped into scores of police guns—some of them secret police. Aina watched him from the back of a police vehicle. Even with his magic, this looked like death, but he was in such pain he hardly cared. He glanced at one of them. A young lord, Thomas guessed—the man had small magic.

"He's just killed four police officers," one of the police said.

"They're still breathing," Thomas said.

"Drop your weapons."

"I'm unarmed," Thomas said.

"The knife."

Thomas dropped his black knife. He still had the concealed blade inside the walking stick. Despite the pain, and the police holding him, he felt his power. No one here possessed what he did, but the guns limited his choices. He looked at the young lord. "Who are you?"

"Lord Keen," the man said. The name was appropriate; the man was excited over his arrest. But he was wary, too. He didn't come too close.

"How did you find me?"

The man grinned, glancing at Aina, but didn't say anything. Thomas stared at her, wondering how this could happen twice. The last time she'd wandered off, the police had found her, but that time she'd got away. She avoided his gaze.

"What now?" Thomas asked as they walked him to the vehicle. It was sturdy, but for Thomas it looked like another weapon he could use. He noted a man put his knife in the front of the vehicle. Thomas didn't care about other weapons, but the black obsidian knife was special. He felt it calling and knew that it would come to him on his call. Even the heavy metal walls of this vehicle wouldn't stop it coming to him. He couldn't say the same for any other weapons he'd possessed.

"I've orders to take you to the tower," Lord Keen said. The man was watching him closely for any reaction, but Thomas merely nodded. "You're a cool one."

Thomas shrugged.

The man looked a little surprised. "You're not afraid of death?"

For the first time, Thomas felt a little surprised when speaking to one of the nobles. "I've faced worse."

"I believe you," the man said as they sat inside the vehicle. Thomas's hands were bound by metal handcuffs, but metal was his friend and spoke to him—vibrating in the way that metals do.

"If you plan to kill me, you'd better do it soon."

"Why?" the lord asked.

"Because I'm going to escape."

Lord Keen laughed, and even one of the Imperial Intelligence officers smiled slightly. "I can see you're hard to kill." He leant forward and slapped a metal band around Thomas's wrist.

Thomas felt its energy and recognized it.

"A magical lock," Lord Keen said. "I can't have you using your magic on the way to the tower."

Thomas tested it with a simple spell of natural magic,

and the band became alive. The lord smiled and then spoke on his phone to someone. Thomas listened telephone conversation; the band around his wrists had no effect on his ability with the True Language. Lord Keen was speaking to someone called Lord Mono. The man's magic vibrated through the phone.

Turning to Aina, he noticed she wore no handcuffs. "What happened?"

"I don't know." Her eyes were red and pleading. She'd been crying. "I was walking along a street when they appeared." She looked into his eyes, waiting for a reply, but Thomas had nothing to say to her. "I didn't contact them! Thomas, believe me!"

He wanted to, and he couldn't detect any deceit, but circumstances were too much. He glanced at Lord Keen, who was grinning. "What?"

The imperial security officer nudged the noble, silencing him. It didn't matter. Thomas had seen the look in his eye. There was something between Aina and the Empire, even if she wasn't aware of it. He returned his attention to his magic. The band worked, to some extent. It blocked some of his natural magic, but it didn't completely block the rock magic that had now become a part of him. He could speak to the metal band and understand its language, even if it ignored him.

Next, he tested the Fire, and pain stabbed him, so he stopped. But the Fire was one of the most powerful sorts of magic he'd experienced. He guessed that if he was willing to experience pain, he could shatter this band into deadly splinters, even aiming some of them at the men opposite. In a sense, shattering the band would be like sawing off his wrist, but not as bad because he'd still be whole after. The thought, though, was not appealing, and he decided that rock magic was the best choice.

"What magic do you study?" Thomas asked. From the widening of Lord Keen's eyes, Thomas knew he'd touched on a subject of interest.

"I think you've experienced our magic enough times to know."

"Black magic."

"That's your word for it."

"What other word is there? It's magic that forces other life to work for it."

"Your orange witch friend does the same with animals."

Thomas hoped the reason he'd not named her was that she'd not been captured. "She asks permission first."

The man rolled his eyes. "You bind earth elementals and command them. I've read reports on you."

"I'm sure you have, but they may have lacked some detail." Thomas glanced out of the darkened window. They were passing through Old Dnaskat, driving along a street he knew.

"My stop," Thomas said. The lord laughed, and Thomas called his rock magic. He heard a squeal from the front of the vehicle as the obsidian knife answered his request.

"What?" Lord Keen asked. The intelligence officer turned to look, then jumped back as an orange shape burnt through the metal. "What's happening?" the lord repeated, becoming alarmed.

The dagger landed in Thomas's palm, and the metal band shattered. He sent the splinters into the men's legs, but one flew high, pinning a guard's arm to the seat. The engine responded to his request and died as they passed an alley.

"This is impossible," Lord Keen said as he pulled two metal splinters from below his knee.

"Sorry about that," Thomas said as he opened the door.

Already regretting his next magical hangover, he took Aina by her hand. He narrowed his eyes at her as he pulled her out of the car. "We need to talk."

27

They ran down the alley, and then another, until Thomas saw the place he was looking for. It'd changed its name to the Pleasure Palace.

"Thomas, I didn't go to them. Please believe me!"

A thickset man blocked the entrance. "I wish to enter," Thomas said.

"Wish all you want, but you're not going in."

Thomas glanced at his bloody clothes. The blood had splashed when he'd broken the band and sent shards into the men opposite. "Open the door." The man still didn't move. "I know the owners of this establishment. They'd want to see me."

"Who?"

"The Landlord and Nancy . . ." He struggled to remember her last name.

"They've gone."

It made no difference; Thomas had to enter. If he was forced to go to the Crown, he'd do it his way.

"They're coming," Aina whispered. "Forget this place, whatever it is."

Thomas reached for the door, and the bouncer took his arm. A sharp shock put the man on the ground. But the door was locked.

"Let's just go!" Aina said.

"We're going inside." Pushing his mind into the metal lock, Thomas felt its components. It was an old-fashioned lock, without any artificial intelligence. In some ways, these were harder to break, but a burst of magic moved the parts, and the door opened. Thomas closed the door, locking it behind him.

The opulent vestibule was as he remembered. A smooth, smiling man, dressed in an expensive suit, walked towards them. Thomas had seen his sort before—his hard eyes gave him away. He waited as the security man approached, taking the chance to study the layout more. The marble stairs that swept around and up to the plush lifts were as he remembered.

But in the centre of the vestibule was a gilded cage, set on a small pillar, about three foot high. Inside the cage was a hyena. Thomas recognized it immediately; it was the one Lucy had befriended. A man was taunting it with a stick.

"I don't like it here," Aina said, eyeing the space warily.

"There's nothing to like. It's just a place we have to pass through."

The security man stopped in front of them. "Can I help you?"

Thomas ignored him and walked to the hyena. The man followed closely. "Do you like animals?"

"Some," Thomas said, glancing at the man. From the sounds of the argument at the door, Thomas guessed he had only seconds before Imperial Security forced their way inside.

"Do you remember me?" Thomas asked the hyena in the

True Language, shoving the man with the stick aside. The hyena growled, and the man glared at Thomas.

"I wouldn't touch the bars if I were you," the security man said.

"You're not me." Thomas showed the hyena an image of Lucy, and the animal cocked his head to one side. He remembered her, even if he'd forgotten him. *"I can free you."*

The animal stared intently, and images came to his mind. Animals such as this had their own intelligence and could speak well at their level. The answer was clear, despite the dangers Thomas showed. The hyena barked.

The security man gripped his arm. He was stronger than he looked in his suit, as Thomas knew he would be, but so was Thomas. And he had magic, too. A push sent the man sliding across the vestibule on his backside. Again Thomas touched the cage door with a shock of magic, shattering the lock.

"Thomas?" Aina said. He grinned.

The hyena knocked the door open and jumped to the polished floor. It skidded as it turned to the taunting man, who backed away with his stick still in his hand. The stick fell to the floor as the hyena bit his neck.

"It'll kill him," Aina said.

Thomas touched the hyena's neck; it turned and nipped him—he'd surprised it. But his skin was hard, apart from any magic. The bite left no more than a graze. The hyena touched its nose to his arm—an apology of sorts. Pointing at the intelligence officers entering the club, Thomas spoke the True Language again.

"Hurt them."

Happy with the suggestion, the hyena charged the men. They'd not expected to be attacked by a wild animal, and they panicked.

The smooth-looking security man looked less smooth as he approached. He drew a gun, and Thomas threw his knife into his throat. Taking the pistol, he shot two of the officers dead; the others rushed for cover.

"Upstairs!" Thomas took Aina's hand and led her up the sweeping staircase.

The beautiful lift attendant looked at him in horror. He knew he looked shocking, not just the bloody clothes, but his blood-red eyes, and his scarred skin. As he stepped into the lift, he whistled, and the hyena bounded up the stairs in seconds, running into the lift. The lift attendant pressed herself against the wall, but the hyena did no more than growl.

"Top floor," Thomas said. The girl nodded, swiping her hand and pressing the button. The intelligence officers were coming out of hiding as the doors closed.

"This is dangerous," Aina said.

He laughed. Then he noticed her staring at the hyena. "Don't stare. Animals like this don't like it."

She looked away. "Won't they be waiting for us?"

"Yes." He didn't have time to explain. The Aina he'd known had never concerned herself with details like this. She'd just done whatever she'd had to.

The top floor was the brothel; the bedrooms were above. But it was the floors above the bedrooms that interested him. The private quarters of whatever criminal gang ran the place held the entrance to the dark passage through the mountain to the Crown. As the lift slowed, Thomas pressed his knife against the doors. He could already see the energy patterns of the four men waiting, their guns pointed at the doors. As they slid open, his knife flew through the gap, and before they'd opened more than three inches, he'd cut deeply into the wrists and arms of the waiting men. When the doors fully opened, the guns fell to the floor, and the knife slapped back into his palm.

The hyena charged, and the men backed off fast. He picked up the pistols.

"Do you need that many?" Aina asked.

"Probably not, but neither do they." He gave Aina two pistols and put the other two in his belt.

They walked through the large room, past naked boys and girls and many half-naked customers. Men watched them, but the guns and hyena seemed to deter them. Only one man blocked their way. He was standing in front of a second set of lifts—the ones that went to the bedrooms above. Thomas pressed his hand against the man's stomach, sending vibrating energy inside. Seconds later the large man was vomiting on the floor.

A woman in her forties rushed over, ignoring the hyena, and the pistol Thomas pointed at her. "You cannot go to the bedrooms," she said.

"I'm not going to the bedrooms."

She frowned. "Where then?"

"To the level above them."

Her eyes widened for a second. "You'll be killed."

He smiled, but she still blocked his way, and Thomas pressed his hand against her forehead. She screamed as the migraine started.

They stepped into the small lift. The hyena had to press against them. He looked quickly for inner guns, but this lift was unarmed, unlike the ones in the prison. Pressing the buttons achieved nothing, so instead, he pressed into its mind. Its ability to think was limited, and he had to burn through the security mechanisms, but there was no time to be careful. The lift would become unusable after their short trip.

"Do you remember any of this?" he asked Aina.

She shook her head. "Have I been here before?"

"Yes. This is where you single-handedly killed half a criminal gang."

She laughed, then stopped. "You're not joking, are you?"

He shook his head. He'd not had the time to figure out what had happened outside between her and Imperial Intelligence, and how much he could trust her. He didn't really want to think about it. As the lift slowed, he pushed against her body with his mind. This time he searched more coldly, and his stomach sank. She was much more machine than he'd thought, although she had human parts, too.

The hyena rushed through the open doors and ran towards the end of the passage. Thomas had already shown him the way. Leaning heavily on the walking stick, Thomas followed the animal along the silent passage, past the padded doors. They reached the metal door at the end of the passage. He touched it.

"Will it be open?" Aina asked.

"Doors are the least of my problems. I don't think there are locks I can't open." The pain was becoming overwhelming; he leant against the door, breathing heavily. Both the hyena and Aina watched him. He placed his palm against the door. It was locked; he didn't even have to try the handle. He had neither the time nor the inclination for finesse. He blasted it with magic, and with a sound like a gunshot, it opened.

"How many criminals do you think there'll be?" she asked.

"If we're lucky, none." But he expected a dozen.

"At least you have magic."

"Yes." And it throbbed. The pain was constant. Only when he called the magic was he allowed relief.

They kept walking up flights of stairs until they reached the top. Again, he used magic to open the door. A familiar corridor led to the meeting room, but it was empty. They walked through the long room where he, Aina, and Orange had killed the Gleemen. The next door led to the private quarters of the gang, and to the dark passage. He listened in the True Language. There were no vibrations—all was at rest in the room. Breathing a sigh of relief, he grinned. "Our luck's turned. It's empty."

He opened the door to the drawing room and stopped, suddenly feeling disoriented. His head jerked back as magic swept over him. He'd just made a huge mistake.

28

A flight of rocs landed breathing fire. Each of the birds radiated power, and each stood twice the height of a human.

"*Who called us?*" a bright red and orange feathered bird asked.

"*I did,*" Lucy said.

He looked down on her. "*A human, a dragon, and an ice demon inside the holy grove.*" Fire dripped from his beak.

"*She is the Fire Bearer,*" Na said.

Lucy felt them push into her mind. "*I'm a friend of Hwith and Pzillis Trillis.*" She knew that they were well known and respected. But these rocs were suspicious, and when they pressed harder, she called the Fire. Light poured from her, and she blazed brighter than the rocs. "*I call the rocs to a war council! The dragon and ice demon are my companions.*" Her message reached beyond the forest glade. The rocs breathed fire, speaking amongst themselves in their singing language. She knew they were uncertain of what to do.

"*I'm Sabden, Leader of High Eyrie. The names of the leader and huntress of Dragon Eyrie are well known.*"

"Dragon Eyrie?" Na said.

"From their special bond with the dragonflies of the forest." Na nodded her understanding.

Lucy wanted to ease their fears and suspicions, and she spoke directly to the forest. Many flowers already shone, but now even the sleepiest flowers and fruits brightened, and tiny faerie creatures tended the vegetation around her feet. Patches of mushrooms rose from the forest floor. All watched her in amazement.

"I invite the ancient forest to the meeting." Tiny faerie creatures were flitting from flower to flower.

"You speak to the Old Ones?" Na asked in wonder.

"They're part of the ancient forest, and yes, I speak to them."

More rocs from different eyries landed, and a circle formed around Lucy, who was now the centre of their attention. She'd charmed them, and many were asking her questions. Many were also chattering in their own language. Then she thought of Hwith and called him. This time she heard a distant response.

"We come. A silver dragon flies with us."

Na became alert.

"Sister," the silver dragon said.

Na blew a burst of fire in excitement before she controlled herself in front of the rocs. *"Seth."*

"We arrive soon."

The rocs arrived later with a silver dragon almost three times the size of Na. As Hwith landed, wind moved Lucy's hair. The silver dragon landed lightly next to Na.

"Hwith. It's good to see you."

"Always good to see you, Lucy."

"Lucy," Pzillis Trillis said. The huntress landed next to her, as did the green and blue Jzzrata and the beautiful Soonasa, the roc who had once sliced off the arm of an imperial lord who had threatened her life. Lucy greeted them all and introduced them to Sabden of High Eyrie.

They all noticed Chloris, and Lucy spoke quickly to avoid any misunderstandings. *"This is my friend, Chloris."* The ice demon stood close to her, her tail twitching, which told Lucy of her nervousness.

"An ice demon as a friend?" Jzzrata said.

"We have the habit of saving each others' lives."

"If you've saved the life of our friend, you're welcome in our forest," Hwith said to Chloris. Chloris nodded her appreciation, and her tail stopped twitching.

"The forest accepts her," Pzillis Trillis added. Lucy remembered, that of all rocs, this huntress was the most attuned to the ancient forest.

The rocs looked at the golden dragon. Na was nestled next to Seth, but she looked up when the rocs turned their attention on her. *"I am Na, Daughter of Fire. I come from the Eastern Rim at the request of Night Sun, First of the Wisdom."*

"You look very young," Jzzrata said.

Na blew a burst of fire in the direction of the green and blue roc.

"I fought on the Moon of Oberon, I've awakened the psychic skills of dragons, and I've come here in search of the Fire Bearers . . . and the rocs."

"I intended no offence," Jzzrata said.

"She's a skilled psychic," Lucy said.

"We already know," Hwith said. *"Welcome, Na. I've spoken to Night Sun many times. He mentioned you."* This seemed to placate Na.

"Who's this?" Lucy asked as the only roc she didn't know, a yellow and blue roc, approached.

"Magni—one of our leaders."

Lucy sensed that Hwith was a leader, too. He seemed to have grown in stature.

"I am."

"*You still have the habit of eavesdropping on my thoughts.*" His laughter echoed in her mind.

Several more flights of rocs arrived, and the rocs chattered amongst themselves in their songlike language while they waited for more to arrive. Hwith took the opportunity to speak to Seth.

An hour later, the grove in the ancient forest contained more than two hundred chattering rocs. *"Are they always this noisy?"* Na asked.

"Always," Lucy said. Something seemed familiar about this dragon, but Lucy couldn't place what. *"What are dragon communities like?"*

"More solitary, but we spend time with our brothers and sisters."

"What about your parents?"

"Dragons hatch into the Tangle. My first memory is swimming in Tangle Top. We never know our parents, but we can see our past lives."

Lucy was fascinated. *"Tell me about your past lives."*

The dragon appeared embarrassed. *"I'm an exception. No one knows why, but I have trouble remembering mine. Sometimes I catch glimpses."*

"I'm sorry." Then Lucy sensed movement from inside the forest. She wasn't the only one. Na had turned her head to look, and Pzillis Trillis and Hwith had lifted into the air, coming down by the edge of the trees.

"Chloris, come with me!" The stationary reptile moved quickly to her side.

"What?"

"I think there may be trouble." She sent her mind out deeper into the forest, touching the trees and plants. She was surprised by what she saw. Some of the rocs screeched, ready to fight. She spoke to the rocs and dragons. *"Let them approach."*

None of the rocs appeared happy when a troop of over a hundred silver basilisks walked and crawled from the forest, but the ancient forest itself remained calm. Pushing aside her personal dislike of the serpent people, she cleared her mind and listened to her intuition. She needed guidance with this species, the traditional enemy of rocs. They were led by a shaman. He walked on two legs, and his silver skin was tattooed, but unlike other basilisk shamans, this one's tattoos were simple natural scenes—not the ornate mythological scenes she'd previously seen.

The silver basilisks seemed surprised, except for the shaman and a party of legless females who slid along on their tails. She immediately sensed their importance in the troop. They appeared to be royalty, perhaps princesses, and looked at the rocs with scorn. They didn't understand their danger.

Several rocs blew fire, scorching some of the basilisk guards. *"Basilisks are not permitted in the ancient forest, and especially not in this grove,"* Magni said. Other rocs squawked loudly.

Lucy stepped forward, and raising her hand to the squawking rocs, she spoke. *"They've been called!,"* Suddenly the grove was quiet. She wondered why everyone was staring at her.

"You did speak loudly," Chloris whispered in her ear.

"Thank you, Bright One," the basilisk shaman said. *"I saw your Fire and answered."* Lucy wondered if this was a shaman king. She knew so little of basilisk society. Her only memory

of silver basilisks was another basilisk sorcerer using the term as an insult.

The shaman turned to address the gathered rocs. *"I am Sallow Loss, shaman of the silver basilisks of the Northern Mountains."*

"You're far from your home," Pzillis Trillis said.

"We were forced from our home by human invaders and other groups of basilisks. Many of us died, and we became separated from our queen. These are her daughters. The ancient forest called us and we entered." The rocs had quietened and were listening to the holy serpent. *"Silver basilisks live apart from the Basilisk Nation and are not involved in its wars. We glide our own way, but I come to pledge our help in the coming war."*

Lucy watched the young princesses as they slid closer. Glide was a more elegant way of putting it. She spoke. *"I welcome the silver basilisks."* The rocs and dragons accepted her words.

"We must talk of war," Hwith said.

Lucy, Chloris, the two dragons, a dozen senior rocs, and the basilisk shaman formed the inner circle of the meeting. Lucy turned to the princess who'd been standing still on her long tail, listening, while her sisters whispered by the trees. *"Come."* The silver basilisk slid forward and took her place next to the shaman.

"Where is the other Bright One?" the shaman asked.

"Thomas?" Lucy said. *"I don't know, and I've not been able to contact him. I left him deep underground."*

"Why didn't he come with you?"

"He wanted to take men to help the Silvan Resistance to fight the Empire."

"A small goal," Sabden said. Some of the rocs agreed.

Lucy was determined to express her true thoughts, and as she looked down at her scarred hands, she felt a rush of emotion. *"Night Sun visited him in visions and dreams and told him that Aina would return. Now he searches for a dead woman. It was a cruel lie. We would've raised the Fire anyway. Why the deception?"*

Na remained quiet, but fire trickled from Seth's mouth, dropping to the ground and burning the mushrooms of the forest floor. *"The Fire is needed, and the dragons had to awaken to defend our world,"* he said.

Lucy bristled. *"You admit to lying in order to achieve your aims?"*

"I do not," Seth said. *"Night Sun is the First of the Wisdom. He would never lie."*

"How can Aina be alive?" Lucy asked. *"The dead don't return fully formed."*

"All are reborn," Sallow Loss hissed.

"That's not the same," Lucy said.

"If Night Sun said this woman will return, then she will," Seth insisted.

Lucy felt the Fire rising within her as her body temperature rose. *"The Fire is changing me. I feel pain after using it."*

"You agreed to this before you were born," Seth said quietly. *"Yet all dragons thank you for the sacrifice."*

Lucy could hardly speak. *"Sacrifice?"*

Hwith flapped his bright wings. *"The story is still unfolding. It's hard to see the future from where we stand. Much may be revealed later."*

"We should focus on what we can achieve," Pzillis Trillis said.

The conversation continued. Pzillis Trillis and Magni wished to defend the forest; Hwith, Soonasa, Sabden, and the dragons argued for a direct attack. *"We have a unique chance to kill the leadership of the Empire in a single strike,"* Hwith said. *"Such an attack might turn the war in our favour."*

"We'll attack the tower," Seth said. "But keep clear of the weapon the Emperor created during the last war."

The rocs nodded and whistled. It was obvious they remembered very well.

"What weapon?" Sallow Loss asked.

"A burnt orange fire that rises from the top of the tower," Seth said. "It steals souls."

The two silver basilisks hissed their disgust.

"The tower is also protected by technology," Lucy said.

"We have magic," Seth said.

Lucy wasn't sure how true this was. If they did, it was different from hers. "But do you have technology?"

"We don't need it," Seth said.

"He's right," Na said. "We have other ways to master their technology."

"The rocs also have ways to deal with technology," Hwith said.

"I'll come with you," Lucy said.

"We cannot fly to the tower," the basilisk princess said, speaking for the first time. "But we'll defend our forest home with our lives." The shaman hissed his agreement. The meeting continued for some time as they discussed details.

Later, Lucy approached Sallow Loss. "You're different from other basilisks."

"As are you from other humans," the shaman said. "I would've liked to meet the other Bright One."

"Perhaps you will," Lucy said.

She watched the procession of silver basilisks reenter the forest, sure she'd never see them again. Leaving the chattering rocs and silver dragon, Lucy walked into the ancient forest. It lit up around her, lightening her spirits. Further ahead, Na sat in a smaller glade. The golden dragon didn't turn as Lucy pushed through the undergrowth close to her.

"Will you return with Seth?" she asked.

"I must. I can enter the minds of the machines better than any other dragon."

Lucy was reminded of Aina, and how she used to do the same. *"So it's not only pride when Seth claims not to need technology."*

Na blasted a patch of mushrooms with fire. *"Seth can be wise or stupid, depending on his mood. We can listen to and control human technology, but the skin of a dragon, although strong, is not the metal of a spaceship."*

Lucy sat on a fallen log next to Na's head and looked at her palms. They were almost the same colour as Na's scales, and the skin had toughened. *"You were right about the colour,"* Lucy said.

The dragon looked. *"You're part dragon, and should be respected as such whenever you meet another of our kind."*

"Will it spread?"

"I've watched it within you. Your natural magic makes no difference to it, but when you use our magic, you change."

"So you really believe the Fire belongs to the dragons?"

"Only dragons can use it safely."

"Then why didn't Night Sun take it himself?"

"He had to watch over the sleeping dragons and our eggs. He was the only one able to do that. If he'd left them unattended, the dragons would have vanished."

"Why did this happen?" Lucy asked. *"I mean, how did it become so bad?"*

Na was quiet for several seconds before replying. *"The first war was worse than we admit. It only brought us a rest from strife."*

They sat in silence for several minutes, before Na spoke again. *"Who is Aina?"*

"The woman Thomas loved. Who I loved," Lucy said. *"And a woman who was loved by the rocs, too. Night Sun saved her life when she was a child alone in the ancient forest, and he joined us at her funeral pyre the day her body was burnt."*

"Do you think Thomas will stand with you against the Empire?"

Lucy stomach churned at the thought of more loss. *"If he's alive, it's certain."*

"I'd like to meet him," Na said.

"You will," Lucy said, a little surprised by the dragon's words. *"We'll meet on the top of the mountain city."*

"We'll meet in battle," Na said softly.

29

A fire burnt in the fireplace, and a man leant against it. Others sat around a table; they turned to look at Thomas. He tried to focus. The pressure of magic stifled his, and he felt his contact with his magic fade. He was only vaguely aware when the hyena ran into the room, attacking the closest figures. Seconds later, it lay crumpled on the floor by the far wall—tossed by an ice demon.

Thomas blinked, trying to understand what he saw. Two ice demons, with red lightning tattooed onto their necks, stood in the shadows. Morgan Red, a mercenary of the Red Legion and a man partly responsible for Aina's death, leant against the fireplace, and two other members of the Red Legion stood by a wooden table.

At the head of the table, a woman wearing a hooded robe sat, watching him. He could only see her mouth as it curled into a smile. He wasn't sure of her age; she looked young—except for her eyes. Thomas had never experienced such powerful magic in another human—not even in Frore. Another wave of power came from her, disorienting him further.

Two other sorcerers sat at the table—imperial lords, a male and a female. He didn't like the look of either. They had power, but even combined it was less than half that of the woman seated at the head of the table. Another man sat watching him.

She stood and pulled back her hood. For a few seconds, Thomas felt a mental fog descend around him; he knew the woman was employing her magic, but he'd been taken too much by surprise to call the Fire. He tried to focus on the woman but couldn't. His pain was too great. The mercenaries disarmed him, throwing his knife and stick to the ground but keeping the guns. Still staring at the sorcerer, he blinked, unable to accept what he saw. Her robe hung open, and her short shirt exposed her belly. In its centre, a mouth moved, chanting spells that sickened him, and growing from her neck was a shrunken head. It twitched as it slept.

Belatedly, he reached for his magic, but the woman reacted with more magic of her own. He found himself on the floor. The pain of his magic combined with the attack of twisted energy left him struggling to breathe.

"Put him in a chair," she said.

One of the mercenaries lifted him, and another placed a chair against the wall, near the body of the hyena. Thomas noticed that it was breathing. He searched for Aina, and then saw her standing next to one of the mercenaries. Her mouth and nose were bleeding.

"She won't help you," the woman said.

"Who are you?" he asked, hardly stopping himself from vomiting.

"I am the Empress of the Nine Planets."

Thomas tried to comprehend what he heard, but the magic disoriented him. He searched the room for a way out, but there was none.

"My husband's busy right now. I've come to finish what he left unfinished."

The three faces of the woman stared at him. "You're hard to kill," she said. "Frore was convinced he'd killed you in the centre of the planet."

"What do you want?" Thomas asked.

"To kill you, of course. You have a habit of disturbing the order and stability of our society." She laughed. "We're a happy society, you know. But first I need to ask some questions." A mercenary tied him to his chair, and again he tried to call his magic, but the attempt brought only nausea.

"You can't do that with me," the Empress said. "You may match a middling magician of my order, but not the Emperor or myself.

Thomas knew she was playing with his mind, and he sealed off as much as he could, causing her to laugh again.

"I have time." The mercenary punched him, but his skin had hardened so much he hardly noticed. "This Fire you carry is interesting," the Empress said, "but it seems to be killing you. Frore doesn't have this side effect."

Thomas wasn't sure it was a side effect; it seemed to be the main effect. "Frore doesn't have the Fire."

The woman's mouth curled into a slight smile. "That's possible. I never noticed much difference after he returned."

Thomas spoke to the rocks. Three feet behind him, through solid rock, was a cave that led to the beginning of the dark passage.

"Sit the girl next to him," the Empress said. "It might be faster to work on her first." A mercenary dragged her across the room.

"What about magic?" the female sorcerer asked.

"I'm already using magic," she said coldly. "This is not

one of your everyday prisoners." The woman nodded, appearing uncomfortable.

As they sat Aina in a chair next to him, Thomas spoke to the rocks, hoping to find an ally like the elemental fire he'd once called when cornered by hellhounds in the mantle of the planet. Then he remembered the life in his pocket. The midnight blue crystals were awake and seemed unaffected by the magic in the room. Their energy soothed him, and he wished he'd spent more time working with them; he'd never explored their other qualities. As he spoke to the crystals, he felt increased clarity. The midnight blue was clearing his mind.

With clarity he saw the situation from a different perspective. The Empress was powerful; she was really three magicians combined. And the two sorcerers were strong, too. Individually, he could best either, perhaps both. But the Empress and the pair of sorcerers together were too much. He needed an ally, and he thought of the midnight blue.

The Empress nodded at Aina. "She's ours, you know." She turned her cold eyes to a mercenary. "Hit her."

Thomas inwardly winced as the mercenary punched her head. If they had created her body, was it possible that they'd created it from an almost dead Aina? Perhaps they'd really augmented her body, and the human parts were really the old Aina. "If she's yours, why this?"

The door of the room opened, and Lord Keen walked in with several intelligence officers. He stopped, and his mouth fell open as he took in the scene.

"Get out!" the Empress yelled.

The young lord was terrified. "I'm sorry, Your Imperial Highness. I had no idea."

"Out!"

An ice demon stepped towards Keen, who quickly back-stepped out of the room, shutting the door hard.

Thomas told the midnight blue to grow, which it did. And as it grew bigger inside his pocket, its soothing effects increased. It seemed to be sucking some of the pain from him.

The Empress returned her attention to Thomas. "We created her with one aim in mind: to bring you to us. You must have noticed her desire to take you to the Crown. But here is good enough." The woman laughed. "Don't tell me you really believed that woman of yours had returned from the dead?" Some of the others appeared amused.

"I don't know you," Aina said through her bloody mouth.

"Of course not. Tools don't know their makers."

Thomas realized that whatever Aina was, she was ignorant of the aims of the Empire. "She's not tagged."

"That would be too obvious; it would be one of the first things you'd check. But she has programming. Didn't you wonder what happened the times she disappeared?"

He'd wondered exactly that, but he didn't blame her. She'd been innocent, used by the Empire, as so many people had been.

"She's a marvel of engineering really," the Empress continued. "Part woman, part machine. Perfect in many ways. But disposable, too. Now, to business. Where's your female companion going?"

"Who?"

"You know who. The Orange Witch and the traitor demon." One of the ice demons hissed at the mention of Chloris.

Thomas felt a little better. Lucy and Chloris were alive, and they may have reached the rocs. The Empress stood close to him. She would have been good-looking if not for the shrunken head growing from her neck, the coldness in her eyes, and the fact she was an evil murderer.

The shrunken head on her neck woke up and screamed. Even the Empress appeared disturbed. "What, sister?"

But Thomas knew before she could telepathically communicate with her sleepy sister. The head had sensed the midnight blue as it absorbed the negative magic. He sent a blast of magic out, and the Empress fell to the floor with a cry. At least the head was now silent. His bonds fell away, and he prepared to rock walk.

"*Come!*" The obsidian knife flew through the thigh of an approaching ice demon, causing the creature to collapse into its colleague. The knife slapped into his palm, and he cut Aina's bonds. It didn't matter whether it was really Aina or not, he couldn't bear the thought of the Empress killing her.

The more powerful of the two sorcerers assisted the Empress. He seemed used to the role, and he soothed the shrunken head. The other sorcerer, a woman in her early twenties, attacked him with magic pressure that sent Aina and him sliding to the floor next to the half-conscious hyena.

Staggering to his feet and grabbing both Aina and the hyena, he surrounded them in a sphere of orange light. A further attack from the woman sent him back into the rock wall behind him. He used the energy and kept falling into the rock, pushing Aina through first. He felt her fall to the cave floor. Holding the hyena closer to his chest, he moved through the rock towards her, hesitating for a second when he heard the commotion in the room. The Empress was at the wall—all three heads were casting a spell. He pushed himself into the rock and pain stabbed him. He began to materialize inside the rock. Forcing himself forward, he slowly fell from the rocks into a cave, dropping the hyena to the ground. He lay on the ground, breathing heavily. The Empress had discovered a way to prevent him rock walking. Slowly, he stood and looked around the cave. A single light had turned on.

"Where are we?" Aina asked.

"Inside a treasure room."

As he led her deeper into the series of treasure rooms, he heard a key enter the door from the criminals' sitting rooms. "We don't have much time." He dreaded the next thing he had to do and prayed that the Empress had stopped her spell. "Here."

They were in the deepest of the rooms, and boxes lined the walls. Thomas pulled and tossed boxes away from the wall as men ran through the outer treasury towards them. Again, Thomas clutched Aina and the hyena and stepped into the rocks. The Empress's magic clawed at him, seeking to slow him down so much that he would materialize inside the rocks. He pushed harder, and his body was wracked by pain, only a little of which was absorbed by the midnight blue. He was grateful the rocks were only a few inches thick, remembering well when he'd watched Orange seal the passage from the treasury. He was shaking, and Aina touched him.

"You're bleeding."

He touched his face and stopped it. Then he sent a spark of magic into the hyena. The animal stood and shook itself.

"We must go!"

Thomas led the disoriented Aina and hyena along the dark passage.

30

"How can you find your way through the darkness?" she asked as Thomas helped her over a boulder.

"I feel life around me." He felt so connected to the mountain that he heard each vibration, from drops of water to insects crawling over the rocks.

She clung to him as they walked, and it slowed him down, but there was no choice. He vaguely wondered whether this was an intentional ploy the Empire had programmed into her, but he rejected the thought; at least, he didn't want to believe it.

The hyena was disoriented and hungry. It was dangerous, and Thomas didn't trust it, but he knew it hated their pursuers intensely—he was surprised by the depth of the animal's emotion. He was aware that the Empress, if she followed, might try to turn it, but he didn't think that would be so easy. It was a stubborn animal, and not prone to suggestion of any kind—although it had taken to heart his suggestion that it could hunt rats. It had already eaten one family.

They were in the dark passage he'd used once before,

and there were only two directions. He could return to the club in Lower Dnaskat, or he could climb to the Crown. They walked for hours, but the journey to the Crown would take about three days, and that was assuming he could find some way to help Aina walk faster through the tunnels. He regretted the loss of his walking stick; it would've been useful. He was silent as he walked, and she'd commented on it, but apart from sometimes needing quiet time, he also needed time to think over certain problems. Food and water were the most basic, staying ahead of the sorcerers was another. But for now, trust was most on his mind. How far could he trust Aina? He didn't believe she was aware of her duplicity, yet the Empress's words rang true.

Thomas sensed water along one of the tunnels ahead. It was an awkward climb up through very low passages that forced them to crawl on their bellies. When Thomas turned to pull the hyena through a particularly tight gap, it bit his hand. A shock of magic made it release its grip.

"Are you all right?" Aina asked.

"Fine," Thomas said. He pulled the hyena the rest of the way, and it stood and shook itself. He felt his hand, and for once, he was glad he couldn't see it. His skin was hard, and the bite had done no more than graze him. Even though the bite was from surprise, not anger, it should have hurt him more, but he wasn't even bleeding. He began to feel his arms, then stopped himself. He'd rather not know the changes the Fire was inflicting on him.

Water ran along the ground, and the hyena had already drunk its fill. As they got closer to the stream, the water became deeper. Although most of the stream flowed into another tunnel, enough of the water spilled over towards them.

"How close are you going to get?" Aina asked.

"Close enough to see if there are fish." He stopped by the stream, sitting and waiting. The hyena seemed content resting.

"Why didn't you detect the magic in the room?" Aina asked.

"I rushed. If I'd been more thorough, I might have heard something." He honestly wasn't sure; the Empress's ability to disguise herself and the others had been impressive.

"And the Emperor is the same?"

"From what I've heard, he's worse."

He sensed her seriousness in the darkness. "Thomas, I've changed my mind. I don't want to go to the Crown anymore. It's too dangerous."

"We don't have much choice. The passages go up or down, and it looks like we're being forced up."

The hyena whined. "What's it doing?" She moved closer to Thomas, nervous of the animal.

When Thomas tried to touch its mind, it barked at him. "I'm not sure." He listened for movement in the caves, but felt none. "I can't hear anything, but that doesn't mean there isn't anything here. We should start moving again."

They had to repeat their journey through the tight spaces before resuming their climb to the peak. He'd forgotten how hard the climb was, and by the end of the day, he was covered in sweat, with no chance to wash. The hyena found another rat, but they had to make do with water from the few pools they found on the way.

Thomas slept uneasily, and he woke up several times in the night. The fourth time he woke, Aina was staring into the darkness and the hyena was gone. The animal often wandered, so he didn't worry about that. "Can't sleep?"

She shook her head. "I don't like it here."

"Who does?" Although the truth was that he usually

enjoyed the feeling of the mountain, but not the ominous feeling that had settled on him recently. He had enough experience being stalked by magical entities that he thought it not a coincidence. "They're coming."

"Where are they?"

"Not very close. But the feeling you're getting is not just the darkness."

"Can they see us?"

"In a sense. We should go. There's no point sitting here waiting."

"What about the hyena?"

"It'll find us."

They carried nothing, apart from the obsidian knife in Thomas's belt. At least they needed no time to get ready. Seconds later they were climbing yet another of the dark passages. As he climbed, Thomas spoke to the hyena. The animal responded by sharing a familiar acrid scent.

He stopped.

"What?" Aina asked, bumping into him.

"Our hyena friend smells an ice demon." He listened to the rocks; the ascent was clear. "I want you to keep climbing until you reach a small cave. It has puddles inside. Wait there."

"Thomas! I don't want you to leave me."

"I'll be back soon."

He knew if he didn't return, she'd die in these tunnels, but if he didn't do something about their pursuers, the same would still be true. The hyena was about twenty feet beneath them; it was trapped near the bottom of a shaft, unable to climb. Now he was alone, he moved freely, and much faster. Making sure the hyena wasn't directly at the bottom of the shaft, he dropped—his rock magic softening his landing.

The hyena was growling at an ice demon. On sensing Thomas's presence, it attacked. If it hadn't been for the restricted space in the tunnel, the hyena would have died quickly, but the lack of space prevented the demon from moving freely. The hyena dodged the acidic spit of the demon with skill. Another ice demon was behind the first, and behind that was one of the mercenaries. Thomas couldn't see the others but felt their presence around the corner.

Thomas's plan was simple. Sending a mental message to the hyena, he charged down the tunnel. The animal stepped to one side, and Thomas threw his knife. It was controlled by intention, and it flew, invisible to the demon, before him. The demon hissed in anticipation but hesitated when Thomas's hands glowed orange in the darkness. It yelped as the knife passed through its body and hit the demon behind. It died as Thomas burnt a hole through it. His whole body was like a burning blade. The second ice demon behind knew its comrade was in trouble, but in the dark and narrow passage, it couldn't see how—until Thomas, surrounded by bright orange light, stepped from the back of its body.

The shocked creature quickly backed up, knocking down the mercenaries behind it, as Thomas ran towards it. He pointed at his knife, lying unseen on the ground where the second demon had tossed it, and it flipped into the air before him. Thomas attacked, darting at the demon with three blades before him: the black one stabbed its head, and the orange shining blades of his hands, arms, and elbows penetrated its body. Behind its body, the mercenaries were shouting, but it did them no good. They were stuck behind the now dead demon.

Thomas ran back, stopping by the other demon and

cutting off both its legs. He tossed them over his shoulder and pocketed his knife. The hyena backed away nervously. He sent it a thought of peace, and it relaxed slightly, but it was still nervous. Risking a bite from the animal, he lifted it. His magic made its body feel lighter than it would otherwise have been, and he ran up the shaft.

Dropping the relieved animal on the ground, he felt the rocks at the top of the shaft, and his mind entered the cracks inside them. He no longer cared about using magic; he had no choice, and his pain was less when he lived in a state of magic. Rapidly expanding and contracting the rocks until they were looser, he then blasted magic through the gaps and cracks, stepping back quickly as part of the shaft collapsed. The clouds of dust blocked his view but not his rock sense. Even with magic, it would take them hours to dig their way through the fallen rocks. Picking up the demon legs, he ran up the tunnel, then climbed the next stretch carrying the hyena, too. A few minutes later, he heard Aina moving into the tunnel.

"Thomas?"

"We have to go!"

She hugged him, then recoiled. "You're covered in blood."

"Not mine, I think."

"What are you carrying?" She gingerly touched one of the legs, then quickly let go.

"Leg of ice demon."

"Why?"

"We need to eat."

Before she could speak, he led her along the tunnel. The hyena was hurt, and he'd been licking his wounds, but he'd survive. Thomas walked confidently up the passages; he just knew the right way. He pushed ahead for hours, despite

Aina's complaints and the hyena's increasing slowness. About five hours later, the hyena collapsed, and Thomas stopped.

"There's a spring in a small cave near here. We can rest there."

"Do you have mental map of the mountain?" Aina asked.

Thomas grinned. "Something like that, but I can only see the places nearby. It's more like shining a torch in the darkness, but my torch shines through solid rock.

He carried the exhausted hyena for another thirty yards, and then placed it close to the spring, splashing water on it. It had proven useful, and he didn't want it to die on them. The water revived it. While Aina washed, he searched for something to start a fire; raw lizard didn't appeal to him. But there was nothing but rocks, so he began to pile them.

"What are you doing?" Aina asked.

"Making a fire."

She crawled along the ground, feeling with her hands. "Thomas?"

"Mmm."

"Stones don't burn."

He smiled in the darkness. "For me they do." Sending magic into the stones, he was pleased to see them start glowing orange. He placed a leg over the hot stones. "Barbecued lizard."

She pulled a face, and this time he could see her with his eyes. She blinked as she studied him. "You need to wash. You're covered in blood." She was right. He washed, then decided to rest for a few moments.

"Thomas. Wake-up."

He woke with a start. Instantly alert, he looked around the small cave. "What?"

"I think the food's ready." He laughed, instantly relaxing.

He realized he'd slept for about two hours, but it felt like minutes. She pulled a face. "But I'm not sure I want to eat it."

"You have to eat it. You need your strength."

The hyena had woken, too, and was watching the cooking leg intently. Thomas took the other leg and tossed it to the animal. It caught it in its large jaws and dragged it away into a dark corner of the cave where it began to eat.

He pulled part of the leg off the hot stones and cut meat from it, passing some to Aina. "It's not bad." For a second he wondered what Chloris would think of them eating one of her old comrades but decided that she wouldn't care. Anyway, she happily ate humans. Aina chewed the meat while Thomas told her what happened in the tunnel.

"So now we only have three mercenaries and three magicians trying to kill us," Aina said.

Thomas shook his head. "Four magicians. I sensed a new magic."

"So it's just got worse."

"Better. We don't have ice demons tracking our scent."

"Not our physical scent."

"Tracking magic is trickier than tracking a physical scent," Thomas said. He was relieved that the ice demons were gone. "Those things have the habit of sneaking up close and killing anything that breathes."

"What about the new magician?" Aina asked.

"Weaker than the others." Thomas looked at the hyena. It'd almost finished the whole leg, and he knew it'd want to rest. "We should sleep for a few hours, then move on."

"It's odd," Aina said. "There's a vast wilderness in the heart of Nassopolis."

"I know. I've thought that before."

Aina cuddled up close to Thomas and fell asleep. He thought about the life here in the mountain. It was not the desert it appeared. Lichens, fungal growths, and insects lived here, but a few smaller mammals survived on the insects, including bats and rats. There were other forms of life, too: those different in type and order from the life of the physical world. Sometimes he felt the presence of the elemental spirits as he listened to the earth. Then he thought of Aina. It was a long time before he slept.

31

Na stood before thousands of dragons. Many had come from distant parts of Prometheus to discuss war, and the mood was antagonistic towards humanity. She needed to ensure that the dragons didn't attack the Fire Bearers when they attacked the tower.

"I've met a human Fire Bearer." A dragon whistled loudly, and Na glared at her. *"She's committed to fighting the invaders. Both Fire Bearers will join us in the final battle at the tower."* Na hoped this would be true and that Thomas would find his way there. *"They are our friends and allies and should be respected as such."*

Incredulous hoots drowned her voice. These dragons were too proud to consider outside help, but whatever happened, they couldn't be allowed to attack, and possibly kill, the Fire Bearers. The hooting continued, and she raised her voice.

"They must not be targeted."

"This isn't a concern of great dragons." The unfamiliar green dragon puffed his body up as he spoke, making Na wonder if he was secretly unsure of himself.

"Later," Night Sun said quietly in her mind.

Na felt too tired to be angry. The conversation had moved on, and the mood had become more belligerent. Night Sun was a senior leader, but he now had to contend with the leaders of other Wisdoms and Thunders. But they lacked his direct experience dealing with humanity.

Feeling suddenly lonely, she looked for Seth, wanting him to be close, but she couldn't see him anywhere. She opened her mind, listening in the True Language for her brother. She thought she heard him far above. Wondering if he'd flown into space, she projected her mind further, but if he was there, he wasn't answering. She decided to search for him one more time, but instead, she felt a darkness in space—it was moving towards them.

She searched for the First of the Wisdom and saw him in the inner circle. *"Night Sun?"* He turned to her. *"I think we have a problem."*

After listening carefully, Night Sun told the assembled dragons what Na had said. As many of them searched in space, Na wasn't sure what they'd find. Most dragons lacked her psychic abilities. *"Can you sense it?"* she asked Night Sun.

"*No.*" Her heart sank.

"There's nothing there," Twrch, leader of one of the outside Thunders said. Several other leaders agreed.

"I feel it," Na said. *"An emptiness in space, and it's moving towards us."*

"And you think this nothingness is an imperial fleet?"

"Yes."

"And what do you propose?" another asked.

"I propose we find out what it is," Na said. *"And if it is an imperial fleet, we must attack."*

"Look for an emptiness?"

"Yes."

The dragons discussed and disagreed. Twrch turned to Night Sun. *"We can't afford to waste time flying into empty space on the imaginings of a juvenile dragon. We have a real fight. We fly to the human colony tomorrow."*

Her Thunder remained, as did the Flights of her group. *"What about us?"* Willa asked.

Night Sun was quiet for several moments. *"Although I respect Na's abilities, as no other dragons can sense this emptiness, I don't think we can spend more time investigating it. We must join the attack on the human colony."*

"Her affection for humanity might have clouded her judgement," Warth said.

Even her brother had turned against her. She'd always trusted her instincts, but as the dragons left her alone on Tangle Top, now she doubted them, too. Perhaps she should join the attack on the human colony tomorrow. Perhaps her imagination was too active. Glancing down, she was pleased to see a new Tangle playing in one of the volcanic pools; some of the young hooted their admiration when rays from the rising sun reflected on her golden scales. A movement above caught her attention. A silver dragon dropped towards her. Her heart lifted to see her brother, *"Seth."* He landed beside her, and she immediately sensed his mixed emotions. *"What's wrong?"*

"We were on a mission between the moons and the planet. I saw nothing, but Kaylie sensed something strange, and she flew alone into space..."

Na's stomach chilled. *"Show me where."* Her brother showed her the emptiness in space, and her fire chilled further.

"She never came back," he said.

"What do you mean, never came back?"

"I looked for her but found nothing. She was gone."

Na called her sister in the True Language, but only heard the silence of space. She called again, more urgently, projecting her mind into the emptiness she'd sensed. Pain and terror seized her, and she staggered, feeling her brother support her. Her inner fire almost went out when she touched a dragon's twisted body with her mind. *"Kaylie!"*

"What?" Seth said.

"She's inside the darkness. Seth, they're killing her. She's in pain. We must go to her!" Pushing him away, she stretched out her wings.

"Not yet," he said. *"I heard your conversation with the others. I need to speak to them, too."*

While Seth spoke to his Flight—he was now flight leader—she spoke again to the Thunder. They listened silently, but Na sensed their answer before they spoke.

"Seth has already searched for her. If he can't find her, how can we?" Spere said.

Na dripped fire onto the rocks.

"Na, we cannot stop the war for the loss of one dragon, however close we are to her. The greater good is our priority," Spere said.

One by one, the dragons tuned out of the conversation, leaving only Seth and herself. Minutes later, a light brown dragon landed beside them. "I will join you." Tan was a dragon she didn't really know, but she suspected he was Kaylie's partner. He, at least, was keen to start the search.

They flew fast into the sky, and then into the upper atmosphere, each taking the oxygen needed. With experience, less oxygen lasted longer. As they flew through space, she felt the emptiness. *"We must move unseen,"* she whispered. The three dragons became invisible to the ships ahead. The largest, the flagship, flew just behind the first ship. A battlecruiser flew to either side, and dozens of other warships followed. Hours of silence passed, and then she spoke.

"Kaylie's in the flagship."

Neither Tan nor Seth could see the fleet, and she could only feel its displacement, but the flagship was clear in her mind as she led them towards it. It was the largest ship she'd encountered, and she felt dwarfed as she flew under its belly. Searching the ship, Na sensed her sister's presence and intuitively chose the precise spot from which to rescue her. They landed silently on the outer surface of the ship, next to a large set of doors. Seconds later, she touched the edges of the ship's metal mind. Some parts of it were unguarded, and she decided to go there first. It didn't notice her brush lightly against it, nor when she went through the log of the crew and guests.

The crew was nothing, but some of the guests were thought important by the ship: seventeen lords and ladies, all arriving to administer parts of the planet. The humans had many levels and ranks, and many orders. It was those belonging to the Imperial Order that posed a threat—they were the ones trained in magic. Seven of them were on this ship. Resisting a desire to vacate their quarters of air, she crept slowly along the underbelly of the ship, stopping upon reaching a door. Seth and Tan were with her.

"What now?" Seth asked.

"Something dangerous. Guard my body while I go deeper into its mind." Slipping into its mind again, she moved through its circuits, flipping switches, until she reached a lock. As soon as she reached for the lock, something started scratching on the other side.

32

Na walked into a trap—she was bound by electrically charged threads. As she pulled away, she saw something move above her. A shimmering spider ran from the centre of a strange cobweb towards her. In revulsion, she sent out a jet of fire. It backed off, but as she pulled away from the web, it jumped at her, biting her leg. Na bellowed in pain as poison entered her body, and she felt her body numbing. It waited.

In the darkness behind the spirit spider, she saw something move. *"Kaylie?"*

Her sister was slumped against a wall. *"Na?"*

"I'm caught in a web."

"Burn its legs. Its body is almost indestructible." Kaylie said. Her voice was weak.

Na wanted to scream. She sent out another jet of fire at one of its legs, which caught fire. It was then she noticed that it only had seven legs.

"I burnt off one of them," Kaylie rasped. *"But I'd wasted too much time trying to burn its body, and I passed out."*

Na was already feeling faint. She burnt two more legs,

and it backed off. Part of the web fell away, and she jumped through, staggering along what was a weird sort of circuit in the ship's brain.

"I lost consciousness for hours," Kaylie said. *"That was then they caught me."*

Na couldn't let that happen to her. Then she felt as if she were breathing fresh air. *"Seth?"*

"I'm breathing healing flames on you."

"Keep doing it!" Na exclaimed in sudden relief. Then she spoke to her sister. *"Show me where you are."* An image of a dirty room in the hold of the vast ship appeared in her mind. *"I know."*

"They have magic," Kaylie said. *"Two of them are dangerous."*

Kaylie's memories shocked her. Na turned in anger and blasted the spirit spider again, and it retreated around a corner. She'd seen the faces of the sorcerers who'd done this to her sister: Lady Byota and Lord Uys.

"I'm coming to get you."

"Na, leave me. There's not much of me left—they've done a lot of damage."

Na's inner fire was boiling. Her only concern was to rescue her sister, and if she could, kill the sorcerers. Her muscles tightened in readiness for battle, and she mentally ran towards Kaylie, not concerning herself with how to get there; to know her destination was enough to take her there. A sudden pain in her tail made her look back. The spider stood behind her with blood dripping from its frilly red mouth, two fangs contracted.

She burnt off another leg—again she felt Seth's healing flame. She blasted it again, sending it crawling back into the dark circuits of the metallic mind. As she moved, it followed at a distance, pulling itself along awkwardly on its three remaining legs.

Realizing that she could move by just thinking, she wished to be in the hold with Kaylie. And then she was. It was huge, big enough for a medium-sized spacecraft to fit inside. Her sister was chained to one of the walls. *"Kaylie!"* Na was shocked by the violence done to her sister. One of her legs had been cut off, and both her wings were broken. Her pale blue body was burnt, and open wounds still bled. The floor was covered in blood.

Her disoriented and weakened sister looked around the room. *"Na?"*

"I'm here." But she wasn't physically there, and Kaylie couldn't see her, so Na drew energy from the spaceship. Kaylie's eyes widened as a hologram of Na appeared before her.

"Help me."

Na found the control systems. *"Unlock!"* The machine body obeyed the machine mind, and Kaylie's shackles fell away, sending her weakened body crashing to the ground. Trying to breathe healing fire over her, Na cursed that she was only there as a projection. *"I have to leave and reenter physically,"* she said.

"Na, come soon."

"I will."

A door opened behind her and three spider bots rushed in. She disabled them, and they crashed to the floor. Then she had an idea. Ordering one to wake, she instructed it to dismantle the others. Soon there was a single spider bot, standing with quivering legs, over the remains of the others. She was wondering what to do with it when two guards entered. *"Attack!"* The spider bot killed them before they could react.

"Who's with you?" Kaylie asked.

"Seth and Tan." She sensed an increase of emotion on hearing Tan's name.

"Only the three of you?"

"The others didn't believe me when I told them about the approaching emptiness."

"That's how I saw it," Kaylie said. *"I tried to turn the shield off."*

Na searched its mind again, going deeper into the more restricted areas. A shape moved silently in the darkness. The burnt and wounded spider moved awkwardly; it was cornered, and no longer shining brightly. Behind it were the security controls for the flagship.

Again, she burnt off one of its legs. On two, it could hardly move, and she easily burnt the final legs off. Its body twitched on the ground. She sent a fine jet of fire into the invisibility control, hoping to disable it. Then Kaylie moaned, and Na was again in the hold of the ship. Seven figures in black entered the hold, followed by soldiers. They couldn't hurt her, but they could kill Kaylie. She ordered the spider bot to attack, but they shot it dead.

They stared at the golden dragon. "Can you capture it, Lady Byota?" one of the figures asked the middle-aged woman.

"It's a hologram, fool! It'll be on the outside of the ship. Send robots to destroy it."

"It's a big ship," Na said through the ship's communication system.

Lady Byota turned back to Na. "Yes, but you're too late," she said as the soldiers ran from the hold. "Your pretty blue friend will soon be dead."

Na recognized the man standing by her side as the torturer, Lord Uys. She had no time to waste. Her hologram vanished, and she resumed her search for the door locking mechanism. She found it and flicked on the mechanical timer. Then she was back in her body.

"Are you okay?" Seth asked.

"Yes." She was shaking, and she knew she wasn't all right. Her inner fire felt erratic, but she forced herself to move her head. *"Kaylie's dying."* Looking around, Na saw the fleet flickering around her. She must have done more damage than she'd thought to the invisibility control.

"How bad is it?" Tan asked.

She shared an image, and Tan's temperature increased. *"The doors will open soon. Kill the humans first. They're dangerous."* She thought about her tender sister and wondered if she still would be after this. *"She might live, but she won't be the same."*

"I'll enter more deeply and destroy what I can," Seth said.

"No." She couldn't bear the thought of losing her brother. *"Just stop anything from entering the hold."* Seth looked at her questioningly. *"Humans don't trust humans. Their instinct is to control, which means they place great power and control in a single location."*

"And you know that location?"

"I do."

The three dragons crouched around the rim of the doorway. The doors opened suddenly, and they waited, watching several soldiers fly into space. No one had expected her to unlock the doors. *"There are seven, and each has magic. Kill them quickly."* Na rushed along the ceiling upside down, breathing fire at the waiting bots. Seth sprinted along the wall to her right, and Tan ran along the wall to her left. A toxic cloud moved along the floor and into space along with the soldiers—the sorcerers had assumed they'd enter using the floor.

The bots reacted faster than the humans, and Tan was hit in his leg, but he burnt the bot and it fell smoking to the ground. Na and Seth destroyed the remaining two bots. One of the sorcerers was holding a heavy gun to Kaylie's head. Na knew it would kill, but she couldn't stop, and neither she nor Kaylie had that weakness so common in humans—a fear of death. They'd made the mistake of choosing a neophyte sorcerer to hold the gun—it showed their lack of understanding of dragons. Na invaded his mind in under a second, burning his brain. He staggered forward and his head burst into flames, but he was already dead.

"What do we do?" a sorcerer asked in a shrill voice. Seth killed him with a jet of fire. Other novice sorcerers grabbed metal shields to protect themselves. Na knew they'd have very little effect. Only Lady Byota and Lord Uys didn't show any fear; they hummed a sickening song, and a dark mist emanated from their skin, then drifted towards them. Na had never known a magic like this, but it seemed familiar, nevertheless.

"What're they doing?" Tan asked.

"Diseased magic," she said. Although she was sure she didn't want to touch it, she really wasn't sure how to deal with it, but Night Sun had once told her that dragon fire contained a magic all of its own. *"Brothers!"* Her voice vibrated clearly through their minds. *"Blast them!"* Together, the three dragons blasted the sorcerers with fire. Even Kaylie breathed a fiery mist. The dark diseased mist caught fire, like oil, and returned home, sticking to many of the less experienced sorcerers. Soon they were dead or dying on the floor.

"You'll pay for this!" Lady Byota shrieked. "Your species is finished."

"You'll pay," Na said.

The three sorcerers staggered back. They had enough power to deflect some of the sticky energetic stuff that sought to return to its creators, but not all. The lord screamed in pain as patches of his returning black magic smoked on his skin. Knowing it was time to finish them off, Na moved forward, but she stopped when Lady Byota reached her hands towards Kaylie.

"No!"

But it was a trick—a distraction. Byota slammed a switch on the wall, and a door opened behind her. She ran through the opening with Uys. The third sorcerer staggered after her. The door shut as Seth's fire slammed into it. The hold doors began to close. *"Faster!"* Tan said. Kaylie was already crawling towards the closing doors. They lifted her and flew into space. The doors closed behind them.

"Invisible!" Na yelled. Around them the guns of dozens of warships had already turned towards them. They flew towards the planet below, but as soon as they became invisible, they swung around. *"Back to the flagship. We must hide there."*

"Hide?" Tan asked as he looped round with Kaylie.

A missile exploded where they would have been, and smaller spaceships were already following their original path back to Prometheus, firing rounds of heavy bullets. Na searched the surface of the flagship. It was huge, and there were hundreds of indented sections. She wanted to avoid any stray bullets, but more importantly, Kaylie needed somewhere to rest. Her invisibility spell was already flickering on and off. She was sicker than Na had imagined and was passing in and out of consciousness. *"There."* The three dragons supported Kaylie, and slowly they moved over the surface. At last they crawled into the space.

"Do you think the dragons will see the fleet?" Seth asked. They watched the fleet flickering in and out of vision.

"Perhaps," Na said. *"I've sent Night Sun messages. But he hasn't replied yet."* She looked at Kaylie.

"They'll scan for our body parts," Seth said. *"And when they don't find them, they'll start searching again."*

Na looked along the surface of the flagship. *"They're already coming."* Hundreds of spider bots ran over the surface of the ship, searching each hiding space they came to.

"They'll kill Kaylie," Seth said. *"We must fly to another ship."*

"They'll hear the vibrations as we leave, and we'd be shot immediately." Na watched the guns of the circling ships. *"They're ready for us this time."*

"All dragons must face death at some time," Tan said.

"Yes, but not yet," Na said. *"I have an idea."*

33

The rocs chattered in their musical language, with Lucy only picking up some of the meaning from the fragments of True Language they sometimes used. Hwith landed nearby.

"How close are they?" she asked.

"They're already inside the ancient forest. They'll be here within a day if we do nothing."

"How many?"

"Twenty thousand."

Lucy was shocked. *"How many rocs?"*

"Almost three thousand. But we have allies in the forest, and our own devices. You only spent a few days with us before. Our homes are more developed than you think."

Lucy eyes widened in surprise. She'd experienced firsthand the lethal flora of the forest, and she knew the rocs were gifted at crafts and could manipulate tools very well with their beaks and claws, but she wasn't sure what kind of devices they could create to counter the Empire's technology.

"We use wood, the shells of insects, the bones of fish, and materials made by insects," Hwith said, reading her mind.

Lucy's hopes diminished. *"But not advanced technology."*

"We don't use metal, nor do we have access to their sources of energy generation, but we have fire. We can harness steam."

"Without metal?"

"Some woods and shells are harder than most metals. The life of the ancient forest possesses its own fire; we can make use of that."

She still couldn't see how some steam device could match the fighters and machines of the Empire.

"We won't use steam this time," Hwith said.

She no longer found Hwith's mind reading unusual, nor particularly annoying. *"They'll have a command post. We need to occupy it and reprogram the soldiers' tags,"* she said. *"Their control of their people is their strength and weakness. If we can access the tags, then we gain a big advantage."*

"Too easy," he said.

"The command post will be camouflaged, and the computers will be well protected, but it's possible."

"Still too easy," Hwith said. *"If that's all, then we'll find and destroy it, but they'll have ways to regain control."*

"Perhaps, but it will be a setback for them. We can't just destroy it, though."

"Why not?"

"Because then the soldiers will continue with their preset programming. We need to gain access to the computers in the command post and reprogram them. But we have to find it."

"Ask the forest."

When Hwith turned his attention to a group of rocs, Lucy walked into the ancient forest. Finding a fallen log, she sat and watched an assassin bug on a nearby branch. She touched its mind and watched it light up. If the rocs could call on insects such as this, then the approaching imperial army would be slowed and inconvenienced, although she couldn't see how it'd make a big difference. But every bit counted.

She asked the forest for the location of the imperial command post. It was silent, and she realized she had to be more active. The rocs were teaching her again—interesting things. Pzillis Trillis had been showing her special ways of moving her mind at a great distance from her body, whilst remaining hidden. At least, that was the theory.

She reached out with her mind, listening to the life around her and searching for anything out of place. The forest was rich with life, and immediately around her it was humming. But as she reached towards the invading army, the pain of the forest almost overwhelmed her. They were firebombing its outer edges. Pushing her mind further, she saw the embers of forest, and beyond that was the imperial army. She continued, projecting her mind beyond the imperial lines, speaking to the plants and insects and listening to their simple replies. Although the fires had destroyed much of the forest around the soldiers, some remained.

She searched for spaces that felt out of place, and she quickly found ten or more. One by one, she studied these spaces. In most cases, it was simply that the advancing army had destroyed even the smallest forms of life, but she singled out two places with the scent of magic. One was at the rear of the army—it was slowly moving forward. Perhaps a moving command post. The smell was sharp and unpleasant. It was moving in some sort of vehicle. She sensed a drive to succeed, a feeling of advancing. It was a familiar feeling. Then she knew him. It was Lord Plane from the police station on 27th. She continued searching.

The other space was further back, and she felt pressure

pushing against her as she tried to project her mind towards it. Her mind numbed as magic resisted her, and the Hag's head appeared in her mind. She broke contact and breathed deeply, feeling a weight being lifted from her. She had an approximate location of the second command post. Next time, she'd sneak in more quietly. A branch snapped behind her, and she started.

"I'm sorry," Chloris said.

"I was projecting my mind," Lucy said. "Where have you been?"

"With the rocs. They were showing me their devices; they're simple but effective."

"Machines?"

"Sorts of devices. Some can fly." Chloris shared an image of a fire balloon.

Getting up from the log, Lucy said, "I want to see for myself."

Once they rejoined the rocs, Lucy understood. Fire balloons made of some sort of silk, which one of the rocs told her had been coated in the droppings of a certain animal. Lucy removed her hands from the object. Apparently the substance, when dried, could withstand great heat. Beneath the balloons were double pods.

"How do they work?" she asked Hwith.

"The pods contain fire oil. The upper one lifts the balloon. As soon as the oil's burnt, the balloon drops, and the second pod explodes when it hits the something. The fire sticks."

"Aren't these dangerous?" Lucy asked.

"Yes," Hwith said.

The rocs began chattering loudly, and Lucy knew they were getting ready to fly. *"Before we fly, I need to tell you what I've found in the forest."* She showed him the first command post and told him of the second.

"We'll deal with the forward command post soon. Come."

The leaves and branches became a blur as they flew through the upper levels of the giant trees, followed by other rocs. Then they flew through a gap in the green protective covering. Lucy was soaked by the hard rain. The ancient forest possessed its own microclimate; outside the forest, the weather was colder and damper. Lucy adjusted the flow of energy in her body, warming and drying herself. They joined the thousands of rocs flying towards the edge of the forest. From the silent chatter of the True Language, she knew that more were flying to join them.

Their first concern was the destruction being caused by the large imperial bombers. The bombers flew high in the grey sky, but without any protection. *"They assume because we lack flying machines that they're safe,"* Hwith said. *"Their first mistake."*

"They may have fighters escorting them," Lucy said.

"The fighters are attacking the dragons. There are forty bombers and nothing else," Hwith said. *"Two hundred rocs will attack them. The others will wait in the forest."*

"For what?" Lucy asked as she looked down on wildfires that covered an area the size of a small city.

"For the second attack."

Wind from the firestorm struck, and the rocs faltered as they flew through it. Clouds of smoke rushed around them, hiding them from the ground but robbing them of air. The rocs were able to compensate, having some natural magic that Lucy was only just beginning to appreciate. She formed a protective bubble around them.

"Thank you," Hwith said. *"I can fly faster if I don't need to think about breathing."*

Lucy caught glimpses of the scorched land beyond the fire. At the outer edge, the imperial army waited to advance over the dying embers of the forest. She gripped Hwith's feathers as he dropped into the forest through a gap in the foliage. Leaves brushed over her body. She didn't like sudden descents, and the rocs could drop like stones when they wanted, only opening their wings at the last moment. They landed on the forest floor, a few hundred yards from the approaching inferno. A stream of dragonflies, each with wings spanning several yards, poured through the hole in the foliage above and landed around them. They carried supplies needed for the fight: sacks—made from plants—in three distinct colours.

"What're inside those sacks?" Lucy asked.

"The blue ones will help slow the fire, the orange ones will burn the soldiers, and the red ones will burn their machines."

The dragonflies with the blue bags rose almost immediately, flying higher and higher, and then disappeared in the leaves hundreds of yards above her.

"Watch," Hwith said.

While he returned to other tasks, she sat on a log and reached out to the flights of dragonflies now flying towards the fire, but she struggled to make a connection. Then she saw a dragonfly with the cords of a blue bag entangled in his wings. It was turning and dragging the bag along the ground but unable to free itself.

She walked up to it. *"Can I help?"*

Although she couldn't hear words, she sensed its assent, and she carefully untangled the cord, stepping back quickly to avoid its wings. It was powerful, its body almost as big as hers, and she held her hair as the wind from its wings blew into her face.

"May I share your vision?" she asked.

Again, she sensed its agreement as it rose up to join his companions. She reached out and was soon looking through the dragonfly's eyes. She gasped as the world brightened and new colours appeared. Lucy sat quickly on a log; its ability to see in different directions at the same time disoriented her. However, the biggest change was that she now saw the world in slow motion, with humans moving at the same speed as sloths.

It flew fast over the treetops, and when it reached edges of the fire, it soared up on the rising hot air. Thousands of dragonflies soared over the flames, and many of them caught fire; their bags burst open, spreading a white dust into the flames. The fire crackled fiercely, but the flames no longer leapt as high. Then, aquamarine insects with strange fattened bodies flew straight into the flames. Swarms flew from the forest and dropped dead in the fire.

"What?" Lucy asked the dragonfly.

"Sacrifice," was all she heard. The watery insects sizzled in the fire, each one slowing it down. And she sensed the creature's sense of accomplishment as its wings melted, and it, too, dropped into the fire.

Pulling her mind from the burning dragonfly, she felt a sense of loss. She'd never imagined these beautiful creatures experienced the world so differently. She wondered how different she really was from the watery insects and dragonflies. She looked at the burns that covered her hands, arms, and legs, and thought about the times she'd risked her life and whether she was sacrificing herself as the other creatures of the forest did.

Chloris ran out of the jungle, straight to Lucy. "Further than I thought," she said. Lucy nodded. She thought Chloris had run fast to catch up with the rocs.

Explosions came from high in the sky, the loudest coming from much further away. *"Not all of the bombers had dropped their bombs,"* Hwith said. *"Humans are being burnt by their own fire."*

From the way they spoke to her, Lucy sometimes wondered if the rocs thought she was some exotic variety of roc, and not a human at all. They chattered and dragonflies buzzed as more bombers exploded in the sky. She watched fragments of images as a huge bomber caught fire and dropped from the sky, engulfing a unit of the imperial army. She imagined that at least a thousand men died in that explosion alone. Other bombers lost control and crashed. She caught glimpses from a passing roc of men running in confusion on the ground. The imperial army had just lost two or three thousand men.

Hwith chirped his satisfaction. *"Now we'll burn them with our fire."*

The rocs could be so boastful that Lucy wasn't sure how true this would be. She watched a second wave of the bright dragonflies rise, this time carrying the orange bags.

"What exactly is in those orange bags?"

The tall roc looked down at the bags and considered how to answer. *"Helicopters."*

"Helicopters?" The bags were quite bulky, but nothing she couldn't carry.

"You'll see."

As the dragonflies rose, she again connected with one, and through its eyes, she saw the fire from above the trees. The watery insects and the white powder had done something, as had the heavy rain, but the fires still burnt, even if the flames no longer reached as high.

Her stomach felt heavy when she realized that the imperial army was again advancing on the forest. The dragonflies flew over the smoking remains, mostly hidden from the soldiers marching. Lucy wondered why the men below didn't look up, but then she noticed they were wearing masks and helmets. It was probably not easy or comfortable marching with that gear, as well as the equipment on their backs.

The dragonflies circled over the army. Then they released their loads. The outer coverings of the sacks fell away, and thousands of helicopter-like seeds whirled down. When the first ones hit the men below, they exploded. These were small explosions: some stunned the men, some burnt them, and some killed. She knew that many seeds on Prometheus were naturally explosive. The soldiers shot into the air, but the dragonflies were already halfway back to the forest.

Before her dragonfly reached the edge of the forest, Lucy asked it to turn. As it did, she saw through its eyes. Thousands of small fires lit the approaching army. She estimated that another thousand men might have been disabled or died. Her dragonfly reentered the forest, and she opened her eyes.

"The red ones." She looked at the red sacks; they were bulkier than the others.

"Fire balloons," Soonasa said. "We must act quickly. Soon they'll send robots."

Lucy grabbed four bags but had to put two down. They were much heavier than she'd thought. She carried two to the edge of the forest. The rocs and dragonflies moved the rest.

A loud crack startled her, and looking up, she saw flashes of light around the edges of the forest. Without asking, she adopted the roc habit of joining the group mind. The forest was defending itself against what it saw as hundreds of tiny metal insects; the imperial army was attacking with swarms of nanobots, but the electrical field around the forest was burning them. An odd metal rain fell for several minutes and then stopped.

Hearing noises behind her, she turned to see the rocs skillfully using their beaks and claws to prepare fire balloons from the materials they and the dragonflies had brought. Each was a pod of fire oil attached to a balloon. The pods were only inches beneath the balloons, and a small but intense fire blasted into the balloons, which were being held down by dragonflies.

No longer having to ask questions, Lucy watched the dragonflies grasp one each and fly no more than a foot from the ground to place the fire balloons amongst the embers along the new edge of the forest. The creatures beat their wings on the ground until small clouds of grey dust covered both the dragonflies and the balloons. Only the glow of the small fire balloons showed their presence, but this could easily be mistaken for the glow of the embers of the forest. The rain did nothing to extinguish these flames. Camouflaged in the ash, the dragonflies waited for the bots to sweep the area. It was a standard imperial protocol before an invasion. The army still advanced.

The bots flew a hundred yards ahead of the running army, and when they reached the dust-covered dragonflies, the insects released the fire balloons, which lifted into the sky. As they rose, many hit the bots, bursting into flames. The soldiers ran ahead, firing in the air, hitting their own bots. On the ash-covered ground, the dragonflies waited motionless. Unexploded fire balloons drifted away from the heat, towards the approaching army. When they'd used up their small supply of fuel, they dropped onto the soldiers below, covering them with burning oil that stuck to their skin.

Lucy watched the scene from the edge of the forest. The

heavy rain had now put out many of the fires. Although smoke still partially obscured her view, some of the dragonflies above shared their vision with her. She estimated that the imperial army had lost about a third of their bots. But still, an army of around sixteen thousand marched towards her.

On Hwith's command, thousands of dragonflies, each one with a body three or four feet long and knife-like pincers, attacked the soldiers. At first, they didn't appear to understand what was happening. The dragonflies stuck to their faces, cutting and slashing deeply. Then a scream went up from the men as the dragonflies dropped the dead and blew jets of fire into the faces of the second line of men. The soldiers responded with gunfire, but the dragonflies fought close up, often using their long tails to wrap around the necks of men and pull them closer before cutting and burning. Within minutes, another two or three thousand men lay dead or dying. The soldiers shot the insects, but Promethean life was tough, and a single bullet was not enough; even multiple bullets often resulted in the dragonfly attaching itself to a man, and then immolating itself as a sacrifice for the world that had given it life. Very few dragonflies survived, but by the time they'd finished, no more than fourteen thousand soldiers advanced on the forest.

"Are you ready?" Hwith asked her. He'd already asked for her help.

"I am."

Lucy spoke silently to the ancient forest, and it moaned in answer. She called on burnt seeds lying in the hot ash, and many of the fire-germinated seeds burst into life. Drawing on her magic, she felt the power of the forest joining with her, accelerating their growth.

She gasped in pain as the magic burnt through her, and

she felt Chloris supporting her. Waiting, she sensed the seeds germinating. Shoots rushed upwards towards the grey skies, growing at an unnatural speed. The fattening fire funnels groaned with the effort of their fast growth. The soldiers looked at the growing plants nervously, but their commanders still ordered them on. When the fire funnels reached chest height, she sent them into a rage, pumping energy into them; she felt her body heating up. The plants groaned and vibrated, and as soldiers roughly pushed past them, they began to glow—first orange, and then red.

"Something's happening to these plants," one man shouted. A yell from his commanding officer silenced him.

"They're almost ready," Lucy said. She felt unsteady on her feet as the flow of magic slowed.

"As soon as they are—"

Lucy called on the fire funnels before Hwith finished his sentence, and they lowered their head towards the soldiers. The glowing red plants shuddered as fireballs flew from their mouths. The army was on fire, and hundreds fell in seconds. A few of the remaining bots were targeted as they fired from above, and they crashed down to more cries from the men below.

Lucy was exhausted. Chloris lifted her up and carried her gently through the forest. The rocs ran quickly, faster than any human, but Chloris had no problem keeping up.

34

Lucy felt weak. She'd lost her energy after accelerating the growth of the plants, but she was breathing more easily.

"Are you okay?" Chloris asked, still running with Lucy in her arms.

"No."

She dreaded the use of magic and was now scared to look at herself. She ran her fingers over the rough skin on her hands. At least her face hadn't been too badly affected yet. Chloris stopped.

"We wait here," Hwith said.

"You're in pain."

Lucy looked up into the grey and yellow plumage of Pzillis Trillis. She tried to laugh but failed as Chloris laid her gently on the ground.

"Don't speak." The roc breathed a light fire on her skin and squawked when Lucy pulled away. *"This is healing flame. Similar to that of the dragons."*

The flames cooled her raging inner Fire, and slowly she calmed. This magic was rougher and stronger than anything she'd experienced before, but now she breathed more easily.

"What's happening to me?"

"Ask the First of the Wisdom. It's dragon magic that burns inside you."

Anger towards the dragons competed with a deep tiredness. They'd used her and Thomas. She called him, but again he didn't answer, and she fell into a deep sleep.

"They come." She woke suddenly, unsure where the voice had come from. "We must move." It was Hwith. She sat up and stretched.

"How long have I been asleep?"

"Five or six hours." Then Hwith was gone, organizing the rocs.

She stood. Chloris lent her a hand when she staggered slightly. She was surprised she'd slept for so long, but she felt better. Rocs were moving through the forest nearby, appearing as flashes of colour running through the trees.

She found Stelling, an older blue, grey, and red roc. She'd seen him before, but they'd never spoken. After a lot of time speaking to rocs, she was finally beginning to understand them the first time they spoke.

"What's happening?"

"They're sending in advance teams of soldiers. One roc will deal with each group. Come with me."

Chloris hissed her dislike of the bird's attitude, but Stelling ignored the ice demon. Lucy looked for Hwith or Pzillis Trillis. She wasn't surprised when the roc picked up on her concerns.

"They're well; they've moved further from here. Run with me."

Lucy ran with the roc and Chloris. She struggled to keep pace, but she didn't have to run far. Stopping, she listened to the ancient forest as it spoke to her in whispers and humming vibrations. Its anger was rising. A platoon of thirty soldiers was forcing its way through the forest, and every inch of the way, the forest resisted. She watched, hidden from their eyes, as they cut and cursed their way forward. The roc looked down on her, and she nodded. She was the best to begin this.

Chloris and Stelling would be able to kill many of the soldiers before they knew what was happening. None of their detectors would work in the electrical field of the forest, and their senses were damaged and distorted by their use of tags. But attacking thirty armed soldiers was dangerous, even for an ice demon and roc, and other groups of soldiers moved through the forest nearby. Listening in the True Language, she heard their noisy minds. Their tags were receiving constant streams of information from the command post.

But it wasn't just information. Lucy was surprised that many of the men listened to loud music as they slashed at the brambles blocking their way. *"They've given up their autonomy,"* Lucy whispered. Chloris quietly hissed her agreement. Stelling just watched the soldiers with his fierce eyes. Of the thirty, all but one were tagged. She'd work on the tagged minds first.

She listened to the incoming information. Not what was being said, but to the way it was entering the men's minds. She saw it as waves washing over the men, and she followed the current back to source. She was inside the first command post and saw Lord Plane searching and sending information. He appeared overwhelmed. She left him to his worries and entered the artificial intelligence the lord was attempting to work with.

With the music blasting in the minds of the men, it was

hard to know how to approach this. She'd hoped to send disturbing thoughts about the forest, but these men were already partially anaesthetized. Although they thought themselves independent, the machine mind suggested, chastised, and enraged them when the Empire wanted. Then she noticed that certain parts of their brains were being stimulated more than others.

Sharing some of their feelings was unpleasant, but it was the only way for her to understand what was happening to them. She realized that the soldiers were being drugged from the constant downloads. It sent constant stimulations to the pleasure centres of their brains. These men were literally being turned on by a computer, but tricked into thinking their thoughts and feelings were their own. Many of the men mumbled along to the inner music, which appeared to be controlling their moods. Lucy was both fascinated and horrified. She'd not realized the control was so extreme.

While Lord Plane was still occupied, she began to make changes. The first change was to their inner music. She created a slower, more creepy sound that chilled even her. The effect was immediate. The soldiers hesitated and looked into the forest, which they seemed now to be seeing for the first time. Then she stopped the stimulation of their pleasure centres and prevented the suppression of pain. Now, the soldiers sweated as they slashed, and they looked from side to side, confused. Stelling took advantage of their confusion. He hopped forward and pecked a man's eyes out before hopping back into the trees. No one but her saw what happened, and even the man seemed to only slowly realize that something was wrong. Then he started screaming, and while the men were distracted, Chloris dragged two men backwards by their throats, which she quickly cut under the cover of the undergrowth. Stelling killed another, dragging her body through the undergrowth.

"What's wrong?" the platoon leader demanded.

The man staggered as he turned to face his officer. The platoon leader started as he looked at the man's empty eye sockets. "Sir, we've lost four men," a soldier said. With their weapons drawn, they formed a circle, facing outwards to the forest. Lucy instructed the vines to whip the men, and they cried out in pain and fear. "The forest's attacking us!" the man shouted.

They fired into the trees, and Lucy, who'd been expecting this, hid behind the particularly tough trunk of a large tree. The roc had flown up to a branch above them. As they shot into the forest, fire rained down on them. Four were immediately engulfed in flames, falling dead on the forest floor. Another two were seriously burnt. They were now calling for help on their tags, and she scrambled the messages, changing the locations of the tags. No one noticed.

Stelling dropped from the branch, slashing and burning the soldiers, and Chloris rushed from the forest, killing the platoon leader. Two men tried to escape and ran straight into Lucy, pointing guns at her in shock. Not knowing what else to do, she reluctantly told their hearts to stop. The men fell dead. She shivered and pushed her aside her unease.

The platoon was no more, apart from seven or eight dying men. Chloris began to feed, while the roc wandered off to find food in the forest. Rocs seldom ate meat, preferring fruit, nuts, and insects. Lucy was pleased they didn't eat humans. She glanced at her friend, but there was nothing much she could do. Although she loved the reptile, she could never approve of her eating habits. As if conscious of Lucy watching her, the ice demon dragged the corpse she fed on into the undergrowth. Lucy walked amongst the dead and dying, and as she did so, she instructed the imperial computers to again pump drugs into their bodies. Although they were her enemy, there was no need for them to die in pain.

Then she noticed the untagged man. He was hiding in a tree. His mouth was badly burnt, and she doubted if he could speak. Easing his pain with her magic, she spoke to him in the True Language, curious why he alone was untagged.

The bright roc appeared next to her, squawking loudly. *"Shall I kill it?"*

The man screamed and fell from the tree.

"No, I want to speak to him."

Chloris had returned to the clearing, and the terrified man stared at the ice demon with an open mouth as she bit into a groaning soldier. Lucy glanced at her friend. "Kill him first!" The man was close to dying, but this was too much.

"Sorry," Chloris said, quickly cutting the man's throat.

Lucy turned back to the untagged man. He'd soiled himself, and she was unsurprised. The man stared at her with wide eyes. "Why are you untagged?" she asked in Dnassian. His gurgled reply made no sense, and she repeated the question in the True Language, hoping to glimpse some of his thoughts.

He answered her in the True Language; he spoke like a child taking his first steps in the telepathic language, but she was still taken aback. *"What are you?"* he asked.

Lucy realized she glowed from the magic. With that and her scarred skin, she must've looked wild. She searched his memories, because he was too unused to the True Language to truly talk, and he couldn't use his burnt mouth. He'd been an artist once, but now he was a soldier. He'd had a desire to free himself of his tag, and she felt overwhelming sadness at what she and the rocs were now being forced to do. She decided to let him live, and she told Chloris and Stelling. It gave her hope that one ordinary soldier had attempted to break free of the Empire, even if he'd not done it consciously.

"All humans must leave the forests of Prometheus." She thought the message would be stronger if expressed in the True Language.

"You?" the man struggled to reply. She was surprised but pleased by his simple ability to express an idea in the True Language.

She wondered what she'd become. Once, she'd identified with humanity; now she identified with all life. She leant towards him, and he pulled away, but relaxed when her golden healing energy soothed him. She eased his pain and set his body on its own course of recovery.

"You must stop the attack," she said, sharing something she'd learnt from the ancient forest. *"All life is one."* Then without another word, she slipped back into the forest with Chloris and Stelling.

They found Hwith and other rocs several hundred yards deeper in the forest. The imperial soldiers were in retreat, but once they'd reached their lines, they'd regroup and return. Reserves already approached the battlefield. *"I've located the forward command post,"* Lucy said. She shared the location with the rocs. *"You must destroy it."*

"We will," Hwith said. Jzzrata and three other rocs lifted into the air and flew towards the battlefield and the retreating army.

"The other command post?" Hwith said.

"The Night Hag," she said. She showed Hwith the rough location. *"I need to do another search. It was difficult; she might*

have known I was there. The pressure pushing me away was intense." She secretly dreaded the encounter.

Forty minutes later, Jzzrata and the rest of his flight landed. *"The forward command post is destroyed. Unfortunately, the sorcerer escaped."*

Lucy felt a change in the forest. *"Something's happening,"* she said.

"I feel nothing," Jzzrata said.

"I feel very strange." It was as if adrenaline was flushing through her body. This was confirmed when the telepathic chattering between rocs suddenly increased. Something was definitely wrong.

The voice of a distant roc confirmed it. *"The humans have gone hysterical; they're throwing away their lives to advance a few feet."*

35

Thomas woke to the growls of the hyena and rolled onto his feet, his knife in his hand. They'd slept too long. He shook Aina, covering her mouth when she tried to speak.

"They're here," he whispered.

He crept to the entrance of the small cave. The hyena had left the cave and was stalking down the passage, growling softly.

Several seconds later, Aina joined Thomas at the mouth of the cave. "Where?"

He pointed in the direction of the growls. He also sensed magic. "We should go the other way." With the strength of the magic coming from the tunnel, he doubted the hyena would survive an encounter with it. He silently called the animal. Seconds later he heard a yelp. Several minutes later, the hyena limped behind them. They ran up the dark tunnel.

"I think we might have lost them," he said. He couldn't sense any movement behind them. Then the hyena growled, and Thomas cursed his lack of care.

"Drop your weapons." Morgan Red stood ten yards in front of them. He flicked on a torch. In his other hand, he held a sub-machine gun.

Thomas had paid too much attention to the magic behind, and not enough attention to movement in the other direction. "Don't try anything or I'll shoot you dead. And that animal," Morgan Red said, glancing at the growling hyena.

From the vibrations within the tunnel floor, Thomas estimated they had about ten minutes before the sorcerers arrived. He had to do something before then. Two other mercenaries waited in the shadows, and another man stood behind them.

"Drop the knife."

The black knife fell to the floor. In some ways, that made it easier to use unobserved. Thomas pressed against the minds of the men in front but felt resistance. It was coming from the fourth figure—the new sorcerer. Turning his attention to this man who stood in the shadows, he listened for his thoughts, but the sorcerer shielded himself. However, his shielding was weak, and Thomas found leaks and pushed through them. The Empress was speaking to the man, but she stopped when she sensed Thomas's presence.

"You might be able to kill this man, but you won't step an inch past me or my husband."

Thomas noticed the junior sorcerer's annoyance on hearing the dismissal of his powers. Thomas wondered why she'd mentioned her husband. He couldn't sense any other strong magical presence. Surely he would've noticed, but after his recent mistake, he checked again. There was no sign of any other powerful magic.

"He's stronger than you can imagine."

"Which head thinks that?"

She didn't rise to his bait. *"You'll discover the nature of his magic soon."*

This discussion was a delaying tactic, and although he was fairly confident he could shield himself, he was concerned they might shoot Aina. But to not act meant the probability of death was high for both of them. Thomas cast an invisibility spell over himself, Aina, and the hyena. Morgan Red's eyes widened as they disappeared.

"He's still there," the sorcerer said.

But Thomas was already moving, and the hyena moved with him. Morgan Red fired into the space where Thomas had been. A second later, the hyena's huge jaws ripped into the mercenary's groin. He screamed and shot the space in front of him, but the hyena had already run for the second mercenary. Morgan Red fell to the ground, groaning. Thomas took his gun. The hyena took the second mercenary by his throat. Thomas called his knife, which slapped into his open hand. A shot from the third mercenary killed the hyena, and Thomas threw his knife into the man's heart. Two of the mercenaries were dead, and Morgan Red was bleeding profusely. He'd be dead soon.

"Who're you?" Thomas asked the sorcerer, allowing his invisibility spell to lapse.

"I'm Lord Page." Thomas raised his gun. "You might kill me, but you can't escape."

Thomas killed him. "I've decided to escape," he said aloud. Aina ran to him. "We have to hurry." She needed no persuading. They ran past the bodies of the four men and animal and up the incline into a narrower part of the tunnel.

"Only three of them left," Thomas said as they squeezed through a gap in the rocks.

"The worst three."

"There is that, but the numbers are getting more manageable. I'll miss the hyena, though."

"He was helpful," Aina said. Then she screamed and fell against the wall. "Thomas! Help me!"

Her hand was missing, and she was bleeding heavily. Thomas searched for the threat, and his magic was alive, but there was nothing to fight.

"Aina!" He ran to her.

She lurched forward, and the world slowed down for him. He caught her as she fell. Her back had been torn from her body. He held her, trying to stop the bleeding. He couldn't understand what had happened—there was no one there.

Tears ran down his hardened face. "Aina, I want you to live!"

"Thomas," she said weakly.

Thomas held her and tried to use his magic to heal her, but she was bleeding heavily. Her metal spine was clearly visible—it had snapped in two. She was dying.

Then he felt a presence in his mind. It was Lucy. *"Thomas! I almost fainted when I felt your pain. What's wrong?"*

"It's Aina. She's dying!" Lucy hesitated. She was searching for a connection. *"Help her!"* Thomas said.

"I'll try." From wherever she was, Lucy sent healing energy into Aina. Thomas held her, sensing Lucy's soothing energy rushing into her.

"Thank you," Aina whispered.

Lucy went quiet. *"I'm so sorry."*

Aina was dead. He sat very still, unable to believe that he'd lost her a second time. Again he held her dead body, and again he willed her to live. He was quiet for a long time, unable to control his tears.

Lucy waited silently, then she spoke.

"Thomas?"

"What?"

"Are you sure this is Aina?"

His eyes opened wide. *"Of course it's Aina! I've been with her for weeks. I know she's a bit different, but it's her. She wasn't dead when we put her on the pyre. A dragon must have taken her to a human hospital; they replaced some parts."*

"Her spirit is different," Lucy said quietly. *"This young woman has a softer, gentler spirit."*

"Aina could be gentle, too," he said, then he closed his mind to Lucy.

He knew this was Aina, even if she was different from before. He still held her, not caring about the blood. Now he felt remorse at not having fully believed her when she'd been alive. Tears burnt his eyes and he could no longer see the dark passage around him, but he felt it with rock magic. He was alone.

"Aina," he said quietly.

Laughter came from the rocks, and he looked up to see a mouth forming in the rock itself. Blood dripped from it as it grinned. This was the thing that had killed Aina.

Thomas attacked it. He had no idea what it was, he just threw all his magic at it. The mouth puckered, then spat. He vapourized whatever came from it. It laughed again, and he melted the rocks, sending surrounding rocks crashing around him. He no longer cared; he held nothing back, striking the obscene mouth again.

Movement from the passage below caught his attention. He saw the Empress and her two magicians rushing forward. They must have disguised themselves. He raised his hands and orange fire poured from him into the obscene mouth. Its grin changed to a scowl. But Thomas continued to attack, no longer caring about whether his body changed again with the Fire. The rocks trembled with his rage, and the face melted.

"Husband!" the Empress cried.

Then the rocks tumbled down the descent towards her and the sorcerers behind her, but Thomas continued to fling fire at the place the mouth had been. Time had slowed for him, and in his fury, he shook the mountain. All around him molten rock flowed, and then, as time passed, more rocks fell as a hard rain. His vision was blurred, and with a breaking heart, he picked up Aina's body and walked into the mountain.

36

"*If you have an idea, now's the time,*" Tan said. The spider bots were less than thirty feet away.

"*I know.*"

"*And the idea is?*" Seth asked.

"*I'm going to blow up the ship.*"

Na entered the machine mind again. She imagined the central controls and moved to a new place, but it wasn't where she wanted to go. Something vibrated, blocking her. She tried again, and each time, she appeared in another place. She saw movement, and she looked more closely. It was the twitching body of the spider, but she was sure that it wasn't this broken creature preventing her from moving. Then she sensed the source of the vibrations.

"*I can do this, too,*" Lady Byota said. A partial image of the sorcerer flickered ahead of her.

"*Do something!*" Seth's distant voice sounded urgent.

Not knowing what else to do, Na scooped up the remains of the spider and threw it headfirst at the sorcerer. The woman screamed as it bit her. "*What have you done to me?*"

She threw the body away from her, but she staggered as its poison entered her system.

Na focussed her mind on the central controls. Lady Byota and the remains of the spider disappeared, and she stood before the self-destruct mechanism. She commanded the ship to self-destruct, but it refused. It needed something else, and she guessed it might be the sorcerer. Hoping the woman was still conscious, Na returned. The surprised woman was pushed against a wall as the spider's body edged towards her. Na lifted them both and returned to the controls. She thrust the spider's red frilly mouth at Lady Byota and pushed into her mind. "The code for the self-destruct mechanism." Lady Byota resisted, and Na rubbed the spiders body against her while demanding the number.

"I won't tell you."

Na thrust the spider's mouth against her neck. "The number." When the spider bit, the number spewed from the sorcerer's mind. The countdown began, and Na locked the mechanism. The sorcerer had already lost consciousness, and she left the spider at her throat.

"Na!" Seth shouted.

"One more thing." She had to know about the two battle-cruisers. There was something strange about them. She searched quickly through the ship's mind. The information she wanted wasn't secret. She recoiled in shock. "We have to destroy the battlecruisers!"

She opened her eyes and blasted the nearest spider bots as they attacked Seth and Tan. *"It's about to explode."* Invisible, they flew away from the ship, but she knew the ships would calculate their trajectory. *"Why aren't they shooting?"* Na asked.

"I think they're waiting for us to drift further from the flagship," Tan said. *"They don't want to risk damaging it."*

Na laughed as the flagship exploded, pushing the four dragons further into space. If not for Kaylie, they would have separated, but their efforts to support her kept them together. Seth and Tan held them physically together, while Na maintained group invisibility. They were drifting closer towards one of the large battlecruisers, a ship that, in size, was almost as large as the flagship had been, and like the flagship, it had many hollows and holes where they could hide. Soon they were flying low over the outer surface of the vessel. She saw a shaded area ahead.

"Let's look," she said.

It was a large hollow, and as they passed over it, they circled down and disappeared inside. Na wasn't sure of the purpose of the space. In the centre of the indentation was a door about the same size as her. Nothing else. They clung to the side of the space and waited.

"You're bleeding," Seth said. She hadn't noticed, but looking down, she saw that her side was covered in blood. Perhaps that was why she felt so weak. While Tan tended Kaylie, Seth examined her wound. She almost fainted when he pulled something from her. *"A piece of the flagship,"* Seth said. He blew healing flame onto her, and it soothed the pain a little.

"I need to attempt to enter the mind of this ship," she said.

"No, you're too weak," Seth said. *"If you're attacked by one of those things again, you might never come out."*

She was worried about that, too, but she had to try. *"When I was inside the flagship, I saw something."* She paused for breath. *"The two battlecruisers are special. They have a new weapon the Empire has developed. Something that could destroy us from space."*

"Even if that's true, it doesn't help us to lose you," Seth said. The ship vibrated. *"What was that?"*

"*A weapon,*" Tan said. The others looked at him. "*It felt like a discharge.*"

It happened again. "*I need to see,*" Na said. But her body was hurting, and she struggled to move.

"*I'll look.*" Tan crawled to the top of the hole. Light glinted on his light-brown body, making him look almost golden. He turned his long head towards them. "*The battle-cruisers are firing on the planet.*"

Another vibration shook the ship, and something hit Na's body. She cried out in pain, but when she looked, she couldn't sense any life, just hundreds of objects flying past her.

"*The door's open,*" Tan said.

She looked deeper into the hole to see the door closing. "*It's a refuse chute,*" she said. Her side hurt, and she was bleeding again. She turned her mind back to the problem. "*I have to enter its mind.*"

"*I'll go,*" Seth said.

She knew Seth was skilled, but she didn't like it. "*I'm better suited to this.*" But he'd already ignored her and entered the machine mind.

"*You should rest,*" Tan said. "*I can keep watch.*"

Na closed her eyes, but the vibrations of the ship stopped her from sleeping. Several minutes later, Seth cried out. She was now alert. "*Seth.*" There was no reply. His eyes were closed, and his body was shaking. She tried to push him from the side of the ship, but it was as if he were stuck with the strongest glue. She was becoming alarmed.

Kaylie opened her eyes. "*Don't go inside its mind, Na. It's too dangerous.*"

Na was relieved to see Kaylie recovering, but she had to help her brother. She reached inside the metal mind and saw Seth stuck on a giant cobweb, surrounded by flickering spiders. He wasn't moving. They turned on her, but then, something else attacked her. It punched out of the artificial mind. She was stunned, and she slipped from the side of the ship. Tan caught her and pulled her back in.

"What happened?"

"Something attacked me." She looked at his body. "And Seth's trapped." She knew that if he died inside the metal mind, he'd die here, too. "I have to go in again."

"No!" Kaylie and Tan said together.

"I have no choice." Then there was another vibration below them. "The door's opening." Impulsively, Na flew deeper into the hole in the side of the ship, towards the opening door.

"Na!" Kaylie called.

But Na kept flying, and just as the doors were closing, she slipped inside. She ran up a dark tunnel, sometimes slipping on the slimy surface. There was another door at the far end, but by the time she reached it, it had closed. It was a solid metal door. It would be impossible to burn open.

She waited. And as she waited, she decided to explore the outer part of the machine mind. Usually, nothing in this part interested her; it was the part being accessed thousands of times a minute by the crew. But it did contain some things of use. She studied the ship's plans and saw where she was, and where she wanted to go. There was a space on the other side of this door, and from that space, dozens of waste disposal chutes led up to various sections of the ship. She also checked the frequency of waste disposal. It was much longer than she wanted. In half an hour, Seth could be dead.

When the door finally opened, she forced her way through a pile of moving waste, her fire burning away the many impurities. Then she rushed towards the chute leading to the computer centre. She squeezed along it, incinerating the waste in her way. Pushing open the small door at the top, she slipped out into a maintenance area close to where the ship's computer mind was located.

The area was large. Easily big enough for dragons to walk around—although a great dragon would need another entry point. A woman walked into the maintenance area and stared at her in surprise, and then she screamed and fled. Na followed along the passageway, but several yards later, turned into the computer centre. Five people sat at desks, and two looked up. Na burnt the main computer, and small explosions caught the attention of the rest of the staff. One spoke on her earphone, and Na killed her first and then the others. When she left the room, the fire was blazing.

"Seth's free," Kaylie said.

Feeling better, Na ran back down the corridor to the maintenance area with the chutes. There was no one there, and she slipped back down the chute. Going down was easier than climbing up, and seconds later, she landed in a pile of waste. She then waded through the sludge until she came to the fourth chute to her right. This one led to a kitchen near the weapons centre—the centre itself had no waste chute she could find. It was harder to climb, and she kept slipping on the grease. But she persisted.

When she was near the top, a cook opened the chute, and she blasted him with fire. He fell back with a scream, and she slipped out. The kitchen staff ran from the kitchen, and she set fire to the stores of food as she left the room. It was certain that the kitchen staff would communicate with security. She was close to the weapons centre, but she knew the doors would be impossible for her to break open. And they'd be guarded. She needed another way.

She quickly entered the outer part of the ship's mind again, and as before, she was one of many searching for information or commanding the ship to perform some small service. Na went to the education centre where she created a hologram of herself, and she walked it along the corridor in front of the weapons centre. The guards fired as the hologram charged at them, blasting them with imaginary fire. A dragon immune to bullets made them move further back along the corridor. Her hologram stood in front of its door and appeared to open it and enter. She even created the sound of it shutting. Standing still, and using her invisibility spell, she waited and watched the passage, hoping someone would enter to check.

Within a minute, a security team led by an imperial lord ran towards the centre. The lord possessed some magic. They opened the door, and she slipped into the centre behind the men. She burnt the soldiers from behind, but the lord was protected. *"A nice trick with the holograms."* He spoke the True Language passably well, but with none of the richness of a dragon. *"But you're only one, and I'm not sure what you think you can do here."*

She looked around the room. There were three technicians sitting at desks, staring at her; there were also racks of torpedoes. She had some ideas. *"Tell them to explode."*

The man laughed. *"That might work, but it might not be as easy as you think, and you'd kill yourself, too. And any dragons on the surface of the ship."*

"The sacrifice would be worthwhile." Although she hoped to find another way.

"Have you heard the news from the planet?" he asked. She was tempted to kill him and start looking for a way, but she hesitated at the mention of Prometheus. *"You must have noticed our weapons. Not just these."* He gestured to the torpedoes and missiles. She knew there were other weapons; perhaps she should've chosen the weapons centre on the

other side of the ship. *"We can now target armies with precision, leaving the surrounding environment almost untouched."*

"So?"

"The imperial navy has just killed half your species, and soon we'll kill the other half."

Na was shocked but hid her emotion. She listened for deceit, and didn't hear any. This man believed what he was saying, but that didn't make it true. Her tail flicked out, decapitating a man sending a message to the bridge. *"No communication."* The other two technicians stared at their dead colleague in shock. They'd understood on an unconscious level.

"I'm not lying," the lord said. *"I don't need to. You're by far the most annoying alien species on the planet, although the giant birds have caused some damage, too."*

"The rocs have hurt you." She was pleased.

"Not as much as we've hurt them. They're protected by the forest, and we want the wood, so we don't want to burn it all down." The door opened and a score of security officers walked in. She'd waited too long. She positioned herself so the lord was between her and the men.

"That will make little difference." He turned to the men.

Na knew his intention, and she blasted him with fire before he ordered his men to shoot. He shielded the blast, which didn't surprise her, but the way the flames flew around him, much faster than they should have, burning the men, did. She liked his shield and continued to blast it, sending the flames rushing around him and scorching the men behind. His look of annoyance told her that this hadn't been his plan. Then she whipped out her tail, knocking the lord and the remaining men to the ground. She leapt at them, breathing fire, and crushing those on the ground. Soon it was only her, the lord, and the two technicians. She was bleeding, but the lord was lying on the floor; his back seemed to be broken.

"*This wasn't supposed to happen,*" the man said.

"*Were the deaths of dragons supposed to happen?*" She wasn't interested in his answer and stamped on his head.

She needed to quickly understand how to detonate the ship's weapons. She turned to the two technicians. They were scared, which made reading their minds easier. She tried the female first, but quickly found out that she was the junior technician. Na quickly switched into the male's mind.

At first it was easy. The man started thinking about how to detonate the torpedoes on her mental suggestion, then he started to suspect that something was wrong. She sent another message into his mind, and he began to think of how he could stop her from detonating the torpedoes. This was more useful, and as he went through various ways of blocking her, she realized that she needed the security code to access the device. "*Do you remember the security code?*"

"*Of course,*" he thought, almost annoyed. And he mentally repeated it.

"*Thank you,*" Na said. She accessed the computer terminal in the True Language—much faster than the voice activation the humans used. She found the weapons controlled and entered the code.

"No!" the man shouted, his face flushed.

From his emotion, she knew she'd done it right. She set the timer for twenty minutes, and then she fused the electric pathways used to access the controls. It would take more than twenty minutes to fix.

"*The ship's going to explode!*" she said to Kaylie. "*Get away!*"

Then, turning to the technicians, she projected an image of a heavy fighter into their minds. They thought of the fighter bay in the huge hangar at the bottom of the ship. *"Take me."* She monitored the messages they sent to security. Hesitating for a moment, Na turned and picked up two rocket launchers from a rack of weapons—each was loaded—and put them over her shoulders. Then they left the room together. She had seventeen minutes left. *"Fast!"*

They ran down passages, sending the crew into doorways, or forcing themselves up against the walls. They were taking her to the large lift and had messaged security. It was a trap. *"Stairs!"* They changed direction, and she scrambled the message they sent. When they reached the lowest level, she repeated the image of the heavy fighter. This time she let them message security.

They ran along a wide corridor. To their left was a huge hangar divided into bays, and every twenty yards there was an entrance. They rushed past the first entrance, but on the second she stopped. They had seven minutes before the ship would explode. The humans kept running, ignoring her attempts to call them, and she melted their tags. They screamed and fell into the walls. *"Stand!"* They staggered to their feet. *"In here."* They reluctantly followed her into the nearest transport bay. They had less than five minutes.

She'd already chosen the vessel she wanted. It was a transport vessel big enough for her to fit in the front, and for four dragons in the back. *"Start the engine."* She heard the vibrations of soldiers' boots on the ground as they rushed towards them. They'd just discovered they'd prepared an ambush in the wrong place. Na placed the missile launchers on the ground and studied them, then she quickly confirmed her thoughts against the woman's memories. Aiming the missile at the outer hangar doors, she fired. Tossing the empty launcher aside, she aimed again with the second one. They had two minutes remaining.

The first missile exploded against the doors, causing a sudden rush of air out of the hangar. The second missile widened the space. The soldiers were now rushing to leave the hangar as it emptied of air. Na jumped into the cockpit, squeezing into the back three seats, while the man and woman sat at the front. She'd already checked to see if they had basic pilot skills, and they did, so when they hesitated, she suggested death. The engine started, and the old transport vessel taxied onto the runway. They had forty seconds left.

"Where are you?" An image came to her. They were too close, but both Seth and Kaylie were injured. *"I'm coming in a human transport vehicle. Get in the back."*

The transport sat on the end of the runway—they had thirty seconds left. *"Go!"* The vessel slowly accelerated towards the large hole in the hangar doors. Na was counting the clock, and at twenty-four seconds they flew through the hole. *"There."*

The humans resisted. *"There!"* she repeated more forcefully, and they flew towards the partially visible dragons. Na could understand the basic controls, and she opened the rear doors. Tan pulled Kaylie in first, then he helped Seth climb in. Na closed the rear door and filled the rear space with oxygen. They had seven seconds left. *"Go!"* The mental image she sent of an explosion was clear. The transporter accelerated away from the battlecruiser at full speed. The explosion lit the darkness of space.

37

Lucy listened to the distant magical rhythms. They were almost musical, a chanting or incantation coming from beyond this world. They were similar to but stranger and stronger than those used in the forward command post. And the magical signature was sadly familiar.

"Show me a way." She was confident her higher self, the deeper part of her spirit, would provide an answer.

A path appeared. And at the end of the path was a mutating forest of the type she knew—the Night Hag was on the astral plane. But as she stepped towards the path, she hesitated. Something touched her. A grey owl—an animal from her oracle—was perched on her shoulder.

"Who are you?" Lucy asked.

"I'm Briallen. I'm your guide."

Lucy had travelled to other realms of existence before without a guide. *"Why now?"*

"You had unseen guides in the past, but this time I must make myself known. You travel a dangerous path."

She felt warmed to have this beautiful bird by her side.

Briallen flew ahead, and she followed into a wooded world where shapes changed, mutated, and blended with others for no apparent reason. It was a world of illusions, but Briallen knew the true way, and she led Lucy to the edge of a glade. There she perched on a branch above her head.

Hidden in the trees, Lucy watched Lady Hay dancing around a glowing grey crystal. Dark spirits, ghouls, and demons were dancing a tight circle around the crystal, and each time they touched it, sparks flew into them. Their dance appeared insane, and some were slashing themselves with their curved claws. She shivered, but the mad dance captivated her. Unseen, she continued to watch the patterns of black magic flowing around the woman.

Briallen hopped onto her shoulder. It was time to go.

"*Lucy?*" Hwith said.

She opened her eyes and rubbed her face, calling her Fire to rid her of a deep chill she felt.

"*I was with the Night Hag. She's calling dark spirits towards her.*"

"*Why?*"

"*They feed on energy. They can rob someone of vitality and life. They're also insane,*" Lucy said.

"*Is this what's sending the human soldiers into a frenzy?*" Hwith asked. "*It's a needless sacrifice, but one that suits us.*"

Lucy had heard the reports that the soldiers were forcing their way through some of the most dangerous parts of the forest, without a concern for their lives, instead of going around them. To save a little time, many lives were being lost.

"*Perhaps.*" She looked up at the rocs and shared an image

of a rear command post in the jungle. "*She's drugged them: dulling and exciting at the same time. All they hear is loud music, and all they feel is the urge to kill. She's combined black magic and technology perfectly; she's draining them of their vitality. They'll die if she continues this for much longer.*"

"*That's not our problem,*" Jzzrata said.

"*The damage their madness inflicts on the forest is,*" Lucy said.

Lucy could hear the sounds of mental chatter coming from the soldiers, some of whom were only sixty or seventy yards away from where they stood, although the thick forest slowed them down a little. "*They're hardly aware of their own bodies, let alone their own minds.*"

Some of the younger rocs wanted to fly to the command post immediately, but Lucy insisted on planning first. Lucy and Chloris stood in the inner circle as the rocs gathered. With them were Hwith, Pzillis Trillis, Soonasa, Jzzrata, and Old Grey. Around them, outer circles of rocs formed, until the massive trees surrounding them prevented more from fitting in. Other rocs sat in the branches above to listen.

The inner circle spoke in turn. Lucy began. "*The destruction of the rear command post mustn't happen until after I've entered and reprogrammed the soldiers' tags. I can send them running.*"

"*Program them to kill each other,*" Stelling said. Other rocs tweeted their agreement.

"*I want them to run,*" Lucy said. "*Programming them to attack each other would create resistance. The humans have given up their autonomy, but they're not automatons. I met a soldier in the forest who'd turned off his own tag. He'd done it instinctively. A tag cannot completely control a man; it only influences. The natural instinct of many of these men is to run. I can add confusion and fear to those feelings.*"

The rocs were quiet for a few moments, then Pzillis Trillis and Hwith simultaneously squawked their agreement, followed by the rest of the inner circle. *"I need help in dealing with the guards, and whatever else is inside the headquarters. I'll deal with the magic of the Hag,"* Lucy said.

"Agreed," Pzillis Trillis said.

Hwith spoke to all present. *"I'll lead the attacks on the army."* The bright roc looked at Lucy. *"You and Chloris go with Pzillis Trillis, Soonasa, and Stelling."* He raised his large head, and five dragonflies flew down from the trees. *"They'll accompany you. We've not scouted that area, but we know the vegetation is quickly growing again, thanks to you. The dragonflies will hardly be noticed as they scout ahead."*

It was agreed. Lucy ran with Chloris and the rocs; the dragonflies flew ahead, scouting the area. Their route was not direct; they had to skirt around the army. However, there were gaps in their lines, and eventually, they reached a place where Pzillis thought they could slip through unseen.

It took a further three hours to reach the smouldering but regrowing part of the forest. They walked over glowing embers, but around them, fire funnels and a few other of the toughest plants grew. Lucy and the rocs spoke to the fire funnels, calming them when they were forced to brush past. The ancient forest helped, too.

Lucy pointed, stifling her urge to speak aloud. *"There."* All knew that the command post would listen to the regrowing forest around it. Even imperial buildings and vehicles possessed basic artificial intelligence.

Chloris hissed quietly, and her tail twitched. She sniffed the air. "Two of my sisters are there," she whispered.

Lucy and the rocs pushed their minds against the protective shield around the squat vehicle. It combined magic and technology, and was dense. After several minutes trying, they stopped.

"It's too well protected," Pzillis Trillis said.

Lucy nodded. *"But the Hag's inside. I can sense her magic. And another magic. I might still be able to find a way inside."*

"Your skill's improved," Soonasa said.

"But I can't see their numbers."

"Never mind their numbers," Chloris hissed. Then she switched to the True Language. *"The size of the vehicle limits the numbers. As long as there's no more than a few sorcerers, we can destroy it."*

And if not? Lucy thought quietly. This is going to be hard.

"Of course," Pzillis said, reading her mind. *"That's why we're here."*

The dragonflies returned from scouting the area. They'd seen two ice demons moving around the command centre.

"We need a distraction," Chloris said. *"I'll call my sisters."*

"Will they come?" Lucy asked aloud.

"If they don't, I'll find them."

This sounded ominous to Lucy. *"The Hag might lock herself inside."* The tank-like vehicle looked incredibly strong.

"Then we'll roast them alive," Pzillis Trillis said. Stelling twittered a laugh.

Chloris was gone, and Lucy sent two dragonflies with her. They were incredibly tough, fire-breathing creatures. They might just make a difference. The ice demons had wandered a little away from the command post. The dragonflies placed them at about forty yards distance.

Lucy studied the eyes of the tank-like vehicle. They were open to the world around them, and she created an illusion of trees. *"I've blinded the metal mind."* Lucy wondered whether she were becoming a dragon or roc, with her ways of expression. *"We must move closer now, while they're blinded."* She ran forward, followed by the three rocs. They stood in the open, protected only by the illusion Lucy had created. The remaining three dragonflies were hidden in patches of fire funnels, awaiting orders.

Screeches in the undergrowth told her that Chloris had met her sisters. The sound was ferocious. She reached for the dragonflies, but one was dead, and the other wasn't responding. The screeching lasted for over a minute, and then there was silence. The door of the command post remained tightly shut, until a bloodied ice demon staggered towards it. One of its eyes was missing.

Lucy closed her eyes in sadness. *"Chloris?"*

"Shhh."

Her eyes opened wide. Chloris was alive. Unsure what was happening, Lucy waited as three men stepped from the command vehicle. One was a sorcerer; the other two belonged to the Red Legion. She wasn't surprised the imperial aristocrat was using mercenaries instead of imperial soldiers.

"What happened?" the lord asked.

"An ice demon attacked us," it said.

"Impossible," the lord said. "The other demon?"

"I didn't see."

"This planet isn't as much under your control as you'd like to believe, green lord," a red legionnaire said.

"My name's Lord Green."

"As you wish." The mercenary looked around. "There could be others. Fix this lizard up. We may need it."

Lord Green's gaze darkened as he looked at the mercenary. Then he turned towards Lucy and the rocs. His jaw hung open.

"I think he's seen us," Lucy said.

Pzillis Trillis and Stelling were already running at the men with fire spraying from their mouths. The injured ice demon leapt away. The mercenary died instantly, and the lord ran screaming into the tank. Despite his magical defence, he was badly burnt. Soonasa sat on top of the tank vehicle and stopped the door from closing. Lucy ordered two of the remaining dragonflies to attack—they flew straight inside. Screams and flames came from the vehicle, and two men fell out. The rocs killed them.

With the doors open, Lucy could sense the life inside. *"There are two of them inside: the Hag and the other sorcerer."* She knew one of the dragonflies she'd ordered inside was dead.

Lord Green leapt out, followed by the remaining dragonfly. Magic swirled around him. The dragonfly died on contact with his magic, and he deflected Soonasa's blast. The three rocs attacked with fire, but he stood unscathed. He was stronger than Lucy had thought, but she had to reach the vehicle.

The forgotten and injured ice demon staggered from behind the tank with a submachine gun in its hands. It shot Stelling repeatedly, and the roc fell to the ground. Chloris ran from the undergrowth with another ice demon. Both of them were injured. Lucy watched with surprise when they knocked the one-eyed ice demon to the ground. Chloris must have turned this ice demon against the others. Lucy wondered if it was one that Chloris had known.

Lord Green fought the two rocs, both of whom were tiring. "Chloris! Help them!" Lucy shouted. Green pushed the rocs back, and then turned and ran into the forest.

Lucy had no time for him. She ran towards the vehicle with a knife in her hand—one she'd already infused with magic. The door was closing again, and she leapt inside. The door slammed shut behind her.

The Hag attacked, and Lucy was thrown against the wall by the psychic punch, but it was the second attack that shocked her. It shouldn't have contained so much power. The Fire blazed inside her, and she struck a blow that sent the Hag across the inside of her command centre and into a control panel at the front. Lucy looked around for anyone else; she felt a presence of some sort.

"You're not bad. You'd make a good imperial lord," the Hag said.

"Surrender," Lucy said.

"You know my answer."

"I'm stronger," Lucy said, uncertain that it was true, but her oracle had insisted it was.

"But I can call aid. Sometimes it's our friends who make all the difference." Assuming she'd ensorcelled a spirit, Lucy prepared herself. But instead of attacking, the Hag was speaking to someone else telepathically. Slightly shocked, Lucy realized that she couldn't hear the conversation.

"The Emperor wants to speak to you."

A vision of the man who controlled the solar system appeared on the vehicle's forward screen. He was more energetic and vibrant than she'd imagined.

"Come to me."

An image of the black tower appeared on the screen, and a desire to travel there softened her. She rubbed her face to get rid of the feeling; the Emperor had tried to plant the suggestion in her mind. She was scared by his power, but she wasn't prepared for the sudden attack of magic through the communication systems of the vehicle. She was flung against the back wall, her Fire blazing in defence.

She noticed that the Hag was moving about inside the

vehicle. Lucy called on her power as she pulled herself to her feet. She no longer cared about the pain. The Emperor vanished, and again she faced the Hag. The woman smiled unpleasantly, and then she stepped forward and touched her. The inside of the command post disappeared, and they fell into another world. The woman watched her. "Do you know where you are?"

Lucy looked at the misty world around her. "I know it well."

The Hag appeared surprised, then she nodded. "We are alike, in some ways."

"We're nothing alike," Lucy said.

They were on the astral plane again. Creatures pressed against both her and the Hag. The shadowy things disgusted her. Nervously, she backed away. The Hag seemed at home as she watched the creatures.

Realizing her fear was paralyzing her, Lucy began to study her surroundings. It seemed to be some sort of ethereal laboratory. She pushed into the Hag's mind, feeling the woman's surprise as she entered. Realizing that the things pressing against her were feeding on her, she searched for a way to remove them. Her magic vibrated, and her mood lifted. Immediately, she felt a lessening of pressure. The creatures and the Hag disappeared.

Lucy opened her eyes and the Hag screamed. They were back inside the tank, and the sorcerer was surrounded by a violently swirling scarlet nimbus of energy. An emergency door blew outwards, and the Night Hag jumped from the vehicle and ran into the undergrowth.

Lucy was stunned, but a ticking brought her mind back. She looked at the control panel: the Hag had activated the vehicle's self-destruct. Chloris joined her. Lucy pointed at the number.

"This thing blows up in five minutes," Chloris said.

"I have to get inside its mind before it does."

"No, you don't," Chloris hissed. "You can leave it and live."

"Give me three minutes." Lucy entered the machine mind warily, but nothing attacked. Perhaps the presence of a psychic attack dog within the machine would simply have been too inconvenient for the sorcerers. Lucy realized now that the woman's work had been explorative. She was researching other planes in search of spirits to ensorcel.

She searched for the controls for the soldiers' tags and soon found them. They were obviously frequently used. It was harder to understand what to do with them. Switching off the download of drugged feeling and stopping the loud inner music were the first things she did. Then she suggested a fear of the forest. The machine's computer mind showed her the changes almost immediately.

The men stopped where they stood, confused. They dropped their weapons but were unsure why. The final thing she did was to download a single word.

"Retreat!"

38

Thomas laid Aina's body to rest in a peaceful chamber deep within the mountain. The chamber was sealed; it had neither an entry nor exit. No one who couldn't walk rock would ever find it. He touched the cave wall, and soon the chamber glowed orange. He didn't need the light to see, but he imagined she'd like it.

He thought back on her deaths. His lack of belief in magic had resulted in her first death; his fear of its power had resulted in her second. He swore that if he ever had a third chance, there would be no hesitation; he'd use his magic without restraint.

Parts of her artificial body showed clearly through her broken skin, but so too did her human flesh. The Empire may have created much of her body, but she'd shown her own spirit. And in the end, she'd fought against them. One way or the other, he was sure it was Aina's spirit. Thomas remembered Orange's words. The troll had once created a bright butterfly from the rocks. When he'd asked Orange if he'd created life, the troll had told him that he'd only created a body; life itself had chosen whether or not to inhabit it. Perhaps it'd been the same with Aina. Perhaps that was the body she'd chosen. Perhaps she'd had no other choice.

He was hardly conscious of time passing as he sat in the glowing chamber, his body burning with the Fire. His thoughts soon turned to vengeance.

"Thomas! Are you all right?"

He sat up straight. *"Lucy."*

"What's happened to you? Your energy feels very disturbed."

Thomas looked at Aina's body as he spoke, and although he tried to prevent it, he couldn't help but share his emotion with his friend. He knew she saw the small chamber, lit in soft orange light, as he did.

"Aina?"

"I've failed her for a second time. She died because my fear of the Fire held me back."

She was silent for several seconds. *"What happened before she died?"*

He showed her from the time he was tied to a chair to the mouth opening up in the wall of the cave. She studied the Empress and was then silent for several seconds, but the warmth of her heart eased his pain a little.

"So the disturbance of energy I felt earlier was that thing appearing in the wall. Are you sure it was the Emperor?"

"His wife called to him when I attacked; she would know."

"Thomas, the magic was strange. Powerful like nothing I've felt before. I think I understand how."

"Tell me."

"The Emperor has a weapon, a sort of device in the tower. A burnt-orange fire. It's used to capture a dragon's soul."

Thomas now had one more reason to hate the Emperor. *"It doesn't completely surprise me,"* he said. *"And it doesn't bode well for us. What's happened to you?"* Thomas asked.

"A lot." She told him about her journey and the Night Hag.

"She sounds unpleasant."

"She's as bad as Frore, and I'll have to face her again." She showed him her meeting with the silver and golden dragons. *"There's something familiar about the golden dragon, Na. I can't place it."*

"We saw a golden dragon in our shared vision after we left the centre of the planet."

"I think it's the same dragon," Lucy said. *"She told me her task is to help us embrace the Fire. She'll join us at the black tower. I fly with the rocs. The dragons are joining us, too. Prometheus has declared war on humanity."*

"But not on you?"

Lucy gave a dry laugh. *"I think the rocs sometimes think I'm a roc, too. But I have to stop them harming the citizens of Silva, at least. Nothing I can say will stop them attacking Nassopolis. We fly to the tower soon. I don't know how this will work out, but the rocs expect to end the empire."*

"I'll be there," Thomas said. *"It's time to end this."*

Then Lucy was gone, and Thomas was alone, planning ways to kill the Emperor.

Thomas knelt next to Aina's body. After several minutes, he laid his hand on her and flames leapt up. She would return to the elements. Her body blazed, and then it was gone.

Without looking back, Thomas walked through the wall and strode through the rock. Without burning the Fire, he moved silently, searching for the nearest tunnels. He found a series of caves near the summit and walked towards them. Half an hour later, he stepped into a cave. A cold wind blew into him; he was no more than a twenty-minute walk to the cave mouth, although he had no idea how far that would be from the citadel.

As he turned to leave, he felt something pulling him. Standing still, Thomas listened in the True Language, prepared to fight whatever it was that reached out to him. But it wasn't imperial; it wasn't even human. He listened again, but he couldn't identify it. Again he walked towards the cave mouth, but this time it pulled more strongly. Thomas had no idea why, but he reached into his pocket and pulled out the midnight blue. It was glowing. Bringing the crystals up to his eyes, he spoke to them.

"What do you want?"

An image of a large cavern came into his mind. He knew where it was; it was the last of this series of caves. He hesitated. He wanted to kill the Emperor and this seemed like a distraction, but this simple life form called him more insistently. Estimating that the final cave was no more than a half hour walk, he sighed and walked back into the mountain. The midnight blue immediately calmed. Experience had taught him it was best to listen to his intuition. For whatever reason, he was being called. He walked faster, hoping that it was simply the midnight blue seeking a new home, and nothing more serious.

The final cavern was one of the biggest he'd seen in his journey through the mountain, and in the middle lay a large rock. He rubbed his hand over it, admiring the pattern of black stripes running through the green rock. It wasn't connected to any of the other rocks and looked as if it'd been placed there. Thomas wondered how it had got there in the first place. Before he could investigate it further, the midnight blue called him again. It wanted him to place it on the wall of the cavern. Thomas walked up to the wall and placed the crystal against it. It tugged at his magic, and with a slight smile, Thomas gently applied his rock magic, helping it attach itself to the cave wall. He stepped back and watched it slowly grow. Crystals like these were the simplest of lifeforms, but as with all life, they had their likes and dislikes, and this one appeared to like this cave. Now free of his obligation to a small life that had saved his, he turned back to the giant rock in the centre. It was unlike any he'd seen. He touched it again, sending his mind into it.

Thomas quickly moved several paces back. It wasn't a rock. A large green eye opened.

"Why do you wake me?" She spoke the True Language with clarity and power.

"I'm sorry. I didn't know you were here."

The dragon moved her giant head stiffly and sniffed the air. Her deep green eyes glowed, and Thomas felt her push into his mind. He pushed her away, and she blasted him with fire, but his Fire was alight, and the flames rushed around him without harm.

"You're not what you appear," the dragon said.

"Neither are you," Thomas said. *"What do you think you see?"*

The dragon uncurled herself, turning so her head faced him. *"I've yet to decide. By what right do you hold the dragon fire?"*

"It's mine by right of travelling to the inner sun and taking it. A dragon asked me to take it."

The dragon listened more intently. Then he realized that she'd reentered his mind more softly and was sifting through his memories. This dragon knew a magic he'd never encountered, and he wasn't sure how to stop it. Instead of trying, Thomas slipped into the dragon's mind. She was an ancient queen. She'd fought during the first great war between humans and dragons but had been asleep ever since. The Fire had woken her and would wake all dragons. Then a deeper thought came unbidden.

"Rhiannon."

A deep rumbling vibrated through the chamber, and fire dripped from her mouth. *"Only a dragon could do that,"* Rhiannon said.

"At least mind reading saves time," Thomas said.

"Indeed. Your story is unique." The dark green eyes regarded him closely. *"But you still know little of dragons."*

"I know that the black dragon came to me in dreams and told me to travel to the centre of the planet and take the Fire.

"What do you know of the other dragon in your dreams?"

"The golden one?"

"I sense that she's important," Rhiannon said.

Thomas moved awkwardly forwards a few steps. The pain from the Fire almost made him faint, and again, he wished for the walking stick he'd lost. He called on the magic to soothe the pain, but it only eased it slightly. The dragon watched him struggle to regain his breath.

"What is this dragon fire?"

"Something no human should possess."

"That's what it's not; what is it?"

The dragon rumbled a laugh. *"You'll soon discover, but it's not for me to tell you."*

"You can try."

A burst of flame came from Rhiannon's mouth, and Thomas took that as a no.

"I'll join the dragons in the war against humanity."

"Against the Empire," Thomas said.

"They're the same."

Thomas shook his head. *"I'm human."*

"Don't underestimate yourself. Now leave me!"

The giant eyes closed, and the dragon called in the True Language—on a level he could hear but not understand. She was speaking to other dragons.

Thomas called the Fire to loosen his joints, and then he ran through caves and tunnels. After about forty minutes he felt the fresh mountain air. When he stepped out onto the white snow, his magic warmed him, and the cold air helped dull the pain. He looked around the white peak and the sea of clouds that surrounded it. He knew that less than a mile away was a bridge over an icy chasm, which led to the black tower.

Thinking of the tower seemed to make it aware of him, and he shuddered when he heard its eerie call. He never remembered hearing it so clearly before.

"A foul thing," Rhiannon said. *"The dragon fire has given you the ability to hear it."*

"It needs razing," Sensing the dragon's agreement, Thomas climbed down towards the icy road beneath him. A long caravan of vehicles moved slowly along it. As he approached, he cast the spell of invisibility while considering which vehicle to take. The luxurious cars were for nobles; he had no wish to sit with them. Further back in the line, he heard minstrels singing—his choice was made. Then he hesitated. Two cars in front of the minstrels was a vehicle exuding a magic that crept along the ground towards him. Carefully, he threaded it around him whilst avoiding its touch. The neophyte sorcerers only saw the white snow.

But if he moved, there was a chance they'd see him. He needed a distraction, and then he heard Rhiannon moving through the mountain. *"I'll give you your distraction."* The top of the mountain exploded, and Thomas sprinted to the minstrels' wagon as the green and black dragon rose into the air. Slipping into the wagon, he found an empty space while the minstrels stared up in wonder. Thomas planted a false memory in their minds—he'd been there all along.

He sensed a distant amusement. *"You're dragon,"* Rhiannon whispered in his mind.

39

"*Where are we going?*" Kaylie asked.

"*To the other battlecruiser,*" Na said. She knew movement caused her sister pain, but she had no choice.

"*I'm not sure I can fight yet.*"

The thought of her mutilated, one-legged sister fighting at all disturbed her. "*If all goes well, you won't need to. You can stay in this boat and watch the humans.*"

"*You're keeping them alive?*" Tan asked.

"*For now.*" They were useful and more intelligent than many she'd met. "*We'll need humans to get us into the other ship. I don't plan on entering via the refuse chutes again.*"

The destruction of the first battlecruiser, following shortly after the loss of the flagship, had shocked the human fleet, and electronic communications were rushing backwards and forwards.

"*How will we get in?*" Kaylie asked.

"*I've given the humans a story,*" she told her sister as they moved towards the battlecruiser. The story she'd devised was that they'd been doing maintenance outside the ship when the explosion happened, and their burnt boat, as she knew it was, had been pushed away. They'd been injured and their tags were broken. That was as complicated as she wanted it to be, and it had taken her more than a dozen attempts before they'd been able to understand.

"Dragons!" Seth said.

Na felt their presence, although they were still invisible.

"Where are you?" It was Twrch, the First of his Thunder.

"Here," Na said, immediately irritated by his tone.

"I'm leading the battle. What are you doing?"

"War leader?"

"For this battle."

That was not the same. *"Where's Night Sun?"*

"The First of Wisdom has disappeared."

This title included all dragons—something had changed on the planet. *"What do you mean?"*

"Many dragons died in the attack on the planet. Many became separated from the others."

"Spere?"

"Gone. Answer my question."

"What do you mean, gone?" Na's fire chilled at the possibility that the fierce but brave First of the Thunder was dead.

"We can't find him."

For a few seconds, she was quiet as she readjusted her inner fire. Then she spoke. *"I have questions, too."*

"Do you always speak like this?"

"Yes." She projected her mind into space, and then she noticed an emptiness drifting towards her. *"I can see you."*

"Answer my questions," Twrch said.

"This isn't a game. Because of foolish decisions, hundreds of dragons have been killed."

"I agree. We've had problems on the planet. I was challenged and forced to kill a dragon."

Na's temperature almost doubled, and the two humans next to her looked at her in alarm. *"It's nothing."*

"What?"

"I'm speaking to my human pilots."

"Human pilots?"

"I've destroyed the flagship, and the first battlecruiser, one of the ships with the new weapons. I'm about to attack the second. Wait until I've destroyed it, and then attack."

"I command," Twrch said.

"I command!" The deep voice vibrated through the minds of all dragons. "I'm First of Thunder."

"Spere!" Na felt love for this fighting red who had a confidence that few possessed—he'd declared himself leader of all dragon Thunders. She felt his warmth momentarily touch her.

"The Daughter of Fire protects dragonkind." Spere's attention turned to Na. *"What can you tell me about the fleet?"*

"There are over seventy ships, but we have to destroy the battlecruiser. You've seen what it can do."

"Are you in the small boat heading straight for the battlecruiser?"

"I am, and I have three dragons with me. Two of them are injured."

"Do you need help?"

"No, it's easier for a small number of dragons to enter secretly."

"Good luck, Na."

And then the great fighting red was gone. He gave her confidence in a way few other dragons did, but she still felt concern for the dragons attacking the fleet, even for her brother, Warth.

"We heard," Kaylie said.

The human pilots next to her began speaking with the

battlecruiser. They had many questions, but no apparent suspicions; they allowed the transport vessel to approach. But when they came within a hundred yards of the massive battlecruiser, its weapon systems came alive.

"What's happening?" Kaylie asked.

"They're killing dragons," Na said. Not all the dragons had been able to maintain invisibility, and as torpedoes hit the first dragons, more of the inexperienced ones became visible. A laser weapon, perhaps the one the empire had recently developed, killed others. Soon dozens of dragons drifted dead in space. Then she saw the body of a young black dragon floating in space. Again her fire chilled. She thought of Allie—that she would never see her sister again. More dragons died before her eyes. She'd never been more determined to kill the invaders. She snapped the screen into opaque mode, despite a request to return it to clear mode from a pilot officer of the battlecruiser.

"Are you ready?" She received affirmations from Seth and Tan. They'd attempt to position the transporter in a remote area of the hangar, telling the pilot that it needed repairs. She was sure repairing an old boat would not be a priority at any time, but especially not in a battle.

She'd already spoken to Kaylie about the power of suggestion in controlling humans. With most humans, it was quite possible to suggest something alluring to them, and they'd happily let themselves be mentally led in all sorts of directions—and hopefully, physically, too. She'd wondered why humans, of all animals, were so easily led astray. She wasn't sure whether it was because they had no idea that such a thing as the True Language even existed, so they wouldn't even think about defending against mental control, or whether they'd weakened themselves so much from continual use of electronic devices. It'd annoyed her the first time she'd discovered how mentally weak they were, but it was an advantage. Trying to ignore the distress calls from dying dragons, she focussed on her task.

The hold doors opened, and they flew in. A robot pilot directed them to a distant corner of the hangar, and a security team came over to check. All the dragons were invisible, and she suggested that there was nothing of interest in the old transporter. They saw nothing—they hardly looked. Na had made sure that her human pilots were ready to talk a lot in order to further distract them. An explosion near the closing hold doors also distracted their attention. Their deception was working, although one of the security officers did ask about the strange smell. Humans smelt strange to her, but it hadn't occurred to her that the same might be true in reverse, nor that she should mask it. When they were alone, she opened the door to the rear of the vehicle and squeezed through. She'd exit through the back with Seth and Tan. They left Kaylie speaking to the humans.

They entered the ship, accompanied by holograms of themselves as humans; their true form was invisible to those they met.

"This is a strange body," Tan said.

Na rumbled a laugh but had to stop herself when a group of humans stared at her. Then one of them bounced off her body, which was considerably larger than her hologram image.

"I think we need to adjust these bodies," Seth said.

Na reached into the education centre where the holograms were created, and hers became a lot fatter. The other two did the same, and now three fat humans walked down the corridor.

"I think we're the only fat humans on the ship," Seth said.

"It can't be helped," Na said. She knew that no one their

size would be on the ship. Only the poorest humans lacked the funds to custom design their bodies. *"We'll just tell people this is for fun."* But no one asked, and Na wasn't sure they really noticed. The crew was busy, and constant announcements were being broadcast into their minds. The dragons were losing the battle.

She led them away from the most crowded areas, and suddenly they were alone. *"Where are we going?"* Tan asked.

"Up the stairs to the bridge. I want to speak to the captain, and the bridge is a better place to access the ship's mind." The two humans had inadvertently told her that it had less locks and restrictions—less nasty shocks, she hoped. She ran through the plan again, and soon they were on the level of the bridge.

"Who are you?" an officer asked. It was the first time they'd been questioned. Two security guards stood by the entrance to the bridge.

"I'm Lady Na, and these are Lords Seth and Tan." But the effect of speaking to the officer in the True Language didn't exactly work.

"Did you speak to me?" He looked at them strangely.

She tried again, but it still didn't work, so she tried suggestion. *"The captain wants to see us."*

He rubbed his head. "Arrest them!"

She blasted the three of them with fire and stepped into the bridge with Seth and Tan behind her. The three fat humans surveyed the hectic activity on the bridge, and slowly they were noticed. A man and woman spoke in the centre of the room, and then they turned to look. She presumed the man was the captain, and a lord, from the presence of magic around him—he was the only human with any trace of magic.

"Who are you?" the captain asked.

"I am Na, Daughter of Fire, and I am taking over this ship."

"Did she speak?" the woman asked. Na guessed that she was the first officer.

"It spoke," the captain said. The man raised his eyebrows, and then Na changed the hologram. The bridge was suddenly filled with golden dragons, and she mingled with them. Seth and Tan did the same.

"What is this?" the captain asked.

"Your ship has been invaded by dragons," Na announced via the communications system.

When the first officer called on her earphone, Na burnt her tag, and the woman fell back in his chair, holding her head. The captain laughed. Na had already suspected that the man was mad. "I've already killed half the dragons. More than half." The man flipped a switch on a control panel behind him and the holograms vanished. Only three dragons remained. "Kill them!" But the remaining two security officers were not keen to approach the dragons.

Dark energy radiated from the captain, but he wasn't the sorcerer that Na had encountered in the ancient forest. He was something unpleasant, but lesser. She blasted the man with fire, but he deflected it. He cried out, though, so it had hurt him. Na repeated the blast.

"My lord, come to me!" the captain said. It was some kind of magical incantation.

Na had no idea what he was calling, but she didn't want any of it. She blasted him again, and this time Seth and Tan joined in. The man caught fire and was soon a blackened patch on the floor of the bridge. "Let's get this over with." Na touched the control panel and accessed the ship's mind. The two humans in the boat had been right—it was much easier. She studied the weapon systems, but realizing that something was wrong, she tried to pull away. She was stuck to the control panel, and something was sucking her strength. She almost fainted. *"Help me."*

Tan touched her and was thrown across the bridge, killing one of the humans and injuring another.

"What?" Seth asked.

"I don't know," Na said. She pulled back, but it held her tight and pain wracked her body. *"I think I'm dying."*

The ship shuddered, and the human crew leapt away from the crackling controls. Electricity was flowing through the ship.

"What's happening?" Kaylie asked.

"Something bad."

The ship's systems were being controlled by this thing, and the humans had no influence over them. She could hear their confused mental chatter. Then the weapons systems came online, and hundreds of torpedoes fired into space, each searching for dragons. A bright laser cannon opened fire, too. She heard distant dragon cries. Spere tried to communicate with her, but she couldn't reply. *"Kaylie!"* She screamed and lost consciousness.

KAYLIE HEARD her sister's silent scream, and her fire chilled. She could no longer hear Tan, and although she sensed Seth, he was barely conscious. Their plans had gone badly wrong. She'd always been highly psychic, and calling on her skill, she reached out into space. But what she saw shocked her. Hundreds of dead dragons were drifting in space. She saw Twrch's body; she searched for Spere but could neither see nor sense him. Others floated, injured and confused. The ship she sat in was attacking them repeatedly. The dragons were being wiped out. Then, noticing two dragons approaching, she tried to warn them away, but they continued to come closer.

"Keep away! We're dying!"

"It's time to finish this," Night Sun said.

Night Sun's voice calmed her. *"You're alive!"*

"I am."

Another dragon, a female, spoke with vibrating words exuding power. *"Have hope."*

"Who are you?"

"Rhiannon."

Kaylie sensed the dragon was old.

"Where's Na?" Night Sun asked. *"We heard her distress call."*

"She went inside, but something went badly wrong. I think she's dying."

"We've almost reached your ship," Night Sun said. *"Can you let us inside?"*

"I think so." Kaylie waited and watched the humans. They were getting more used to her. She'd already had them prepare the procedure for opening the outer doors. And when the two dragons approached, she told them to open the doors. The invisible dragons flew inside, and she told the humans to apologize to the hangar pilot for their error.

She saw the invisible green and black Rhiannon shimmering next to the glowing black Night Sun. Rhiannon was the biggest dragon she'd seen. *"I don't think you can fit any deeper into the ship."*

"No need," Rhiannon said. *"We could do this from outside the ship, but it's wise to breathe oxygen while we can."*

∽

Na fell from the wall breathing deeply, shocked by the power of the human Emperor that had held and weakened her. But she sensed another change.

"Kaylie. What's happened?"

"Na! You're alive," Kaylie said. *"Night Sun and another dragon are inside the ship."*

The news lightened her heart. *"Another dragon?"* Na looked through Kaylie's eyes.

"Rhiannon."

Na's eyes widened in surprise. She'd never seen such a large dragon, nor one that smelt so strongly of magic.

The new dragon was already inside the ship's mind. Na gingerly touched the wall again. Immediately, she sensed a battle of wills between Rhiannon and the Emperor. She lent her support to Rhiannon, and for several second she held her own, but then she was thrust from the wall, smashing into a control console and sending humans running.

Standing up awkwardly, Na looked around the bridge. Seth and Tan were both breathing, but neither was well. The humans were staring at the moving walls. Eyes and a mouth had appeared, and they moved in different directions. A red eye stared at her. And then it was gone.

"You understand this metal mind," Rhiannon said. *"Do your stuff!"*

Na didn't hesitate. She pushed into the ship's mind again. The Emperor had gone. Again she was attacked by spirit spiders, but in the few seconds she'd helped this dragon, she'd learnt a lot about fighting these chained spirits. Na burnt the hidden chains that bound the spirits, and they vanished. Searching for the ship's weapons system, she found it and silenced the guns. And then she used the ship's sensors to feel her way into space. The spaceships around her glistened like a school of silver fish. No more than two or three of the seventy ships had been destroyed by the dragons, yet seven hundred or more dragons drifted dead in space. Hundreds more were injured. Na was hardly able to comprehend the loss. She watched a grey dragon float past her. Her inner fire burnt cold. Shocked—she watched in a daze. *"They're all dead."*

"Kill the humans," the ancient queen said.

Na imposed her wishes onto the metal mind. She knew that usually the humans would attempt to countermand her orders, but she'd felt the vibrations from Tan and Seth. They were moving around the bridge. She watched the gun battery on the top of the battlecruiser turn towards the largest of the spaceships; the barrels lowered. One by one, she trained the other gun batteries onto other ships. They waited patiently for her command. It was a start, but she really wanted the torpedoes; gaining access to them was harder. It must have been some sort of safety mechanism.

Eventually, she found the controls she wanted inside the torpedoes themselves. Each one was intelligent and their minds were tightly closed. Starting with the first, she charmed it with a brush of magic. She felt as if she were singing a lullaby to a fat metal baby, slowly sending it to sleep. Then she was in, and one by one, she programmed the torpedoes to hit the largest ships. Next, she turned her attention to the advanced weapons system—some type of laser weapon. It was easier to gain access to than the torpedoes.

"Get ready to leave," she said to all dragons.

"Na."

It was Warth. *"Brother?"*

"I was wrong."

She breathed deeply, unable to think of a reply. Then

her proud brother was dead, gunfire from a destroyer ripping into his body.

Choking back tears, she launched her attack. The torpedoes flew silently through space, and then she commanded the guns and laser weapon to fire. Some of the nearest ships exploded. The communications systems of the vessels buzzed into life with questions and condemnations. "Have you gone mad?" a commander of a sleek white destroyer asked.

Using the computers, Na answered. "The dragons are striking back." She watched as the destroyer was engulfed in flames. "For my brother."

A wave of explosions spread outwards from the battlecruiser. She heard distress calls being sent to Prometheus, and a few minutes later, an order to attack the battlecruiser was sent from the planet. A third of the fleet was burning, including eight long tankers, which burnt as oxygen and oil spewed from their sides. A slick of black oil spread through space. And the torpedoes still flew silently towards the largest of the outer vessels.

A white yacht was sailing towards the battlecruiser. She'd not programmed any torpedoes to hit this. It'd seemed too small; it was one of the unarmed civilian boats carrying administrators for the empire.

"This is strange," Na said. She read the information on the ship, but it was nothing unusual.

"The Emperor returns," Rhiannon said.

Forked fire came from the yacht, and a nearby dragon died. Then she heard the cries of the remaining dragons. The remnants of the fleet had come to life and was attacking the dragons. Jagged debris cut into them. She wanted to distract whatever was inside the yacht, but she received a mental punch that stunned her. She felt light-headed and tears ran down her inner lenses as she watched in disbelief and bewilderment as yet more dragons died.

Rhiannon flew towards the yacht and roared a challenge; it returned the challenge with forked fire. Na closed her eyes, not wanting to see the death of this special dragon, but when she opened them again, the black and green dragon was alight with energy. Her fire struck the yacht, and it exploded. Then it was over. The fleet drifted lifelessly once again, and the remaining dragons gathered around this ancient queen.

"The human Fire Bearers already move to attack the enemy. We will aid them."

No one argued about helping the two humans now, not in front of this glowing magical queen. And Na wanted to join them, too.

She turned to Seth and Tan. *"Let's go."*

She'd already vented most of the battlecruiser of oxygen, and now she vented the rest, and the three dragons ran through lifeless areas of the vast ship until they reached the hangar. Kaylie was waiting for them. *"I'll fly by myself,"* Na said. She wanted to be alone in space. Seth and Tan flew, too, while Kaylie followed in the transporter flown by the two humans.

As they left the ships, Na reached out to it for a final time. She'd left the last torpedo inside the belly of the ship, and even that torpedo had a mind of its own. But it was a simple one, and she gave it a simple command. *"Explode!"*

"Daughter of Fire, fly with us."

Na approached the three great dragons: Rhiannon,

Night Sun, and the burnt and battered Spere. She noticed that the First of Thunder had lost a hand.

She flew closer to the ancient queen, who shone with a bright magic. Night Sun and Spere, too, shone with the old magic. They were followed by Kaylie in her transporter, Seth, Tan, and about forty dragons. So few had survived. When Rhiannon spoke, Na knew no other dragon, apart from Night Sun and herself, could hear her words.

"You've saved the dragons from their foolishness, but now you must do more," Rhiannon said

"How could a human gain so much power?" Na asked.

"The Emperor is hardly human—he's gained his power through consuming the life force of others."

"Can you kill him?" Na asked.

"That's the task of the Fire Bearers, and you must help them."

Na was a little surprised by this answer. *"Wouldn't it have been better for a dragon to raise the Fire?"*

"A dragon with the Fire would unwittingly aid the enemy. The human Fire Bearers possess different qualities."

Although Na trusted Night Sun's judgement and liked Lucy, the appearance of this queen, with her confidence in the Fire Bearers, removed Na's final doubts about helping the humans. She no longer considered them completely human. Lucy, at least, was becoming something more. And Lucy's placing of the needs of the ancient forest above the desires of her species was something Na respected. Rhiannon flew ahead with Night Sun by her side, and she sensed Night Sun speaking to the queen but couldn't quite hear. Na studied the glistening magic dancing around the queen, and with shock, she recognized the magic of the Old Ones.

Rhiannon rumbled a gentle laugh. *"Dragons have long worked with the magical creatures of Prometheus."*

Rhiannon glanced at Night Sun, and again Na heard whispers of a yet deeper level of the True Language.

"Is she what I think she is?"

Night Sun turned to the ancient queen. *"We will soon see."*

40

The omnibus bumped and slid along the icy road. Although the tower wasn't visible through the snowstorm, Thomas sensed its presence as a pressure. It stood apart from the rest of the imperial citadel and could only be accessed by crossing a deep abyss via a metal bridge. The minstrels quietened, and the jokes dried up as they crossed the bridge.

The bus entered the black obsidian tower, and Thomas girded himself for the fight. He looked at the black rock; his knife was made of the same material, but the energy infused by black magic was so different from that the giant of the underworld had imbued in his work. The tower had attitude and imposed it on those within. The gates scanned them—his tag buzzed and then was silent. He'd taken the most expensive tags and blockers. If sold, they'd fund an extravagant life for months. Normally, he'd modify his emotions to match the darker thoughts of the tower, but his thoughts were of murder, and his emotions needed little modification. What he did consciously, those around him did unconsciously at the behest of the tower. Thomas was aware that adjusting his emotions and spirit to the tower further damaged his body, but after losing Aina a second time, he didn't care. His thoughts turned to Lucy, and she appeared in his mind.

"I can see you," she said.

Thomas knew she could see what he saw. *"Am I early?"*

"A little. I'm with the rocs." He saw the burning forest. *"They burnt us, and we burnt them back. For now they've pulled back. We still have a few things to finish. We'll reach the tower in a few hours."*

Thomas couldn't wait; his only thought was to kill the Emperor.

"Thomas, be careful. The energy of the tower's different, darker..."

"I know."

A court official waited as they alighted. The servants were now alert. The official walked ahead, cane in hand, and led them into an unadorned room. There was something about the man that Thomas disliked immediately.

"Address me as Master Houser." The man's moods almost perfectly matched those of the tower. Thomas disconnected from his tag but observed its actions. It downloaded submissive behaviour into the servants' minds. "The tower is special. It monitors your moods and reads your minds. Is that understood?"

The servants chanted affirmation, then Houser divided the group into strong and weak, but Thomas puzzled him. He moved very close and stared. Thomas was acutely aware of the scarring on his face and body, and he struggled to stand straight, being forced to increase the magic flowing within him.

"What are you?" Master Houser asked.

"Strong," Thomas said, hoping to be placed in the strong

group. He could kill the man, but killing would draw attention to himself—it'd more efficient to accept a task that took him to the higher levels. The weak were already being assigned to cleaning tasks on the lower floors, and he didn't want to go there.

"You're the ugliest servant I've ever seen. Your eyes?"

"I had an accident, but I'm strong."

The man grabbed his arm and squeezed. He raised his eyebrows. "You're in the strong group."

Thomas's first job was fetching heavy items from some of the vehicles and taking them to one of the middle levels. Although he remembered the tower having lifts, they were told to use the servants' stairs. It suited him well enough. Meeting the aristocracy could wait. The stairs were half empty, and when he reached the middle levels, he kept climbing. He almost didn't notice the heavy box he carried.

But as he climbed, he noticed a strange energy coming from the centre of the tower—it was both attractive and repulsive at the same time—and he wanted to investigate. Stopping on a landing between two flights of stairs, he walked to the door. It opened suddenly, and he was almost overwhelmed by the energy. A lord looked at him.

"Who are you?"

"I have a delivery, my lord," Thomas said. The man wore a grey cloak, making him a lesser sorcerer.

"That's strange. I've ordered nothing today." The man looked closely at Thomas. "What's wrong with your face and eyes?"

"An accident, my lord."

"Well, bring it in. Perhaps it's for someone else."

Thomas followed the lord along a dark passageway. He knew that, like himself and Lucy, some of the lords could see in the dark. The man glanced back at him, unaware that Thomas could see him clearly, too.

They walked into a dark flickering hall. His breath was almost taken away. A shaft of burnt-orange fire, unlike any he had ever seen, occupied the centre of the vast room. It pulled at him. One thing he clearly knew—this fire was deadly.

He glanced at the two other lords standing by the flames. There was something strange about them—their energy fluctuated. The man who had led him into the room spoke to them, and he noticed the same thing about him. Thomas often saw a person's energy, just as he saw that of a rock, and their energy was indistinct and fuzzy.

All three were minor sorcerers. The one in a yellow robe possessed more magic than the others, but not enough to interest him. He studied the orange fire again. It appeared to be coming from the sides of the shaft.

"Interested?" Thomas realized he'd been staring.

"What is it, my lord?"

Another one laughed. "A curious servant?"

"Come here," the lord wearing yellow ordered. From the way the other two quietened, Thomas guessed that this one was the most senior. The man probed his mind, but Thomas gently led him astray. "There's something strange about him."

"His eyes are odd," one said.

"It's something else," the man in yellow said. Thomas wondered whether the man could read his mind, but he couldn't sense anything. "Something's not right about him." Thomas decided to stop acting. He walked towards the orange flames in the centre but stopped halfway, then slowly moved back. They made him nauseous, and their pull almost made his heart stop.

"What is it?"

"Servants don't ask questions," the man in yellow said. "Who are you?" He was attempting to access Thomas's tag. It fused, and Thomas removed it, tossing it into the fire, but he retained the blocker. They didn't recognize him yet.

"He's untagged," one of the men said. "He was using a temporary one."

"A very expensive one," Thomas added. He studied the flames again. "What happens if someone falls into it?"

"Would you like to see?" The three men approached him.

"I meant, what happens to the energy?" He turned to the three lords.

Two of the men took hold of him, but Thomas was used to wrestling strong men, and these men weren't. He threw the lord who'd led him into the room around, and the man stumbled, falling into the flames. The tower murmured as if satisfied.

"It's as if it's feeding," Thomas said, looking at the walls around him. They seemed to shine a little brighter. He turned back to the pair of lords. One was sending a message. Thomas stepped forward and punched him and then threw the dazed man into the flames. "That just leaves the two of us," he said.

"I'm an imperial lord," the man in yellow said.

Without any subterfuge, Thomas probed his mind. The lord was overwhelmed and tried to send a message. Thomas touched his head, and he screamed.

"What did you do to me?"

"Melted a part of your brain." Thomas was impressed with his accuracy; he'd half expected to kill the man, but he still seemed to function, even without his tag. Continuing to push, he flicked through the man's knowledge of the orange fire.

"No!" The man was now experiencing a shocking intrusion into his mind, and his memories would be flashing before him.

A thought popped into his mind. It was the device Lucy had mentioned—the one angering the dragons. "A weapon?" The man didn't seem to know. He wasn't surprised; the Emperor seldom shared information. He pushed harder, but the man was close to panic. He charged at Thomas, attempting to push him into the flames. Thomas stepped aside and kicked him into the shaft.

THOMAS EMPTIED the box he'd entered with and rejoined the main stairway, carrying the now-empty box. He walked up four floors without meeting anyone. On the fifth, the stairs ended abruptly, and he entered a large reception, but with his rock sense, he saw another flight of steps behind a grey metal door.

A woman and a man watched him.

"What do you want?" the woman asked.

"To deliver this box."

"There're no deliveries scheduled. What's in it?"

Thomas knew from her tone that discussion would not go very far. "It's empty." Dropping the box, he walked to the grey door. He sensed Lucy's fleeting presence—it was almost time. The man took hold of him. He was strong and knew how to apply armlocks. But so did Thomas. All grappling techniques had gaps or leakages, and he felt for the gap. Seconds later, the man was sitting on the floor, staring at him in surprise. The woman drew a pistol, and Thomas walked straight through the metal door. On the other side, with his magic alive, he thrust his glowing orange hand into the lock and melted the mechanism.

He walked up the stairway to a food preparation area. Servants were taking pre-prepared food from several small lifts. They stopped working and stared at him. Some of them backed away. He became aware that smoke was coming from his skin, and suddenly he was anxious that he might die before he could kill the Emperor.

Leaving the frightened servants, he ran up the final flight of stairs to the base of one of the four turrets. There were two metal doors: one leading to the top of the turret, the other to the roof of the tower. He heard a lift vibrating in the middle of the turret. This was how the aristocracy ascended to the roof. Stopping for a few moments, Thomas looked through the wall with his rock sense.

A strange image formed in his mind. People moved around the tops of the turrets and the walkways along the outer wall that joined them. The one opposite reeked of toxic magic, and the figures shimmered in his mind. It was the imperial turret. But the strangest part was the floor of the roof; he had to stare for several seconds to understand what he saw. Two magics moved around each other: the outer orange fire was something he understood, but the inner magic was darker, the same burnt-orange magic he'd seen inside the tower.

Thomas contemplated his next move as if he were playing chess. The Emperor was in the opposite turret, and he had to reach him, and kill him, before he was killed or died from the dragon magic. Thomas considered the enemy's pieces: the Emperor, the Empress, the senior sorcerers, the minor sorcerers, and the soldiers. His pieces were further away—for the moment, they were himself and his knife.

But in a chess game, the location of the pieces also made a difference. Although the Emperor possessed the more powerful pieces, they were not well positioned. With smoke pouring from his skin, Thomas stepped onto the roof of the tower.

41

The roof was a sticky orange marsh with jets of flame sporadically shooting from its moving surface. In the centre, burnt-orange flames rose higher into the air, blocking the view of the imperial turret. The tower appeared to be melting, but in the turrets and along the walkways connecting them, waiters served cocktails to the lords and ladies. Slightly to the left of the central orange flames, a table with two men, one seated on either side, was slowly being sucked towards it.

Thomas saw the pattern of energies at the top of the tower with both his physical and his inner eyes. He walked towards the table, and with each step he felt the surface's stickiness, but the orange substance burnt on contact with his magic, allowing him to move freely. However, the draw from the central fire tugged strongly, forcing him to adjust his own Fire. He estimated that the men had less than half an hour before they reached the central flames. They'd be dead before that; their bodies had already blistered from exposure. One of the men stared at him with an open mouth. Thomas sensed a small magic around the man.

Fire Rising

From their smouldering clothes, he guessed they were lords who'd displeased the Emperor.

"Who are you?" the man asked. The other man gazed dully ahead.

"Thomas Brand."

From behind, something clutched at Thomas. He changed the flow of energy within himself—this was becoming uncomfortable. The dying man moaned. A translucent bubble quivered about him. Thomas blinked. He saw with his inner eye, but he didn't want to believe what he was seeing. The man gasped as the flames sucked him and the bubble expanded. Thomas cut his throat, and the man died in relief. Thomas swallowed hard in disgust.

"Thank you," the first man said. "You know what it is?"

Thomas nodded, pushing the dead man onto the orange surface and sitting down. The man's body caught fire. The burnt orange flames had been sucking the man's soul from his body. He became aware of the silence on the top of the tower.

The Emperor watched him from his black obsidian throne—one decorated with strange patterns. The Empress, Lord Frore, and the sorcerer known as the Night Hag also watched him with a piercing intensity. The lesser lords and ladies simply seemed amused by the spectacle of the smoking man.

"Who are you?" Thomas asked the man at the table.

"I was a lord, but I learnt too much."

"The nature of the orange fire?"

The man nodded and gasped.

Thomas saw the same translucent substance quivering about his body. "But he doesn't need a special fire to take souls."

"I know." The man said it so firmly that Thomas guessed

he'd had personal experience of this. Breathing heavily, the man continued. "He can suck the souls from a man with a thought, but not a dragon."

"And this can kill a dragon?"

The man nodded.

Thomas couldn't really see how effective it would be, unless they flew too close. But he knew from Lucy that the dragons hated the Emperor for this.

The man's skin was smoking. "Why are you here?"

"To kill the Emperor."

"Good luck." The man's soul billowed out towards the black fire. "Kill me!"

Thomas cut the man's throat, and his billowing soul rushed back towards his body before dissipating in the air around him. If the burnt-orange fire could do this to a man's soul, what would it do to the martial magic of the sorcerers?

Producing a small magic flame from his finger stub, he watched it pulled towards the fire. He sat back in the chair and searched for a way to kill the Emperor.

"Stalemate."

"Not stalemate," the Emperor said aloud. "You're losing. You've already lost your lovers, your friends, and your supporters. You've lost."

Thomas thought of the deaths of Aina—and of retribution. He recognized the magical power in the Emperor's voice, but it only made him more determined.

"Why the orange fire?" Thomas asked.

The Emperor just stared, and the rest of his retinue waited.

"Why do you need so many souls?"

The Emperor's expression passed from amusement to anger.

Thomas turned to the lords and ladies inside the imperial turret. "Do you know that your Emperor lives by stealing his subjects' souls?" The faces of the senior sorcerers were unreadable as they watched their Emperor.

"Kill him!" the Emperor said.

His voice reverberated through the tower as if he was using the stones themselves to speak. Thomas suspected he was. A group of nine reluctant imperial guards ran towards him, but as they ran over the orange surface, they became stuck. The Emperor raised his eyebrows in amusement as they slid slowly towards Thomas, but his face became stony when Thomas threw his black knife into the heart of the nearest man. With a flick of his wrist, he sent it through the throats of the others before recalling it. The Emperor was testing him—assessing his strengths. Despite his hatred of the man, Thomas waited. The Emperor had all the pieces, and Thomas knew that for now, he stood in the best position. Once he moved, he'd be vulnerable to attack.

"Imperial Order," the Emperor said.

Lord Frore ordered a group of five third-rate sorcerers forward. They glanced nervously at each other as they slowly approached him. These men didn't stick to the ground, but neither were they skilled magic users.

They were a sacrifice. A further test while the senior sorcerers watched and studied his techniques. The nearest man attempted a basic magic whip—elementary but enough to kill most men. Thomas knew how to counter such an attack, but he also knew he didn't need to. He'd made sure that the orange fire was not directly behind him —he had no wish to be skewered.

The man whipped at Thomas, but the black whip of magic was pulled to Thomas's right and sucked into the orange flames, feeding them. Two more sorcerers attacked, and each time their magical attacks were distorted and pulled away by the central flames. When one of the sorcerers tried to place himself so Thomas would be directly between himself and the orange fire, Thomas directed his knife into the man's throat.

"Cut him down!" the Emperor yelled.

Two sorcerers launched more determined attacks, and again, the magic was pulled into the central flames, but this time they overexerted themselves and couldn't turn it off. A stream of energy flowed from each one into the flames. Exchanging worried glances, the other sorcerers stepped back. The two men were dying—slowly their life energy was sucked into the orange fire, and their desiccated bodies dropped to the ground before bursting into flames.

The two remaining sorcerers drew their guns. Finally embracing the Fire, Thomas burst into flames. Reaching out with his mind, he fused the mechanism of the guns. In his thoroughness, they caught fire and the sorcerers cried out, dropping them into the orange marsh. The two scared sorcerers backed away, but a shout from the Emperor stopped them. Thomas killed them with a burst of magic.

Nothing felt good about this—he wanted to engage with the Emperor but was unsure how. The orange fire would pull his magic, too. For a moment he wondered whether the Emperor had really set up a situation he couldn't lose. It was time to finish it—he only needed to live long enough to kill one man.

Thomas flickered in and out of visibility as he sprinted across the orange marsh. He leapt onto the side of the turret, and with rock magic and the Fire blazing in and around his body, he hardly changed pace as he ran up its outer wall.

Second-level sorcerers stood by the battlements. They backed off as Thomas, blazing with fire, attacked, killing a lord with a blast of magic as the sorcerer led a group against him. Thomas kept the sorcerers between himself and the senior lords, but his attack left him exposed to those closest. Lord Green weaved a strange web of magic with scores of creatures sitting at strategic points. It looked like a combination of spiderwebs, each with a creature in the centre of its own web. It wrapped around Thomas, stifling him, and the creatures, created by black magic, bit into him. Even with his hardened skin, they hurt. Lord Plane stood on Thomas's left with a whip in his hand, watching, but unable to join the attack because of the danger of being entangled in Green's net.

Thomas staggered as Green pulled the net tighter. He could hardly move his arms, but he could control his knife, and it cut through the threads of the net. Thomas moved through Lord Green's magical attack, cutting each spider-like creature as it attacked. Each one was dangerous, but none by itself was lethal. It was slow work, and if any higher-level magic users attacked, he'd be vulnerable. But they seemed content to watch. Perhaps they were so confident in their ability, they didn't care.

Green looked nervous as Thomas approached; he was thinking too much. He struggled to tighten his creation. When much of the net was cut, Thomas focussed his mind on his knife and it flew at Green. The sorcerer had no defense for such a direct attack, and the blade lodged in his throat. As the man died, Thomas pulled each of the wriggling creatures of black magic from the pieces of net that still clung to him and flung them at Lord Plane. The man frantically knocked the things away.

Holding his hand towards the dead Lord Green, he called his knife. But instead of flying back to him, he moved it sideways and slashed at Lord Plane. The surprised lord was still pulling the spider things from himself and only just jumped back in time. But Thomas controlled it, and instead of falling to the ground, the blade penetrated his left knee. This was the distraction he needed, and Thomas attacked with his hands—each one was an energetic blade, and they cut into the surprised man. Lord Plane fell to the ground. The remaining spider things covered his body as they fed.

42

"*I'm here!*"

Thomas breathed out in relief as Lucy flew through the air, landing beside him. Smoke poured from her body. A roc veered away, avoiding an imperial attack. His throat was so dry he could hardly speak. She looked at his burning skin.

"Thomas, I don't like this," she said.

"Neither do I." He could tell she was shocked. He was, too. "I don't know what the dragons have done to us."

Bright rocs attacked the outside of the tower with fire, and others clung to the outside of the tower with the sole purpose of accessing and sabotaging the imperial weapons systems. The more complex the weapons, the easier this would be. The sorcerers around the Emperor spread out, sending flashes of magic outwards, attacking the giant birds. Guns rattled from positions on the side of the tower, and groups of attack bots flew towards the rocs.

"Stop shooting!" the Emperor shouted. His officers looked at him in surprise. The guns were silenced. The sorcerers and others waited, appearing unsure what to do.

This gave both Thomas and Lucy a momentary break while a line of lesser sorcerers, no more than twenty feet away, nervously watched them.

"What's he doing?" Lucy asked.

"He's greedy. He doesn't want the rocs to die on the mountain, he wants to feed on them. With every roc or dragon he gains enormous power."

Thomas remembered the anger on the Emperor's face when he'd killed the seated lords. He hadn't cared about their deaths, only that their energy hadn't come to him.

"We may be reaching the fulfillment of the prophecy," she said.

He remembered it well. *When the shadow of a dark leader stretches throughout the nine planets, a force shall arise to counter the evil. From the stars, Bright Ones shall come and counter the evil with fire."* After all that had happened, he no longer disbelieved, but he didn't feel like a hero.

The Emperor issued a command, and four groups of lesser sorcerers, each situated on one of the four turrets, conjured dark clouds. Thomas had experienced these before. The groups on the other turrets sent their clouds upwards and outwards towards the rocs, but the sorcerers nearest them sent their crawling cloud over the floor towards them.

"He's sacrificing them," Lucy said, her mouth falling open.

"That's something he does."

Together they burnt the edges of the black cloud, and with the power of the Fire, the cloud exploded, sticking to the lesser sorcerers' skin. They screamed and died in agony.

Lucy looked away.

"It's a hard way to die," Thomas said, turning to Lucy.

Fire was spurting from her smoking body. "The Fire's taking you, too."

Thomas looked over the smoking ashes of the lesser sorcerers. The Emperor led the attacks on the rocs and was working closely with the Night Hag and Frore. The Empress chanted in a strange language, and a green slime oozed from the battlements and down the sides of the tower. A bright green and blue roc squawked as the substance touched him; the smoking bird fell from the tower.

"Jzzrata!" He felt her shock as if it were his own. He remembered Hwith's friend. The green slime touched another roc too slow to move, and it screamed, dropping to the ground. It didn't move.

Lord Frore and the Night Hag strode towards them, walking over the ashes of the dead sorcerers. Behind them followed a group of five lesser sorcerers.

"It's starting," Lucy said. Her Fire flickered around her.

Thomas nodded grimly. The sorcerers stopped, and the lesser sorcerers attacked, running between him and Lucy. Both he and Lucy killed one each. Two more rushed at him, forcing him back, but one came too close, and Thomas's hand, which was now a flaming blade, sliced off his arm. The final one persisted, but he was overexerting himself and gasping for breath. Thomas told the man's lungs to contract, and he went straight down.

Lucy was ten yards away. She looked down at the two bodies of her attackers. Then Thomas understood the purpose of the attack. These people had given their lives to separate him from Lucy. Perhaps Frore remembered the times he and Lucy had fought against him together—the times when their magic had combined into something more. Thomas cursed silently that he'd let this happen. Then the Night Hag attacked him. Confident in his magic, he waited as the woman approached. She was alive with a sticky black magic, tendrils of which clung to his arm and pulled. He burnt them off, but his arm stung; however, the pain further cleared his mind.

The Hag pushed at his mind. A spear shimmered in her hands. Without warning, she thrust the weapon at him. His dagger deflected her strike, but then her spear turned and cut a hole in the air. It popped open and scores of small demons flew from a hole. They came rapidly, attacking without pausing, and stung when they touched him. His attempts to burn them off merely resulted in the demons leaping in the air and then rushing back to bite him again. It was his martial, rather than magic, skills that helped him. His knife cut and killed the closest. The only problem was their speed; once they sensed his knife approach, they darted away, only to return seconds later. They tried to suck his strength. Dozens of them crawled through the tiny hole—too many to fight, and he could hardly keep them away.

Then he sensed something else on the other side of the hole—something older and colder. He was feeling light-headed, and tried to will the hole closed but nothing happened. He was already having difficulty breathing. Another opponent could kill him.

Knowing that black magic forced spirits to act, and that these demons were slaves, Thomas changed his approach, cutting through the air behind the demons in the places he imagined invisible threads connecting them to the Hag. The effect was instantaneous. The first shrieked, and as if attached by elastic, it snapped back towards her, striking her on her forehead. She cried out and leapt back. Thomas quickly cut the bonds of every demon he could reach, and soon dozens of demons bit the Hag.

The Night Hag cast small spells, and one by one the

small demons flew back through the hole. As it began to close, Thomas instinctively reached through to the other place. An older and colder spirit stared at him.

"What are you?" Thomas asked. It looked like a haggard tree, but it moved slowly. It too was chained.

"Free me, and I'll grant a boon." It spoke in a strange dialect of the True Language.

He hesitated, wondering what worse thing he might release on himself, but a look of fear that passed over the Hag's face persuaded him. He cut the spirit free.

"At last." He heard its thoughts clearly. *"Your wish?"*

"Kill the Night Hag."

Its laughter chilled him. The Hag's spear was pulled into the hole. "What've you done?" She was breathing heavily.

Thomas wasn't really sure. Roots reached from the hole and weaved towards her. Her magic had no effect on them. Then they whipped out, wrapping themselves around her leg.

"Not this," she screamed. And then the roots dragged her from this world.

43

Lucy stepped back from the man's punch. A woman followed up with a kick. They seemed to have decided they could beat her physically, without resorting to magic. They were both bigger than her and might be able to overpower her. Perhaps they thought she lacked the will to attack with magic if they didn't. She caught a second kick, using martial magic Thomas had taught her. Her hand followed the trajectory of the kick, taking it in a full circle, forcing the woman to do a backward flip. The sorcerer landed awkwardly on her back.

The man punched to her face, and she slapped his fist with enough magic to break the bones in his hand. He leapt back with a scream.

All the time, Lord Frore stood watching her in a way that made her skin crawl. But her attention was taken up by her attackers. At least she had only two to deal with. The man rushed forward, punching with one hand. He'd magically infused his punches, and they stung and disoriented her, but the Fire absorbed some of the pain. Becoming frustrated by his lack of progress, the man tried to slam into her. She touched him on his chest and told his heart to stop. He staggered back and fell to the ground. He was trying to use magic to revive himself.

"I showed you!" Frore said. The woman protected herself with a field of magic around her body.

Changing her tactics, Lucy sought to confuse. She suggested the woman sleep. She staggered back, but it didn't work. Lucy threw her knife as the woman went for a gun, magically guiding it into her wrist. The woman dropped the pistol, but unfortunately, Lucy lacked the ability to call back a knife. When the woman attacked again, this time with grey magical mist that flowed from her fingertips, Lucy let go of her remaining inhibitions, and fire leapt from her fingers.

A spark ignited the grey mist, and the woman screamed, running at Lucy, who stepped to the side, kicking her backside. The woman flew from the battlements. Lucy briefly noticed Thomas alight with magic, slashing a sorcerer with bright hands, but then Lord Frore stepped towards her.

She'd dreaded this encounter, and his familiar magic pushing against her reminded her of the previous times she'd faced him. She'd never been able to best him in a straight fight. His swirling red eye disturbed her, despite it being her creation. She'd needed a distraction when they'd been in the centre of the planet. Asking the fire wasps to enter his eye had provided it. He hadn't known it'd been her suggestion, believing instead that the Fire had chosen him. He still didn't know. "We meet again," he said. She readied herself for an attack. "You're stronger than I thought, and sneakier." She wasn't sure what he was talking about. "So you passed more of the tests than I thought." She wasn't going to give him any information about what had happened in the inner sun. "This is your last chance to join with me."

His power almost overwhelmed her, and she had to fight to speak. "You failed the tests."

"I have the Fire."

She prayed that was untrue, but feeling his presence pushing against her, she wondered whether he'd gained more than she had thought.

"So what's your answer?"

"To what?" As she spoke, she pushed through his defences and sought to enter his mind.

Frore laughed and attacked, and she flew into the battlements. She quickly slipped away from a patch of green slime; just the smell of it burnt her nostrils. Without warning she stepped forward and punched Frore's face. However, even a magically enhanced punch had little effect on him, although she saw him wince as she struck. But she was too slow to withdraw her hand, and he grabbed her wrist, pulling her closer.

His skin was damp and shiny—an unhealthy grey. And liquid oozed from it, then it turned to a choking vapour. She felt light-headed. "You're mine," he said as his grip strengthened. "Perhaps I'll save you." He pushed into her mind, but she was faster, and she pushed back, slipping past his defences. "You may be able to slip in, but you can't do anything inside—you'll just become a part of me."

She shuddered at the thought but continued to probe, and she found a recent thought. Looking up at him, she spoke. "You've found a way to my world." She felt sick.

He grinned. "I'll take you with me, even if it's only your memories."

"And other worlds." She saw flashes of a red fiery world, and then the green forest world where she'd battled Frore before. She felt a rush of concern for the creatures of that world.

"You were right. I thought the world an illusion, but apparently the green forest planet really exists. It's ripe for exploitation."

Lucy screamed as the pressure in her mind intensified, but still she pushed past the pain to the secret place she'd previously found when she'd stood, bathed in the golden light of mushrooms, in the faerie world. He'd called her the Queen of the Underworld. The seed she'd planted was still there. She now called on it to awake.

"What've you done?" He was confused.

The seed sprouted, and Frore's eyes widened as he revisited repressed childhood memories of pain—a memory of rejected love. For a few seconds, he hesitated, and she was free. She called the fire wasps swirling in his eye, and they listened, remembering her voice from the inner sun.

"Your home is dying, return to the inner sun." She showed them a way to the centre of the planet. Some of them burrowed through the back of his eyeball, burning through the sorcerer's body, some crawled out and fell as fiery tears.

Frore screamed. "What have you done to me?"

Others flew directly from Frore's eye. He staggered away from her. But he was healing himself.

"Stop!" she commanded. She spoke to all of his bodily systems.

But despite losing his fiery eye, and despite the internal damage he was suffering, Lord Frore called more magic, repairing himself almost as fast as he'd been damaged.

Lucy was becoming desperate. How could she kill this man? She attacked with blasts of energetic magic, sending the sorcerer staggering further back. Lucy's eyes widened in disbelief at his strength.

"My fire!" Frore cried.

"You never had the Fire!" Lucy shouted.

Lord Frore screamed, swiping at the remaining wasps as they stung him. He rushed at Lucy, but she slipped out of his way, and the Fire flowed through her body and out of her hands, hitting him hard. He fell against the battlements, his magic flailing around him as the wasps stung. Losing balance, he fell into the orange swamp.

Slowly standing, and ignoring the wasps, Frore called on his magic, and Lucy felt a vibration pass through the air. She felt dread at what he might do, and she desperately thought of a way to kill him. But his power was so intense. A black cloud formed around him, and with determination, she struck him with another blast of Fire, and he fell back onto the orange marsh.

Her palms felt different, and she glanced at them, surprised to see that the almost crystalline centre was still glowing. A movement near Frore caught her attention. A forked tongue of burnt-orange flame flicked along the surface of the roof, licking around him. Lord Frore screamed as the fire dragged him towards the central Fire. *"Help me!"*

Knowing he was still trying to manipulate her, she raised her hands and blasted him again. He burst into flames. Seconds later, Lord Frore was dead. Feeling attention on her, she looked up to see the Emperor glowering at her. She was unsure whether it was because she'd killed one of his top men or because she'd denied him his dinner.

A scream from behind made her turn, and she saw the Night Hag vanish. She felt only relief.

Thomas looked exhausted as he walked closer. He was shaking, and flames were burning erratically around him. She reached out to support him. "I'm finished," he said.

"No!" She was tired, too, but they couldn't stop now. She

stared, trying to hide her concern but failing. She was shocked by the flames leaping from his body, but his eyes were the most disturbing.

"What?" he asked.

"Your eyes are glowing red."

"The magic's killing me." Thomas's eyes focussed as he regained his breath.

Lucy became aware of the fight around them. The rocs had launched a new attack on the Emperor. Hwith led the attack with an intense burst of fire, and the man staggered back, but seconds later he sent scores of needles of black magic towards the bright roc, and as Hwith twisted in the air, the flight of needles followed.

"Hwith!" Lucy cried out. As she prepared to defend Hwith, the air around her vibrated.

A bright golden dragon dropped from the sky, striking the Emperor with a bolt of fire, flinging him to the ground. Wild magic spurted from his body, but he recovered and sent a fierce burst of flames at Hwith and Na. They escaped, joining the other dragons and rocs as they circled the tower.

The lesser sorcerers struggled to maintain their defensive shields against thousands of dragons and rocs; they screamed as two turrets collapsed, sending scores of them to their deaths.

44

Lucy gripped Thomas's arm. "Look!"

A dark orange stream flowed from the central fire to the Emperor's throne; it was changing. The engravings covering it glowed red; some of them were cracking open and bleeding. They were obviously not just ornamental. The Emperor's skin shone, radiating power.

Despite the heat, Thomas shivered as he looked at the device transmitting stored life energy to the Emperor.

"He's tapping into the energy of the souls trapped in the tower," Lucy said.

"I think so." He felt nauseous, but he also became more determined to kill this man. The only problem was how.

Lines of energy spread from the throne to the Emperor's skin, lacing it with bright red lines. His eyes burnt red. His force of magic was a menacing pressure pushing against them.

"Thomas?"

He felt her fear, too.

"Be steadfast," Na whispered as she landed next to Thomas and Lucy. *"We'll find a way to kill him."*

Thomas just couldn't see how.

The Empress stood beside her husband, adding her own magic to his. The head on her neck watched Thomas, and the mouth on her belly chanted some sort of lullaby. He was sure its aim was to pacify them—and its effects were hard to fight. Perhaps this was why he was feeling negative, and why they hadn't attacked yet. Thomas rubbed his face. Lord Nimor leant close to the Empress, whispering something in her ear. A score of lesser sorcerers stood behind the three figures.

Dozens of dragons and rocs lined the battlements and thousands more were circling the tower. They too were a power, but the Emperor didn't seem to care. Thomas knew that they had the advantage, but something was wrong.

"He's too confident," Lucy said.

A faint smile passed the Emperor's face, and Thomas guessed he'd heard their inner conversation. "Your Fire's fascinating. It's a magic I'd like to have studied, but now it's too late. Frore claimed to hold this Fire, but I wasn't impressed."

"His Fire was fake," Thomas said.

"My wife told me what you said. Perhaps it was true." The Emperor's voice carried around the top of the tower. "I admit that I never thought you'd better him nor Lady Hay, but ultimately, it makes no difference. You've fulfilled your purpose as much as the young woman we created fulfilled hers."

"Purpose?" Thomas asked.

"We should kill them now," Na whispered.

The Emperor glanced at the golden dragon and then turned back to Thomas and Lucy. "To bring you here."

Thomas searched for a trap but couldn't see one. Despite the power radiating from the Emperor, and the danger of his Empress and her lord, they were only three. The lesser sorcerers hardly counted. He was, however, disturbed by the burnt-orange fire that flickered dangerously in the centre of the tower. But he still doubted that they could match the combined power of their Fire, as well as the power of thousands of dragons and rocs.

Thomas noted the concern on Lucy's face as she translated all the Emperor said into the True Language.

"Your magic is powerful," Thomas said. "But your sick weapon is static." He prayed it was true; he knew that magic could coax flames to leap.

The Emperor stood and smiled, but his eyes remained cold. "Magic isn't everything. That's why I use technology, too." He paused. "Look up."

"Thomas!" Lucy stared into the sky.

Although Thomas was reluctant to take his attention from the sorcerers, in case of deception, he nevertheless glanced up. His stomach sank. Hundreds of silvery spaceships glittered in the sky. The Emperor had hidden a fleet.

Na looked carefully. *"A third battlecruiser."*

Two of these ships had already killed half the dragon species. They all knew that the dragons and rocs with them represented the last living adults of their respective species.

The Emperor spoke. *"In thirty minutes the dragons will be extinct. Then I will be able to fit the final piece of my imperial jigsaw together."*

"Is this just a game to you?" Lucy said.

"In a sense."

The dragons and rocs rose into the air.

"No!" Lucy shouted.

"Why not?" Na asked, her eyes burning brightly. She was the only dragon not to have taken to the air—assigned, as

she was, to be their helper. Thomas nevertheless felt her desire to join her brothers and sisters.

"You'll be exposed—between his fire and the spaceships. You'll be dead in minutes."

Lucy's emotion and reason touched the dragons and rocs, and they alighted, this time on the sides of the tower. Thomas silently thanked her—he guessed that the number reaching space would be zero.

"Dragons don't hide," Na said.

"It's a tactic," Thomas said. And he thought once more of strategy. How could he kill the Emperor and Empress?

For the first time, the Emperor showed his displeasure with a scowl. Thomas prepared himself.

"I outclass you," the Emperor said, glancing at Thomas. "Magic has its uses, but you've missed the big picture."

"So you admit black magic has limits?" Thomas asked, playing for time.

The Emperor appeared amused. "It has focus. But I didn't become Emperor of the Nine Planets because of it."

Thomas had often wondered at this. Natural magic worked, but didn't always work on command. However, the Fire did—it was burning around him now.

Thomas whispered as quietly as he could, *"Do you see any way out of this?"* He knew Night Sun, Spere, and Rhiannon heard.

The great dragons looked at him, but there was silence.

The Emperor spoke to Lucy. "Your mistake is in asking the universe instead of understanding its nature and then commanding it."

"The universe is bigger than any of us," Lucy said.

"Meekness has never appealed to me," the Emperor said. The Empress's spare head cackled.

"He talks a lot," Na said. Fire dripped from her mouth.

The Empress glanced up. "It's time." Her husband nodded.

Flaming torpedoes flew from the outer atmosphere towards the mountains; they targeted the few dozen rocs and dragons still circling the tower. They dropped to their deaths—the rest clung to the side of the tower, waiting.

Thomas, Lucy, and Na blasted the Emperor and Empress with Fire, but they remained unharmed. The Emperor raised his hands, and a wave of power washed over them. Na's claws dug into the ground as she tried to avoid being thrown into the burnt-orange fire. Thomas and Lucy fell to their knees. Despite his toughened skin, Thomas was bruised and bleeding.

From the battlements, dozens of dragons and rocs sent focussed streams of fire at the Emperor and Empress. Both husband and wife staggered but quickly recovered as a chorus of lesser sorcerers chanted, seeming to lessen the intensity of the flames.

Then the attack changed. The fleet spread across the sky and, like lightning, smaller fiery torpedoes struck the rocs and dragons. The burnt-orange flames blazed from the centre of the tower in anticipation.

"Attack!" Spere ordered. The dragons and rocs took to the air. Many became invisible, but many of the younger ones faltered, flickering in and out of view.

"Thomas!" Lucy cried.

It was raining dead dragons and rocs.

Na was frantic, and she attacked the three sorcerers repeatedly, joining a group of three dragons and three rocs that sent continuous streams of fire at the Empress. But each time Na's fire touched the Emperor, she was swatted away, and each time she took longer to recover. Then she lifted into the air.

"*I must help.*"

"*Remain with the Fire Bearers!*" Night Sun commanded.

Na landed next to them again, but her pain at the loss of young dragons, many of whom she'd trained, poured from her uncontrolled. To be next to a dragon in grief was a powerful experience—both Thomas and Lucy trembled as they literally shared her heartbreak.

"*We have to do something!*" Lucy shouted.

"*Raise the Fire!*" Rhiannon cried. She blinked out of sight, becoming invisible as she rose towards the spaceships.

"*We've raised it!*" Lucy said.

Thomas felt her desperation wash over him in waves, adding to Na's pain and to his own despair. Alight with magic, Lucy detonated a fiery torpedo that flew towards them. The Emperor seemed content to keep them away; he appeared more concerned in coordinating the attack on the dragons, and in attempting to drive them into his weapon.

The three of them attacked again but were thrown back into the rubble of the collapsed turrets. The next time they attacked, part of the wall fell in on them, and they struggled to free themselves.

Thomas remembered Aina's first death. In his anger and pain, he'd used rock magic to call on the power of Prometheus. That was how he'd killed Lord Anlair, the ex-governor of Prometheus. Again, as he clawed his way out of a pile of rubble, he felt deep into the planet—seeking help.

Then he knew. He staggered to his feet. "*I have to raise the Fire.*"

"*Thomas?*" Lucy said. Despite her fiery form he felt her fear. "*I don't understand.*"

"*We need to raise the full power of Prometheus, not just our personal pieces of power.*"

Lucy shook her head, not seeming to understand, but Na's large fiery eyes fixed him with a stare. *"Perhaps I see."*

"Protect me!"

Without waiting for a reply, part of his mind sank into the planet. He felt Lucy's and Na's energy surrounding and supporting him as his spirit and mind descended deeper, first through the rocky crust, then on through the softer mantle, until he reached the inner molten sea. He saw the shining elemental cities clinging to the edges of the inner sea. Then, crossing the bright sea, he reached the inner sun. Thomas stood in fire, surrounded by the power of the planet.

"I summon the Fire!"

Thomas sensed intelligence in the flames, and it flared around him—he heard a whisper.

"At last."

He wasn't sure whether he'd heard a part of himself, or whether Prometheus had spoken. He called again.

"Come!"

Incredible power arose around him, and it was his friend. He flew across the fiery inner sea, sending goblin barges onto the rocks of the Faerie Isles. He caught a glimpse of a tattooed albino troll saluting him, and then he hurtled back through the mantle. Behind him, a giant volcanic vent formed, and a river of molten lava laced with magic rushed upwards. He was no longer alone—something greater surrounded him. The power of the planet moved with him, and he rushed towards the black tower. Nassopolis shook as he ascended, sending rocks cascading down onto the Hanging Cities and into the valleys below. The power of the Fire was overwhelming.

His body quivered as his mind returned, and Fire exploded from the roof of the tower, rushing into the sky, and then on through the atmosphere and into the darkness of space. And, for a few seconds, white light beamed from the tower, turning it into a lighthouse with the power of a star. Then the white light faded, leaving only the ascending torrent of Fire.

"Look!" Lucy said. Tiny lights emerged from the tower and rose into the sky. *"The trapped souls."*

The Emperor's eyes widened; the burnt-orange flames of his weapon were gone. "What have you done?" One of his legs was already on fire, and he lurched into the Empress as smoke rose from his back. Thomas was aware of the Empress backing away in shock, helped by Lord Nimor.

The tower was a torch, and flames rushed around them. Thomas felt as if his body was pulling itself apart.

Lucy screamed. *"I can't see. What's happening to me? I'm burning."*

"Absorb the energy," Na said.

"It's killing us," she said.

"Not kill—do it!"

Na moved closer to them, and within the roaring Fire. Thomas was very aware of the golden dragon beside him—it felt as if time stood still. She seemed familiar. *"I had a vision of you,"* Thomas said. *"You flew at the head of a flight of dragons."*

"And I've dreamt of you. I feel I know you," Na said. *"But unlike other dragons, I don't have memories of my past lives."*

Their magic mingled—three minds became one. *"My memories,"* Na said, rushing through past lives faster than Thomas could follow, but he felt her surprise. "*Look!*" Thomas saw her memories like a movie playing before him. She showed him an image of them both together in the ancient forest.

"I don't understand." Then she showed him more memories of their past life together. *"Aina?"*

"Yes."

"But..." He thought of the Aina killed by the Emperor.

"She was an innocent; someone abused by the Emperor," Lucy said.

"You acted well towards her," Na added.

Thomas felt overwhelming sadness. He'd finally found Aina, but it was too late. *"Why now? I'm dying."*

"No!" She shook him. *"I can see what you can't. Embrace the Fire. Make it part of you."*

Thomas felt himself change. His body flickered with magical energy. Little was clear, except that he was growing bigger.

"You're transforming," Na said.

Then she screamed, and he felt her pain. Her golden body darkened. Something had attached itself to her.

"The Emperor!" Lucy cried.

Thomas attacked the dark shape on her body, but it stuck to her. It was sucking her life. Na weakened.

"Thomas, not again!"

His heartbeat raced; she was dying in his arms for a third time.

Lucy's magic snapped around the darkness, making it relax its grip, but it was still there.

"Use the Fire," Na said faintly. *"Embrace it."*

Thomas became Fire.

He flung the Emperor away, again blasting him with Fire. The burning man crawled away and collapsed in the rubble as fire engulfed him. The ruler of the Empire was dying.

A deep orange dragon moved beside him. *"It's me, Thomas."* The voice was Lucy's.

"What's happened?" Thomas asked. He looked at his new copper body. He was a dragon, too.

"You've changed into a rock dragon."

"Aina?"

"I'm Na. Aina is my human form." She moved closer.

Thomas wasn't sure whether he wanted to be a dragon, but the energy felt good. And he had wings.

A fiery torpedo flew from the sky, hitting the side of the tower. "The dragons!" Na cried.

They flew upwards within the rising jet of Fire rushing from the centre of the planet to the darkness of space. Lucy cried out as a burning roc fell past them. "Old Grey." Her friend, the roc poet, was dead. Thomas felt her fury. She was now a dragon, and her feelings, as his, were dragon. *"Kill them."* Na bellowed agreement.

The Fire gushed into the blackness of space and they flew towards the battle. When Thomas saw a dragon being pursued by a frigate, he set an intention of burning, and a spear of fire shot into it. Seconds later the ship was engulfed in flames. All around them the dragons fought the fleet, but so many were dead. Thomas felt the loss.

"Look!" Na said.

The battlecruiser had turned its weapons on them. They shared a thought, and dozens of flaming spears flew towards the warship, penetrating its armoured body. It shuddered as a wave of energy passed through it. Then it exploded. Burning pieces of ship, many the size of the smaller ships, fell towards the planet.

They sent more spears into smaller cruisers. Behind them the giant stream of Fire reached hundreds of miles into space. Changing his tactic, Thomas called it, and forks of fire leapt from the greater stream engulfing gunboats, frigates, and the sleek white destroyers.

Lucy and Na copied him, and as they flew through the fleet, each set clear intentions of destruction, and each time, the Fire forked, first at the destroyers, and then at the smaller frigates and gunboats, and finally at the fiery torpedoes still killing dragons.

Ship by ship, they destroyed the imperial fleet.

"The Emperor was wrong," Lucy said. *"It's bigger than us."*

"I know." Thomas was very conscious of the power being channelled through him. Despite the power he wielded, he felt small.

"We've become forces for nature," Lucy said.

It was true. The imperial fleet was burning or floating listlessly in space. It was a graveyard of ships.

"We've destroyed them," Na said. But there was no triumph in her voice.

Thomas felt her aching heart as if it was his, and his inner fire also chilled as he looked around at the dead dragons drifting between the lifeless ships. Of ten thousand dragons, there were only hundreds left. It was a bitter victory. He flew close to her, instinctively knowing the dragon ways of comfort. Lucy flew close, too. For the first time he called her sister.

"We must help the rocs," Lucy said. She trumpeted, calling the remaining dragons, including Rhiannon, Spere, and Night Sun. Seth was there, too. And then she dropped through the atmosphere.

All the dragons followed.

The rocs had fared little better than the dragons. Many were dead and many more lay injured on the mountains. But with the dragons' help, they quickly finished off the remaining imperial fighters.

And then the world was silent. Thomas looked down.

For once there were few clouds. Flames rose from Nassopolis. Many parts of the mountain city were burning.

But the blazing tower still stood.

"Is the Emperor dead?" Lucy asked.

"I saw his burning body," Thomas said. *"But we must check. This must be finished."*

They landed on the roof. The Empress and her lord had gone, but a group of lesser sorcerers remained, forming a circle amongst the remains of a fallen turret. Something moved in the centre of their circle. Lucy called out, and Thomas sensed the danger, but he was too slow. The sorcerers screamed as their life was stolen, and a wave of black magic hit them, flinging them and dozens of other dragons into the smoking piles of rubble.

The charred body of the Emperor rose from the burning ruins—around him lay a circle of withered men and women. "I didn't expect that," he rasped, his voice rough. "But it seems your source of power's subsiding."

Thomas glanced at the receding spout of Fire. It now only rose twenty or thirty feet into the air. He called to it, but it was weaker than before—still, something came to him.

"I admit, magic does have some uses," the Emperor said. Fire came from his hands, knocking Na into a fallen turret. Thomas and Lucy were flung back into the Fire, which again flared.

The Emperor pulled at his life energy as he'd pulled the life from the lesser sorcerers. But Thomas resisted. Lucy and Na stood near him, covered in dust. The Emperor then changed his tactic. Instead of pulling, he sent an overwhelming force of magic at them. Na fell against him. Other dragons slid backwards towards the battlements.

"Absorb the energy," Lucy said.

They embraced the overpowering energies rushing

through their bodies, and the three shining dragons, crackling with electricity, transformed again. As they changed, they sucked the strength from the Emperor as he had the sorcerers.

"This shouldn't be happening." The Emperor's voice weakened. "I've achieved so much." He fell into the dirt.

Now full of power, Thomas, Na, and Lucy blasted him with Fire. Rhiannon, Night Sun, Spere, Hwith, and Pzillis Trillis sent their fire, too. The Emperor screamed as he burst into flames. When all that remained of the Emperor was a blackened husk, Rhiannon stamped on his body, returning it to dust.

"The Emperor's dead!" Thomas said.

He felt light-headed. He was no longer a dragon and was unsure how to feel. He looked at Aina, who stood next to him. Her skin was golden brown and glowing with magic.

"We're human," he said.

She grinned. *"You should see your eyes."*

He looked at hers. And for a few seconds, they burnt like bright red embers. *"Perhaps not completely human."* He looked at his arms. They were still copper coloured, but the scarring had subsided, and he could breathe without pain.

Lucy, too, had changed. *"I feel very different."*

"Has the magic gone?" Thomas wondered aloud. Whatever had happened to him, he felt less magic than before.

Rhiannon rumbled a laugh. *"Something remains."*

45

"*The humans must go,*" Rhiannon said, melting the ice in front of her.

"*Some must stay,*" Lucy said.

"*They go!*" Rhiannon roared, and almost every dragon bellowed agreement.

"*The three humans present are Promethean,*" Hwith said.

"*They're dragon,*" Rhiannon said. "*I speak of the others.*"

Thomas looked at the small group of prisoners Pzillis Trillis had brought out from the tower. She'd sensed they might be important. Lucetta First and three other members of the Silvan Resistance sat apart from the meeting, staring at the rocs, dragons, and three bright humans, unable to hear them speak.

"*Silva remains,*" Lucy repeated both aloud and in the True Language. She ignored the smoke rising from the dragons.

"*She's right,*" Thomas said. "*The Silvans have lived in peace for over a century on Prometheus. They have no connection with the Empire.*"

The dragons hissed disapproval, while the rocs held

mixed opinions. They'd known Aina in another lifetime, and Lucy in this. But the majority wished the humans to leave.

Aina's words vibrated through every mind at the meeting. *"I'm dragon and I'm human. The Silvans were my people—they stay."* The argument went backwards and forwards, but despite the noise, neither Lucy, Aina, nor Thomas wavered in their opinion.

When Pzillis Trillis spoke, all listened carefully. *"These three humans, who are part dragon, and part roc, too,"* Lucy felt Pzillis Trillis's attention pause on her for a second, *"have saved our world. We owe them a lot. The ancient forest has also chosen them, and the leviathans sing their song. The country of Silva can remain."*

"I stand with Lucy," Magni, the yellow and blue flight leader, said.

"And I," Soonasa said. More rocs gave support for the idea.

Lucy translated for the small group of Silvans. "Thank you. We owe you our lives," Lucetta First said.

"Dragons?" Aina said, her eyes burning like bright embers.

"Silva may remain," Night Sun said. Spere nodded his great head in assent.

"I agree," Seth said. Kaylie had agreed with her sister from the beginning.

A chorus rose from the seas and oceans of Prometheus

"Listen," Night Sun said.

They sang in the True Language. Tears came to Lucy's eyes as she realized that thousands of vast creatures she'd felt but never seen supported her wishes.

The great green and black dragon stilled herself, and for a few moments there was silence amongst the dragons and rocs. Then she turned her head to the humans. *"The leviathans speak, and I too accept. But the others must die."*

"I'll arrange for them to leave the planet," Lucy said.

Rhiannon pushed her head, which was three times the size of a human, against her.

Lucy shone more brightly but didn't move. *"In your heart, you know this is right."*

The giant dragon gave a short hoot. *"Very well, little dragon. But we must deal with this army."*

No one objected.

THEN THEY DISCUSSED DRAGON BUSINESS: Spere, Seth, and Kaylie joined the Wisdom, Night Sun was named Father of Fire, and Rhiannon Mother of Fire. Honorific titles, but ones with meaning for dragons. *"There's more,"* Rhiannon said. *"The three little dragons will be recognized as such. And Na joins the Wisdom."*

Aina was startled. *"But..."*

"She's human," a crimson dragon said.

Aina strode up to the newly arrived crimson dragon, her anger simmering within. He'd arrived late in the battle, and his name was Bo—a strange name for a dragon. That was all she knew about him.

"What?" Bo said.

She raised her hands and blasted his scales with fire. He leapt back, immediately retaliating with his own fire. Protected by her magic, she stood proudly and scorched his belly.

"Was that wise?" a dragon asked.

"Is it wise to let a sore fester?" Aina said.

Rhiannon laughed. *"Na expresses herself through fire; the*

other expresses himself with hot air." All dragons approved of Na's action.

A ROC SENT word of a human army advancing through the blizzard. *"It's time we spoke to them,"* Thomas said. He found a piece of cloth and attached it to a stick.

"Surrendering, little dragon?" Rhiannon asked.

"Asking for their surrender."

She rumbled her amusement. *"And will they agree?"*

"We'll see. Be ready if they don't."

Aina turned from her conversation with her siblings. *"I'll listen for any problems."*

He nodded. He was worried that she was still too much of a dragon to deal with humans yet. "Let's go," Lucy said. Night Sun and Hwith took them closer, and then waited, hidden in the snowstorm as Lucy and Thomas walked down the snowy slope towards the line of soldiers.

"What happened to the Empress?" Thomas asked.

"Soonasa saw her disappear with some of her sorcerers."

"Do you think they escaped alive?"

"Perhaps," she said. "Thomas?"

He glanced at her.

"Have you noticed our hands?"

"I know." He looked at his palms. In the centre, the skin was not only stronger—all of his skin was stronger—but it looked like crystal.

"What do you think it is?"

He grinned. "You saw what Aina just did with that dragon."

She nodded. "So we really are part dragon." Her eyes

drifted to the lines of men waiting as they approached. "Do you think they'll shoot?"

"I don't think so. They'll understand we want to parley, and they'll be hoping they can avoid direct conflict. I think they'll want to hear what we have to say. Where's Chloris?"

"She's been busy with the ice demons. She has something to say, but she can say it better herself."

Thomas wasn't in a rush. He was more concerned about his body. It'd changed twice, and his energy fluctuated. He had sudden urges to transform into a dragon but wasn't sure whether he could.

She grinned. "Do you want to change?"

Thomas gave her a sidelong look but accepted her ability to read minds—he sometimes did it himself. "Perhaps."

They reached the army and waited, waving the makeshift flag in the air. The blizzard was weakening, and the army in front of them was becoming more visible. A pair of aristocrats walked towards them. "Do you recognize them?" Thomas asked. Lucy shook her head; he felt her searching their energy. He listened in the True Language, too. "At least we kept something," he said.

She smiled. "We've kept a lot: natural magic, fluency in the True Language. And something from the dragons. This pair have no magic."

"Who are you?" the man asked.

"I'm Thomas Brand, and this is Lucy Thomson. We speak for Prometheus." He opened his mind to allow Aina to hear. "Who are you?"

"My name is Lord Hall, and I'm the administrator of the Outer Citadel. This is Lady Morris, my assistant."

"So you run everything up here except the tower?" Thomas said.

The man glanced at the burning tower—the rocs and dragons had decided to reignite the flames. He nodded curtly. "My conditions. The animals must be euthanized immediately. Lady Morris has the resources to assist." She nodded.

"Just kill them!" Rhiannon rumbled in the distance.

"Nobody will kill them," Thomas said.

"The dragons and rocs are intelligent species," Lucy said. "Their right to live here supersedes your own."

"Because they were here first?"

"It's their world," Lucy said.

"If they're intelligent, why can't they speak?" Lady Morris asked.

"They're telepathic."

"Telepathy has never been proven," she said.

Thomas was surprised by her comment, but then he noticed she wore a blue sash, the colours of the Order of Science, around her waist. She wouldn't know about the inner science of magic, which was how Thomas now viewed his manipulation of energy. The other noble wore a red and grey sash. "Which order do you belong to?"

The man seemed surprised by the question. "The Order of Bankers."

Thomas laughed and the man's face darkened. "Either you kill the animals or we do."

"And then?" Thomas asked.

"Then you'll surrender."

"To who? You understand that the Emperor and the senior aristocrats are dead?"

"We have no information about their whereabouts."

Thomas gestured to the burning tower. "Their bodies are there. The Empire has no leader."

"Even if that were true, and I do not believe it is, the Empire still stands. The Empress—"

"Is no longer with us," Lucy finished. Thomas hoped that was true.

"I have five thousand soldiers here, a full division of attack bots, and a brigade of ice demons."

"Let's just arrest them," Lady Morris said. "The bots can kill the animals." Hall nodded.

"You'd break a parley?" Thomas asked.

"You're enemies of the Empire," Morris said. "You have no rights." She turned and shouted an order. A dozen armed men ran towards them.

"They've broken trust," Lucy said. *"They're preparing to attack you with robots."*

"We're ready," Aina replied.

Neither Thomas nor Lucy resisted arrest. But when the soldiers tried to drag them away, Thomas spoke. "You've not heard our terms."

Lord Hall raised his hands towards the soldiers, and they stopped. "Well?"

"The Empire will leave Prometheus. The evacuation of Nassopolis will begin immediately. Those living in any other imperial settlements will also leave. We've negotiated separate terms for Silva, which will remain as an independent country."

Lady Morris and Lord Hall glanced at each other with open mouths, then Hall shook his head and started speaking on his earphone. "Kill the animals." Hundreds of attack bots lifted into the air and flew up the hill. The dragons and rocs launched themselves into the air and blasted them with fire. There were more dragons and rocs than bots. The encounter was one-sided, and the bots were soon destroyed. Lady Morris looked at Lord Hall with raised eyebrows.

"Send in the army," Lord Hall said.

Both Thomas and Lucy knew that hundreds of rocs and dragons would win any encounter with the five thousand soldiers who lacked any heavy weapons. But neither wanted to see more death.

"The ice demons are coming," a soldier said. A brigade of two hundred ice demons ran over the snow. The regular army quickly stepped back to make way.

"Why're they running this way?" Lady Morris asked.

Lord Hall frowned and spoke again on his earphone, then he shook his head. "They want to discuss tactics."

Thomas grinned at Lucy. *"Lucky we're dealing with a banker and a scientist."*

"With you?" Lady Morris whispered.

Chloris approached. A large male ice demon moved beside her—they were flanked by several other demons. The pair of administrators seemed to shrink in their presence.

"How did it go?" Lucy asked.

"We're ready," Chloris said.

"Any problems?"

"No," she hissed. "The supervisors died quickly."

"What're you talking about?" Lord Hall asked, nervously. The soldiers had moved further back. No one wanted to stand next to two hundred battle-bred demons, all armed with modern weaponry.

"We're negotiating the establishment of an ice demon nation," Lucy said. "And then we'll negotiate your surrender."

The roc and dragon stepped forward. Aina was with

them. Thomas was almost mesmerized by her golden aura. *"Thanks,"* she whispered, standing next to him.

"This is Hwith, a leader of the rocs; Night Sun, First of Wisdom, leader of dragons; and Aina, a human leader of Silva," Lucy said.

Morris and Hall glanced at each other, bewildered.

"We request permission to form a nation of ice demons in the forests of Prometheus," Chloris said.

"You're an alien species," Hwith said. *"Why should we allow you to live on Prometheus?"*

"We need a home. And we'll fight to defend Prometheus."

"We've already defeated the enemy," Night Sun said, *"even if they don't understand that yet."*

"I can make it much easier," Chloris said.

The fierce male ice demon next to Chloris presented a box to Lucy. *"A gift."*

Lucy's eyes fell on a silver knife in the ice demon's belt. "Chloris gave you Lazolteotl's knife."

The ice demon's jaws opened, sending Lady Morris backwards into Lord Hall, but Lucy knew that it was only an ice demon grin. She opened the box.

"A tag controller!" Lord Hall was silenced by an ice demon's claw at his throat.

"He's right," Chloris said. *"With this you can access all the tagged minds on this planet. We took this from a fleeing lord."*

Lucy showed it to the roc and dragon. *"Can you use it?"*

"We can," they said.

Appearing to peck the device, Hwith psychically entered and commanded it. Cries came from the army as the soldiers dropped their weapons. "What's happening?" Hall asked. When no one answered him, he shouted an order. A man attempted to respond, but seconds later he lay dead on the ground.

Hwith spoke to the combined human minds of Nassopolis. The roc was dramatic. The viewers saw a flourish of bright colours and then his fierce eye. *"The Emperor is dead, and the Empire is no more on Prometheus. You'll leave this planet: the first will leave within days, the rest over the following months. By the end of the year, Nassopolis will be abandoned."* The message was sent to every tagged mind on Prometheus.

"You've betrayed humanity!" Lord Hall said to Thomas and Lucy. He stared at them with wide eyes.

"We've saved lives," Lucy said.

"Thank you for the gift," Hwith said.

Hwith and Night Sun communicated with the rocs and dragons.

Night Sun spoke first. *"If the rocs agree with the formation of an ice demon nation, then we do, too. But they must decide, for it's the rocs, as caretakers of the forest, who'll be most affected."*

The rocs sang for several minutes, the sound clear from the lower part of the mountain. Then they switched to the True Language. *"We accept the right of the ice demons to live in our forests if they swear to protect our world and respect life—including the ancient forest."*

The ice demons hissed and spat as they spoke together. *"What of food?"* Chloris asked.

"You can kill to eat, but some species are protected," Hwith said.

A flurry of hisses came from the ice demons. *"We agree,"* Chloris said. The ice demon turned to Hall and Morris. "Send a message to the nine planets: an ice demon nation has formed in the forests of Prometheus. All brothers and sisters are welcome."

"Who's this?" Lucy asked, indicating the large ice demon next to Chloris.

"Masson," Chloris hissed.

"Respect," Masson said to Lucy. She knew this was the closest an ice demon could come to expressing affection.

"We'll form the ice demon nation together."

Lucy nodded. *"Do you trust the dragons and rocs now?"* she asked quietly.

"I trust you," Chloris replied.

"We created you," Lady Morris said. "You belong to us."

Chloris pushed her mouth against the woman, who fell back into Hall. "No longer," she hissed.

"Help us deal with these soldiers," Thomas said.

"We can do that. The controller." Hwith returned it, and then, two hundred ice demons ran over the snow collecting the fallen weapons. They were soon joined by hundreds of rocs and dragons. The imperial subjects began to walk back to the citadel.

"Will they just leave?" Aina asked.

"Their leadership is gone, so is most of their heavy weaponry, and we control their minds," Night Sun said. *"Simply stopping the downloading of recreational drugs into their minds could be enough. The Emperor's love of control was a great strength and great weakness."*

"Tonight we have a final task." Hwith said.

"The magic?" Night Sun asked.

"The song of life."

EPILOGUE

A bright company of rocs, dragons, and humans stood on the mountain. Magic radiated from each one. The great leviathans joined them in mind, and together they watched the distant tower burn against the darkening sky.

"It's time," Hwith said.

They began the song of life. Their song was heard around the mountain, but on a deeper level, the song was a thought, forming a centre, from which it rippled through space, from galaxy to galaxy, and on through the many universes that lay so closely together that few could distinguish between them.

The singers were conscious of the deep magic of their song—within its poetry was purpose.

Life burst forth.

Plants flourished, animals basked contentedly, and even on the bleakest edges of the universe, life pushed into being. The song touched all. And although most were unaware, they were not unaffected. And, for a moment, from London to Lusaka, and from Damascus to Detroit, there was peace, and strangers greeted one another as friends.

The minds of the bright company expanded across the universe. Sensing a pressure of life, Lucy watched. *"Look."* Their minds touched hers.

Thomas saw a dark moon on the edges of the universe.

"There's nothing there," Aina said.

"Wait."

On that desolate shore of the darkling sea, a flower bloomed.

FREE STORIES

Find out about Aina's young life in the forests of Prometheus. Visit NedMarcus.com, sign-up to my newsletter and get two exciting prequels to the Blue Prometheus series for free.

PLEASE LEAVE A REVIEW

If you enjoyed Fire Rising, please leave a review. Reviews can help a writer's work be read by more readers and help promote their career, so allowing more books to be written. Thank you!

BOOKS BY NED MARCUS

Blue Prometheus Series

- Young Aina #0
- Blue Prometheus #1
- The Darkling Odyssey #2
- Fire Rising #3

Orange Storm Series

- Orange Storm #1
- The Orange Witch #2 (forthcoming)

ABOUT THE AUTHOR

Ned Marcus is an author of fantasy and science fiction. He lives and writes in the mountains of northern Taiwan.

NedMarcus.com

ACKNOWLEDGMENTS

Thank you to my editor, Parisa Zolfaghari; my proofreader, Deborah Dove; Owain McKimm; and members of Taipei Fantasy and Sci-fi Writers' Group for help with this novel.

www.ingramcontent.com/pod-product-compliance
Lightning Source LLC
LaVergne TN
LVHW091658070526
838199LV00050B/2202